THE INVICTUS CHRONICLES 1

LIKE A HERO

COURAGE CAN BE COSTLY

MICHAEL J. BOWLER

Like A Hero
Copyright © 2022 by Michael J. Bowler
All rights reserved.
First Edition: 2022

Paperback ISBN: 978-0-9903063-9-9
eBook ISBN: 978-1-7333290-2-6

Hardback ISBN - 979-8-9862241-7-6

Editor: Loretta Sylvestre
Cover and Formatting: Streetlight Graphics

CHAPTER ONE

WHO WOULD PAY MONEY FOR YOU?

C OURAGE CAN BE COSTLY.

Dennis recalled his father's words as he squirmed on a plastic chair on the soccer field, awaiting his diploma and glaring over the heads of his classmates at the empty seat next to James and Linda.

Vincent's seat.

James met his gaze a moment and Dennis detected annoyance. Linda offered a sympathetic look, but Dennis focused his simmering anger on that empty chair next to his godparents and shuddered at the memory of how Vincent's persistent tardiness had destroyed their family. After all they'd been through since that horrible night, and with all the preparations to put their plan into action this summer, Dennis was *sure* his brother had changed.

Obviously, not.

Feeling disgust well up within him, he turned back to face the stage. The light breeze pushed his hair in front of his eyes and, irritated, he shoved it aside.

Principal Rodriguez, wearing a fancy blue dress, stood at the microphone praising the graduates for their hard work. Behind her sat the other administrators and those teachers who'd be presenting awards to the highest-achieving graduates.

Ms. Ellis—Dennis's art teacher—caught his eye and smiled.

Despite his smoldering anger at his brother, Dennis couldn't help but smile back. Ms. Ellis was his favorite teacher and she had a huge, infectious smile that always brightened his day. She would present the "Best Artist" award to him, an achievement that filled him with pride. He saw it as a small stepping stone toward becoming a professional comic book illustrator.

Behind them, held up by several tether-ball poles, a banner proclaimed "CONGRATS PARKER MIDDLE SCHOOL GRADUATES."

"This is one of my favorite classes in ten years at Parker," Ms. Rodriguez said with a grin. "Give yourselves a round of—"

The class burst into thunderous applause before she could even finish, and she laughed.

Dennis clapped half-heartedly, thinking of his parents and involuntarily glancing off to the side once again at that empty seat. His chest pulled tight, and sadness weighed on him because he knew how proud his parents would be of his award and top-ten GPA standing.

Vincent had said the right words—"Great job, bro"—when Dennis told him he was graduating with honors, but there'd been no passion behind those words, like always.

Dennis forced himself to stifle the painful memories of growing up in Vincent's shadow, and never measuring up. Since the accident, they'd gotten closer than they'd ever been, especially while creating Invictus, but Dennis desperately wanted that closeness to get stronger.

I'll make you proud of me, Vince. Somehow.

Ms. Rodriguez concluded her remarks, and applause arose from all over the field. She'd just turned to introduce the teachers when loud gunshots sounded from the direction of the administration buildings.

As Dennis spun around, he heard, "Nobody move unless you want a bunch of dead kids!"

A large number of masked men carrying military-grade weapons stormed the field, surrounding the graduates and their parents.

Vincent, wearing dress pants and shoes, but no shirt, hurriedly rummaged through his closet. He pulled out a shirt and eyed it. The shirt was wrinkled. Frowning with disgust, Vincent tossed it onto his bed and grabbed another. This one was also wrinkled. With a sigh of frustration, he pitched it atop the other. Snatching a third, he examined it, squinting through his round wire rim glasses for any sign of wrinkles.

He knew his obsession with neatness and perfection was, for the most part, unhealthy, especially at times like this when he was *very* late for Dennis's graduation, but he couldn't help himself. It was a deep-seeded compulsion, one that had admittedly served him well in school and martial arts. Deciding this shirt would do, he removed it from its hanger and replaced the hanger exactly where it had been on the clothes rack. He'd just slipped one arm through the sleeve when he heard Dennis's police scanner squawking from the other bedroom.

He never turns anything off!

Annoyed, he slipped on the shirt and stepped into Dennis's room across the hall. As always, it looked like a bomb had gone off. Feeling disgust in the pit of his stomach as he stepped over piles of dirty clothes, he approached the desk. It was strewn with artwork, comics, and poetry books. The scanner sat beside Dennis's computer, continuing to squawk. He reached out to snap it off, but a crackling voice burst forth from the tinny speaker and froze him where he stood.

"All units in the vicinity of Parker Middle School. Hostage situation in effect. Unnamed perps are holding approximately two hundred children and their parents hostage. Captain Torres is on route. Report to him outside the campus. This situation is fluid. Do not attempt to engage perps without authorization."

Vincent realized he'd stop breathing, and let out a loud, gasping breath.

Dennis!

He spotted one of Dennis's drawings next to the scanner. It was the final Invictus costume, just as his brother had designed it.

Vincent bolted from the room.

Dennis lay face down on the soccer field, while men in ski masks strolled among his prone classmates waving semi-automatic weapons at anyone who moved. He considered employing his martial arts skills, but being skinny and only passably good, such foolish courage would probably get him killed.

He shook his hair from in front of his eyes with a slight jerking motion and focused on James and Linda, lying on the field off to the side with the rest of the parents.

James had his head slightly raised and Dennis caught his eye. When a gunman approached, James quickly returned his face to the grass. James wanted to intervene. That was obvious by the way he kept looking around for some kind of opening. But could he do anything without getting people killed?

The masked men called themselves "anarchists" and were well armed. Despite lying prone for the past forty minutes, Dennis had managed to spot sentries patrolling the rooftops, apparently stationed there to prevent the cops outside from storming the school and making their way to the field. He'd also noted the types of weapons these guys carried and considered how best each could be disarmed if this was a comic book scenario.

Except it wasn't.

He considered the anarchists' claims. They said they were "anti-capitalism" and "anti-public school indoctrination," but then they demanded twenty million as ransom for not killing him and his classmates, which sounded pretty capitalistic to him.

Raising his eyes once more, he noted a big, broad-shouldered dude wearing a black and blue ski mask, staring right at him while chatting with a burly guy holding an Uzi. Dennis averted his eyes and hoped he hadn't called too much attention to himself. He'd overheard them earlier as they conversed by walkie-talkie. Masked guy was called "C-1" and burly guy "C-2" by the other anarchists, so he figured they ran the show.

He glanced over at Jackson and Kenny lying a few feet away. His two best friends looked terrified. Jackson's curly hair partially hid his brown eyes, but Kenny's bright blue ones screamed pure fear. Dennis tried for an encouraging smile, but it was difficult with his cheek pressed against the grass.

All his comic book scenarios started much like this one, except the hero always knew what to do. As annoying as Robin could be, he'd know what to do even if Batman wasn't around. Dennis's mind raced with ideas. He knew James was packing—on duty or off, James always packed. But if he pulled his gun, kids would die.

I wish I'd thought of something when these guys first showed up.

Instead, he'd frozen with fear when the masked men flooded onto the field. And now with everything that had gone down since, Dennis trembled with the terrifying possibility that someone would die. Maybe him. Sadly, he wasn't the hero of his dreams.

He peered at the administration buildings. Long and single story, the two main wings spread the length of the field. His gaze traveled up and he squinted with confusion. The sentry who'd been on duty at the north end was gone.

What the…?

Dennis knew his weaponry from playing *Call of Duty* and other war games, and that guy had been patrolling with an Artic Warfare Super Magnum sniper rifle, likely a .338 Lapua Magnum, but Dennis was too far away to be sure of the model.

Only now the guy was gone. With C-2 barely ten feet away, Dennis used caution to scan the south roof. That sentry was gone, too. SWAT maybe? He knew James' mean-ass boss would have called in the big guns for something like this. But he was *also* sure those sentries had been up there no more than two minutes ago.

Could it be Invictus?

His heart thumped with hope. Vincent *must* know about this by now. Dennis pressed his face into the grass and pretended to look scared. Hell, he didn't have to pretend. He *was* scared!

Ms. Rodriguez and the administrators sat tied to their chairs. Several armed men surrounded them, including C-1 and C-2. Ms. Ellis squirmed against her restraints and happened to glance his way. She looked petrified.

"Why don't you just let the children go?" Ms. Rodriguez pleaded.

"Why would I do that? Who would pay money for *you*?" C-1 raised a walkie-talkie to his mouth. "North roof, check in."

Static shot from the speaker.

He looked up at the far roof of the administration building and stiffened.

"South roof, check in."

Again, his only answer was static.

He gazed out over the row upon row of horizontal bodies.

"Roof sentries aren't answering," C-1 told C-2, loud enough for Dennis to hear. "Somethin's wrong."

"Think the cops got 'em?" C-2 asked, hefting his Uzi.

"How? Ain't been a peep." He paused a moment to scan the roof. Then he swept his eyes over the field. "Alert the chopper. Tell 'em we may need 'em early. I'm gonna check the perimeters."

C-1 stepped off the stage and moved toward another perp.

"Be ready," he warned in a low tone. "Somethin's wrong."

Dennis eyed the masked leader, whose booted feet passed within inches of his head. He could have reached out and tripped him. But could he take the weapon away before getting shot by the other guy? Not likely. So, he remained rigid and allowed the boots to pass out of range. Not sure why, he raised his eyes to the empty roof once more, and sucked in a slight breath.

A shadow rose just above the lip of the roof, barely visible in the twilight. The shadow raised something that looked like a small handgun.

Dennis craned his neck around to observe the gunmen at the periphery of the field. One by one, each swatted at his neck in annoyance, as though driving away a pesky fly. But Dennis knew it wasn't a fly. He lowered his face and grinned into the prickly grass.

Invictus was here.

C-1 stopped beside the motionless group of parents and consulted with another perp holding a cell phone.

"Still got them pigs on the line?"

The man handed over the phone.

C-1 pressed the speakerphone button. "Captain Torres, I know what you're tryin' to do and it's gonna cost you."

Dennis barely made out a muffled "We haven't done anything" from the speakerphone.

"Then where are my men that was on the roof, eh, Captain?" C-1 retorted, clearly angry.

"We never touched your guys." poured forth from the speaker. "And we brought no snipers, per your demands."

C-1 chuckled. "Course you got snipers. You guys always do." He surveyed the field of parents and students, and then spoke into the phone again. "Any word on the money?"

"No," came over the phone. "We're waiting on the mayor."

C-1 cursed and held the phone closer, gripping his firearm tightly in the other hand.

"Your time is up, Captain. Maybe if we start reducing class size around here, you'll take us seriously."

He ended the call and tossed the phone back to the tall man. He looked right at Dennis and moved in his direction.

Dennis stiffened, and his heart pounded against his chest. They were gonna start killing kids and C-1 was headed straight for him!

The guy snapped his fingers at several thugs and pointed to four kids lying on the grass. The men stooped and yanked the kids to their feet. Two were girls and two were boys. The girls whimpered and the boys looked rigid with fear. All four wore looks of wide-eyed shock.

Distracted by their struggles, Dennis nearly jumped with surprise when a shadow fell across his face. His eyes registered a pair of boots before he was roughly pulled to his feet and dragged toward the others. He caught a glimpse of the black and blue ski mask as he tried to turn his head.

The man shoved him hard.

"Keep your eyes ahead, punk."

Dennis smelled peppermint, as though the guy wanted to make sure he had fresh breath when he murdered innocent kids.

The men pushed and dragged the five struggling teens to the edge of the field near the administration buildings. Dennis caught James's eye as he was shunted past. Then C-1 gave him a brutal shove that sent him to his knees. He threw out both hands to break his fall and jammed his wrists hard as he toppled forward. But he managed to avoid face-planting into the hard field, rolling slightly and landing on his back, shaggy hair covering his eyes. He whipped up a hand to brush it away.

C-1 loomed over him. "You're the prize, so we'll start with your sorry ass."

Dennis's heart pounded. The prize? Start with you? His mind whirled.

But, I never even got my award! And I'm barely fourteen!

C-2 handed off his Uzi to C-1 and grabbed the front of Dennis's blue graduation gown, wrenching him to his feet. One thick arm encircled his throat, cutting off his air supply. The other hand floated before his eyes brandishing a serrated hunting knife.

Dennis struggled and fought, but the man was built like a grizzly bear and he could barely squirm.

C-1 waved over the guy with the cell phone. That guy shifted the phone around like he was framing his shot for a movie.

"Make it gory as hell," C-1 said. "I want them to know we're serious."

Dennis heard C-2 grunt with approval. He could smell the man's fetid breath as the vise grip loosened to expose part of his throat. The arm remained pressed around his torso, locking him against the huge man and preventing him from even lifting his hands.

The knife danced before his eyes. It glinted red beneath the setting sun. The blade moved closer.

The other guy held out the phone.

C-1 laughed.

The blade came closer. It brushed the soft flesh of Dennis's throat.

Dennis felt weak in the knees. He forgot to breathe. His heart hammered, and he snapped his eyes shut.

CHAPTER TWO

RUN!

"**P**OLICE, FREEZE!"

The voice came from behind Dennis.

James!

C-2 lowered the knife and spun Dennis around like he was a stuffed animal.

James stood amidst the ocean of prone bodies, legs apart, arms outstretched with his service weapon pointed straight at them.

Dennis felt momentary relief until he heard C-1 chuckle beside him. He barely had a second to catch his breath before the leader opened fire.

James dropped to the grass and rolled behind a row of chairs. Bullets ripped through the backs of the chairs and sprayed splinters of white-painted wood into the air. Linda rolled behind another row of chairs, but there was nowhere to hide.

"Freeze!" Dennis heard from behind him.

Once more he felt himself spun around like a loose rag in a washing machine, and faced the administration building. James' boss, Captain Torres, and a boatload of SWAT and heavily armored LAPD officers poured forth from the buildings, their weapons aimed at the anarchists.

C-1 called out, "Kill the pigs!"

From everywhere around the field, his followers unloaded on the police.

The kids being restrained kicked and struggled against their attackers. One of the girls screamed as bullets whizzed past her head.

Torres popped off a few rounds at a guy to his left. The bullets struck the man in the chest, but he didn't go down.

Dennis absently realized the guy must be wearing body armor as he fought and squirmed, causing C-2 to clamp down harder with his left arm.

C-2 dropped his knife as C-1 tossed him the Uzi, and then both of them fired on Torres.

The stocky little man ducked behind a SWAT shield and returned fire. One bullet struck C-1, but he remained standing and kept on firing. Bullets bounced off Torres's body-length shield and sailed out in all directions.

Dennis heard whimpering cries of fear from behind him.

A helicopter appeared in the sky above the field accompanied by a loud *whup whup whup* sound. Machine guns mounted to the sides of the chopper took aim at the police. The guns sprayed bullets at the crouching officers.

Pop! Pop! Pop! Pop! Pop!

Several cops fell to the ground and the others ducked for cover behind the large planters fronting the building.

Bullets ricocheted off the concrete walkway. One whooshed so close to Dennis's face he felt the air moving. He fought to break free, but the thick arm around his torso nearly cut off his breath.

"Fall back!" Torres shouted, leaping through the heavy glass administration doors as the glass shattered all around him under a barrage of gunfire.

Another officer went down as cops scrambled for the safety of the building. Two men grabbed the fallen officer and dragged him inside as the helicopter completed its deafening path and rose again into the sky.

Odd, Dennis thought. *They don't sound that loud in Call of Duty. Wait, did I just think something that stupid?*

He struggled all the harder to break free of the iron grip.

Then he noticed an anarchist stagger, as though drunk, and topple hard to the grass, the weapon spilling from his grasp. A second guy collapsed. Then a third.

Finally!

Dennis looked up at the roof of the administration building.

In the growing twilight, the silhouetted figure of Invictus rose up. The setting sun cast him in dappled shades of red and gold and black. Between the mask over the face and the black cape billowing in the breeze, Dennis felt momentary awe, especially when Invictus raised the shield to protect his body from gunfire.

But will Invictus be enough against all these guys?

C-1 and C-2 momentarily froze, and Invictus leapt into action. He dropped to the lower roof that extended out above the administration entrance, and then did a forward flip to land on his feet in front of C-2 and Dennis. He spun into a kick and planted one black shoe squarely into the man's face. C-2 grunted and staggered backward, releasing Dennis and pinwheeling with his arms to keep from toppling onto his back. Dennis dropped and scrabbled away on hands and knees. Spotting the knife C-2 had dropped, Dennis snatched it up with one trembling hand.

Invictus whirled and slammed his shield into the face of the perp restraining one of the girls, while simultaneously leaping up and kicking another hard in the knee. Both men staggered back and collapsed to the grass as the kids broke free.

"Run!" Invictus commanded the kids.

They didn't need to be told twice. They scrambled for cover toward the school buildings.

Dennis jumped to his feet with the knife and ran toward the stage to free the teachers and administrators.

The *whup whup whup* of the helicopter blades grew louder.

C-1 and another perp trained their guns on Invictus and opened fire. From the corner of his eye as he reached the stage, Dennis saw Invictus raise his shield, and watched the bullets bounce off. They ricocheted out over the field, sending terrified parents and students scrambling for safety.

Dennis dropped to a squat behind Ms. Ellis and sliced through the rope knotted around her wrists, all the while keeping the action in his field of vision. No way would Batman be caught unawares, and he wasn't about to be, either.

The two perps stopped firing and Invictus hurled his shield at them like a Frisbee. It plowed into them, sending both men sprawling, their guns clattering onto the walkway.

Dennis grinned as the shield arced in the air and returned to Invictus like a boomerang.

The perp holding a tall boy took aim at Invictus. In a swirl of long, black hair, Invictus leapt up and planted both feet against the man's chest, flinging him backward onto the grass. The boy remained frozen in place. Cape fluttering, Invictus landed on his feet and shoved the boy toward the buildings.

"Go!"

The boy bolted.

Torres waved him on. "Hurry, kid!"

The boy flew through the shattered doors.

Ms. Ellis yanked her hands free and offered Dennis a smile of gratitude. Dennis nodded, but went to work on the bonds securing Ms. Rodriguez, while Ms. Ellis helped untie the terrified vice-principal, Mr. Lattimore.

The chopper swooped low over the field, triggering a whirlwind of air that blew graduation programs every which way. Dennis ducked behind a chair, but no gunfire erupted this time.

People panicked. Some ran for the safety of the bleachers, while others raced desperately for side doors into the administration building.

The chopper lowered a rope ladder.

C-1 dashed across the field toward it.

Dennis watched James stand and shoot at him, but the man was too far away. C-1 leaped up and snagged the rope ladder with both hands and clambered up as the chopper rose higher into the air.

Invictus crouched and turned his shield on its side. The shield sprouted a sharp blade around half its circumference and Invictus flung it at the chopper.

Dennis grinned at the sight, even as he freed Ms. Rodriguez.

James stood with his mouth open as the sharp blades sliced through the rope ladder and sent C-1 plummeting fifteen feet to slam into an unmoving heap on the field. The shield arced around and returned to Invictus. As he snatched it out of the air, the blades retracted.

Yes!

Despite his racing heart, Dennis couldn't contain his excitement. Invictus was performing better than he'd ever expected!

The chopper banked a turn and headed back toward the field.

Invictus called out, "Run for cover!"

The kids on the grass jumped up and sprinted for the bleachers. The chopper moved in their direction, strafing the field with bullets and kicking up clods of dirt. A longhaired boy went down.

Oh, no! That's Bobby!

Dennis remained in a crouched position, but felt his heart lurch at the sight of his classmate down and unmoving.

Another boy cried out as a bullet struck him and blood spurted from his leg. He began to topple, but the girl beside him grabbed his arm and kept him upright. She pulled him toward the safety of the bleachers, where at least a hundred kids were cowering. The last stragglers raced across the field to join them.

James crouched low near the stage and took a few shots at the chopper. The bullets bounced off, but the pilot veered left to avoid being struck again.

Dennis eyed Bobby, still motionless on his stomach. The rest of the kids and parents had ducked beneath the bleachers. Horrified, Dennis watched as Bobby's brother, Todd, suddenly rose and started back onto the field. A girl pulled him back.

"Let me go! I gotta get my brother!"

He yanked his hand loose and sprinted toward Bobby's motionless form.

"Get back!" James shouted, but Todd ignored him.

James leapt up and sprinted in that direction.

Invictus raced toward the fallen Bobby.

Todd dropped to his knees beside the unmoving form of his brother.

"Don't move him!" James called out, but he wasn't close enough to offer assistance.

The chopper swung around and opened fired on James.

Pop! Pop! Pop! Pop!

James spun right. Bullets ripped divots into the grass as he dove beneath the bleachers where Linda already crouched with a group of graduates. The chopper veered back toward the field.

Dennis couldn't pull his eyes from the scene. Most of the teachers and administrators were either hunkering low behind the stage or untying each other. But Dennis was riveted to the action on the field.

Invictus reached Todd and Bobby, planting himself between them and the approaching chopper. Bullets burst from the machine guns, but Invictus held out his shield and the bullets ricocheted off to the sides.

The chopper soared overhead and banked around for another pass.

Invictus bent and examined Bobby.

"He's alive."

"We gotta move him!" Todd shouted as the chopper approached.

Invictus eyed the incoming helicopter. "No time."

He stood and stepped out in front of the two kids, his gaze locked on the chopper. The machine guns spun. Bullets spewed forth, striking the grass and kicking up dirt in a straight-line right toward him.

Dennis froze, his body tight with dread.

"I hope you know what you're doing, Vince," he muttered. "I can't lose you, too!"

Invictus stood his ground, shield at his side. Todd crouched low to protect his fallen brother.

"That's right," Invictus mumbled. "Keep coming."

Bullets tore up the field.

Pop! Pop! Pop! Pop! Pop!

Invictus lifted his shield in an arcing motion. The bullets hit the shield, but rather than ricochet off to the sides, they bounced upward, striking the bottom of the helicopter.

Dennis gasped as black smoke billowed forth and the chopper veered sharply to its left, the pilot either dead or unable to control the massive machine. It tilted slightly and plummeted downward, slamming into the field so hard the ground rumbled. The front rotor struck the wooden bleachers and sliced through them before snapping off from the impact. The kids beneath screamed and scuttled back from the crumbling rows of seats.

Fire erupted within the cockpit and smoke poured forth.

James shouted at the kids beneath the bleachers, "Get back, everyone!"

Kids and parents scrambled as fast as they could away from the downed copter, pressing in against each other beneath the wooden bleachers.

Invictus pelted across the grass toward the burning chopper and used one gloved hand to yank open the cockpit door. He reached in and flung the pilot over his shoulders and then stumbled away from the smoke and flame. He dumped the pilot onto the grass and sprinted back to the wreck.

Invictus reached back into the burning cockpit and dragged the other perp out onto the grass. He dropped his shield long enough to scoop the guy up over his shoulders. Then gripping the shield handle he rose unsteadily to his feet and staggered away from the wreckage. Oily black smoke filled the field.

James shouted, "Get down, it's gonna blow!"

The few stragglers flung themselves to the ground, and James wrapped his arms around Linda.

Dennis crouched low behind the stage.

The chopper exploded in a massive fireball that sent flames in all directions. The explosion flung bits of burning debris all over the field, igniting small fires everywhere.

Dennis raised his head and eyed the bleachers, where everyone was trapped by the heat and flames from the burning helicopter.

Do something, Vince!

Invictus emerged from the billowing smoke and observed the burning copter. He studied the flaming bleachers, and then swung his gaze up to the old water tower that stood just outside the school grounds.

Dennis held his breath.

Invictus reached into a small pouch on his belt and pulled out some of his explosive pellets. He affixed them to different spots along the circumference of the shield, gripped it like a Frisbee, and flung it hard up at the water tower.

Dennis watched with wide eyes as the shield arced toward the wooden legs that held the old tank aloft. The shield struck the front leg. There was a visible explosion and a *snap* of wood. The tower began to topple. The shield continued its arc and struck the second leg. Another explosion ensued, followed by a *crack* of breaking wood.

The entire tower toppled forward, right onto the flaming helicopter. The tank shattered. Rather than water—which would have spread the burning gasoline—what poured from the splintered tank was… sand?

Yes!

Dennis had no idea how his brother knew about the sand, but he wanted to throw his arms into the air with triumph.

The sand doused the flames, spreading outward across the field toward the bleachers and putting out the residual fires, leaving only small patches of grass still aflame.

Kids and parents scrambled out from under the burning bleachers and bolted from the danger zone.

James assisted Linda to her feet.

Parents ran to their kids and engulfed them with hugs and affirmations of love.

Invictus panted from his exertions and watched the area beneath the flaming bleachers empty out.

Dennis wanted to run to him, to make sure he was alright. But he couldn't do that. It would blow their cover before they even started.

One girl, her blue graduation gown smudged with grass stains and singed by fire, eyed Invictus with awe.

"Who are you?"

"My name's Invictus. I'm a kind of guardian angel, I guess. You okay?"

She nodded just as a man in a suit and a woman wearing a flowery summer dress raced over to drag her away.

Todd, still crouching beside the unconscious Bobby, jumped aside as paramedics raced over to attend him.

Torres, his officers, and the SWAT team charged from the administration buildings toward the fallen anarchists.

Todd glanced at the medical personnel attending to Bobby, and then marched over to where Invictus remained watching.

"Why did you save them?" he practically screamed, pointing to the two unmoving men from the helicopter. "They shot my brother!"

Invictus took a step back. "Well, I, uh, why kill someone if you don't have to? I believe in justice, not revenge.

"Payback is justice!" Todd spit into Invictus's face. The spittle landed on the mask, just above the nose, and slid slowly down one cheek.

Invictus reared back in apparent shock, and raised one gloved hand to wipe away the spit.

A harried man rushed to Todd and grabbed him around the shoulders, dragging him back to where the paramedics were placing Bobby onto a stretcher.

Invictus turned and looked right at Dennis.

Dennis stood so his brother could see he was unharmed, but his mind reeled by what Todd had just done!

Invictus gave a slight nod, then darted past the remnants of the helicopter out of sight.

Dennis left the stage area and sprinted toward James and Linda.

"Dennis!"

Linda engulfed him in a crushing hug.

Over her shoulder, Dennis noticed James sag with relief as he holstered his gun

"You okay?" James asked, his gaze sweeping over Dennis for injuries.

Still smothered by Linda, Dennis nodded.

Linda released him, but kept her arm around his shoulders, as though he might disappear if she didn't.

"Who was that guy, anyway?" she asked in amazement.

James eyed the smoldering wreckage beyond which Invictus had vanished. "Good question."

Dennis felt a mix of relief and elation. Everyone was alive, and his creation had performed with spectacular success. He couldn't help but smile.

CHAPTER THREE

THEY DON'T UNDERSTAND YET

Vincent watched with helpless frustration as three police vehicles, lights flashing and si-rens blaring, pursued a BMW, but the details were hazy. The Beemer careened around a corner and the three cop cars followed. A white Ford Explorer entered the intersection – and Vincent didn't need clear vision to recognize it. He stood in his front entry hall wearing his lab coat, cell phone in hand.

"Loookkkk Oooouuttt!" he screamed into the phone.

The BMW plowed into the side of the Explorer, crumpling it inward and propel-ling it forward into a power pole. The Explorer erupted into an explosive fireball that engulfed the BMW along with it.

"Nooooo!"

VINCENT SNAPPED HIS EYES OPEN and lifted his head in a jerking fash-ion, the dream images quickly fading. His heart pounded. His breaths came in fits and starts. His wire-rimmed glasses were askew and he fumbled to adjust them, gradually taking in his surroundings. Several young people in lab coats stared at him with a mix of surprise and sympathy.

Had he screamed out loud or only in his dream?

Glancing around the lab, Vincent could clearly see on the faces of his co-workers that he had, in fact, screamed. Some of them were startled, others a bit spooked. Some stared at him like they thought he should see a shrink.

"Sorry," he mumbled. Tossing his long, black ponytail over his shoulder he returned his gaze to the Spectrophotometer in front of him and studied the solu-tion within. He saw movement at the corner of his eye - a white lab coat drifting in his direction.

Oh, no…

The movement stopped and Vincent turned to look into the craggy face of Professor Chin. He was a small, frail-looking man with close-cropped, receding gray hair, but his apparent fragility masked an indomitable spirit and a brilliant mind. Chin's thin lips sloped downward in a frown.

"Still not sleeping well?"

Vincent glanced away a moment, feeling weak. "No. I haven't had a good night's sleep since…."

He let the thought trail off. Chin already knew the rest.

"I understand your loss, but I need you focused, Vincent," he said, his voice low and gravelly. "Concentrate on your work and your classes."

He walked away. Vincent felt eyes on him and glanced around the lab. His fellow grad students looked away.

He focused on the equipment before him. He needed this job, not just for his PhD, but also to supplement the money and life insurance his parents had left him and Dennis. The research project UCLA had undertaken on behalf of both the government and the private sector was enormous in scope. The results of their endeavors would be used to shape public policy in all fifty states for decades. He'd been flabbergasted, and deeply honored, when Professor Chin of the prestigious Institute for Neuroscience and Human Behavior had invited him on board.

"Only the best for this research, Vincent," Chin had told him last year when extending the invite. "And you're the best grad student I have."

Vincent had become fascinated by human behavior while doing community service work in high school with kids who'd gotten in trouble with the law. His interactions with them and the way they thought, as well as with the people who worked so diligently to get those kids back on track, filled him with a burning desire to understand how the human brain shapes every choice we make.

Insanely shy, his high school and undergrad years had pretty much been "nose in a book twenty-four seven." His taking of every possible AP course and resulting 4.82 GPA had earned him valedictorian status and easy entry into UCLA. He still recalled how terrified he'd been delivering his speech. His body had trembled the entire time, not just because he was speaking in front of hundreds of people, but because, as he stood on that podium gazing out at his classmates, he realized that he barely knew any of them. And they didn't know him because he'd never given them a chance.

He'd sailed through undergrad in two and half years and now, at twenty-one, he found himself PhD-bound doing significant brain research with one of the foremost researchers in the field.

Other than martial arts competitions, which his dad had gotten him into at a young age, he'd never had anything that could be described as a social life. He knew libraries and labs better than he did movie theaters or clubs.

Maybe that's better, he thought as he resumed his work. Most people self-obsessed too much and the city was declining as a result. His brother had the right idea, but after yesterday, Vincent knew that fulfilling "The Dream" wouldn't be as simple as he thought.

For now, work beckoned. And work paid the bills.

Vincent loved the sloping hills and lush foliage that made up the UCLA campus, and the Romanesque revival-style buildings gave him a sense of stepping backward in time. He'd parked in one of the upper lots because he had to use Sunset Boulevard to access the dreaded 405 Freeway, the only direct route from UCLA to the San Fernando Valley.

As he strolled past Royce Hall, lost in thought about yesterday's events, he heard his name called out.

"Vincent, wait up!"

He turned, and froze. A gorgeous blonde jogged across the grass in his direction, lugging her backpack and lumbering slightly under its weight.

Of course, he knew Lisa; she was the knockout in Professor Chin's Neuroscience class, and even Vincent "nose in a book" Villanueva couldn't help but check her out whenever he had the opportunity. Her smooth features were perfect for modeling, especially since she wore minimal makeup. She favored light-colored shirts and jeans, but that hair, though. He loved her hair!

He'd been letting his own hair grow since he was ten, despite his parents' disapproval. In high school, whenever a girl commented that Asians had the most beautiful hair, he would always remind her that Filipinos weren't technically Asian, but Pacific Islander. Such remarks had only cemented his "weird" status on campus and kept girls at a distance.

But Lisa's hair, with its gentle yellow-blond color and waterfall quality as it slipped down her back and danced in the breeze, well, in Vincent's mind, put his to shame any day of the week.

"Can I walk with you?" she was saying, and Vincent suddenly realized she was standing directly in front of him. Had she said anything else? He hoped not!

"Uh, yeah, sure."

He shifted his backpack to one shoulder so he could take hers.

She smiled and happily relinquished it. "Thanks. It weighs a ton."

He pretended to grimace as he hefted it over his empty shoulder. "Sure does. I'm getting my workout in for today." He chuckled, knowing how pathetic that sounded, but unsure what he should say.

She eyed his taut, veiny forearms and biceps. "I think it takes more than my backpack to give you a workout. I should call you Vein Boy."

Since it was summer, he'd worn a tank top beneath his lab coat at work, and had left the coat in his locker. He felt both pleased and a bit embarrassed by her compliment since he wasn't accustomed to being noticed.

"Uh, thanks," he replied. "I do martial arts with my brother and my…" He stopped, his chest tightening, his breathing suddenly on hold.

Her face clouded over and she put a hand lightly on his arm. "I'm sorry. I heard about your parents."

Forcing composure onto his face, he offered a sad smile. "Still adjusting."

She removed her hand.

He wished she'd put it back.

They walked a few moments in silence.

"I saw on the news about your brother's graduation yesterday," she finally offered in a conversational tone. "Were you really scared?"

"I, um, I was late getting out of here and by the time I got there the police had cordoned off the school. But Dennis said it was terrifying."

"They keep showing the video on the news of the guy who saved everybody," she went on, shaking her head in amazement. "I don't know if he's really brave or really stupid, but it was so exciting to watch. Better than a movie."

Vincent stopped and shuffled uncomfortably. He feared looking into her eyes, but forced himself anyway. "Yeah, well, listen, Lisa, I really need to get home. To make sure Dennis is okay and finish some homework. I'll see you in class, okay?"

She seemed disappointed, which mystified Vincent since most people didn't seek him out for conversation. His "loner" status was well known on campus.

"Oh, okay."

He slipped off her backpack and helped her loop it around both shoulders.

She offered a smile that seemed so perfect and inviting that Vincent almost let his mouth drop open. He spun around toward the parking structure.

You're being paranoid, Vince! How could she know anything?

And then he stopped. Of course, she doesn't know anything!

He turned back around. She stood where he'd left her, that disappointed look still shading her delicate features. He wanted to say something, but nothing came.

Her frown morphed into a smile. "Yes, I'd love to go out with you on Friday. I thought you'd never ask."

His mouth dropped open. *Huh?*

She jogged over, but Vincent didn't know what to do.

Did she just ask me out?

"Uh, let me get out some, uh, paper to write down your number." He started to slip off his backpack.

She laughed. "Boy, you don't date much, do you?"

He almost blushed, but it was true! How about 'don't date ever'?

"Let me have your phone."

Momentarily overcome by paranoia, he quickly realized what she meant to do and slipped his phone from his jeans pocket. He swiped open the screen and handed it over.

With deft, smooth movements, she input her name and number and handed him back the phone.

"Seven's good for me." She smiled.

He returned the phone to his pocket. "Uh, works for me, too."

She raised a hand in a light wave. "See ya, Vein Boy."

She sauntered off in a different direction across campus.

Dumbfounded, Vincent headed for the parking structure.

He slid the silver Volt into the left side of his three-car garage and parked. The thirty-eight-mile all-electric range of this car meant he could travel to UCLA every day without gas, charge the car there, and return home without gas. His parents had always been smart with money.

Just that thought caused him to look over at the empty space where the Explorer used to rest when it wasn't in use. The vacantness of the spot sent another surge of melancholy into his soul and he quickly squelched it. Emotions were the enemy of intellect. Professor Chin always said that, and Vincent agreed.

He stepped from the car and went around back to plug it in. As he did, his eyes settled on the motorcycle he'd bought. He'd taken classes on how to ride it, had just gotten his license two months ago, and had been practicing every chance he got, especially in places where he could push the speed without risking a ticket. Maybe it was his intense martial arts training over the years, but he'd not felt a moment's fear on the cycle. Riding it provided the kind of adrenalin rush he savored. Of course, he had to keep the throttle low when leaving the garage since James and Linda lived just a few houses down, and they could never know he had it.

Dennis sat in the family room watching the sixty-inch flat screen with rising excitement. On every channel he flipped to, his graduation and the appearance of the "mysterious costumed vigilant known as Invictus," as CNN had dubbed him, unspooled with numerous cell phone videos that kids had apparently been shooting while lying on the field.

Dennis chuckled. His generation just couldn't resist the temptation to film everything, even when their lives were in mortal danger.

Vincent stepped into the room from the kitchen and tossed his backpack onto the couch.

"We're famous, bro!" Dennis exclaimed, his heart racing almost as fast as it did when he was heavily into a *Call of Duty* session with Jack and Kenny. He muted the sound just as video of Todd spitting on Invictus unspooled on screen.

Vincent groaned. "How often do they show that part?"

Dennis noted Vincent's rigid stance and the distressed look on his face.

"It doesn't matter, Vince. You blew 'em away, totally stupendous! How'd you know that tower had sand in it?"

Vincent shrugged. "I didn't for sure. Just remembered one of my teachers saying it did when I went to that school."

Dennis grinned and shook his head in admiration. "Well, we couldn't have picked a better debut for Invictus, that's for sure. You being late was a good thing, for once."

The moment he uttered those words, he felt his chest tighten and his breathing pause. Vincent opened his mouth to say something, but Dennis turned away. He couldn't talk about Mom and Dad. From the corner of his eye he noted Vincent opening his mouth to speak, so he pointed the remote at the TV.

"Look, there's James." He unmuted the sound and pointed at the tall African American with close-cropped hair, thick mustache, and dark suit standing in the background.

Vincent looked at the television.

Dennis recognized the setting as the pressroom at Parker Center, headquarters of the LAPD, because he'd seen press conferences in the past, including the one about…

No! Focus, Dennis!

James stood with some officers and detectives behind Captain Torres. Torres was a short, stocky man with a buzz cut, jowly cheeks, and a booming voice that pounded forth like a bullhorn on steroids.

"…and I don't care how it turned out," Torres was saying when Dennis unmuted the sound, "a number of my officers were wounded. Not to mention the civilians who were hurt. Bobby Kendall, the boy shot in the back, is in critical condition, but expected to survive." Torres practically mad-dogged the camera, Dennis noted, but then again, that was his usual expression. "The interference from this so-called 'guardian angel' directly caused those injuries."

Dennis felt anger surge through him. "That's not true! The big guy was about to cut my throat open!"

"Chill, Dennis." Vincent took the remote and raised the volume a notch.

"This clown is nothing but a two-bit vigilante who reads too many comic books," Torres went on forcefully. Laughter from the unseen press corps filled the room. All the officers chuckled, except James.

"He got the comic book part right." Vincent offered a tiny smile.

But Dennis was still mad and ignored the attempt to calm him.

"This 'Invictus,' or whatever he calls himself, is no guardian angel, folks," Torres asserted with passionate conviction. "Like every other citizen, he cannot operate outside the law. If he's spotted again, he will be arrested and booked for interfering with police operations. That's all I have to say at this time. Questions?"

As hands flew into the air, Vincent muted the sound.

Dennis glared a moment longer at Torres and then paused. Using the breathing techniques he'd learned through martial arts, he gradually slowed his heart rate and felt his body settle itself into a reasonable semblance of calm. He took note of the doubts flitting across Vincent's face.

"We knew it wouldn't be easy, Vince," he offered, standing to take the remote from his silent brother. He flicked off the TV.

"True, but I didn't expect to save somebody's life and then have him spit on me. That's not a logical response."

"Todd was angry. That part made sense. But the other part, the payback mentality, *that's* what we're trying to change. You know that. And we *will* change it, at least in some people."

"It's not just him. It was all those people. They didn't clap or say thank you or offer any support. They simply stared at me like I should be institutionalized."

"You freaked 'em, bro, and they don't understand yet. They will."

"I don't know, Dennis. Maybe Dad was—"

Dennis felt his chest constrict again. "We better get ready. James and Linda are expecting us for dinner."

"Oh, right, I forgot." Vincent snatched up his backpack and made for the stairs. "Oh," he added, turning back. "Please, don't let me forget that I actually have a date on Friday."

That news surprised Dennis big time. He'd never known Vincent to go on a "real" date before. "Is this that Lisa chick you talk about sometimes?"

Vincent practically blushed. "Yeah. She asked *me* out."

"Why shouldn't she? You're hot, you have kick ass hair, and you're a superhero." He stopped himself, not having planned to gush so much. Where had all that come from?

Vincent looked shocked. "Wow. Thanks. Except she doesn't know about the superhero part."

Dennis hadn't meant 'Invictus' when he'd said that, but let the comment pass.

"She'll figure it out one of these days if you don't do the man bun thing with your hair like I been saying."

"You and the man bun. The mask covers most of my face. No one will recognize my hair."

"We'll see. Gimme your phone. I'll make sure the Lisa gig is on your calendar."

Vincent fished out his phone, handing it over. "Thanks, bro. Don't know what I'd do without you." He ascended the stairs.

Dennis studied the phone a moment and then caught sight of something to his right. Atop a curio cabinet against the wall sat a large framed photo of the family. Dennis stepped closer and picked it up. This one had been taken during a vacation to the Philippines, when they visited his grandparents. Dennis had been eight at the time, Vincent fifteen. He noted how small and skinny he looked compared to Vincent. His brother even then had lots of muscle and veins and, despite his shyness, tons of secret admirers at school. If only Vincent could see himself the way other people saw him.

Especially me.

Dennis forced himself to gaze at his mother. Her hair framed a round face marked by big dimples and a smile that killed. Everyone always said she should be in movies with that smile. Dad gazed seriously into the camera. His wire-rimmed glasses and short hair made him look younger than he was, and Dennis could clearly see Vincent in him. *He* took after his mom, except maybe in the smile department. But he did have dimples that got him tons of attention, much of it mockery from guys who claimed he "looked like a cartoon," but occasionally compliments from girls who thought the dimples were "cute."

As he gazed at his parents, Dennis felt that tightening of his chest and the onset of erratic breathing. PTSD had been the diagnosis when he'd begun having these episodes shortly after the funeral. He slammed the photo face downward with a sharp *crack* of wood against wood and raced up the stairs to his room.

Vincent had practically grown up in James and Linda's house. Across the street and a few houses down from theirs, it had been his and Dennis's home away from home, with James and Linda like second parents to both of them, not just their godson, Dennis. Unlike their house, this one was single story, but it had long hallways, a huge kitchen because Linda loved to cook, and a big sparring room off the garage.

Vincent's dad had installed his own workout room at the house, but James's was larger and he'd incorporated strength training equipment that the boys had used over the years to strengthen their joints and muscles.

The Villanueva clan had spent many a laugh-filled Thanksgiving or Christmas at the Stevens home, and the large brightly lit dining room felt hauntingly empty without his parents sitting at the table with them. Loy and James had been partners in the police department as far back as Vincent could remember, and the families were more like one than two.

Sitting at the burnished wood table passing bowls of rice back and forth choked off most of the words he considered saying because too many memories intruded. Dennis, he knew, felt their missing parents even more acutely.

James shoveled mashed potatoes into his mouth and swigged from a glass of water. "I still can't get over what happened yesterday," he offered. "Only Dennis could have a graduation like that."

He tried for a smile, but Dennis half-heartedly returned it as he chewed on his chicken.

Yeah, he's fighting the PTSD again, Vincent realized.

Linda said, "I would've preferred to watch the excitement from Vincent's vantage point – the parking lot." She smiled and reached out to cup Dennis's hand with one of hers. "I was so terrified for you, baby."

Dennis swallowed his food. "Yeah, me too. Lucky Invictus showed up, huh, James?"

James grunted as he swallowed a bite of chicken and placed his fork down onto his plate. "Truth be told, he did save your life, Dennis. He saved everyone. Torres was wrong."

"You tried to save me," Dennis added. "Thanks for that."

"I'd do anything for you boys, you know that," James affirmed, his face set with determination. "I promised your dad I'd–"

Dennis flinched and averted his eyes.

"Well, uh, I'm happy Invictus showed up when he did," Vincent tossed out, knowing it sounded lame, but wanting to distract Dennis. "I'm the only one allowed to take down my baby brother."

He elbowed Dennis and drew out the smile he loved.

"Only cuz you outweigh me, Vince," Dennis said, the fire returning to his voice. "You know I can kick your ass by catching you off-guard."

"Exactly how many times have you managed to do that?"

Dennis laughed. "Okay, once. But I'll do it again."

Vincent returned the laugh and they high-fived.

Linda chuckled. "I almost had a heart attack yesterday and these two laugh about it."

"That's us guys for you, Linda," James said, and they resumed eating.

Vincent scooped some rice onto his plate and passed the bowl to Dennis. Trying to sound casual, he said, "So James, are you and Torres really gonna treat Invictus like a criminal? I mean, he saved Dennis and those other people, right?"

"No choice, Vince," James said around a mouthful of asparagus. "Like Torres said, nobody can be allowed to operate outside the law."

"Even if they're doing something good?" Dennis asked.

"Even then," James responded. "If we let guys like that do their thing, order eventually breaks down and we end up with chaos. Your d—" He stopped himself quickly. "You'll understand that better when you're older. Life isn't a comic book."

"It could be," Dennis offered before focusing on his food.

Vincent noted James and Linda exchange a confused look and hoped they weren't making the older couple suspicious. Then James said something that almost stopped his heart.

"You know, Linda, there was something about his fighting style."

"Whose?"

"Invictus," James went on, pausing with his utensils in mid-air. "I was just telling Torres today that there was something familiar about his fighting style. Did you notice anything, hun? You've trained half the young black belts in L.A."

She considered a moment. "Now that you mention it, there *was* something about the fluidity of the body, the way he spun into those kicks."

"It'll come to me. I never forget a fighting style."

Vincent kept his head down, but stole a quick glance at Dennis. His brother was looking his way and wore the same facial expression.

This wasn't a good development.

CHAPTER FOUR

I ASSUME YOU HAD NO TROUBLE HACKING INTO THE LAPD?

DENNIS SAT AT HIS DESK with his twenty-seven-inch monitor fired up and linked into the LAPD mainframe. A police-band scanner sat beside the monitor. Scattered all over the desk were comic books – mostly Batman – and paperback books of poetry.

Despite his room being cluttered, with clothes scattered everywhere, Dennis felt safe there. By contrast, Vincent's room was like a museum, everything always put away exactly where it belonged. They were polar opposites in this arena. But then, Vincent was ordered and logical and scientific, whereas Dennis had always been a dreamer.

He'd taught himself how to hack at an early age, but never used it for criminal purposes or even to screw with somebody who treated him like crap at school. He and Vincent had been raised believing that their purpose on earth was to make the planet better, not worse.

"Each according to his gifts," their mom would always say. Both parents lived that belief, and the boys had adopted it. In large measure, it was this belief that had led to the creation of Invictus.

Vincent entered wearing the costume and carrying the mask. His long hair trailed behind him and his wire-rimmed glasses glinted beneath Dennis's overhead light.

"Am I allowed to iron Kevlar?"

Dennis gave him an exasperated look. "Of course not."

Vincent looked disappointed. "You sure?"

"Who made the costume?"

"Oh, right."

Dennis couldn't help but be amused. He gazed at his brother a moment to admire his handwork. The two of them had agonized over the look of the costume for many long hours, with Dennis's ideas finally accepted by Vincent. There was a belt containing six small pouches in which Invictus would keep his tools. One such tool was the modified airsoft gun he'd used to shoot knockout darts at the school thugs. Other pouches contained various defensive items Vincent had created in the lab late at night when everyone else had gone home.

They'd decided that the entire costume needed to be black. It had never made sense to Dennis for Batman to have that big yellow seal right on his chest. It was easily visible in the dark and the perfect target for bullets. So Invictus wore all black. Even the small cape was black, though Dennis had sewn on the Invictus logo in white near the top. The logo consisted of a "V" with an "I" set within it. He'd painted the same symbol into the center of the shield and added white bands in between the black. The use of white here was necessary, he'd explained to Vincent, who insisted the white would make him a target for bullets.

"Bro, the shield is bullet proof," he reminded Vincent with exasperation. "That's where we *want* the bad guys to aim."

The shield itself was made from Graphene, a super-strong, lightweight metal that UCLA had bought for the creation of new super capacitors. Some clever biochemistry students "borrowed" some of it and got together with friends from the engineering department to build a Captain America-style shield. They'd even added pop-out blades along half of the circumference. Dennis never got the whole story, but the students had been expelled for stealing a valuable element and costing the university thousands of dollars. Rather than have their creation confiscated, the guys hid it somewhere on campus and never told anyone where, until Dennis found them via social media a few months back and explained his plan.

Of course, he'd coded his message to make sure it wasn't backtracked to him, but the guys were so excited to hear their bullet-resistant shield would be tested in the field that they eagerly coughed up the location. Vincent stayed late one night at work on some pretense and when everyone had gone home, he went straight to the gap between walls where the guys said to look, and sure enough, the Invictus shield was born. Vincent had driven them both out to vacant hillsides in Canyon Country to get the feel for how to throw the shield. It took numerous hours of practice, but he was finally able to arc it so the shield retuned to him most of the time.

"It's all in the wrist," he said with a tired grin.

Acquiring the Kevlar had required some sleight of hand, but it had been worth it. Dennis ordered it from a place in Ohio and had, naturally, hidden his actual name and address. He'd routed the package through several states and different addresses before it ended up at a P.O. box Vincent opened using the fake I.D. he'd bought down in McArthur Park. He'd later mailed the company a money order and made sure it wasn't traceable to either of them. Kevlar in hand, he set about creating the suit.

The cape, however, had been a major bone of contention. Vincent insisted it would hamper his martial arts moves, but Dennis maintained that he had to have a cape because, well, "Batman does." In the end, he'd sparred with Vincent wearing various cape sizes to determine just the right length so it wouldn't be obstructive. The final version was thin and stopped just below Vincent's waist. Based on the episode at the school, the length was just right.

"I assume you had no trouble hacking into the LAPD?" Vincent stepped over a pile of clothes and stood beside his brother's desk.

"Piece of cake," Dennis replied, feeling good that there was something he could top his brother at.

Vincent leaned in to examine the information on the screen.

"Now," Dennis began, "there are some major ongoing investigations, drug rings, sting operations, hate crimes, stuff like that. A number of those hate crimes are against Asians, by the way."

He glanced at Vincent and saw his brother nod in agreement. In certain parts of Los Angeles there was always tension between races.

"I think it's too early for you to get into the big stuff," Dennis went on like he was Batman talking to Robin. "Besides, we're not trying to win over the cops, just the people. I've been monitoring the scanner and there's plenty of street crime for you to tackle. There's been an armed robbery, a gang shooting, and a carjacking. And that's only in the last fifteen minutes."

Vincent stood and gazed a moment at the mask. "I got it. C'mon, help me get the damned motorcycle started."

Despite his training, Vincent still had difficulty starting the cycle, which amused Dennis to no end.

Vincent clambered over the piles of clothes and exited the room.

"Don't forget your contact lenses," Dennis called out.

"I knew I forgot something," Vincent's voice wafted in from the hallway.

Dennis shook his head.

A few minutes later, he stood with his arms crossed trying not to laugh as Vincent struggled to start the motorcycle. Mask on, his long hair noticeably trailing out from beneath it, shield attached to the front of the bike, Vincent cranked the throttle and the choke. The cycle sputtered and died. Sputtered and died.

"Damned choke. I either leave it on too long or not long enough!"

"Told you a car would be better." Dennis tried not to sound smug.

Vincent turned to him and Dennis was sure he was going to say something nasty, but he laughed instead. "Yeah, you did. A car might be acceptable in Gotham City, but not with the traffic congestion in L.A."

He'd bought a black motorcycle so it would be harder to see in the dark, and he'd removed the license plate after his last practice session. It would not be good for the police to capture his plate number on camera or via satellite. He'd also painted over every identifiable logo so the cycle would look as generic as possible.

He tried the choke and throttle again and the bike rumbled to life beneath him. Dennis pressed the "Up" button and the garage door rolled open on its tracks.

"Be careful not to stall out. I'll monitor the scanner and send you where the action is. Keep your GPS on."

Vincent switched on the small GPS device mounted just inside his windshield.

"Later, bro." He shifted into first gear and then eased the clutch lever out.

Dennis observed Invictus swing around to the small alley that ran behind the houses and then vanish from his sight. They'd decided the darker alley would hopefully keep neighbors from spotting his comings and goings. Dennis felt by turns excited and envious that, as always, his big brother got to have all the fun.

Fool, he thought as he closed the garage door and watched it roll and creak its way down. *You're the one who always said there was no way Batman or any other hero would take a young kid into the streets with him. It was just too dangerous.*

He regretted those words now.

Entering the kitchen, he heard several meows from the back yard and looked through the window. His group of strays crossed the rear lawn toward the house.

Oh, no, I forgot to feed them!

He darted to the cupboard above the microwave and dragged out several cans of cat food. Vincent chided him for "helping every stray that comes along," and

Dennis always replied that he couldn't help himself. These cats were homeless and hungry and needed help.

Always the rational one, Vincent would say they should call Animal Control and have the cats picked up. Horrified, Dennis told him most of those cats ended up being put to sleep.

Vincent finally gave up, as Dennis knew he would. It was true that he seemed to attract more strays every day, but he couldn't *not* help them. Life was too precious to waste.

He laid the bowls in the backyard beside the flower garden and his furry friends dug right in. Dennis grinned and then hurried back into the house to become the eyes and ears of L.A.'s first and only super hero.

Invictus avoided freeways, navigating his way across the Valley and over Laurel Canyon into the Hollywood area, heading for downtown Los Angeles. He didn't want his cape and costume distracting other drivers, and he needed to avoid the police.

As he rode along surface streets, he heard Dennis in the Bluetooth earpiece underneath his mask rattling off crime reports from various parts of the city, but these incidents had already happened and he'd be too late to be of any assistance.

Being the sons of an LAPD detective, they knew the department didn't have any reliable way to track Bluetooth signals or even hack into someone's Bluetooth device unless they were within a radius of thirty feet. Invictus had no intention of getting that close to any police officer, not if he could help it.

He'd also bought a separate cell phone with a number distinct from his regular phone, and he'd used the fake ID to set up the account. The Supreme Court had ruled that the federal government trolling phone records was illegal, and though he knew the LAPD didn't have that kind of infrastructure set up anyway, he would take no chances.

He decided to park his bike somewhere and do "the Batman thing," as Dennis called it – sit on a rooftop and observe the streets for any sign of trouble. Dennis would use his location to monitor the surrounding area and if any 911 calls came in, "Invictus" could be there before the police.

In a suitably seedy neighborhood notorious for drug dealing, Invictus rode into an alley. With less finesse than he'd have liked, he eased the bike to a stop and killed the engine. Dismounting, he rolled the motorcycle behind a row of large dumpsters. Opening the compartment in the seat, he slipped out a cycle cover. Having treated it with his special Chameleon Chemical, as Dennis had dubbed it, he knew it would keep his bike safe from prying eyes. He'd gone through numerous combinations of chemicals, with many trials and errors, before he found the perfect amalgam. He enveloped the motorcycle and watched the pale color of the cover morph into black and grey, matching the surrounding environment. Pleased at witnessing one of his experiments coming to successful fruition, he slunk from the alley.

He used old-fashioned fire escape ladders to ascend to the first building and then parkoured his way across to several others, seeking a good vantage point. The streets below were not busy. Perhaps the dealers didn't come out until later, he surmised. This area was mostly a business district and everything was closed. A square of yellow light shone from the back window of Margaret's Notary Public, illuminating the single car in the parking lot, a shiny new Lexus coup with fancy wire rims and dark-tinted windows.

He decided to sit on the parapet and observe this one car for a while.

Just in case.

The city smells different up here, he mused, *and feels different.*

On the street the smell of car fumes was more pungent, not to mention odors from dumpsters or even pleasant smells like the wafting presence of perfume from a lady passing him in a crowd. Atop the three-story building, however, the light breeze mixed those scents together and muted them somehow. He could even smell dirty water and decided he must not be far from the L.A. River.

Invictus felt like a bird watching the world below. Up high, the city belonged to him and him alone.

"There's nothing going on here, Dennis," he said after twenty tedious minutes, knowing his brother could hear him through the Bluetooth. "I'm about ready to head back and do my homework. I guess nothing happens when you wait for it, even crime."

Movement below caught his eye and he paused. A woman emerged from Margaret's and locked the front door. As she moved toward the parking lot, Invictus observed two men slink from the shadows of an alley to follow.

"Uh, oh, gotta go." Invictus ended the call. He leapt up and swung himself over the side of the building with a flourish of his cape.

The woman arrived at the Lexus, which sat gleaming beneath the overhead streetlights, and held out a key fob. With an audible click, the driver's door popped open. She scanned the area before slipping into the front seat. As she reached out to close the door, a tall man darted from behind the car and yanked the door back. The woman screamed. Another man, shorter and holding a knife in his outstretched hand, popped up from around the passenger side.

Invictus watched from his hiding place behind the parking lot dumpster. The tall man grabbed the woman by the wrist and yanked her roughly from the car. She cried out again.

"Please don't kill me," she begged. "You can have the car!"

He snatched the fob from her hand and shoved her roughly to the ground. With a startled cry of pain, she collapsed onto the dirty asphalt of the parking lot. The shorter man raised the knife.

Invictus was up and over that dumpster in seconds. He flipped in the air and landed in front of the guy with the knife. He spun into a kick and sent the man flying back into the car with a thud. The knife flew from his hand and landed on the ground several feet away.

The taller guy fumbled a gun from beneath his baggy flannel shirt and took unsteady aim. Invictus leaped in front of the woman and raised the shield. The sound of the gun firing punctured the quiet of the night like a series of explosions. Bullets bounced off the shield and ricocheted in every direction.

The woman cried out in terror.

The gunman looked confused and stared at his gun like it had failed him. Beneath the streetlight, Invictus saw the gun hand trembling.

Probably high, he thought as he plowed forward to slam the shield against the man, knocking the gun from his hand and sending him sprawling to the ground in a daze.

Kicking the gun away, Invictus hurried back to extend a hand to the fallen woman. "Are you–" He stopped, and then in a deeper voice repeated, "Are you all right?"

She slapped his hand away with a grunt of disgust. "I'm fine, no thanks to you!"

She struggled to her feet.

In his shock at her response, Invictus noticed that her knees were scraped, but otherwise she seemed uninjured.

"But, uh, I just–" he began, feeling confused.

"Almost got me killed, that's what!" she snapped, strutting to the fallen man and snatching up her fob from where it lay beside him. He groaned, but made no move to stop her. She swept disheveled hair off her face.

"I have an anti-carjacking device in my car. These punks wouldn't have gotten two blocks!"

Invictus stared at her, open-mouthed.

She stalked back to her car and tossed him another furious look. "I don't know who you are, but if you want to play superhero, do it somewhere else!"

She practically threw herself behind the wheel, slammed the door, gunned the engine, and roared out of the parking lot.

Invictus stood frozen in place.

The guy was gonna stab her. Did I miss something?

Shaking his head in bewilderment, he set about tying up the two men so he could leave them for the police. Using the Wi-Fi on his hidden belt camera, he'd relay the footage to Dennis, who'd then send it anonymously to the cops along with the location.

So far, he thought as he slipped thin twine from a pouch on his belt, *this super hero idea has been a miserable failure. Maybe Dennis was wrong, after all.*

After uploading the video, he started along the dimly lit sidewalk back toward where he left his bike. A woman's scream of terror pierced the night somewhere behind him and he took off running.

CHAPTER FIVE

WHAT'S UP WITH THE COSTUME?

H E HEARD A MALE VOICE grunting, and muffled screams, like the guy had a hand over the woman's mouth. He sprinted down another alley that ended at a wall. He could make out two figures struggling on the ground, rolling and fighting for an advantage. The alley reeked of urine, and trash abounded.

He reached the struggling couple before the man even sensed his presence. The guy had one hand pressed against the woman's mouth while his other hand tore at her clothes. Her eyes, wet with smudged mascara, bulged wide when Invictus grabbed the man around the collar and yanked him back. He was big and thick and Invictus had to pull hard.

Caught off-guard, the guy rolled over onto his back, but quickly spun and righted himself. "The fu–"

Invictus didn't let him finish. He lashed out with one foot and caught the guy across the jaw, snapping his head back and sending him sprawling onto the dirty asphalt. To his surprise, the guy wasn't knocked out. Eyes bulging with fury, he leapt at Invictus.

Invictus spun into a roundhouse kick and planted one foot squarely against the man's chest.

The guy must weigh two-fifty, he thought, as the impact sent him staggering back a few steps. But the kick propelled the man backwards where the prone woman was able to kick out at his knees and send him stumbling into a dumpster.

Invictus charged forward and slammed his shield into the man as he started to turn. The impact sent the guy pitching back into the brick wall. Stunned, he slumped downward into a crumpled heap.

The woman pressed her torn blouse up over her exposed bra and cowered.

"Are you all right?"

He reached out a hand to her. Hesitantly, she took it and he helped her stand. She staggered, but he kept her aloft and when she seemed steady enough, he let go.

"Want me to call–"

She shoved him aside and bolted for the mouth of the ally.

"What're you running for?" he called out in shock. "I'm the good guy."

She vanished around the corner without looking back.

"I think."

Invictus felt like he'd been sucker-punched. What was wrong with people these days? Stifling a yawn, he slipped out more of his twine and set about securing the assailant for the police to collect.

Dennis picked up a Batman comic sitting beside his squawking police scanner and flipped it open. The double page spread showed Bruce Wayne training a teenaged Tim Drake in the Bat Cave using a variety of self-defense and fighting techniques. Dennis found himself recalling a time a few years back when he and Vincent were sparring in the backyard. Despite having practiced martial arts since he could walk, just like Vincent, Dennis wasn't a natural. Vincent's body flowed like water, smooth and sleek and almost without restraint. Dennis would never be that good, and he knew it. He'd known it for as long as he could remember.

As he recalled that particular sparring match, he saw his short, well-muscled brother barely crack a sweat as he dodged and danced around every move Dennis made. Both wore karate pants and no shirt. Dennis's upper body had been coated with sweat, and his breathing ragged, while Vincent looked as though he hadn't even begun the match.

Finally, Dennis quit. He'd stalked over to the table and plopped into a lawn chair. Vincent approached and Dennis couldn't help but admire his brother's impressive physique, and even more impressive ability for composure.

"It's okay, Squirt," he offered.

Dennis swept his damp hair off his forehead. "No, It's not. I'll never even be half as good as you."

Vincent sat beside him. "That's true. You're not even a quarter as good."

Dennis scowled. "Thanks for the support."

Vincent seemed puzzled, as though not realizing he'd said something insulting. "I was just trying to be precise. Dad doesn't care if you're good at martial arts."

Dennis recalled the humiliation he'd felt. "I know," he'd replied wistfully. "I just wish…."

"Wish what?"

"Nothing."

Vincent had looked confused, and Dennis glanced away in shame.

Stifling the memory, Dennis snapped the comic book closed and tossed it onto his desk.

It had always been his dream to create a superhero. And now he had. Except he could never *be* the hero he'd created. Sure, once the people followed, he'd know he was the one who'd put the Dream into motion. But he still wanted to prove to Vincent that he could be useful in the field.

Fool, he thought. *You wanna prove it to yourself.*

Invictus pressed tightly against the wall, knowing the Chameleon Chemical in his suit had shifted the color and blended him into the background.

He observed a skinny African-American teen who appeared to be eighteen or nineteen selling a bag of white powder to tiny little boy who looked eight or nine. He couldn't believe it!

Anger surging through him, he stepped away from the wall and sprinted forward. The small boy's eyes widened in surprise, causing the teen to spin around. Invictus grabbed the teen by the collar and slammed him against the alley wall. The teen grunted as air whooshed from his lungs, and Invictus snatched the bag of powder from his hand.

The little boy jumped back, but didn't run. From the corner of his eye, Invictus saw him crouched like a cat, fascinated and curious.

"What you be doin' messing wit my business?" the teen spat, his voice hoarse because Invictus kept a tight grip on his collar.

"It isn't right."

"What's *right* gotta do wit business?" the angry teen shot back, struggling to free himself.

"Everything."

The teen squinted and studied Invictus's face a moment. Then he sneered. "You're a slant, ain't ya?"

Invictus heard a slight gasp from the little boy, but kept his gaze fixed on the teen's smirking, acne-scarred face. His temper rose, but he forced it back down.

"And you're a racist," he said quietly. "But I'm not going to kick your ass for being a racist. I am going to kick it for selling this garbage to kids!"

He slammed the bag down hard on top of the skinny boy's head. It exploded and white powder flew everywhere. If it hadn't been such a deadly drug, the snow-like misting of the air would have seemed hauntingly ethereal. Invictus could tell by the smell that this was meth. He'd performed numerous experiments with meth as part of his thesis project.

The youth coughed and spluttered as flecks of powder assaulted his nose. His black hair was dusted with white, and his face had become ghost-like. Invictus landed a firm, but measured, punch to his gut, sending him crumpling to the ground, gasping for air and rolling around in pain. Extracting more twine, he rapidly trussed up the teen before turning to face the little boy.

He froze. The boy crawled on the ground, running his tongue over the scattered remnants of meth, like a dog licking up some juice that had spilled. Invictus felt revulsion well up from deep within him. The little boy was oblivious to everything except each smidgen of powder he could lick off the ground or inhale from the air. He'd lift his head and sniff wherever he spotted residual clouds of meth drifting downward.

The young dealer chuckled. "Look at the little brown dog."

Invictus hauled off and slapped him hard across the face with one gloved hand. Red blossomed on the powder-whitened cheek and the youth's eyes turned stormy. Invictus snatched up a dirty, torn shirt someone had tossed on the ground and when the teen opened his mouth to protest he shoved the shirt into it.

The small boy licked his chapped lips to get every speck of the poison into his system. He was Latino, with scruffy black hair that brushed past his torn T-shirt collar, wary brown eyes with large bags beneath them, light brown skin that looked sallow and pinched around the cheeks. His skinny frame with its ragged clothes made Invictus think of a scarecrow he'd seen once in a horror film.

The child crouched, his body taut and ready for flight. Invictus stayed where he was. He didn't want to spook the kid.

"What's your name?"

The boy inched backward. "What's yours?"

"Invictus."

The boy pulled a face. "The hell kinda name is that?"

Invictus shrugged and offered a smile. "It's the one I have. What's yours?"

The boy hesitated. "Franky."

"How old are you, Franky?"

"Just turned ten."

Invictus gasped. "How long have you been an addict?" He wasn't sure he wanted to know the answer.

The boy guffawed. "Addict? I'm a tweaker, fool, since I's four or five. Can't remember."

"Didn't your parents try to help you?"

"My mama's the one who started me."

"The hell?" Invictus felt his heart hammering.

The boy shrugged nonchalantly. "It's the only thing we do together, mama and me."

His body eased itself out of its coiled state and he rose to his feet. He still eyed Invictus warily, but made no move to bolt. In fact, his eyes took in the costume and the shield with child-like curiosity.

Invictus didn't know what to say. All of his work with troubled kids, all of his brain studies and classes on psychology – none of them had prepared him for a mother intentionally addicting her four-year-old son to crystal meth.

"What's up with the costume?" Franky asked, the wary tone gone. "You some kinda superhero?"

"No," Invictus replied. "Just a guy trying to make a difference out here."

"By getting my ass whupped?" Franky shot back.

"How am I doing that?"

"Mama sent me out to buy," Franky said, his voice heavy with sadness, as though he hated his life, but was resigned to it. "When I come back with nothing, she'll be flailing somethin' crazy and beat my ass bad."

Invictus flinched. "What's 'flailing' mean?"

Franky shook his head. "You don't know nuthin' 'bout the streets, do you, superhero?"

"Not much, no," Invictus reluctantly admitted. He was as book smart as they come, but completely ignorant about what went on in the daily lives of so many Angelenos.

"She be needing her stuff that I didn't get." Then he laughed. "I got mine, though." He stuck out his tongue. It was raw and bloody from scraping it along the pavement. Residual specks of white peppered the red. "I'm small so it don't take much for me."

Again, Invictus felt paralyzed with disgust, and the realization that fighting crime wasn't like Dennis's comic books. He could take out every drug dealer in this area and it wouldn't help Franky.

Franky stepped forward impulsively and brushed his dirty fingertips against the shield. "Is it bullet-proof?"

"Pretty much."

Franky grinned. "Just like Cap."

"You like superheroes?"

"Used to. 'Fore I learned they couldn't save me."

Once again, Invictus felt his heart pull tightly in his chest. This boy touched him in ways he hadn't thought possible.

"Would you like to hold it?" He extended the shield.

Franky's eyes bulged so wide they made the sallowness of his cheeks look almost skeletal. He hesitated, as though he thought Invictus might slam the shield into his face. Tentatively, he reached out. Invictus turned the shield around so Franky could slip his small fingers around the handgrip.

"Use both hands, Franky. It's heavy."

Franky entwined the fingers of his other hand around the handgrip and Invictus let go. The shield dropped and struck the ground with a dull thud.

"Oh, crap!" Franky exclaimed. "You wasn't joking. You must be super strong."

"I do all right."

He watched the boy heft the large shield and hold it in front of him, twisting his face into an expression of determination, as though he hoped the shield could magically protect him from his mother, the meth, the world at large. The lost innocence on Franky's face was almost too much to bear.

How can people treat children like this?

Franky reverently returned the shield.

"No reason you can't be a superhero, too, Franky," Invictus offered, his voice steadier than his heart.

"Me? Yeah, right! Look at me, man. I'm a skinny-ass little tweaker who can't fight."

"It's not about fighting or how big you are. Look at *me* – not exactly the Hulk over here."

Franky laughed and Invictus liked the natural sound of it.

"Sure, I know how to fight because I've done martial arts my whole life," Invictus went on, his voice gentle and calm. "But a real superhero is the guy who steps away from the crowd to do what's right, even if he's the only one doing it."

Franky considered that a moment. "That kinda guy'll probably get his ass kicked out here."

"Or he'll start a revolution for other people to follow," Invictus responded with conviction, hoping he sounded more confident than he felt. Dennis was the dreamer in the family, not him.

Franky looked thoughtful a moment.

"Let me take you somewhere, Franky," Invictus offered. "Somewhere safe."

The boy lurched back. "I can't leave mama."

"But she hurts you."

"She's my mama." He backed away, once more the wild animal wary of a trap. "Thanks for letting me play with your shield."

He dashed from the alley.

Invictus watched him vanish into the night, his heart heavy, his worldview awhirl with doubts and insecurities. He observed the trussed up drug dealer. The kid's eyes no longer danced with mockery. They were filled with the same sense of wonder that Franky had shown while holding the shield.

Before he could change his mind, Invictus strode to the teen and yanked the ragged shirt from his mouth. The kid was stunned when Invictus reached around to untie his hands.

"I'll probably regret this," he mumbled as he undid the twine and stepped back. The teen remained on the ground, as though he feared another beating. "Don't let me catch you selling again," he threatened in his deepest voice. "Or else!"

He stepped back a few feet. The confused youth hesitated. Then he jumped up and fled the ally like a scared jackrabbit.

Feeling a desperate need to talk with Dennis, Invictus headed back to where he'd parked his bike.

Time to call it a night.

CHAPTER SIX
YOU HAVE SEEN THE HERO

Tired and disillusioned after his encounter with Franky, the last thing Invictus needed was the motorcycle to give him trouble.

You should've bought a new one.

Dennis's words rang in his ears as he struggled with the choke and the throttle. Yeah, he probably should've, but he was trying to save money. Dennis still had college in four years and unless he got a full ride, that would mean exorbitant sums of money.

"Need some company tonight?"

The question startled him and he realized how off-guard he'd been. *Focus, Vince*, he shouted silently into his brain as he observed a tall, lanky teen approaching from the mouth of the alley. The boy stopped up short upon noting Invictus's costume and the shield affixed to the front of his bike.

Sadly, naïve as he was about many monstrous things humans did to each other, he wasn't unfamiliar with kids on the streets having to sell their bodies to survive.

Annoyed with himself, he shot back, "Do I look like I'm out here to pick up boys?"

Seeing the shocked and confused reaction on the teen's lean face, he instantly felt bad. But the boy didn't seem fazed by the comment. He looked excited.

"I saw you on TV when I's chilling on the boulevard last night," the boy exclaimed. "They were playing the news in those crap-ass electronics stores. Man, you really kicked ass on those guys at the school!"

The admiration in his voice was unmistakable, and Invictus regretted his earlier tone.

"Thanks."

The boy stepped closer and stopped beneath the meager pool of light provided by a dirty bulb high above. He was taller than Invictus, though being taller than five foot six wasn't much of an achievement, wearing tight jeans and a white tank top. He was African-American, with what looked like a four inch 'fro, a small mouth, and very active eyes that seemed to take in everything at once.

"How old are you?" Invictus asked.

"Fourteen. How old're you?"

"My God," Invictus whispered. "This is how you live?"

The boy stiffened. "It's not like I want to."

"Where's your family?"

"Dunno." He shrugged. The sheer casualness of that shrug sent shivers up Invictus's spine. "I ran away last year. Then they took off for Mississippi or somewhere."

"Why'd you run away?"

"They found out I was queer." He used the air quotes for "queer." Then he offered a hollow laugh. "My dad actually said, 'No real black man is a faggot' and that I'd be better off to be a gangbanger than an effing queer. 'Cept he used the word."

"That's evil." Once again, Invictus felt his entire chest tighten, almost like he couldn't breathe. Could he adapt to how things were out here? He'd have to if he wanted to make a difference.

"It's how people are." He studied Invictus a moment. "What'd they call you again?"

"Invictus."

The boy mulled that over. "Sounds familiar." Then he stuck out a hand. "Name's Joe."

Invictus shook his hand.

"I saw you a few streets over breaking up Franky's deal."

"You know Franky?"

"Sure. He's like my little brother, you know?"

Invictus heard sincerity in Joe's voice and a deep affection for Franky. He felt some relief that Franky had a friend watching his back. Not that Joe looked formidable enough to protect the smaller boy if something went down, but at least he was there.

"You mean what you said to him? All that superhero bull crap?"

"Every word."

Joe shook his head, shuffling his feet at the same time. "That's kid stuff, man. Reminds me of my best bud back in fourth grade. You gotta grow up and face the world, hero."

"I am facing it," Invictus stated with conviction. "It's equal parts ugly and beautiful. But each of us can stand up and make it better."

"Whatever, man. People want what they can get for themselves. That's just how it is out here and you're not gonna change it."

"We'll see. Right now I'm taking you to Runaway House."

"No can do, man. Been there already. Said there's no more beds. Fire rules or somethin'."

Invictus eyed him with firm conviction. He wanted the boy to understand that one person could truly have a positive impact. "They'll make room."

He tried the choke and throttle again and the bike stalled.

"You're flooding it," Joe offered, stepping closer to observe. "Turn off the choke and turn the throttle gently. Then hit the starter."

Invictus followed his instructions.

"Now ease off the throttle."

Invictus did, and the bike purred to life beneath him.

Joe laughed. "Some superhero."

Invictus bit back the sarcastic retort. "I'm no superhero. Just a guy. Hop on."

Joe sprang deftly onto the back of the bike, as though he'd done it a hundred times. Invictus felt thin arms envelop his torso and then he sped off into the night.

Runaway House was located off Hollywood Boulevard because, as Vincent had learned when he volunteered there a few years back, runaway kids always gravitated to Hollywood. The artificial quest for fame was in large part why there were so many problems in America. Kids wanted to be famous YouTubers instead of doing something out in the community that might benefit others and, as a result, became self-absorbed and out of touch.

Joe kept a tight grip across his torso as Invictus navigated his way through side streets. In addition to being wanted by the cops, he didn't want to ride too fast when Joe had no helmet. The kid prattled on about which dealers worked which corners and what drugs they sold and for how much. He insisted he wasn't a user, but had lots of friends on the street who were. His clarity of thought and attention to minute details of the landscape, in addition to specific incidents he recounted, convinced Invictus that he was telling the truth. If he'd been using meth for even a short time, or marijuana, for that matter, his memory wouldn't be so precise.

They stood in silence at the front door of Runaway House after Joe rang the bell. Invictus heard it chime from deep within the two story building, and then waited, with only traffic sounds from the 101 freeway coming to his ears.

"He's not gonna let me stay," Joe proclaimed, a touch of smugness in his voice.

Invictus eyed him a moment. "Yes, he will."

The door opened and a bearded, older man stood on the threshold. He sighed with exasperation upon seeing Joe.

"I told you before–"

Invictus stepped forward, directly beneath the overhead light, and the man gasped.

"You're the one from the school," he said, sounding almost breathless with worry. "The vigilante the police are after."

"In the flesh," Invictus said proudly. "Now you need to let this boy in."

The man inched back. He wore pajamas and had obviously been awakened from his sleep. "As I explained to the boy when he came by earlier, there are no more beds available for tonight."

"Says who?"

The man eyed Invictus like he was a moron. "If we exceed our allotted number, we violate housing and fire codes, as well as jeopardize our funding base. We could be severely fined or even shut down."

"Only if those people find out," Invictus asserted.

"I can't take that chance."

Joe chuckled. "Told ya he was a hardass."

Invictus took a step forward and the man flinched back in fear.

"Codes, fire regulations, and money are all paper. This is a human being and he sure as hell better be more important."

He paused and forced calm into his mind and body. Not every encounter was a martial arts competition. He needed another approach.

"Do you have kids of your own, sir?"

The man nodded, still eyeing him with fear. "Two. Grown now and on their own."

"When your kids were Joe's age, wouldn't you have wanted someone to bend the rules if they were desperate and needed help?"

The man's look changed from fear to sudden comprehension, like he'd never thought of his job in that way before.

"Yeah, I would." He studied Joe in the shadows of the front stoop as though seeing his own son homeless on the streets. "I can put you on a couch for the night. But please don't tell anyone or I could lose my job."

"I won't say a word," Joe assured him.

"Me, either," Invictus added, feeling relieved.

The man moved away from the open door so Joe could enter.

Joe eyed Invictus with respect. "You're chill, man. Oh, and I remember where I heard your name before."

"Yeah?"

"It's a poem." He smirked, clearly pleased with himself.

"How'd you know that?" Invictus hadn't thought many people, especially kids this age, would recognize the origin of his name.

Joe frowned. "I might be a dropout, but I'm not stupid."

"I never said you were."

Joe appraised him a moment. "No, you didn't. You're different." He stepped past the man into the building, and then glanced back. "Your hair kicks ass, by the way. Oh, and don't forget that choke."

He grinned before the man closed the door.

As he started the bike—with ease this time by following Joe's instructions—and rode off into the night for home, Invictus realized he'd need help out on the streets, even above and beyond Dennis's ability to hack into the LAPD mainframe. He needed eyes and ears out here if he was going to make any real dent in the drug trade. Joe and Franky could very well be those eyes and ears. If they were willing, of course.

Dennis sat on the bottom stair dressed in a jacket and tie reading a Batman comic book. His phone sat by his feet on the carpeted floor. The front door burst open and Vincent breathlessly entered, wearing his lab coat and hauling his backpack over one shoulder.

Dennis picked up his phone and glanced at the time. "Vincent, we're gonna be late."

Vincent dropped his pack and slipped his phone from his pocket. "I'll call."

He punched in the number.

Dennis's face screwed up with horror, as though he just realized something. "Vincent, nooooo!"

Vincent ignored him and raised the phone to his ear.

"Vincent!" Dennis shrieked again.

Dennis whipped his head up from the desk and looked around in terror.

Vincent burst into the room, wearing the costume, but without the mask. He leaped over the piles of clothes to his brother. Wide-eyed with terror, Dennis threw his arms around him and held on as though his life depended on it, pressing his face against his brother's chest.

Vincent gently rocked him back and forth. "It's okay, Dennis, it was just a nightmare, that's all. I've been having them, too."

Dennis didn't let go. He was shaking and couldn't stop. Every time he had that dream, it was the same - he couldn't stop shaking.

"Let's get you into bed," Vincent offered, and eased him up and over to the bed.

Dennis sat on the side of the bed while Vincent laid him down, pulling the rumpled covers up and over him. Dennis felt groggy, but anxious.

As Vincent stood back from the bed, he shot a hand out from under the covers and snatched one of his brother's. "Stay with me, please? I don't wanna be alone."

Vincent gazed at him and Dennis saw the exhaustion, but he needed him tonight, more than usual. Maybe it was that nightmare, or maybe just because Vincent had been on the streets play-acting his creation without him. But he needed his brother.

"You want me to read to you, like mom used to do when you were little?"

Dennis nodded. That sounded like a great idea. And he had the perfect book. He reached over to his night table and slipped open the drawer. Pulling out a dog-eared paperback of *The Velveteen Rabbit*, he handed the book over.

Vincent took it and pulled over Dennis's desk chair, eying the book. "I remember this one. Still your favorite, even after all the books you've read?"

"It always makes me feel real."

Vincent tilted his head, as though considering the meaning of that remark.

"Start on page eight, 'kay?" Dennis asked quietly. He didn't need the whole story—just the most important part.

Vincent passed over the first few pages, stifling a yawn as he did. Then he began to read.

"'What is REAL?' asked the Rabbit one day. 'Does it mean having things that buzz inside you and a stick-out handle?'

'Real isn't how you are made,' said the Skin Horse. 'It's a thing that happens to you. When a child loves you for a long, long time, not just to play with, but REALLY loves you, then you become Real.'

'Does it hurt?'

'Sometimes.' For he was always truthful. 'When you are Real you don't mind being hurt.'

'Does it happen all at once, like being wound up, or bit by bit?'

'It doesn't happen all at once. You become. It takes a long time. That's why it doesn't often happen to people who break easily, or who have sharp edges, or who have to be carefully kept. Generally, by the time you are Real, most of your hair has been loved off, and your eyes drop out and you get loose in the joints and very shabby. But these things don't matter at all, because once you are Real you can't be ugly, except to people who don't understand. Once you are Real you can't become unreal again. It lasts for always.'"

Dennis soaked up those words, and the tension in his body uncoiled.

Vincent paused and studied him. "That's your favorite part, isn't it?"

Dennis nodded.

"Dennis, you're the most real person I know."

Dennis heard the conviction in his voice. "Yeah?"

"Yeah."

"Stay with me tonight?" He knew he sounded weak, and especially hated acting weak in front of Vincent. But that dream about the night his parents died, and his self-doubts and, well, everything seemed to be pushing on him, holding him down and suffocating him. It was the PTSD, he knew, causing his mind and body to convulse with reactions he couldn't control. But he didn't want to be alone.

"Scoot over, Squirt."

Dennis smiled as he slid to one side of his bed. "You haven't called me that in the longest."

Vincent lay on top of the covers beside his brother. "That's because for the longest I've been the squirt, not you."

Dennis laughed. "You always told me little brothers weren't supposed to get taller than their big ones."

"You didn't listen."

"I finally beat you at something," Dennis said quietly as he settled into his pillow. He caught the confused look on Vincent's face and added, "How'd it go out there?"

Vincent yawned. "I'm wiped out. Tell you in the morning. But I think Filipino parents are the only ones who teach their kids to say 'thank you.'"

And then he was asleep, his chest rising and falling with peaceful regularity. Dennis switched off the table lamp and scooted closer to his brother. He wasn't sure he'd sleep much, but having Vincent there made him feel safe.

Demon parked the Mercedes in his usual spot inside the loading dock, and pressed the remote button to lower the truck doors. Since the warehouse never stored large boxes, and trucks never came and went, there was plenty of room for him and his cohorts to park their cars.

Young Z popped open the passenger door and stepped out onto the hard concrete. Z, a year younger and the closest thing Demon had to a friend, peeled off toward the lab to turn in his report on their distribution. The Mistress demanded an accurate accounting.

Demon headed for the metal stairs leading three floors up to the Video Room. Other than his echoing footsteps, the air around him was quiet. He considered The Mistress's latest fixation - the so-called superhero guy who'd brought down the takeover of the school. She'd been obsessively watching video footage of him for days.

Demon knew he shouldn't feel jealous. After all, he was twenty-one and The Mistress at least ten years older. She'd always seen him as a little brother from the moment she'd recruited him when he was twelve. She'd said her name was Cat, that she was Korean, and he would address her as "Mistress." That had been the beginning.

She'd taken him under her wing, taught him how to fight and treated him like family. But even as he grew into a man, she'd never looked at him as "a man." In fact, she had no lovers that he ever heard of, and since embarking on her current operation she'd been fixated on nothing else.

"This is a short and long term operation, Demon," she'd told him one night while sparring with him. "I trust you will remain at my side?"

She stepped back to give him space. "Yes, Mistress. I am yours forever."

She'd smiled. It was a beautiful smile that always caught Demon's breath in his throat. But behind her eyes lurked menace and coiled anger. That night she had stepped so close that their bodies touched, and raised one well-manicured hand to stroke his cheek.

"Good. I wouldn't want you running off with some useless female and abandoning me."

Demon felt his body temperature rise, as it did every time she touched him. "Never, Mistress. I am yours to use as you see fit."

He secretly hoped she would use him for other things besides running operations on the street, but knew that wasn't ever going to happen. She had too much self-control to let anyone use her in any way, even if she initiated it.

He was fairly sure she wasn't interested in this so-called hero in that way, but he did wonder, in the back of his mind, if it might be possible

Forcing such thoughts aside, he stopped outside the third-floor door and touched the fingerprint sensor. The door popped open. At least he was still the only one besides herself who had access to the heart of her organization.

The Mistress stood gazing at a bank of video monitors that filled an entire wall. Computer stations abounded. She had hacked into surveillance cameras throughout the city and her monitors shifted from image to image every ten seconds. Other monitors flitted between images of this warehouse and the grounds surrounding it. Some monitors displayed images from the body cams her foot soldiers were required to wear. In this way she kept tabs on all of her operations at once.

Demon knew she had *a lot* going on, but even he didn't know her deepest secrets. She kept those hidden within the darkness of her heart.

"You have seen the hero." She turned amidst a swirl of long, black hair, excitement dancing across her lovely features. "I saw glimpses on my monitor, but you were hidden from his view and the sound quality was poor. Tell me of him, Demon. Tell me everything."

He stood at attention. "We sold the stuff to a black guy, like we been doin', and then he sold it to little Franky. The guy you call 'Hero' showed up and kicked the black guy's ass."

"What else did he do?"

Demon recounted what Invictus told Franky about being a superhero.

She laughed. "He's a foolish dreamer."

Several screens displayed footage of Invictus taking down the school kidnappers. On another screen, Invictus was leaving the alley after his encounter with Franky.

"But he fights well," she commented.

He instantly stepped forward, his pride stung. "I can take him."

She reached out a hand to his shoulder and he shivered. "You'll have your chance, Demon. In the meantime, continue to recruit our people. The more of us working together, the greater the damage we can inflict."

She removed her hand. "Yes, Mistress."

Trembling slightly from her touch, Demon stepped back. Her gaze remained on images of Invictus. She looked mesmerized.

"With all due respect, Mistress, why not stop this 'Hero' now?"

She gave him an enigmatic look. Even after all these years, he still couldn't sense what went on behind those dark eyes.

"I have plans for him."

He didn't like the sound of that, but knew better than to press her further. He bowed and left the room.

CHAPTER SEVEN
COURAGE CAN BE COSTLY

"**V**INCENT, WAKE UP!"

Vincent stirred. His head felt fuzzy with sleep, his body fatigued. He shook violently. Earthquake? That thought shot through him and he sat up, only to find Dennis shaking him hard enough to rattle teeth.

"You're late for school again!"

Those words pierced his sleep-addled brain. "Oh, no, not again!"

"Go!"

Dennis practically pushed him off the bed and Vincent fumbled and stumbled his way over the piles of clothes. At the door he turned back. "You okay?"

"I'm fine. Go!"

Vincent didn't need to be told twice. Chin would kill him!

By the time he got to UCLA, he was forty minutes late for his Neuroscience class and had to park farther away than usual. He'd only had time to jump in the shower and throw on pants and a tank top before barreling down the street in his car. Backpack slung over his shoulders, ponytail trailing behind him like a horse's mane, Vincent sprinted across campus to the Molecular Sciences Building.

Professor Chin stood at the front of the lecture hall engaged in his presentation. Images of the human brain were projected on the smart screen behind him. As Vincent burst through the door at the top of the hall, his backpack tumbled to the floor. The loud *thud* drew the attention of most of his classmates. Chin glanced up from below and frowned.

Vincent stared at the man he couldn't afford to dissatisfy, and saw even from this distance that he had, once again, disappointed him.

"You're late, Mr. Villanueva," the professor said tartly. "Again." Then he resumed his lecture and everyone went back to note taking. Lisa waved to him from one of the upper rows, indicating the empty seat beside her.

Feeling like a little boy scolded by the principal, he brushed his errant hair back over his shoulder and adjusted his slipping glasses. Retrieving his backpack, he inched his way past annoyed students to plop down into the empty seat.

She leaned in and whispered, "I had to fight to save this seat."

Embarrassed, he glanced over. "Thanks."

She handed him a slip of paper. He opened it and saw an address. Confused, he raised his eyebrows questioningly.

"My address," she whispered. "For tomorrow night."

Vincent almost flinched. He'd completely forgotten! He hoped she didn't notice his confusion as he took the paper and slid it into his pocket. He felt a squeeze on his upper arm and saw her hand wrapped around it. She smiled, and he returned it.

She let go, and he fumbled for a pen and his notepad. Time to find out how much he'd missed.

James stood beside Sergeant Janson, a man he knew by reputation, but not personally. The reputation was of a gung-ho cop who'd often go too far in pursuit of a suspect, forsaking prudence for results. That hyper-aggressive attitude ran completely counter to how James worked his cases.

Torres stood before them in the briefing room, a map of Los Angeles projected onto a smart board behind him. Blue lights flashed at several locations in and around downtown, and one in Hollywood. Torres pointed to each as he spoke.

"Last night he was seen here, here, here, and finally here." His finger ended up in Hollywood. "Runaway House. He was spotted with a kid talking to someone at the door. We found out this morning he made the night man take in that kid in violation of the rules."

The captain's tone indicated he thought such an offense was tantamount to murder.

James wanted to say something, but held his tongue.

"As of now, Detective Stevens, I'm teaming you with Janson."

That caught James by surprise. "Whoa, Captain. I haven't had a partner since–"

"Since we lost Villanueva, I know," Torres said, cutting him off. "It's been six months, Stevens, and we have to move on. This vigilante case is your top priority."

James glanced at Janson and didn't like the self-satisfied smirk on his face. Younger than him, Janson had blond hair and blue eyes and a cockier-than-hell attitude.

"Captain, so far this vigilante hasn't broken any major laws that we know of," James insisted quietly, but he hoped forcefully. "He saved us at the school and last night he nabbed those carjackers."

"He's operating outside the law and that in itself is a crime."

"But–"

"No buts, Detective," Torres snapped. "You and Janson have one job – arrest that vigilante."

"Yes, sir."

"Now, we picked up the kid he dropped off at Runaway House," Torres went on. "He's a known prostitute so we might be able to squeeze him for information on this weirdo."

James didn't like where this was going. "Captain, a child forced to live on the streets is a victim of trafficking."

"Spare me the bleeding heart song and dance, Detective," Torres shot back. "He's in interrogation room three. We can't hold him for long, so push hard. See if he knows where the freak holes up."

"Yes, sir," Janson said with authority. "Detective Stevens and I will apprehend this guy. Right, Detective?"

James tried not to grimace. Torres dismissed them and he followed Janson out of the room.

"I told you I don't know anything about him," Joe insisted for the fifth time. "And the guy at Runaway House felt sorry for me. Invictus didn't force him to do anything."

Janson leaned right into his face. "Sure Invictus wasn't one of your customers and that's why he helped you?"

James pulled Janson back. "Back off, Janson. That's an order."

Joe looked aghast at Janson, and shook his head in amazement. "You cops are asshats. No wonder everybody hates your guts."

"Sorry, kid, my *partner* got carried away," James said with disgust and hating Torres for this pairing.

Joe glared at him. "No, he didn't. It's how you guys always are with kids. Even when we're homeless you treat us like garbage to get what you want. Because what you want is always more important than us. 'Cept it isn't. Invictus helped me when no one else did. Thanks to him, I got me a regular spot at Runaway House to crash at night. He's more about justice than this a-hole."

He jerked a thumb at Janson. The blond detective's face screwed up with anger and he lunged forward to grab Joe by his tank top. James shoved Janson hard and he released Joe.

"You're going to let this little prick talk to me that way?"

"Yeah, I am."

Joe pulled the tank strap back over his shoulder.

Janson opened his mouth to protest, but James held up a hand and focused on Joe. "I can call social services to come get you."

"I'll just run first chance I get."

James studied him a moment. "Is home that bad, Joe?"

Joe nodded.

James knew there was no point in forcing the issue. "Okay, you're free to go."

Joe mad-dogged Janson as he moved to the door and pulled it open.

"You tell that freak we're going to nail his ass," Janson said in a low, threatening tone.

Joe studied Janson a moment, and then hurried from the interrogation room.

"You were outta line, Janson."

Janson looked defiant. "Sweet talking faggots like him isn't going to get us anywhere."

James flinched. Having assisted Linda with her martial arts classes, and especially through his job, he'd dealt with a large number of gay kids over the years and he hated that word. Way too close to the "N" word he'd had hurled at him growing up.

"Sergeant, do not let me hear you use that or any other derogatory epithet in my presence. Are we clear?"

Janson appeared chastised, but James knew this was only the beginning of their conflicts. It was beyond him how a loose cannon like Janson ever made sergeant.

"Go home and get some sleep," James commanded.

"Why? The captain said–"

"The captain said to catch the vigilante," James went on, already feeling exasperated. "And the vigilante only comes out at night. That means, sergeant, we'll be on night patrol for the duration."

Janson lost the smug look. "Oh, right."

"Meet back here at eight," James ordered.

"Yes, sir." Janson left the room.

James considered what Joe had said about cops and how they treated kids. Had he ever done that when he'd been a beat cop on the streets? Pumped some kid for information, threatened him if he didn't snitch on his friends or turn over evidence? He hoped he hadn't, but suspected he had. It was how they'd been trained, after all. Joe was right. Cops were supposed to protect kids, not threaten them or force them to become informants or snitches. This Invictus guy might be operating outside the law, but was he operating outside of *justice*?

Pondering that question, James left the station and headed for home.

Dorothy Ellis stood in front of her summer school class of squirrelly sixth graders. Since the terrifying graduation incident the week before, she'd become obsessed with Invictus and followed every news story she could find. His heroics excited her, gave her hope for her city and the people in it. And she hoped he might inspire her students to think beyond the next selfie or video game.

She'd sketched a very detailed drawing of the hero, sixteen by twenty, and placed it on an easel in front of her art students. Her assignment was for them to "interpret" Invictus in their own way – take what they knew about him and make him relevant to each of them.

She wanted to get Dennis Villanueva to drop by and share what it felt like to be rescued by the hero. The police were calling him a vigilante and wanted him arrested, but she thought what he was doing was beyond important and hated how narrow-minded the authorities always were with anyone who thought or acted outside the box. That's what she hated about the school system, too – the one size fits all mentality.

Common sense told her, and anyone else who had a brain, that all kids were *not* the same and each one needed a different approach to teaching and learning. That's why she favored assignments like this one. The kids could individualize Invictus however they saw him and draw him in whatever style they liked. Some of them drew him manga style, others comic book. Some took an abstract approach. But she hoped that however they "saw" him, he might inspire each of them to be a force for change.

She made a mental note to call Dennis on her lunch break. With all the drama of graduation, he'd never even gotten his art award.

Dennis sat at his desk working on detailed sketches of the Invictus costume. Several similar drawings lay on top of his poetry books, all done prior to his creating the outfit. He loved to add more and more detail to these images in case at some point they decided to upgrade his hero's "look."

He picked up a sketch, and his breath caught in his throat. Beneath it rested a photo of his dad and Vincent. They were laughing and arm wrestling. Dennis felt his heart rate increase and his breathing start to escalate. He practiced his calming techniques and after a few moments everything returned to normal. He reached out and picked up the photo. A memory surfaced.

The memory.

The family gathering that begat Invictus.

It had been Thanksgiving last year, their final Thanksgiving as a family. As such, Dennis had obsessed over committing every detail to memory.

James and Linda were over for dinner and everyone sat around the table laughing and enjoying the feast his mom had prepared. The turkey dripped with juice. The fresh cranberries smelled like they'd just been picked. The stuffing melted in his mouth. There was rice, of course, because they ate rice with every meal. But his mom had also mashed up fresh potatoes. She'd seasoned them with spices Dennis couldn't name, but his tongue savored each and every one. The adults drank wine while he and Vincent swigged sparkling apple cider, one of his favorites.

As wonderful as those memories were, Dennis vividly recalled his somber mood. He hadn't planned on spoiling the festive atmosphere, but he must've been wearing a sad face because Mom asked, "What's wrong, sweetie?"

Dennis glanced at Vincent because Vincent already knew. "I'm sorry. Just a little down."

"Why?" dad asked in his usual quiet tone.

Dennis looked around the table. Everyone had stopped eating, including his godparents, awaiting his answer. "It's because of Tommy, that kid from my old school, the one who got sentenced to life in prison yesterday."

"The bully kid who beat another kid to death?" James exclaimed. He looked shocked that Dennis would worry about someone like that.

"He didn't beat the kid to death, James," Dennis corrected. "They got into a fight and the other kid died when he hit his head on the ground. That's manslaughter, not murder. Even I know that."

"The kid had a long history, Dennis," James went on soberly. "You know that. He's one of the reasons your parents moved out of the old neighborhood."

"That's true, son," Loy added, studying Dennis with care.

"Did either of you read the story in L.A. Weekly?" Vincent put in, and Dennis felt relief that his brother had finally spoken up.

No one had.

"Tommy was beaten up since the first grade by his stepfather," Dennis said, his voice hitching slightly. "And his mom let the guy do that to him. Sure, he was a bully in school. He even punked some of my friends. But now I understand why."

"But the law didn't care about that," Vincent put in, sounding frustrated, "and even charged him with second degree murder to get him a longer sentence. How is that fair, or even right?"

Loy studied Vincent a moment before responding. That was something Dennis loved about his dad – he never gave a flippant or off the cuff opinion. He always paused before speaking.

"I think the answer is complex, Vincent. Americans seem to feel the need for punishment, regardless of the circumstances that led to a crime, or even the age and background of the perpetrator. Would you agree, James? I wasn't born here, remember."

He offered a gentle smile. In his mind's eye, Dennis saw the exact angle of his dad's hand as he held the fork, the glint of candlelight off the wire-rimmed glasses that so resembled the ones Vincent wore now, and even the loving glance he cast toward Mom beside him.

James nodded around a mouthful of yams. "I agree to a point, Loy. You and I have had this discussion before. To give Americans the benefit of the doubt, I think people here believe in accountability for our actions."

"How is putting a fourteen-year-old in prison for life holding him accountable when the man who made him that way goes unpunished?" Vincent had asked, putting down his knife and fork. Dennis recalled his brother's stiff posture, and the smell of Tabasco sauce wafting off Vincent's plate because he'd doused his turkey in it.

"He killed another boy, Vincent," James said, as though that was the entire story. "Dennis, you like to say that all life is precious, right?"

Dennis nodded, hating how his godfather always focused on the letter of the law. "But life is complicated too. Back in fourth grade I thought Tommy was just a bully. Now I know he's not any different from me. If I'd grown up like that, I'd probably be where he is right now."

"He's right, James," Vincent went on. "Tommy isn't any different than the kids I worked with, except those kids got help before they spun out of control."

"What about adults, Vincent, who commit heinous crimes?" their mom put in, sipping her wine. "Like those men who beat that poor Korean man to death. That was clearly a hate crime, one of many against Asians, as you well know."

"That kind of hate is sickening," Linda offered, her face scrunched up with disgust. She set down her fork as though she'd just lost her appetite.

"They gloated over being released from custody because we couldn't get any hard evidence," James put in, his tone laced with recrimination. "It's not just white guys who get off scot-free, no matter what the media says."

"Don't you get tired," Vincent said, casting his gaze around the table at each of the adults, "of hearing people complain about the corruption in society when they never do anything to make things better?"

"People in this country have too many freedoms and too little sense of obligation," Loy said calmly. "They say they want to make the city better, but how many give up parts of their lives to make it happen? Courage can be costly, son. To make a difference requires sacrifice, and most people will never go that far. It's a sad trait of human nature."

"Maybe they're just afraid to help," Dennis offered. "Perhaps everything terrible is, in its deepest being, something helpless that wants help from us."

When they all stared at him quizzically, Dennis gave a tiny smile. "It's from a poem I like by Ranier Maria Rilke. Seemed to fit."

Loy raised his glass in a toast. "To my son. He has the soul of a poet."

"I second that," Merriam attested and raised her glass of wine.

Vincent raised his sparkling cider. "Me, too."

"Here, here." Linda raised her glass, and James followed suit.

Dennis still felt the gush of emotion, the acceptance and love within that simple toast and those gentle words from the father he so desperately missed. He lowered the photo and brushed away a tear.

That had been the genesis of Invictus - Tommy's conviction and that conversation around the Thanksgiving table. Dennis felt his heart tug in his chest.

"I miss you, Daddy," he mumbled to his empty room.

His ringtone blasted forth and he jumped slightly. Rifling through papers on his desk, he found the phone and pressed the green button, placing the handset to his ear.

"Hello?" He listened a moment. "Oh, hi, Ms. Ellis." He listened again. "Sure I can come talk with your class. Yeah, I'm free for fifth period. Okay, see you then."

He ended the call and sat back in his chair. He'd agreed to talk with her class because he was bored. Jack and Kenny had begged off a *Call of Duty* session because they were headed to the mall with friends. They'd invited him, but the plan was to stay and see a movie after and he needed to be here when Vincent got home so he could be "the eyes and ears of Invictus."

But now that he thought about his hasty decision, answering questions in Ms. Ellis's class about the graduation incident could be risky. His whole body tightened with dread at the remembrance of how close he'd come to dying that day, and how inadequate he felt about his own response. Sure, he had untied the principal and Ms. Ellis and the other administrators and helped them to safety…

But that was after almost peeing my pants when that guy held the knife in front of me.

He shivered and breathed in and out slowly to calm his pounding heart.

It made him feel good, however, that Ms. Ellis sounded so fired up about Invictus.

That's why you created him, Dennis reminded himself, *to inspire people. Just be careful and be like dad – pause before you speak.*

Having decided, he rose to put on clean clothes.

CHAPTER EIGHT

THAT WAS COOL, WHAT YOU DID

IT FELT ODDLY COMFORTING TO be back in Ms. Ellis's classroom. Dennis felt as though he'd never left. The smell of paints and markers, the student art adorning the walls—some of it his own creations—the easels, the art tables filled with summer bridge students – it all conspired to bring Dennis comfort.

He recognized a few of these kids from recruitment visits to the elementary schools, when he'd urged them to attend Parker Middle. But *all* of them recognized him from the graduation videos that had been broadcast twenty-four seven since Sunday night. Especially unnerving to Dennis had been the recovered cell phone footage of him – close-ups of his terrified face and wide eyes as the knife grazed the soft flesh of his throat. He hated watching those because they made him seem weak. But then, he'd been petrified, so how else was he supposed to look?

Ms. Ellis introduced him to the class. Being summer school, there were only twenty students, rather than the usual thirty-six during the school year. She presented him his art award and the class applauded. Most of them, anyway. A dark-skinned Latino kid and an African-American next to him seemed to be goofing with each other and didn't clap at all.

"I also want to personally thank Dennis for helping me and the administrators get away last Sunday. That was beyond brave."

She leaned in for a side hug and Dennis blushed with embarrassment. But he also felt his insides fill with pride for what he'd done and her acknowledgment of it.

Most of the kids clapped even harder, smacking sounds filling the room, and Dennis grinned.

When Ms. Ellis opened the class up to questions about the graduation, that's when everything went to crap. Later, as he reflected on the afternoon, he didn't think the kids realized how much they'd hurt him.

One girl raised her hand. Dennis noted the paint stains on her fingers and felt right at home. "On a scale of one to ten, how scared were you when that guy was about to cut your throat?"

Dennis's pride was stung, but he couldn't pretend. The video was proof. "About a fifteen," he admitted with a chuckle.

The class laughed and the room brightened with a moment of fellowship.

A boy raised his hand and Ms. Ellis said, "Introduce yourself before you ask your question." She turned to the first girl. "Sorry, Shayna, I forgot to remind you."

She shrugged and the boy said, "My name is Donte. Why didn't you kick that ass–sorry, that punk in the knee and make him drop the knife? What I would a done."

The kid next to him gave a high-five. Their palms slapping together punctuated the air.

Dennis flinched. "Guess I was too scared to think of it."

"Pussy," he heard mumbled from the back of the class.

"That's enough, Santiago," Ms. Ellis snapped angrily. "Dennis is our guest. I have a question, Dennis."

Relieved, he faced her.

"What's your opinion of Invictus? He saved your life and mine and everyone else's. Do you think he should be arrested?"

Careful, his brain warned. Time for the pause his dad modeled so well. He considered his answer.

"No, I don't think he should be arrested. He's out there helping others. There should be more people like him."

"Why don't you go out and help?" came from the back of the room.

It was the African American kid smirking at him, the one who'd been goofing with his friend earlier. He wore a baggy jersey and had a small 'fro.

"That's enough, DeAndre!" Ms. Ellis barked.

Dennis felt a surge of anger well up within him and before he could pause he blurted, "I do my part!"

The kid's smirk grew even larger. "How, by hiding in the bushes when some bad guy comes along?"

"DeAndre!" Ms. Ellis glowered at DeAndre.

Dennis's whole body stiffened and he lost control.

"If you're so brave, why aren't you out there making things better, huh?" Dennis challenged him. "That goes for all of you. I *am* doing my part. You don't have to kick ass on bad guys to be a hero, you know."

"Dennis…."

That was Ms. Ellis, but Dennis couldn't bring himself to stop. He thought of calming himself, fought the tightness in his stomach, knew he should pause and take a deep breath.

But I can't let DeAndre win.

If he accepted that view of himself as a coward, he'd have nothing left.

"Every single one of you can do something to make this school and this city better than it is. You just don't want to cause you're selfish and scared. I'm doing more than all of you put together, so go on and laugh because a guy almost cut my throat and I got scared. You would've been too! So, get off your asses and get your faces out of your damned phones and look around for ways to help other people and stop talking crap about me!"

He stopped suddenly because every one of them had his or her mouth hanging open in stunned surprise. Even DeAndre looked dumbstruck.

Dennis felt hands on his trembling shoulders. He turned to find Ms. Ellis eyeing him with compassion. His heart pounded and he knew he'd messed up big time. Maybe even given himself away.

I'm sorry, Daddy…

"Why not head on home, Dennis?" Ms. Ellis suggested, guiding him to the door.

He felt eyes on him and glanced back to find the entire class watching him.

"Thanks for coming by."

She eased him out the door and whispered, "I'm sorry, Dennis, for letting them upset you."

He couldn't bring himself to speak. He clutched the art award to his chest and made his way slowly to where he'd parked his bike.

When Vincent returned home that afternoon, Dennis felt too embarrassed to tell him about his meltdown in Ms. Ellis's class. He'd always been more emotional than Vincent, so he knew his brother would understand, but he felt like he'd let

Invictus down, somehow, by losing his temper. So he kept quiet and prepared dinner for the two of them. For some reason, cooking calmed him. He also knew that Vincent couldn't make anything except hotdogs and cereal, so the cooking duties were up to him if he wanted anything decent to eat.

He made marinara sauce from scratch and prepared heaping bowls of pasta to go with it. He figured the carbs would give Vincent tons of energy for his night crawling duties. He'd always heard pasta helped marathon runners, anyway.

When they sat down to eat, Dennis noted how distracted Vincent seemed. He hadn't even changed his tank top. "What's wrong, bro?"

Vincent explained how angry Professor Chin had been about him being late. "I know I have to go out every night so people start to know Invictus is there," he continued. "But I really can't afford to lose my job at the institute. It'll cost me my PhD, our income, and, well, everything."

"I could help."

"How?"

"I could be Invictus sometimes" Dennis suggested, his heart pumping with excitement. "Wear the suit, stop some low level crime. Be like Azrael when Batman got his back broken and the people of Gotham needed to think Batman was still active. Remember? Azrael put on the suit and–"

"No."

Dennis stopped and gazed across the table at his brother.

Vincent looked determined. "I will not let you put your life in danger. That's final."

"But you do it," Dennis protested. He knew this whole discussion was pointless. They'd had it before Invictus was even born.

"I'm an adult," Vincent asserted. "I can take better care of myself out there than you can. You yourself said a real Batman would never allow a kid like Robin on the streets."

"But I helped save Ms. Ellis and the principal, and I–"

"That's final."

Dennis knew the discussion was over.

"I'll have to shorten my hours on school nights. That's all."

Dennis met his brother's gaze. "Okay."

They finished their meal in silence.

As Invictus patrolled the streets that night, he kept his eyes open for police cruisers, but let his thoughts go to what Linda had told him. James had a new partner, and they'd been assigned to "arrest the vigilante" on sight. That was one of the reasons he'd been so uncommunicative during dinner. His dad had been James's partner for most of his life, and all of Dennis's, and since he couldn't imagine James working with anyone else, he hadn't the heart to tell Dennis the news. It also worried him to live so close to the man who was supposed to arrest him. What would James do if he learned the truth? Knowing James's adherence to the letter of the law, Invictus hoped he never had to find out.

Dennis alerted him to possible gang activity on South Central Avenue in downtown, but while he headed in that direction, he found himself passing through Skid Row. During his work with homeless and crime-affiliated youth, he'd learned that Skid Row covered more than fifty city blocks in and around San Pedro Street, but he'd never been there before. As he rode south along Seventh Street, tent after tent seemed to appear out of nowhere, both on Seventh and down all the cross streets. Shopping carts and blankets abounded, and people shuffled around in tattered clothes. Their faces were dirty and scarred, their arms unnaturally thin, their gait shambling and unnatural. It was like a zombie movie come to life.

His heart pounded with shock as he spotted small children—even younger than Franky—huddled against their parents for warmth. He turned left onto San Julian Street and the tents became a city unto themselves. There were also cardboard appliance boxes, and blankets laid out behind dumpsters. And people. Shattered, hopeless, discarded people. Even the smell was unlike anything he'd ever experienced, like a cross between a dirty locker room and a dumpster filled with rotting food.

His family had lived in L.A. when he was young, but moved to the Valley while Dennis was still in elementary school because his parents wanted better schools and a better neighborhood. Seeing how these poor souls had to live, he offered a silent prayer of thanks to his parents for what they'd sacrificed for him and his brother.

A group of homeless had gathered at the corner of Fifth and San Julian and Invictus rolled to a stop, wary in case anyone tried to jump him from behind. The people ceased their mumbled conversations and stared at him with suspicion.

"I'd like to help you if I can," he told them, not sure why he stopped or what he could possibly do. There were hundreds of people scattered through these streets like discarded trash.

"The hell are you?" That came from an older man with a dirty face, scruffy beard, filthy hair, and rags for clothes. "This ain't Halloween, man!"

"My name is Invictus," he offered, not sure what to say or do. This situation was huge, way beyond anything his martial arts or biochemistry background could solve.

"I seen 'im on the news, Jasper," a crone-like lady croaked. Stooped and frail, she looked like she'd snap in a light breeze. "He saved them kids at that rich school."

People laughed and Invictus felt himself redden beneath the mask. Yes, compared to this area and these people, all the kids at Parker Middle were rich.

"Nuthin' to save here, man, 'less you can pull homes and food outta that mask you be wearin'," Jasper grumbled, his voice raspy from smoking.

Invictus scanned the area. Everyone stared at him. His mind raced. How could he help them? Then he recalled what he'd seen on the streets surrounding this area.

"Not homes," he muttered to himself. "But maybe… Don't go away."

He cranked the idling throttle and the engine roared loudly. As he tore off down the street, he heard "Where the hell we'd go?"

But he had already left the tent city behind and sped back toward Main Street. Using his phone, he located a number of possibilities for his plan. At the first place he stopped, the owner took one look at the costume and threatened to call the police. At his second stop, the proprietor seemed amused by the "getup," as he called it, and brought him in to show his patrons. Most laughed and offered a number of derisive comments. But one couple clapped. When asked by another patron why the applause, they explained, "Because he saved those kids at the school."

The proprietor took him more seriously after that, and listened while Invictus shared his idea. At first, the man said no because it was against the law.

"But you're not giving it away, sir. You're simply placing it out back at closing time because you're getting ready to throw it away later. It isn't your fault if it's not there when you finally go out to do that, is it?"

The man smiled, and Invictus decided this was a guy who'd likely been screwed over by "regulations" in the past and didn't mind giving the city the finger. He agreed.

"It's out back at two o'clock, when we close," he asserted firmly. "Dumped at three."

Invictus smiled and shook his hand. "Got it, sir."

He spent several hours going to every establishment within walking distance of the tent city. Dennis interrupted a few times with crimes Invictus could tackle, and he felt guilty for being unable to respond to them. He told Dennis to hold off on anything new until he finished what he was doing.

At first, the owners or managers were wary of him, and balked at his proposal. But he kept at them, reminding each that if he or she were homeless, wouldn't they hope for an act of kindness like he'd proposed? They all agreed they would. One man admitted that he'd done business in the area for so many years that he no longer even "saw" the homeless. They'd become like mailboxes – part of the landscape.

It was one-twenty in the morning when Invictus finally headed back to the tent city on San Julian. He'd hit up eighteen establishments, and all but the first one had agreed to his illegal, but moral idea.

Even though it had been hours since he'd left, Jasper, the elderly lady, and all the others still huddled at the corner of San Julian and Fifth. The air was cool, but not cold like it sometimes got in the wintertime.

"What'chu doin' back here?" Jasper croaked, and then lapsed into a fit of coughing. A hand went to his mouth and Invictus noted the fingerless gloves covering it. He also spotted the bloody phlegm the man coughed up.

"I found food for you," Invictus announced, and that got the attention of everyone within earshot.

People crowded around him and he felt nervous. If they rushed him there was no way he could fight everyone at once, no matter what condition they were in. He explained what he'd accomplished, and told the location of each establishment and the rules for getting the leftover food. He'd written down the address of each restaurant on a piece of paper and handed it to Jasper, since he seemed to be the elder in charge.

Dirty fingers clutched the paper and Jasper squinted at the words written on it. "You for real?"

"Yes, sir," Invictus assured him. "The closest one is up on Main. C'mon, follow me."

He twisted the throttle and gunned the bike engine, thinking at the back of his mind that Joe would be proud of him. He hadn't stalled out once tonight.

He started north on Fifth Street toward Main. At first, no one moved. Then Jasper followed. The rest shuffled into formation behind him. Invictus despised the degradation these people had to endure, being stripped of almost everything that made them human. But he wanted them to know that one thing could never be taken away from anyone – the ability to share.

James drove while Janson rode shotgun. James had never minded Loy driving, but there was no way he'd put a hothead like Janson behind the wheel of any vehicle he was in.

They'd been patrolling the streets for hours, responding to various 911 calls, thinking those incidents would have attracted Invictus. But none panned out and the two of them were frustrated. Janson talked nonstop and James wanted to punch the man just to shut him up.

At one fifty-five, a call came through from dispatch: "All units in the vicinity of Main and Fifth Streets. A suspect matching the description of the vigilante known as Invictus spotted riding a motorcycle and leading a large number of homeless in a northbound direction."

"The hell?" Janson whipped up the microphone to respond.

"Tell dispatch to call off all units. We'll handle this."

James reached out to switch on his siren, and then thought better of it. He spun the unmarked sedan into a U-Turn and headed back toward downtown.

Just after two a.m., Invictus eased his bike into an alley behind the restaurant and slowed to an idle outside the dimly lit rear entrance. Trays of fresh food sat next to the closed dumpsters, as though waiting for someone to "accidentally" find them.

Jasper, followed by his horde of homeless, approached. Invictus extended an arm toward the trays. There was enough food to feed at least twenty-five people, he surmised, and this was only the first stop.

Jasper stared in disbelief. The old woman gaped, looking as though the smell of food intoxicated her.

"There's more at the other restaurants I showed you," Invictus explained. "But it will be dumped at three if it's not picked up. Please don't take the trays."

Jasper gazed long and hard at him, as though seeing a miracle. Then he and the others descended on the food like locusts on a field of wheat.

Invictus felt his earpiece vibrate and pressed the on button.

"Vince, the cops are coming," Dennis said urgently into his ear. "To be exact, James and another guy. They'll be there in five minutes."

Invictus was surprised to hear about James, but then recalled what Linda told him. "Got it, Dennis. Out."

He observed the crowd passing food hand over hand to those in back. "Listen up, everyone. Looks like someone saw me. Cops are on their way. Grab what you can and get out of here. Head to the other locations. Cops don't know about them."

Jasper eyed him a moment, as though wondering if he'd set them up somehow. Then he called out, "You heard the man! Git!"

Clutching what food they'd managed to grab hold of, everyone shuffled faster than Invictus would have imagined down the alley and back onto the street. He suspected they'd spent most of their adult lives dodging the police, so they knew how to move fast when necessary.

He heard clapping from behind him and whirled to find Joe lounging against the retaining wall.

Invictus relaxed as the boy sauntered over. "Flood it yet tonight?"

"Not once." He was keenly aware that he had mere minutes to escape. "Aren't you supposed to be at Runaway House in your bed?"

"Night man'll let me in any time," Joe replied with confidence. "Thanks to my badass superhero friend."

"I told you before, I'm not a superhero."

"I know what you said." He paused and indicated the scattered and empty food trays. "That was cool, what you did."

Invictus reacted with surprise. "You stalking me now?"

Joe shrugged. "Just watching. Need to see what a real superhero does."

"I told you–"

Joe grinned broadly.

Invictus stopped, then chuckled. "Never mind. Hop on. I'll take you home. Otherwise we both get arrested."

Joe clambered onto the back of the bike. "I already got hauled in today." He gripped Invictus tightly around the waist.

Invictus twisted his head around toward the boy. "What for?"

"I know a place we can talk. Unless you wanna face the cops."

Invictus shifted the throttle. The motorcycle engine gunned and he ripped out of the alley onto Main Street. He banked a sharp turn down the nearest side street and stopped the bike just as James's sedan sped past them at high speed.

"That's the cop," Joe called into his ear as they sped away in the opposite direction.

"Did he see us?" Invictus called out.

There was a pause. "No tail, so I guess not. That was close, man."

"You don't know the half of it."

"Huh?"

"Never mind. Where to?"

"Just drive. I'll show you."

Invictus utilized less-travelled streets and Joe directed him to a small pocket park off DeLongpre Street, not far from Hollywood Blvd and Runaway House. The boulevard was busy like always, but they approached the park from June Street and no one paid any attention.

He stopped the bike and allowed Joe to dismount. Then he clambered off and killed the engine. Pushing the motorcycle like a bike, they entered the dimly lit park. At two forty-five in the morning, it was deserted.

Invictus parked the cycle next to a bench and they sat. Despite his lack of exertion this time around, the long days and short nights were taking their toll, and his shoulders slumped with exhaustion.

Can't be late for work tomorrow, he thought as he listened to Joe detail his experience at the police station.

"Which guy threatened you?"

"The white guy. The black guy was chill."

Invictus relaxed, and his reaction wasn't lost on Joe. "You know those cops?"

Invictus knew he had to be careful. "The African American guy was at the school. I remembered him when I saw the news."

He knew that sounded lame, but Joe seemed to accept it. "I think there's something going down out here you should know about."

His tone caught Invictus's attention. "Yeah, what?"

Joe scanned the park cautiously, as though fearful of being overheard. Invictus leaned in. His nose itched under the mask and he needed to lift it and scratch. He forced his hands to stay in his lap.

"There's some new kind a super-drugs on the streets," Joe said quietly, his tone one of utmost seriousness. "*Your* people are selling."

"My people?"

Joe pointed at Invictus's eyes. "Yeah, you know, Asian."

Almost instinctively, Invictus replied, "Technically, I'm–" He stopped before he could give himself away. *You're tired, Vince!* "Never mind. Which Asian gang is it?"

"That's the thing, they aren't a gang," Joe whispered. "More like a business. Head guy on the street calls himself 'Demon.' He supposed to be as bad as bad can be. Him and his homies are selling everything to kids for a tenth of the price everyone else does. They're driving dealers outta business. And, get this, they never sell to Asian kids, only the other races."

Invictus mulled over this information. Okay. Selling drugs dirt-cheap meant one of two things – either these guys got the drugs for free or they *really* wanted kids to buy their drugs and not other dealers' stuff. But why? And why only non-Asians? That suggested a racist angle that went beyond profits.

"What do you think is the game plan?" he asked.

"Supposedly there's something in these drugs that does more damage."

"What kind of damage? Like brain damage?"

"No idea. I don't mess with that stuff. Asian guys've tried to sell to me and I said no." He shivered slightly. "Sometimes johns try to force me, but I kick 'em in the nuts and run. No joke there."

Invictus felt that punch to the gut sensation again. Here was a kid his brother's age talking about grown men using him for… It made his skin crawl!

The traffic sounds from Hollywood Boulevard reinforced the sickening reality that some of those cars were driven by men cruising the streets for kids like Joe. His anger surged, and the cool breeze against his chin did nothing to calm him. He forced his mind to focus on the information Joe had just given him. It sounded like someone wanted kids other than Asians addicted to drugs, specifically some new super drugs. If he could get some samples…

"Could you get me some of these drugs?"

Joe shook his head. "If I start buying, people'll know something's up. Franky's your man."

Invictus flinched. "Franky's a little boy."

Darkness flitted across Joe's young features like clouds covering the sun. "Not out here he's not. And he's a regular. Mostly crystal, but sometimes he buys weed to resell so he can eat."

Invictus called up the face of that small boy in his mind—the chapped lips, the furtive eyes, the scraped tongue, the sallow cheeks—and felt his heart lurch.

"I don't want to put him in danger. Sounds like this operation is a big one."

"Your call, man. But he already buys from them."

Invictus yawned. He hadn't saved a single citizen tonight and yet he was burned out. And Friday was a full workday. He didn't like coffee, but knew he'd be drinking it anyway. Recalling his upcoming date with Lisa, he added, "I won't be out tomorrow night, so maybe we can track him down on Saturday."

Joe recoiled with surprise. "The scumbags come out in force on Fridays, man. What kind a superhero takes *that* night off?"

"I'm not–" Invictus started to reply, but Joe wasn't smiling. His comment had been a serious one. A feeling crept over Invictus that this commitment might be bigger than he'd ever considered.

"If you're on the streets, I'll find you," Joe assured him.

Invictus caught what sounded like disappointment in the boy's tone, especially how he'd uttered the word "if."

"Time to get you home."

Joe snorted. "That place ain't home. Just a rest stop."

Invictus pushed the motorcycle through the park and back to the street. Would cast-off kids like Joe ever have a real home? The thought weighed him down and they didn't speak for the remainder of the ride.

CHAPTER NINE

BEING A HERO IS MORE THAN KICKING ASS

Vincent found Dennis slumped over his desk sound asleep. The police scanner crackled with occasional updates and Dennis's screensaver displayed interweaving quotations from some of his favorite poems. He'd made memes for each and they drifted in and out like a mosaic. One meme caught Vincent's eye as it floated past:

'I need not gloom my days with futile dread,

Because I see a part and not the whole.

Contemplating the strange, I'm comforted

By this narcotic thought: I know my soul.

–Claude McKay'

"You do know your soul, Dennis," Vincent murmured. "I wish I knew mine."

He eased his brother up and carefully laid him out on the bed, covering him beneath the Batman comforter. He studied the delicate features of this boy he loved more than anyone in the world. Why was it so hard to tell him so? Because it wasn't "manly?" He watched the quiet rise and fall of Dennis's chest and cursed his inability to deal with genuine emotion.

He returned to his room and collapsed onto the bed. As he went under, he realized he'd forgotten to set his alarm. Panic gripped him and he struggled to pull himself awake, but weariness took him and he knew no more.

He felt himself shaking. Another earthquake? His dream-addled brain couldn't quite make sense of the movement. But then he opened his eyes and found Dennis gazing down at him.

"Am I late?" he exclaimed, sitting bolt upright in bed.

Dennis yawned and shook his head. "I set my alarm this time. It's six o'clock."

"Phew!" Vincent collapsed back onto his pillow and Dennis sat on the bed beside him.

"So what happened last night? You didn't call me back."

Dennis sounded hurt, and that tone sliced through Vincent like a knife. "I got caught up with a bunch of homeless people."

Dennis raised his eyebrows in surprise. Vincent sat up against the headboard and described the previous night's events.

"I'm sorry, Dennis," he apologized when he finished. "I know you had real crimes for me to tackle, but it took me all night to convince those restaurant owners."

Dennis screwed his face into an astonished look. "Are you kidding? What you did was massive, bro!"

"But I didn't save anybody."

"Course you did," Dennis gushed. "Being a hero is more than kicking ass. You think too much, Vincent, about numbers and brain cells. You helped real *people* last night, in a way that will *keep* helping them. That's golden."

Vincent recalled Joe's affirmation and realized that, once again, Dennis's oh-so-human heart was right again. "Thanks, Squirt."

Dennis grinned. "Sure wish I could a been out there to see that."

Vincent frowned, worrying again about his brother's desire to run the streets with him.

But Dennis didn't seem upset. "I'll get breakfast ready." He stood and walked to the door. "Oh, and Jackson and Kenny are coming by today for some video game action. That okay?"

"Course. Tell them hi for me."

"Will do."

"Oh, and Dennis?"

"Yeah?"

"I got a tip last night that there's some nasty new drugs on the street. Guy in charge is named Demon. If you come across that name while eavesdropping on the cops, let me know, all right?"

Dennis narrowed his eyes. "Who gave you that tip?"

Vincent realized his blunder too late. He couldn't tell Dennis about a kid helping him on the streets because then Dennis would feel even more left out. "Uh, just somebody on the streets."

Dennis studied him a moment before exiting the room. Cursing his stupidity, Vincent rose to shower.

He brought a large thermos with extra-strong coffee into the lab with him. Professor Chin seemed happy to see him on time and gave him a pat on the back. With his hair tied in its usual ponytail and sporting his glasses, Vincent went to his locker and pulled out his white lab coat. Slipping it on, he took the coffee to his station and resumed work.

Chin kept the lab spotless and, other than secured drink containers for water or coffee, the professor allowed no food or drink. Computers abounded, not to mention Spectrophotometers used for determining the equilibrium constant of a solution, CT stations, and an MRI – all delicate equipment that could be ruined with even a single spill of water. Vincent had long ago gotten used to the smell of chemicals and drugs wafting through the air as various tests were performed. A powerful ventilation system kept fresh air circulating constantly so these smells would not linger and adversely affect the lab technicians. When certain experiments were performed that could involve a strong reaction, Chin ordered everyone to don facemasks for added protection.

Vincent's conversation with Joe the night before kept intruding, mainly because it so directly tied into the research project this team was working on. They'd received a grant to study the short and long term effects of drugs on the human brain at all stages of its development. This meant over-the-counter medications to psych meds to recreational street drugs. It meant infancy to old age. The scope and breadth of the research was enormous and Chin had assembled a team of twenty-five of the brightest grad students from around the country.

Vincent knew that kids his brother's age were routinely called "young adults" in the media, and in courtrooms. In fact, he'd seen that fallacious title applied to ten-year-olds. Even when Dennis was sixteen his brain would only be about sixty per cent complete in its maturation. *Hell,* Vincent often reminded himself, *mine isn't finished yet!*

His father had told him that pretending kids were adults within the criminal justice system had to do with money because everything in America had to do with money, which made sense in a sick kind of way. That boy Tommy, sentenced to life in prison, was a perfect example of the system not giving kids a second chance, especially when they'd had such horrific upbringings.

States legalizing marijuana, which would make it much more accessible to teens, chose to ignore the fact that drugs – all drugs – affected the developing brain of a child or adolescent in vastly more destructive ways than they did the brains of adults, which biologically speaking finished maturation somewhere after age twenty-one, and closer to twenty-six in many people.

He was part of the analysis team attempting to pinpoint which ingredients in any given drug specifically affected which parts of the brain and how the effect differed based on the age of the user.

So Joe's story of a new "super" drug, or maybe just a super "additive" to existing drugs, intrigued him. He needed multiple samples, not as Invictus, but as Vincent, research assistant and PhD candidate.

You're going to use a ten-year-old for that?

He didn't know.

But if he's taking it and you figure out what the added ingredient is and what it does, you'll be helping him, right?

Maybe.

The whole idea made him shiver and weighed him down with indecision.

He spotted Chin heading his way and forced those thoughts aside. He stifled a yawn and leaned closer to his computer screen.

Torres had been extremely unhappy when James and Janson reported in that morning before heading home, especially because the story was all over the news. Channel 4 proclaimed: "The vigilante known as Invictus helps feed homeless people on Skid Row."

"And none of those bums could give you a better description?" Torres bellowed.

"No, Captain," James replied.

"They just talked about how *wonderful* he was," Janson said in a mocking tone.

"Uh, Captain, it's worth noting that he didn't break any laws last night," James added cautiously, knowing he was on dangerous ground. When Torres got a bug up his butt about a suspect, it didn't matter if that suspect was Mother Theresa.

"That we know of. None of those vagrants said where he got that food he gave them," the captain asserted. "You're back out tonight. Cruise through Skid Row, but he doesn't seem to hang around the same area twice, so if you don't spot him right away, move on. My guess is he's monitoring 911 calls and will go wherever he thinks he can get the most publicity."

"I agree," Janson declared.

"So far, Captain, Invictus doesn't appear to be doing this for self-aggrandizement."

"Course he is, Detective," Torres snapped. "Nobody does something for nothing."

James grudgingly admitted to himself the truth of the captain's words. He saw self-absorption everywhere he went, especially on this job. The days of the Good Samaritan seemed long gone.

"Dismiss."

"Yes, sir," he replied and followed Janson out of the office.

Vincent's bed was strewn with multiple shirts that he'd tried on, taken off, tried on again. He'd been into Dennis's room at least ten times for an opinion. He'd never been on a "real" date before and wanted to look just right. Short-sleeve or long? Lisa liked his veins so he opted for short.

What if she thinks I'm showing off?

He went with long. They were going to a restaurant for dinner so long was better, right?

But maybe this looks too formal?

Off came that shirt and he snatched up another.

"Vincent," Dennis called out from down the hall. "We're needed."

Oh, no…

Shirtless, he bounded from his room and down to his brother's. Dennis sat in front of his computer.

The police scanner sizzled with activity: "All units in the vicinity of Panorama City, robbery and potential hostage situation in progress at A & M Gun Cellars. Multiple gunmen, exact number unknown. Approach with caution."

Dennis twisted the volume dial to "Low" and eyed Vincent expectantly.

Vincent glanced at the shirt in his hand. "The police can handle it."

Dennis stared at him.

"I have a date," he added, almost desperately.

Dennis remained silent. He looked like he understood, but also wore an expression of disappointment; the same look Joe wore when Vincent told him that Invictus was taking Friday off.

"This is an important date," he tried feebly.

Dennis's disappointment melted into a look of genuine sympathy. "I know it is, Vince. But I've been monitoring this situation. Sounds like the hostages are in a bad way. If the police storm the place…"

He let the thought trail off, but Vincent understood the rest.

Could I live with myself if I went out with Lisa and those people died? Especially if I might be able to help?

He knew the answer was *No*.

"I'll suit up. Just let me call–"

"I'll call Lisa," Dennis interjected, reaching for his phone. "You get ready."

Vincent bolted from the room.

James watched the unfolding operation with anxiety. He scanned the area, but saw only police and SWAT vehicles surrounding the front of the gun store. Officers and SWAT team members crouched behind their vehicles pointing a wide array of weapons at the storefront.

"We have you surrounded," the SWAT leader called out through a bullhorn. "Release your hostages and come out with your hands up!" His voice echoed off surrounding buildings.

James had parked his car beyond the perimeter alongside press vehicles and flashed his badge to gain entry. He and Janson crouched behind one police cruiser at the back of the standoff. It wasn't his operation and he didn't want to be in the way.

"What are we doing here, Stevens?" Janson asked irritably. "We're supposed to be tracking the vigilante."

James eyed him with irritation. He *really* disliked this guy! "And this is exactly the kind of situation that would attract his attention."

"Good thinking, Detective."

James squinted a moment before returning his gaze to the scene before him. The vigilante could try to sneak in through the back and rescue the hostages that way, but there was only one small door leading in from the back alley and no rear windows. No, if he were going to try anything it would likely be from out front.

But would he be stupid enough to risk capture with so many cops around?

James pondered that question as he scanned the rooftops surrounding the parking lot. Something told him this guy didn't much care about arrest or publicity, despite Torres's assessment. His gut instincts after twenty-five years on the force convinced him this wasn't about the proverbial fifteen minutes. So what was it about?

Invictus lay on his stomach atop the gun store building, his costume now the same gray color as the rooftop. His Chameleon Chemical would only hide him for so long from the police and news choppers circling over the area, so he had to move fast.

He lay beside a dirty skylight positioned directly above the main floor of the store. He couldn't see much down below because the perps had killed the lights. But Dennis spoke into his ear and relayed all that he'd learned from monitoring the police.

"You better hurry, Vince," he heard. "The cops are about to storm the place. They think the gunmen are going to kill the hostages."

"Roger that," Invictus murmured. He'd been using a corrosive chemical to eat through the lock clamping the skylight to the roof and it finally sizzled its way through. The skylight lifted on hinges, and he suspected those might squeak. They looked rusty. "Can you tell where the hostages are relative to me?"

"Hold on."

Invictus waited. The *whup whup whup* of helicopters, and another challenge of the SWAT leader through the bullhorn below to "Come out now!" were all he heard. The red and blue flashing lights gave the buildings around him a Hollywood opening-night kind of feel, while the hot asphalt roof heated up the costume and fueled his thumping heart.

"Okay, Vince, according to the police chatter, one of the gunmen has the owner and his wife behind the counter. The other three perps are crouched down below the front windows, preparing to take on the cops. Are you facing the front of the building?"

"Yes."

"If you drop through the skylight facing front, the counter will be directly to your left, and the perp should be about five feet away, if I calculate correctly."

Invictus considered. He had no way of knowing how close the gun was to either hostage. "What are the hostages' names, Dennis?"

"Um, hold up a sec." Invictus waited. "I'm back. Marty and Alice."

Invictus paused and listened. The SWAT leader was initialing a countdown. That couldn't be good. And the helicopters were headed his way. It was now or never. Gripping the edge of the skylight with one gloved hand, he lifted it slowly. It creaked, but the helicopter sounds drowned out the noise. He tilted it all the way back and laid the Plexiglas side against the roof. He glanced up. The police chopper was almost on him, its bright light weaving about like monstrous alien eye.

He pulled himself up to a crouch and balanced on the lip of the skylight. He gauged the angle of his shield. It would barely fit if he tilted it just so. He positioned it to throw the second he landed.

The countdown out front continued: "Seven, six, five—"

He dropped through the hole in the roof. The floor rushed up at him with alarming speed. To his left he spotted someone wearing a clown mask standing behind a portly, middle-aged man with thinning hair and a slightly overweight middle-aged woman. The clown held a high-powered handgun aimed at the woman's head. His entrance momentarily stunned all three of them.

While still in midair, Invictus shouted, "Marty, Alice, down!"

To their credit, the terrified couple dropped to the floor. Before the startled gunman could react, Invictus flung his shield. He landed hard and dropped into a shoulder roll as the shield slammed into the gunman's chest and propelled him back against the gun racks. The handgun flew from his grasp and he staggered.

Marty snatched up the gun and used the butt to *thwack* the gunman over the head, sending him unconscious to the floor.

Invictus jumped up to find Alice handing him the shield. She looked scared, but still in control, and he suspected this wasn't the first robbery they'd experienced.

The three by the windows had spun when he landed, and outside the SWAT leader shouted, "One! All right, men, move in, shields raised."

Invictus didn't wait for people to die. He leaped up onto the counter and raced along it, sailing off and wrapping his legs in a scissor lock around the neck of the closest gunman, flipping the man over and slamming him to the floor. The man lay there, dazed and disoriented. Invictus jumped up and whipped his shield in front of him as the other two unloaded their weapons. Bullets ricocheted everywhere and he feared an explosion if one happened to strike an ammo cache.

Shield up, he plowed forward into both men, driving them back until all three of them smashed through the plate glass window into the parking lot outside.

CHAPTER TEN

DENNIS, YOU STILL THERE?

James watched the armored SWAT team raise their body-length shields and start toward the gun store. Still no sign of Invictus. *Maybe I was–*

He never got time to complete the thought. Gunfire erupted from inside the store. The SWAT leader barked, "Down!" and all his officers ducked low behind their shields. Then the glass of the store window shattered outward and three bodies tumbled to the pavement of the parking lot.

James rose to get a better view, Janson beside him.

"Look, Stevens, it's the vigilante!"

Sure enough, Invictus was engaged in hand-to-hand combat with two men. James watched in silent awe as Invictus stood and swung his shield at one of the perps, propelling him backwards. The second staggered to his feet, weapon raised. Invictus spun around so fast James almost missed it and planted one booted foot in the face of the perp. Even from his distant position, James heard the man's jaw snap as he staggered back, dropping his weapon and clutching at his battered face.

The one who'd been knocked down scrambled for his gun and rose staggeringly to his feet. Invictus spun with the shield. The bullets bounced off with a *rat a tat tat* sound. Then Invictus leaped into the air and twisted into a high kick. His boot struck the perp in the upper chest and sent him flying back through the shattered window. He did not reappear.

Panting from his exertions, Invictus gazed out at the stunned, silent police pointing their weapons at him. Even the SWAT leader looked momentarily confused.

James rose to his full height, gun out, and started forward. Janson trailed him.

"You, vigilante, hold it right there!" James called out as he darted between police cruisers and SWAT vehicles.

Invictus paused a moment as James lurched to a stop beside the SWAT leader. "You're under arrest."

Invictus met James's eye a long moment, and James froze. Something about that stance, those moves he'd seen, the long hair. Something....

His hesitation was all Invictus needed. Before anyone could react, he threw a small pellet at the ground. Thick white smoke billowed up around him, filling the parking lot and cutting off James's view.

James jumped forward into the cloud. Janson followed. The SWAT officers moved in. There was mass confusion. Voices grunted and shields clanged into each other.

"I got him, Stevens!" Janson shouted in the thick cloud.

"You got me, Janson," James said in disgust.

"Oh, sorry."

The cloud dispersed and James pointed his gun in every direction. Janson was directly behind him and the officers surrounded them.

But no sign of Invictus.

The vigilante had vanished.

James sat behind the wheel and listened to Torres shouting through the radio. He had to turn down the volume during the captain's tirade.

"You had the little prick and you let him get away!"

James could picture the man's face turning red as he bellowed.

"Captain, we didn't let him—"

"No excuses, Stevens!"

The radio clicked off and James glanced at Janson. The younger man eyed him accusingly.

"What?"

"You *did* let him get away, Detective. You had him at point blank range and could have taken him down."

James felt anger and disgust well up within him in equal measure. No wonder cops got such a bad rep, with guys like Janson on the force!

"Our orders are to arrest him, not shoot down an unarmed man in cold blood. The hell's wrong with you?"

Janson didn't look apologetic. "Captain wants him because his interference is going to get people killed, probably cops. That what you want?"

James gripped the steering wheel so hard his knuckles paled. He focused on his breathing. "It sure looked to me like those hostages were toast and SWAT barging in would've finished them for sure. Thanks to Invictus, nobody got hurt."

Janson shrugged. "He got lucky this time. It'll happen. You'll see."

James glared a moment, but Janson glared right back. James started the car and left the crime scene behind.

As he cruised along side streets on his way toward Hollywood, Invictus felt good about what he'd accomplished, how he'd ended the standoff with no loss of life, or even anyone getting shot.

"But the cops'll still call me a bad guy," he told Dennis through his Bluetooth as he sped along.

"Probably," he heard in his ear. "But look at how long everybody thought Spiderman was a bad guy. Even Batman wasn't trusted at first. You're in good company, bro."

Invictus grunted. "Yeah, I guess."

"Oh, and those people you saved must've seen your eyes cuz now the cops are calling you the *Asian* Vigilante."

"Oh, Daddy'd love that. Remember how he used to correct everybody who called us Asian?"

Dennis didn't respond.

Invictus tapped the Bluetooth volume button. "You there, Dennis?"

"Yeah, I'm here," he heard, but the voice sounded slightly breathless.

"You okay?"

"Golden."

The voice sounded 'off', and Invictus realized the PTSD must be kicking in again. He paused, and then changed the subject. "How mad was Lisa?"

Dennis snorted with amusement.

"What?"

"I said you got an emergency call from an old high school friend who was downtown at the police station for drunk and disorderly conduct."

"Huh?"

"I had to think fast, okay?" Dennis responded, a bit huffily. "I said your friend was going to be booked if someone didn't pick him up and you were the first person he could get hold of."

Invictus turned a corner to avoid a busy intersection up ahead. "And she believed that?"

"Seemed like it, yeah. I mean, she doesn't know you have no friends. Said for you to call her tomorrow."

Invictus flinched. He knew Dennis wasn't trying to be cruel, but the comment hurt just the same. Then he considered Lisa. Was this the best time to try for a relationship? Did doing so make him selfish? Was it fair to her, even though *she'd* asked *him* out?

"Thanks, Dennis."

"Where you off to now?"

"I'm heading downtown to follow-up on that drug tip I got last night," he answered, turning another corner and speeding up.

There was a long pause on the other end.

"Dennis? You still there?"

"Yeah," he heard. "Keep me in the loop. I'll monitor the scanner. Out."

The phone clicked off in his ear and Invictus focused on his steering. Was Dennis angry? Sure sounded like it. But why? He pondered his brother's behavior for the rest of his ride.

He patrolled the streets. People milled around and cars drifted past. It was ten o'clock on a Friday night, so even the seedy parts of town bubbled with life. He kept his eyes open for any Asians who appeared to be dealing, but didn't see any. He cruised into the alley where he'd met Joe and rolled to a stop. He was just about to park and "do the Batman thing" on the rooftops when Dennis called in about a possible home invasion over in Echo Park.

Invictus responded, "On my way."

He'd just gunned the throttle when he heard, "Need some company tonight?"

He spun around in the seat, only to find Joe laughing at his reaction. "Got ya."

Invictus chuckled and dismounted the bike, turning off the engine and kicking out the stand. "Been looking for you, Joe," he began, but then spread his arms wide. "But I gotta go. Home invasion–"

"Scratch that," Dennis said into his ear. "False alarm."

Invictus relaxed and tapped his ear. "False alarm," he told Joe.

"You got Bluetooth under there?"

"Yeah."

"Sweet." Joe stepped closer. "Thought you were taking tonight off."

"Somebody reminded me about priorities."

Joe grinned. He was dressed in a regular T-shirt and normal size jeans.

"You're not out here looking for…, you know, are you?" Invictus still couldn't even utter the evil that was a child having to sell his body.

"Nope. Thanks to a certain superhero, I got me a pad every night. And food."

Invictus didn't even try to correct him on the "superhero" comment. He knew Joe was just messing with him.

Joe hesitated, almost looking like a kid on his first date.

"What?"

He reached into one jeans pocket, pulled out a piece of paper, and handed it over.

Invictus opened the paper and squinted in the meager light at a list of intersections within the city, and some in the Valley. "What's this?"

"Biggest dealer corners," Joe replied with a shrug. "Those Asian guys show up at a lot of 'em ahead of the gangs so they can undercut business."

"I haven't heard news reports of turf wars."

Joe shrugged. "Asians are slick. Everybody knows Demon's name, but no one I know could point him out."

Invictus studied the boy a moment, but Joe kept his eyes downcast. "Thanks."

There was a pause. "I always wanted to be a superhero when I's a kid so, you know, this way, by helping you, I kinda get to be."

Invictus felt his heart start to pound.

When Joe looked up, his face seemed for a split second so soft and innocent, so like the boy he must've been before the street had ravaged his youth and stolen his humanity.

Invictus placed one hand on Joe's bony shoulder. "You still *are* a kid, Joe."

Joe's eyes welled up and he swiped at the tears with the hem of his shirt. "Not after what I been through."

Invictus squeezed his trembling shoulder and they stood a few moments, the silence and surrounding city sounds their only companions.

"So, uh, have you seen Franky tonight?" Invictus finally asked, still conflicted about whether or not he should involve the little boy.

Joe studied him a moment. "Yeah. Can we, uh, bring him some food? He never gets enough and the meth eats him up."

Invictus patted a pouch on his belt. "I brought money."

"There's a McDonald's around the corner. Hide the bike and I'll take ya."

Invictus waited in the shadows of a large tree while Joe entered McDonald's. His body was tensed for flight as he observed cars at the drive-through, keeping an eye out for cops cruising in for coffee or a late-night meal.

Joe emerged a few minutes later still holding the twenty Invictus had given him. "Manager told me to scram cuz I'm a known transient and prostitute and he didn't want me in his es*tab*lishment." He used air quotes for "establishment."

Invictus felt his blood boil. "Gimme." He reached for the money and Joe handed it over. "C'mon."

He knew he was taking a big risk, that people inside would be snapping his picture with their phones, and the manager would likely call the police, but he couldn't allow that man to get away with such cruelty to a kid in need.

He barged through the glass door, shield at one side, Joe at his other. All sounds and speech ceased. Whether they were filling up drinks or already seated or standing in line at the register, each patron gaped at him in stunned surprise. Those already in line stepped to one side and let him go first.

The man at the register was Latino and probably middle-aged, though he had no gray in his hair, with a thick mustache and a prominent beer belly. He recoiled as Invictus slammed his twenty down on the counter.

"My friend here," – he indicated Joe –"told me you wouldn't take his money because he's poor and homeless and has been forced to live like an animal on the streets." His voice rose in intensity as he spoke, and he fought to keep his temper under control. "Only a monster would even think to do something like that."

Remember, Vince, life isn't a martial arts contest.

He forced himself to breathe in and out slowly.

"Somebody call the police," the manager begged his patrons.

Invictus glanced around at the stupefied employees and the equally stunned patrons.

No one moved.

He turned to the silent patrons, still frozen in shock. Some took out their phones, but no one spoke.

"How many of you think my friend here doesn't have the right to buy food? He's just a kid and he's hungry."

He placed his free hand on Joe's shoulder.

A man with two young children standing at the soda dispenser turned to the manager. "What's wrong wit you, man? You too high and mighty to serve poor folk? Sell the kid his food."

Several others nodded their assent.

A girl, who looked to be in high school, hovered near the register. She glanced at the manager.

The man who'd spoken up glowered, and other patrons were already filming the exchange with their phones.

The manager turned to regard Invictus and Joe. He exhaled deeply with resignation and waved the girl forward.

She stared with awe at the shield and mask. "What can I get for you?"

Joe gave her the order. Invictus kept his eyes on the manager. He knew the guy would probably call the cops the second they left. He just didn't want them to arrive before Joe got his food.

The entire restaurant seemed frozen in time while they awaited the order. Servers scrambled to bag up the food. Invictus saw phones filming and heard the clicking of camera shutters and knew he'd be all over Twitter and Snapchat before he even left.

Hands gripping the five bags tightly, Joe headed for the door and held it open.

Invictus thanked the girl. "Your kindness is appreciated."

He and Joe were out into the parking lot and down the street within seconds.

CHAPTER ELEVEN

YOU'RE KINDA LIKE BATMAN, RIGHT?

THEY FOUND FRANKY SLEEPING IN piles of old clothes behind a Laundromat. Joe explained that this was where Franky slept when his mother was out of control. He woke the small boy, and Franky pulled away, his eyes darting from side to side, widening with terror at seeing Invictus.

"Whoa, Franky," Joe said, hands outstretched to calm the boy. "Chill, buddy. Just Joe and the superhero."

Invictus gazed long and hard at Franky. Even in the shadowy darkness of this back alley, he saw beads of sweat on the small, dirty forehead, and the shaking of his body and limbs.

"We brought food, man." Joe planted his lanky frame onto the pavement beside Franky and laid out the five bags. The little boy's eyes bulged with amazement.

"Where'd you get all this?"

Joe threw a thumb back over his shoulder. "Super Hero bought it."

Franky grinned. Then he tore open the first bag and engulfed a Big Mac within seconds, washing it down with bottled water.

Joe bit into his own burger. "Told ya he'd be starving."

Invictus nodded. His emotions were too roiled for him to speak. Watching these lost boys devour the food as though it might be their last meal made him feel weak in the knees. He scanned the area for any prying eyes. Seeing no one, he sat cross-legged beside them and nibbled on a french fry while they ate.

Less than ten minutes later, every speck of food and drop of water had been consumed. Invictus had never seen what true hunger looked like until now.

Chapped lips greasy with dripping fat and ketchup, Franky lounged back in his pile of clothes and belched loudly. He was so skinny that his stomach bulged from ingesting so much food. It protruded from the bottom of his threadbare tee shirt like an early-stage pregnancy.

"Man, I ate too fast. Stomach hurts."

That worried Invictus. He didn't know what eating so much food so fast might do to a boy in his condition. "Just lay back and let the food settle."

Franky stretched out his legs and placed both hands over his distended stomach.

The earpiece vibrated and Invictus tapped the side of his mask. "Yeah?"

"Vincent, where are you?" Dennis asked in his ear. "There's a report of a man with a gun at an apartment complex not far from your location. Over."

"Got it, Den–" He saw Joe eyeing him with interest and cursed himself for almost giving away Dennis's name. "Hold on. I'm in the middle of something."

"'Kay."

Joe dropped peacefully onto the pile beside Franky. The small boy wrapped both arms around Joe and held him close.

"Thank you, Joe," he gushed, his voice trembling slightly. "And thank you, Super Hero."

Invictus smiled as best he could manage. Everything about the way society forced these children to live sickened him. He felt nauseated, and it wasn't from the fast food or the nasty smells permeating the alley.

As Franky shifted under the overhead light, Invictus stiffened. The boy had a yellowish bruise under his left eye. "Mom was angry the other night because you didn't bring anything home?"

Franky nodded, and Invictus felt rigid with guilt. It was his interference that had broken up the deal. Sure, that meant Franky hadn't ingested more crystal, but it also meant a beating from his addicted mother.

"I'm sorry, Franky," he offered, realizing how crazy he sounded to apologize for keeping a ten-year-old away from deadly street drugs.

Franky shrugged, and shivered at the same time. "It's no biggie. But I gotta score somethin' tonight. Can't take this no more."

Joe wrapped his arms around the shaking boy. "You gotta let that food settle first or you'll be tossing it up." He pulled Franky to a sitting position and cradled his head against his scrawny chest.

They sat in silence for fifteen minutes while Franky relaxed and his face gradually lost the pained expression.

"A little better, Franky?" Invictus asked, his body taut with tension.

Franky nodded and smiled.

"Super Hero has a job for you, Franky," Joe said quietly.

Franky pulled his face out of Joe's shirt and cast a wary look at Invictus. His eyes settled on the shield, mostly. He seemed drawn to it. Invictus held it out and Franky wrapped his small, filthy fingers around the handgrip. He pulled the shield over him and Joe as though it might protect them from all the evils of the world.

"What'chu want from me, Super Hero?" Franky's voice cracked slightly, and his ragged breathing didn't help his enunciation.

Invictus explained what he needed, and the small boy listened with wide eyes and trembling limbs.

"I can't give you no meth." He sounded apologetic. "I gotta give that to mama. And me. Could score some weed, tho, maybe coke. I don't mess with coke."

"I just need a little, Franky." Invictus's mind spun with the rightness and wrongness of this course of action. He couldn't live with himself if something happened to this boy. But he really needed some of those drugs so he could help Franky. Or was that the real reason? Could it just be scientific curiosity, a way to reclaim his good graces with Chin?

No.

He needed to know because these drugs were hurting kids. And maybe he could stop that.

"You have money to buy?"

The small boy shook his head. His big, sad eyes tugged at Invictus's heart. "I used the last of my mama's GR the other night. That's why she got so pissed."

"GR?" Invictus asked.

"General Relief," Joe answered.

Invictus nodded.

"It's not all about right and wrong out here, Super Hero," Joe offered, his deepening voice filled with a mix of sadness and assurance. "If he doesn't score something soon, he won't make it."

Invictus scrutinized Frankie more closely. The pasty complexion, the sweating, the constant tremors. He knew from his research that going cold turkey with meth was almost always fatal, especially with a small body and weak constitution.

Feeling like he was making a deal with the Devil, Invictus stood and reached into a belt pouch, pulling out another twenty. He held it between thumb and forefinger, hesitating.

"If it makes you feel better, I can give it to him." Joe held out his hand.

Invictus stared at the thin, dark hand and the skinny arm to which it was attached. He could pretend it was Joe who did this, but that would never be true. No matter what ultimately happened because of his choice, it had to be *his* choice, and his heart pounded with the understanding that it could be the worst one he ever made.

He gripped the bill tightly, close to his body as the debate raged within him.

Frankie needs some or he might die. I need some to understand what it's doing to him.

Was there any other way? He couldn't see one at that moment, so he handed the bill to Franky, who took it with round, grateful eyes.

Franky stuffed the bill into the pocket of his torn short pants and then disentangled himself from Joe. Rising on shaky legs, he hefted the shield up before him and reverently handed it back to Invictus, who took it in one hand and lowered it to his side.

"Meet me back here tomorrow night and I'll have something for you."

Invictus studied this small boy who would now go in search of drugs that could easily kill him.

You could call 911 right now and get him to the ER, he thought, his mind whirling with "maybes" and "what if's." *The doctors can keep him alive without the meth.*

Except he knew Franky would vanish like a magician during a stage show if he heard anything close to a siren approaching.

The small boy started down the alley, lurching back and forth on his short, weak legs.

Invictus watched him with a sober look in his eyes.

Franky turned and waddled back toward them.

"You're kinda like Batman, right?"

"I guess so."

Franky considered something a moment. Invictus could almost see the gears of his drug-addled brain slowly turning. "So if I help you, does that make me Robin?"

Invictus felt his chest tighten. At first, he couldn't speak.

The little boy awaited an answer.

"Uh, yeah," he finally spoke, struggling to keep his voice steady. "I guess that makes you Robin."

Franky broke into the most beautiful smile Invictus had ever seen on a human being. It spread across his dirty face and radiated lost innocence, hope, and the purity that only a child can display.

"That's so cool. I always wanted to be Robin when I was little."

He lurched from the alley out of sight.

Invictus felt his eyes well with tears. He couldn't help it. His contacts blurred his vision.

"How it is out here, man." There was genuine sadness in Joe's voice.

Invictus nodded, unable to think of anything to say. He reached out a hand. Joe took it and Invictus hefted him to his feet. They mounted the motorcycle and rode off into the night.

Dennis sat back from his desk, cell phone in hand. Vincent had forgotten to end the call, and Dennis heard the entire exchange with two kids his brother had never mentioned. He pushed the red button on the phone, switched off the police scanner, and considered everything he'd heard. It disturbed him on multiple levels.

Was Vincent deliberately hiding his association with these kids because he knew how much Dennis wanted to be out there with him? Or did he feel guilty for using the kids in the first place and was too embarrassed to say anything?

Dennis understood at an intellectual level that the world was diseased. Even comic books portrayed the selfish, abusive nature of human beings rather graphically. But he'd never experienced it at this level before now. Until he was in fifth grade, the family had lived in Los Angeles and the neighborhood hadn't been the greatest. That's why his parents had moved to the Valley.

What Vincent was seeing and experiencing was the real world for way too many kids… and adults, too. Dennis had known this before, and so had Vincent. That was how The Dream came to exist, how Invictus came to be born, why they so desperately wanted to wake up the people of this city so those who "had" might step up and help those who "had not." It was volunteerism they sought to increase, people giving of themselves and their talents and their money to those in need.

It sickened him to picture kids living on the streets, strung out on drugs, with mothers who beat them if they didn't bring home meth. His heart ached for that boy, Franky, whom he'd never met. He didn't know how old the kid was, but the high voice suggested a very young child. Dennis wished he could swoop in and give that boy a real home. He wanted so desperately to do more than just sit and monitor the police scanner every night. He wanted to help people hands-on.

Am I selfish? Do I just want to be in on the action?

He knew that was partly true, and it bothered him. But it bothered him more that Vincent didn't think he was able to take care of himself in a potentially dangerous situation. It tortured him that Vincent saw him as "weak" and "incapable" and still a child.

He decided not to say anything about what he'd overheard. He'd wait and see if Vincent told him about "Robin" and Joe. He'd give Vincent the benefit of his guilt for involving kids because he knew that, above all else, Vincent didn't want anyone getting hurt.

Especially me.

He picked up one of his poetry books. He needed to feel hope again, hope that the world could yet be healed.

They spoke not a word all the way back to Runaway House. What was there to say? Invictus understood more than ever that life was not a comic book and that right and wrong had shades of gray. Sure, his volunteer work had opened his eyes somewhat, but all his book learning and lab work had insulated him from reality. And reality was ugly.

Will what I'm doing now make a difference?

He wasn't sure anymore.

He dropped off Joe and watched him enter the shelter before heading for home.

Passing through Van Nuys, taking the side streets as always, he heard a commotion up ahead, like a large-scale fight. Turning his bike into a small alley, he parked and locked it. Shield in hand, he sprinted off in the direction of the tumult.

Following The Mistress's directive, Demon and his crew continued recruiting new members for the organization. While not a gang—The Mistress would never allow them to even call themselves something so demeaning—the "recruitment" process involved the prospective member participating in some "deals" and then holding his own against three seasoned fighters. In part, this approach demonstrated if the newbie had both the desire to belong and the fighting skills needed when actual gang members tried to muscle in on their business dealings. The only other requirement for membership was a matter of birth – they had to be Asian.

Demon observed his team in action. All were his age, or close, and all sported the shaved head and thin black rattail that signified membership in The Mistress's organization. The new recruit, a Chinese guy who called himself Spider, already had a shaved head and would have to grow out his rattail, but he fought well for a small guy, and Demon liked what he saw. He'd stepped back into the shadows to observe when his eye caught movement at the mouth of the alley.

The Hero pelted around the corner holding his shield.

Demon grinned. This night just got a whole lot more fun.

"Hey!" the Hero shouted at the fighters.

Startled, they stopped kicking the Chinese guy, who lay curled on the ground, and faced the newcomer.

Demon stepped from the shadows and the Hero glanced in his direction.

"The Hero," he announced with glee. "Kick his ass."

Without hesitation, they abandoned Spider and leapt at the Hero. Spider rolled upward into a crouch to watch.

Demon was impressed by how quickly the Hero reacted. He leapt to one side and spun into a sidekick, catching Young Z in the chest and sending him sprawling. Almost at the same time he slammed his shield into the face of K-Dog, one of his biggest and best fighters. Dog grunted and crumpled, hands to his bloody face as he dropped to his knees.

Demon frowned. His body temperature rose with anger and he wanted to intervene, but The Mistress had ordered him not to engage the Hero himself – only observe and report.

Little One, the smallest of his team, dove beneath the shield at the Hero's legs, but was kicked aside before he could make contact.

This guy is good, Demon thought. *Really good.*

His two remaining fighters lunged at the Hero from different directions. Despite the shield, the Hero leapt into the air and kicked out in both directions at the same time. He caught B-Boy right in the balls and the man cried out in agony as he toppled. The other foot landed solidly in the gut of Phamoz and sent him pin wheeling back to slam into the brick wall with an audible *thud*.

Demon was pleased to see Young Z crouched to spring. As the Hero glanced over at Phamoz toppling to the ground, Z leapt up and threw a high kick, connecting with the Hero's face and sending him staggering sideways.

The Hero groaned and stumbled, one hand going to his right eye as though something was wrong.

Demon watched closely. The Hero seemed disoriented, but not from the kick. He appeared not to see Z leaping at him with a follow-up kick. At the last second he spun and swung the shield. It struck Z a glancing blow, but Z managed to keep his footing.

Spider jumped up to join the fight, but the Hero fumbled in a pouch attached to his belt and scattered white powder into the air. Demon smelled something acrid and spun around as Z and the others cried out, covering their watery eyes with trembling hands.

Very clever, Demon thought, backing away to avoid floating traces of the powder.

The sound of sirens came to his ears, approaching fast. He clapped twice.

Staggering from the fight, his team stumbled from the alley. Only Spider remained, still reeling from the blinding powder.

Demon thought to grab him, but the Hero was too close. At this point, he didn't want the Hero to see his face more clearly than he already had. He slunk along the wall and chased after his men.

Invictus turned toward the mouth of the alley as his five attackers stumbled away. A movement caught his eye and he glimpsed a baldhead and trailing rattail running after them.

That guy gave the orders. Must be the leader, he realized. Then he remembered the guy getting beat up.

His right eye only detected blurred movement, but his left clearly saw the bruised and bloodied young man clambering to his feet. The young man's eyes watered from the blinding powder and he squinted with anger.

"The hell you butt in for?" he hissed. "I was doin' fine!"

Invictus still felt the kick to his head, and the blurred vision didn't help.

"Huh?"

"They was jumpin' me in, fool!" the young man spat as he staggered toward the alley mouth. "Next time, mind your own!"

Invictus watched him disappear. The sirens were almost on top of him. Time to disappear, too.

The street was empty. Feeling like he was watching a 3D movie with the glasses only covering one eye, he found his way back to his motorcycle and clambered on.

The earpiece vibrated. He cranked up the cycle and tapped the Bluetooth.

"Vincent, get out of there. Someone saw you fighting a bunch of guys. Cops are almost there. Oh, crap, I hear the sirens!"

"Hold on, Dennis." He twisted the throttle and gunned the engine, whipping out of the alley into the street. The sirens seemed to be coming from his right, so he swung left and raced away as fast as he could. His blurry right eye made steering precarious, so once the sirens receded into the distance, he slowed. Thankfully, he wasn't far from home.

"Vincent, are you all right?" Dennis sounded frantic.

"Yeah, I'm fine, except…." He felt weak and disgusted with himself. If not for the sirens, he could've been in big trouble back there.

"Except what?"

"Except I lost a damned contact lens!"

He heard a sigh of relief on the other end.

"I'll be home soon."

He ended the call and focused on not crashing into anything.

Dennis heard Vincent enter the house and tromp up the stairs. The bathroom door in the hall opened and closed. He waited. After a minute or so he heard the door re-open. And then nothing.

"Vincent?"

Dennis navigated his way through the clothes to his door and stepped into the hallway. The light was on, but there was no sign of Vincent. He moved to the open bathroom door and glanced in. Vincent's contact lens solution sat on the counter next to the case he kept his lenses in, but otherwise nothing had been disturbed.

Dennis continued to the next room and peeked in. Vincent lay sprawled on top of his bed, still wearing the full Invictus costume, mask in one hand. He was sound asleep.

Dennis watched his brother's chest rise and fall, saw the look of sadness on his sleeping features, and felt a mix of conflicting emotions. The despondency on Vincent's face touched him to the core because he understood why it was there. He saw a young man trying to be all things to all people, something Dennis was beginning to realize wasn't possible.

He returned to his own room and snatched his rumpled blanket from the bed. He flipped off the light and made his way back to Vincent's room. Gently, with great care, he laid the blanket over his brother's slumbering form and then turned off the overhead light. Slipping under the blanket, he snuggled close to Vincent and studied his brother's face in the dark.

"Out of the night that covers me, black as the pit from pole to pole," he whispered to the sleeping man beside him, "I thank whatever gods may be for my unconquerable soul." He paused a moment. "For *your* unconquerable soul."

He watched a moment longer, and then rolled over onto his side and fell asleep within minutes.

The Mistress stood before her monitors watching news coverage of the gun store standoff when Demon entered. She didn't even turn.

"Approach, Demon."

He moved to her side and watched the news footage of the Hero fighting the armed men. On another monitor, people in front of a McDonald's were being interviewed while footage unspooled of the Hero trying to convince a big Latino guy behind the counter to sell food to some kid. Yet another monitor showed *his* camera's POV of the Hero fighting his team in the ally.

"He is impressive," Cat mumbled, almost to herself, and Demon didn't like her tone. "And he bested you all."

Of course, she'd watched the entire fight. The body cameras they wore allowed for no secrets.

"We had him, Mistress," Demon insisted. "But as you saw, he used some kind of chemical."

She chuckled. "He outsmarted you."

Demon felt his blood boil with rage. He'd been called stupid and useless throughout his childhood and he was neither!

"No, Mistress, he is not smarter. If the sirens had not…." He paused and met her gaze, something she forbade her subordinates to do. He was the only one. "Let me take him down."

"Patience, Demon," she purred, her voice soft and alluring and so tempting he had to force himself to remain immobile. "I am spinning a web, and he is the fly."

She returned her attention to the monitors. Demon stood and watched a moment longer. Then he bowed and left the room.

CHAPTER TWELVE
HE'S STILL TRYING TO ARREST INVICTUS?

VINCENT SLEPT UNTIL TWO P.M. that Saturday, and Dennis almost as long. He woke at one, but lay beside Vincent in silence, thinking about everything that had happened in the past week.

When Vincent stirred and opened his eyes, he reacted with surprise at finding Dennis there.

"You okay?"

Dennis leaned on his elbow. "Yeah. Just felt like staying with you last night."

Vincent yawned and stretched. He suddenly realized he still wore the costume and groaned. "I guess I crashed, huh?"

"Yeah. You were wiped out. It's two o'clock."

Vincent's eyes bulged and he sat up. "Oh, wow, that's crazy. I never sleep this much."

Dennis brushed hair off his forehead and slid his bare feet out from beneath the blanket.

"I'll make us something to eat." He stood and padded around the bed to Vincent's side and examined his face. "You have a little bruise. You got kicked?"

Vincent looked embarrassed. "That's how I lost the contact. Do I have any more?"

"Yeah, I ordered extras in case something like this happened. I also got some makeup to cover bruises."

Vincent gazed at him with amazement. "You think of everything."

Dennis shrugged.

"Let's get dressed and I'll take my most amazing brother out to lunch."

Dennis grinned. "I'd like that." Then he scrunched up his nose and waved a hand in front of his face. "After you shower, though. You reek."

Vincent laughed and Dennis joined him.

They chose a local Applebee's that fit Vincent's budget, but that also had televisions mounted in various locations. Dennis suspected some of these would be tuned to news channels covering "The Invictus Phenomenon," and they could watch while they ate.

"I don't think it's working," Vincent commented as they slid into the Volt.

"Because people never saw anyone like you for real," Dennis reassured him as he snapped on his seatbelt. "They will come, Vincent. You'll see."

Seated in the busy eatery munching on burgers and fries, Dennis felt anxious as he listened to comments from surrounding tables. Applebee's featured large burnished wood booths suitable for families, lots of wood paneling, a large bar set right in the center by the kitchen entrance, and numerous flat screens mounted high up near the ceiling. At three o'clock, the place wasn't crowded, but several booths were occupied by chattering adults or couples with their children, and a few guys sat at the bar gulping beer and watching a Dodger game on one of the TVs.

Other screens featured national news outlets, all of which were covering Invictus. Fox News had two people Dennis didn't recognize debating the pros and cons of working outside the law to help people in need.

Different channels featured footage of Invictus from the school incident and the gun store robbery, and even interviews with the McDonald's manager. He grumbled, "That weirdo embarrassed me in front of my customers."

"That's not true," Vincent hissed. "His customers were on my side!"

He'd put on sunglasses to hide the bruise, even though the makeup fully covered it. Dennis suspected Vincent still felt exposed in public, like he always had in high school. Maybe that insecurity was more acute now because of his dual identity.

As McDonald's patrons spoke with reporters, they defended Invictus and said the manager was out of line. Some said they'd no longer eat at that McDonald's because of the manager's behavior.

Dennis kept his gaze fixed on the kid who stood with Invictus in the McDonald's cell phone videos being broadcast. He could tell the kid was tall and skinny and Black, but the face was behind Invictus from most of the camera angles and blurred out by the network in others, so Dennis couldn't get a clear picture of what he looked like.

He fought that rising tide of jealousy. Or maybe it was envy. He wasn't sure, but he beat it back and focused on the reactions of people in the eatery.

Kids with their parents seemed to be excited, chattering on about the shield and the costume.

One little boy asked, "Can I be Invictus for Halloween?" His parents laughed.

Dennis grinned at Vincent and was pleased to see his brother smile.

But some adults in surrounding booths seemed to feel Invictus was just seeking attention.

"Probably for a new YouTube channel or something," one man commented, shaking his head with disgust.

It was hard for Dennis to get a consensus of opinion from random comments he heard, but near as he could tell, most adults seemed to think Invictus had an angle, that he wasn't helping people just to help, but that he expected something in return, maybe that "fifteen minutes of fame."

Dennis saw how these comments weighed his brother down, and decided they should head home.

Looking forlorn, Vincent agreed and handed money to the perky waitress who gushed, "This Invictus thing is cool, isn't it?"

Dennis agreed, and Vincent mumbled, "Yeah, it is."

She offered one of those dreamy smiles only young women could muster. "My friends and I are betting he's hot. Hopefully, one day he'll take off the mask."

She drifted over to the next table. Dennis eyed Vincent, who looked paralyzed with amazement.

"Well, she's right about the hot part," Dennis offered with a chuckle.

Vincent shook his head. "You're nuts, squirt."

Just then Linda stopped at their table and offered a huge smile. "Hi, guys. How's it going?"

Dennis grinned. "Big bro bought me lunch. Seeing as I do all the cooking, it's about time."

Vincent shrugged. "He still hasn't taught me how to cook."

Linda chuckled. Her hair was tied back and she was dressed in her martial arts outfit. She looked happy to see them.

"I'm always available to teach you, Vincent, if you ever have the time to learn. You're so busy with school and work, but the offer's open."

"Thanks, Linda," he responded. "Hope I can take you up on it someday."

"So, what brings you here?" Dennis asked, wanting to divert her attention away from Vincent's activities.

"Take-out for James," she answered with a sigh, brushing errant strands of hair away from her face. "He's sleeping now and I teach classes the rest of the day, so I wanted something ready for him before he goes on patrol."

"He's still trying to arrest Invictus?" Vincent asked.

Dennis eyed him with caution, but Vincent focused on Linda.

"Yep. Captain's orders."

"Why is Torres being such a hardass about this guy?" Vincent asked, his tone one of rising annoyance.

Dennis shook his head slightly to get his brother's attention, but Vincent didn't notice. Or chose not to notice.

Linda knew them better than anyone and Dennis hoped Vincent would not raise her suspicions.

"Torres sometimes fancies himself judge and jury these days, but he's mostly a letter-of-the-law guy, Vincent," she answered matter-of-factly. "Like James."

"What about the spirit of the law?" Dennis offered, hoping to steer this conversation in a safer direction.

"You're right, Dennis, and James has come around to that way of thinking over the years. But not Torres. In his mind, Invictus is working outside the law, even though he's helping people, and that makes him a lawbreaker."

"Laws are supposed to protect people," Vincent said tightly, his body coiled with tension. "Laws that keep people from helping each other are bad laws."

"I agree," Dennis offered.

She smiled warmly. "And so do I. If we aren't allowed to help each other, we don't have much of a community, do we?"

"No," Vincent answered. "And if people are too afraid to step up and help because they might be arrested or sued, what kind of society have we created?"

"One that doesn't work," Dennis offered, this time catching his brother's eye. He shook his head slightly.

Linda studied them a moment and then grinned. "You two are incredible. Another reason I love you so much."

"Thanks, Linda," Vincent said. "We don't know what we'd do without you."

"And James," Dennis put in quickly.

"Speaking of which, I need to pick up his food." She glanced at her Apple watch. "Drop by any time."

"We will," Vincent assured her.

She hurried off to the Take-Out counter to pick up her order.

"We gotta be careful, Vince, especially around her and James."

Vincent removed the sunglasses and set them on the table, and Dennis perceived something in his brother's eyes that he'd never seen there before. He couldn't quite explain it, but those eyes looked like they could "see" better than before. No, not better. Just "more." Like they could see more than what was right in front of them.

"I know," he answered quietly. "Torres's attitude just pisses me off."

"Yeah, me too."

The perky waitress returned Vincent's change and thanked them with a big, toothy smile. Then she danced off to another table. Vincent slid a twenty over to Dennis.

"What's that for?"

"In case you want to hang out with Jackson and Kenny. I know I said we might see a movie, but I didn't factor in sleeping all day." He looked apologetic and guilty. "I have midterms next week."

Dennis understood. "No problem. And thanks." He pocketed the money. He didn't have the heart to tell Vincent that his friends always wanted to go out at night when he was unavailable. He didn't want Vincent feeling guilty about going out every night and leaving him alone. Especially since The Dream had been his idea.

They left the restaurant. The warm summer sun lifted Dennis's spirits and he thanked Vincent for lunch.

"And for just spending time with me. Means the world."

Vincent smiled. "You're welcome, Squirt. We need to hang out more often, like the old days."

Dennis grinned broadly. "I'm down for that."

Vincent threw an arm around his shoulders and they walked back to the car.

Vincent stayed in his room the rest of the day catching up on homework and studying for midterms. Dennis played *Call of Duty* for a couple of hours, but it wasn't as much fun playing against online strangers as it was with his friends.

As he'd feared, he called Jackson after returning home from lunch to see if he and Kenny could come over, but they had already made plans to go out with other kids to watch an Angels game. One of their parents had free tickets.

"Sorry, man." Jackson always spoke in a super serious voice. "You been so busy these days I didn't even think to call you. Next time, 'kay?"

Dennis felt like the wind had been knocked out of him. It had only been a week of him begging off outings with his friends and they'd already given up on him?

"Yeah, next time."

After the lackluster *Call of Duty* session, Dennis retreated to his room to sketch new designs. He envisioned that at some point there might be an Invictus comic book and he wanted to be one of the artists.

Because they'd had such a late lunch, Vincent didn't eat much prior to going out, and Dennis wasn't hungry, either. He so wanted to ask if Vincent would meet up with "Robin" tonight, but bit back the question. He stood in the garage and watched his big brother fire up the cycle and head out.

First order of business for Invictus was to track down Franky, in part to determine if he'd been able to score some weed from the Asian group, but mainly to make sure the child was safe. Invictus could not rid his mind of the little boy's angelic smile when he'd "become" Robin.

He rode back to downtown and cruised the side streets. He wanted to be seen by more people so they'd know he was present, but had to be on constant alert for the police, so side streets had to, for the present, remain his principal avenues of travel. He kept his eyes open for any crimes he could thwart, but mostly searched for Franky. He returned several times to the pile of clothes behind the Laundromat. The first two visits proved fruitless. On the third, he spotted a small form curled up in a tight ball beside the dumpster.

As Invictus cruised to a stop beside him, Franky sat up and broke into a huge smile, the deep cracks around his mouth producing a grin more suited to the Joker than Robin.

"Hi, Batman."

Invictus shut off the bike's engine and dismounted. He crinkled his nose at the rotten food stench emanating from the dumpster.

"Hey, Robin." He offered a high five and kept his face turned away from the smell.

The boy sat up and slapped his palm. Invictus crouched down so they could be eye to eye.

"How are you tonight?"

Franky's eyes were dilated and he fidgeted.

"I'm okay," he chirped in his high voice. "My mama's tripping real bad so I came here to chill."

"How much did you take?"

Franky laughed. "Not so much this time." He seemed to sink into himself, as though struggling hard to recall something. Then his eyes went wide. "Now I remember what I was gonna give you."

He dove into his pocket with one dirty hand and pulled out a small plastic bag. Invictus observed crumpled greens that he presumed were weed. It looked like the samples he'd been analyzing at Chin's lab.

Feeling dirty, he shivered and slipped the bag into a belt pouch. "Uh, Thanks."

"Did I do good?"

Invictus felt that lump in his throat again. "You did great."

Franky sat up more and scooted closer. "What's next, Batman?"

Invictus paused a moment. "I wish you'd let me find you a real place to live."

Franky recoiled. "I can't leave my mama."

"But she can't take care of you, Franky," Invictus insisted, hoping he could reason with the child.

"I take care of *her*," he answered matter-of-factly.

Invictus flinched.

"If they take me away, who's gonna do that?"

"There are people who could take care of her," Invictus assured him cautiously. *Were there?* He wasn't sure.

Franky shook his head.

Invictus so wanted to help this boy that he spoke the next words without that pause his father always modeled. "What if I could find you a real home? And a place where mom could get help?"

Franky's eyes turned into saucers of surprise. "You could do that?"

Invictus hesitated only a second. "Yeah. Mom could get her act together without worrying about you. And you'll have a good home."

Franky considered this idea. His tongue kept washing over his dry lips, but there was no saliva to wet them. "Superheroes don't lie, right?"

Invictus realized at that moment he might have just made a terrible mistake.

"No, they don't. If you want it, I promise to find you a good home, a real home with people who love you."

Did I just say that? What the hell, Vince, how can you do that?

Franky screwed up his face, as though thinking about something so big was a strain on his brain. Then he looked Invictus in the eye. "I'll think about it."

Invictus nodded, knowing that was the best he'd get out of the boy. He also wondered how he could keep his promise.

Franky leapt up and Invictus saw his scrawny limbs almost buzzing with trembling energy. "I'm gonna go home now, check on mama."

He started away toward the mouth of the alley. Then he turned back and grinned. "I'll get more stuff for you. I like being Robin."

"Uh, Robin, wait– "

But the boy had already vanished from the mouth of the alley.

Do I want him getting more "stuff?" Sure, the more samples I have, the more I can learn about the added ingredients. But he could get hurt play-acting Robin. Or worse.

Invictus clambered onto his motorcycle, struggling with the rightness and wrongness of involving a child in such dangerous business.

From behind the dumpster, he heard, "You Santa Claus now, too?"

Startled, he saw Joe step out of the shadows with an angry look on his face.

"What do you mean?"

Joe approached and stood before him, arms folded across his chest. "You promised him a home, man. How you gonna deliver on that?"

Invictus winced at Joe's anger. "I'll find a way."

Joe stared at him in amazement. Then he shook his head and unfolded his arms. "Anybody else said that, I'd say he was full of it. But you? You just might pull it off."

"I don't make promises I can't keep." Up till now, that had been true.

Joe tilted his head. "So what about me, Santa Claus?"

"What about you?"

"I gotta be out of Runaway House by the end of August."

That shocked Invictus. "Why? You have nowhere to go."

Joe shrugged, as though kicking kids into the street was the most natural course of action in the world. Apparently, it was.

"It's a temp shelter," he explained. "After ninety days with no parents coming to claim us, DCFS takes over. They'll put me in a group home and try to find my parents. I don't wanna see them ever again!"

His body stiffened and his hands became fists.

Once again, Invictus felt disgust for a legal system that hurt the kids it was supposed to help. Despite Dennis's thinking to the contrary, Vincent was beginning to act *too much* from the heart, and he spoke again without that pause.

"I'll find you a home, too."

Joe's eyes widened almost as much as Franky's. "Yeah?"

Invictus stuck out one gloved hand. "You have my word."

Joe reached out and shook his hand, but said nothing. He just nodded and looked like he might cry at any moment.

Invictus pulled back his hand and studied the boy's trembling lip and misting eyes and prayed that he could deliver on both promises he made tonight.

Determination welled up within him. *I will keep them!*

"Hop on, I'll take you back."

After dropping off Joe, Invictus followed Dennis's directives that led him to stop a gang fight, intervene in a domestic argument that could have escalated into violence, stop a home invasion robbery in progress, and break up a drunk and disorderly fight outside a seedy looking bar.

That last one was worse than the gang fight. The gang members didn't like his interference, but seemed relieved when he forced them to go their separate ways, as though happy no one had to die that night. He disarmed them first, however, which they didn't like, and deposited the weapons near a police station, whereby Dennis alerted the cops to their presence. The gang kids had gone off grumbling, but alive.

The drunken men brawling in front of the Oil Skin Bar were another story. Invictus had to knock two of them unconscious before the others seemed to get the message. At that point, approaching sirens could be heard and everyone scattered, including Invictus.

All he thought of on the way home were the promises he'd made to Franky and Joe. Could he keep them?

I have to!

Somehow.

CHAPTER THIRTEEN

THEY WILL COME, VINCENT

VINCENT SLEPT LATE AGAIN ON Sunday and didn't appear till mid-day. Dennis spent the morning working on his comic book. Despite not knowing what Joe or Franky looked like, or even their ages, he drew Invictus's two "helpers" as he envisioned them, opposite a panel of himself alone in his room with only the computer and police scanner for company.

When Vincent did finally get up and eat lunch, he seemed sullen and withdrawn, like something had happened to him the night before that darkened his spirits. All Dennis could get out of him were bits and pieces of what had gone down, and the news that he'd acquired some weed to test at the lab.

"What do you think you'll find?" he asked, trying to draw his brother out.

Vincent swallowed a bite of his grilled cheese sandwich and shrugged. "No idea till I test it. I'll let you know."

And that was the last time Dennis saw him all day. He stayed in his room cramming for midterms and catching up on other work. Only when darkness fell and Invictus appeared at his bedroom door did he even know his brother was in the house.

"I'm only staying out a few hours tonight, Dennis," he announced. "Tomorrow's my all-class day and I have to work after that."

Dennis studied him a moment, and listened to the tone of his voice. It sounded weary. He knew Vincent needed some validation from the populace at large to keep his spirits up.

"They will come, Vincent. I promise."

Vincent flinched at the word "promise," which confused Dennis. Then the mask was over his head and he was out of the room.

Dennis heard the motorcycle roaring off down the street as he hacked into the police mainframe and cranked up his scanner.

He'd done nothing all day but work on his comic book and play a few video games. He hadn't heard from Jackson or Kenny, and didn't expect to. He could always call them, but for what purpose? Only to say he *couldn't* hang out with them? His excuse that Vincent needed his help with something had already gotten old, and he didn't have anything better to replace it.

He directed Vincent to a number of 911 calls that he thought might generate some level of gratitude on the part of the people involved, and listened in whenever Vincent kept the phone call active.

A domestic disturbance turned into a call to the police to "arrest the crazy guy in the costume."

"At least," Dennis told his brother after Invictus fled the scene, "they stopped fighting with each other."

He'd tried to sound light, but Invictus only grunted in disgust.

Invictus went on to foil three attempted auto thefts and a mini-mart holdup. The mini-mart owner told him he'd already used his silent alarm to alert the police and that the interference from Invictus might have gotten him killed.

"You also might've been dead by the time the cops arrived," Invictus grumbled as he hurried from the scene.

As the night wore on, he sounded more dispirited and decided at midnight to head back home.

"Busy day tomorrow," Dennis heard over the phone. But he knew better.

And what did you accomplish today, Dennis? He could almost hear his dad's voice in his head.

Absolutely nothing, Dad, he silently replied, feeling weak and useless and lonely. *I drew, read some poetry, and watched stupid videos on YouTube. All by myself. And I wasn't even able to lift Vincent's spirits about being Invictus!*

Feeling weighed down with feelings he couldn't quite pinpoint, Dennis put his computer to sleep and turned off the scanner. Slipping off his shirt and pants, he switched out the light and slipped into bed, pulling the sheet up to his chin. He felt exhausted even though he'd done nothing physical the entire day.

How weird is that?

His final thought before drifting off was, *I wonder if Vincent hung out with his partners tonight.*

Vincent managed to get to Professor Chin's class on time and once again found Lisa saving him a spot. He stopped dead when he saw her and almost slapped his forehead in shock. He'd completely forgotten to call her over the weekend. Her look of annoyance convinced him she'd expected that call.

He eased his way into the row and sat cautiously beside her, pretending to slip off his backpack and slide it beneath his seat so he wouldn't have to look at her. When he finally sat up, he found her blue eyes wide with anger.

"What happened?" she whispered, her tone clipped and tight. "You never called me."

Still needing something to do, Vincent adjusted his wire-rimmed glasses and tried to look as apologetic as possible. "I'm so sorry, Lisa, I got–"

He was cut off by a loud, "Good morning, class," as Professor Chin entered and stood at his podium surveying the lecture hall. Somehow, he knew the professor was searching for him, and his suspicions were confirmed when the man's squinting eyes paused on him a few seconds before moving on.

"After class." He fumbled in his pack for a notepad and pen. When he sat back up, he found her eyeing him. That look said it all – *this had better be good.* As Chin started his lecture and Vincent took notes, he suddenly had a terrifying thought. What excuse had Dennis given her on Friday? He couldn't remember!

I'm dead!

He pushed those thoughts to one side of his brain while he assimilated the data Chin was outlining. There was so much significant information being presented that he didn't dare stop to text Dennis and ask, especially with Lisa eyeing him every so often.

The back of his mind replayed that conversation with Dennis on Friday, but he came up empty. He kept thinking about that promise he'd made to Franky. And the second one to Joe. Promises that might be impossible to keep.

By the time class ended ninety minutes later and a hundred students rose to exit the lecture hall, Vincent still couldn't recall the lie Dennis had concocted. Despite having a full day of back-to-back classes, he knew he'd have to tell Lisa something before they went their separate ways.

Backpack over one shoulder, he toyed with his ponytail as he followed chattering young people up the steps to the exit. Lisa was right behind him. Once they exited the auditorium, Vincent reluctantly faced her.

She looked as beautiful as ever with her head tilted slightly and her lips curled into a frown. Those eyes, though. They dove right into him with their questions.

"I'm really, sorry, Lisa, about Friday," he began, hoping and praying the right words would come to him. And then, like lightning from heaven, they did. "Didn't Dennis tell you what happened?"

"Yeah." Her tone reeked of annoyance. "I got that you had to pick up your friend from the police station. But you could've called me when you got back."

Thank you, God!

Vincent felt so relieved he almost smiled, and that would've made her furious.

"He was in the drunk tank and they made me wait around all night for him to sober up before I could take him," he explained, hating the lie, but knowing his new lifestyle would likely necessitate a great deal of lying. He'd best get used to it. "I ran out in a hurry and forgot my phone or I'd have called you from the station."

He watched her digest his story and hoped he sounded convincing. He'd never been a good liar, even as a kid.

"I understand," she finally replied. "My older brother parties too much. But why didn't you call me Saturday or Sunday?"

Now that one he hadn't thought of. The truth was simple – he'd forgotten all about her. Not a good way to begin a relationship.

He didn't have to try looking embarrassed because he was mortified. "Honestly, I slept most of Saturday and Sunday." That part was true, at least. "And with midterms this week and being behind on homework, I just… forgot." He stared at his Nike cross trainers. "I'm sorry."

She seemed like she wanted to be mad, but Vincent must've looked sincerely morose because she ended up laughing instead.

"I've been there, Vein Boy." She punched him lightly on the shoulder. "Swamped with work. What about this coming weekend?"

Like being slapped in the face, Vincent froze. How could he go out with her on weekends when Invictus needed to patrol? As though another bolt of lightning struck, he thought up a new lie as easily as the first.

"Uh, unfortunately I start a second job this week." He tried for a disappointed tone. "Restaurant. Dishwasher. I have to work almost every night starting tonight."

"A second job? Vincent, you have no time as it is."

She seemed genuinely shocked and sympathetic, which made the lie feel all the worse. "I have to, Lisa, for Dennis. We need the extra money."

Disappointment filled her face, which shocked Vincent even more. She must genuinely like him, he realized, and wasn't sure how to process knowledge of that sort. It was unheard of in his life experience.

"Um, we could have lunch," he suggested, but then slapped a hand to his forehead. "Stupid me. I'm in class and work all day today. Maybe another day this week?"

He knew he sounded like a fool.

Her face registered confusion and a trace of hurt.

"I'm busy, too, Vincent," she said curtly. "Call me when you're sure and I'll let you know if I'm free. Gotta get to class now."

She disappeared into the crowd of milling students. Dejected, Vincent headed in the opposite direction. He was going to be late again.

He got through the rest of his classes without dosing off more than once. One of his professors obviously noticed because Vincent caught a disapproving look directed his way and he experienced a memory lapse about what was being said at the podium. Despite sleeping in over the weekend, his body was debilitated after just one week of juggling so many activities and not resting enough. More significantly, his brain function had slowed because the brain needed as much "down time" as the body. But what could he do?

Lisa's anger ate at him throughout the day, and he wanted to make it up to her. But how? When would he have the time to give her anything but mere moments? Sure, she'd asked *him* out, but still… Was he a fool for thinking he could have everything he wanted? Was being in a relationship right now as important as what he was doing? If he became effective as Invictus and inspired the masses like Dennis hoped, of course *that* would be more important. A relationship primarily benefited him. Invictus, if successful, could benefit thousands.

"To make a difference requires sacrifice, and most people will never go that far."

His father's words echoed through his mind as he approached the Neurology Institute. He hadn't considered all the far-reaching ramifications before embarking on this current venture, even though it had been in large measure those words that had created Invictus. Did being a hero mean he'd be alone for the rest of his life like Bruce Wayne in the comics?

What are you willing to sacrifice?

That question weighed him down, and when he slogged into Professor Chin's lab at two p.m., the professor eyed him disapprovingly. Vincent trudged to his locker and stuffed his backpack inside. He slipped his white lab coat on over his tank top. When he turned around, his heart jumped at finding Chin directly behind him. He hadn't even heard the man approach.

"Vincent, I'm becoming more and more concerned about you," he intoned gravely. "I've noted errors in your work this past week."

Vincent felt guilt and shame wash over him. "I'm sorry, professor. I had no idea I was making errors in my calculations."

"Of course, you didn't, Vincent," Chin replied. "Your brain is too fatigued. I know the stress you have been under and I sympathize. But our funding, and your future, could be jeopardized if your work deteriorates further."

Vincent felt his body go numb with horror. He could lose everything.

What are you willing to sacrifice?

"I'll get it together, Professor," he said with quiet assurance. "I promise."

There you go, Vince, another promise you might not be able to keep.

"That's what I want to hear." Chin clapped him on the shoulder and moved off to consult with another grad student who was waving him over.

Vincent found himself shivering, feeling more fear at what the professor told him than he had out on the streets. He couldn't kick his way to a PhD, nor could he help Chin keep his funding by getting Franky to buy drugs for him.

Or could he?

Glancing around to make certain no one was watching, he reached into his backpack side pocket and slipped out the small baggie Franky had given him. If what Joe told him was true and there had been something new added to common street drugs, and if he could isolate it, that discovery would give even greater credibility to Chin's program and assure funding for years to come.

Slipping the bag into his coat pocket, he greeted fellow workers on the way to his station. He eyed the lab as his computer powered up. He knew everyone working there, but not very well. He'd always been the loner of the group and never hung out with any of them socially. Of course, he'd needed to get home right after work to check on Dennis and spend time with him, but that was only part of the truth. With an inward sigh, Vincent acknowledged that he didn't much like socializing, which was odd considering this project was designed to help people.

When he opened up his work file, he noted several yellow highlights where Chin had tagged his errors. He fixed them and updated his conclusions. Then he slipped the baggie from his pocket and poured its contents into a glass container. If anyone observed his work from this point on, they'd assume the sample had been donated by the Drug Enforcement Agency.

The primary method used for separating the components of each drug was Thin-Layer Chromatography or TLC. Vincent added five milliliters of ethyl acetate/acetic acid to a developing chamber that contained a paper wick. Then, using a flat-bladed spatula, he ground some of the weed into powder on a watch glass before transferring the powder to a small test tube. He added two-point-five milliliters of one-to-one ethanol/dichloromethane to the tube. With a stirring rod, he dissolved the powder into the liquid. Using a pipet filled with cotton to act as a filter, he transferred the solution to a small vial, leaving residual solid matter behind in the test tube.

At this point, he used TLC to identify the individual components. He prepared a plate coated with a thin layer of absorbent silicone-based material and added some of the solution distilled from the marijuana to this plate. Solvents would be drawn up the plate due to capillary action and separate out into distinct components.

While he awaited the results, Vincent toyed with his ponytail and glanced around the lab. He spotted Chin watching him and offered a thumbs up. Chin turned back to his computer.

Examining the results of his separation, Vincent frowned. All the standard components of marijuana, primarily THC, were present. But there was something else, something he'd never seen in any of the drug samples the DEA had provided.

What the hell is this?

He studied the chemical breakdown of the substance and the combination was foreign to him. He would need to run these components through the computer one by one, and in conjunction with each other, to determine the precise effect each would have on the human brain before he could draw any conclusions.

He sat back and realized something else. He needed more samples. He needed to know how the added ingredient broke down within meth, cocaine, heroin, and whatever other drugs it had been added to. And he needed to find Demon to learn where the supply came from.

Though tired and hungry—he'd had twenty minutes for lunch and had consumed only a protein bar—he suddenly felt a real connection between his life in this lab and his life as Invictus. Though it had not been part of his or Dennis's plan when they'd conceived The Dream, serendipity had a way of bringing things together in ways they couldn't have planned for.

Demon reported to the Video Center as ordered, where he found Young Z in the presence of The Mistress. Z bowed to her and glided past Demon on his way out, an impassive expression on his young face. Demon approached and bowed.

"I'm at your command, Mistress."

Her hair was tied back in a ponytail and she wore a black leather jumpsuit. Was she planning to go out? He never knew her comings and goings.

"You and your team will take command of the Valley operation," she informed him, her tone all business. "Casper has disappointed me and has been dealt with."

Demon knew what "dealt with" meant – they'd never see Casper, a young Chinese immigrant, alive again.

"There are two reasons for my choosing you, Demon," she went on, looking him up and down as though determining his suitability for the job. "There is real money in the Valley and you are the best man to bring it here. American youth live frivolous lives. They have an entitlement mentality. Not to mention far too much wealth without the understanding of how real wealth is acquired. Had they grown up as did my brother and I on the streets of Seoul, they might appreciate the value of money. In any case, they will buy our product, especially at our *reduced* prices."

She chuckled. While he didn't know why, he did know she'd reduced the price of her "product" well below current street value and severely punished any of her runners who tried to charge more. That was another reason every one of her servants wore body cams. The penalty for turning off one's body camera was a severe beating. If it happened twice, well, there *was* no second chance.

"I've heard there's rich Asians in the Valley, Mistress. Should we sell to them if they want it?"

Her features darkened like an incoming storm. "Never. Try to convince them to work for me. Appeal to their innate intelligence. Remind them of their superiority. Our people should never degrade themselves."

"Yes, Mistress. And the second reason?"

She pursed her lips. The garish red lipstick shimmered beneath the overhead lights. "Rumor has it the Hero knows of you by name."

"I am not afraid of him, Mistress," he assured her, puffing out his chest and standing as tall as possible.

"I never said you were, Demon," she replied with a smile. "But there are reasons I do not want you engaging the Hero just yet. You'll have your chance."

He knew he would get nothing more from her. "I'm honored to take on this new responsibility."

"And so you should be." She stepped closer. "There's something else I need for you to do."

He raised his eyebrows as she explained what she wanted. It made no sense to him, but he'd long ago learned that it wasn't his job to comprehend her plans, only to execute them.

"It shall be done, Mistress."

"Assemble your team. You start tomorrow."

He bowed and left her alone.

CHAPTER FOURTEEN

THEY CALL ME DREAMER

NVICTUS DIDN'T SEE FRANKY UNTIL Thursday of that week and he expressed visible shock when the child handed him several small bags of drugs.

"Did Robin do good, Batman?" he asked with a toothy grin.

Invictus noted the sallow cheeks, but there seemed to be a bit more color to his skin than usual.

"You did amazingly good, Robin," Invictus replied. He raised a fist and the small boy bumped it with his scabbed and dirty one.

Invictus held up the bags and examined them. "You're giving me some crystal? Will mom be mad and…."

He couldn't finish, but Franky obviously knew what he meant. "She don't know." He chuckled. "I'm tryin' to bring her down. Me, too. So I don't give her all of it. I told her the dealers jacked up the price."

He looked very pleased with himself, and Invictus stood speechless for a moment.

"That's awesome, Franky."

They sat cross-legged beside each other on the clothes pile to eat the food he'd brought.

Franky dug into his burger and fries as though he hadn't eaten in days.

"So what made you decide to wean you and your mom off?" Invictus asked, struggling to take a bite out of his own burger. The mask fit snugly around his cheeks and mouth and made eating difficult.

"I figure," Franky explained while swigging his Coke, "If I'm gonna be Robin out here, I gotta get it together."

Invictus nearly gagged on his food and stared in astonishment at Franky's wide, expectant face.

"That's…." He paused to collect his thoughts. "That's golden, Robin. You just keep at it day by day."

The boy beamed. The dirt on his face and in his hair somehow accentuated that smile and made him look even younger than his ten years.

"You got it, Batman."

He dug into his fries while Invictus nibbled on his burger. His heart thumped with wildly conflicting emotions. He never thought he could love someone as much as he loved Dennis, but this boy had snuck in and stolen his heart right out from under his brain. He knew in his mind that he shouldn't get close to anyone out here. But his heart seemed to have a mind of its own, which was something his brain studies had never taught him.

They ate the rest of their meal in silence.

Dennis spent his week largely alone. Jackson and Kenny didn't call, which wasn't surprising, and he didn't reach out to them. He understood that the more he invited them over or hung out with them during the day, the more suspicious they'd become over why he could never hang out at night.

He was lonely. Day after day of video games began to bore him. His comic book was shaping up well enough, and he still wrote and read poetry. But other than taking a daily run through the neighborhood, he almost never left the house. And that wasn't him. He liked being social.

He'd tried again to convince his brother to take him out some nights, not to be part of the action, but just to watch from a safe distance. Vincent steadfastly refused. He never gave a good reason except, "It's too dangerous," and that angered Dennis.

You have Joe and Franky helping you out there, he always wanted to say. But Vincent didn't know he knew about the two sidekicks, so he bit his tongue and said nothing.

In addition, Lisa had phoned to ask if he knew why Vincent kept saying he'd call her, but had not. She'd seen him in class on Wednesday and he'd promised again, but still no phone call. Not even a text.

He apologized for "my brother's sucky social skills," and she laughed. He went on to add that Vincent was "super busy" these days and probably just forgot.

She swore him to secrecy about her call, and he agreed.

When Lisa ended her call, she sat back in her desk chair and considered everything she knew about Vincent. From the first day she saw him in Chin's summer session class, she'd found him attractive, especially the super long black hair, which she adored. People always complimented her on her blonde locks, but on guys she much preferred black. She wasn't sure why, but that straight black hair on Asian and Native American guys grabbed her attention every time. She even liked Vincent's round, wire-rimmed glasses and his shy demeanor.

She'd asked around about him and the same word kept cropping up – loner. She could see right off the bat that he was an introvert and very intellectual, and figured his lack of social skills probably went back to high school. Just the way he'd responded to being asked out had been almost junior-highish, but she rather liked that. Too many guys hit on her every day just to hit on her.

Not Vincent. She could tell he liked her, was drawn to her, but not in any lustful, hook-up kind of way. Maybe it was because he spent so much time looking at books and into microscopes, but when he studied her from behind those glasses she felt like he was looking at everything she was, at her thoughts and feelings and everything that made her Lisa Burrows, medical graduate student at UCLA.

So why had he suddenly backed off? He seemed genuinely interested in going out with her. Not for a second did she buy his lame attempts to lie, or Dennis's either when he'd called her that Friday. No, there was something going on in Vincent's life and she wanted to know what it was.

She slipped out her phone and opened her photo folder. She'd snapped some pictures of him when he wasn't looking, both in class and walking across campus last week. She scrolled through the photos, studying each one. Then it hit her. The hair! He always wore his hair in a ponytail, except for the other day when he'd been late and hadn't had time to tie it back.

Unrestrained, his hair draped his shoulders and spilled down his back and… looked familiar. As a hair connoisseur, she knew she'd seen this hair on someone else. But how could that be?

Setting her phone down on the desk, she flipped open her Anatomy book to finish an assignment. But she made a vow to find out Vincent's secret, and where she'd seen that hair. Whether or not she ever went on a date with him, he was a mystery, and she loved solving mysteries.

Dennis had been monitoring the police scanner for any mention of that Demon guy Vincent had mentioned. Either the police didn't know him by name or he was laying low, but there was no chatter regarding the drug dealer.

Before heading in to work that Friday, Vincent showed him the drugs he'd acquired, though he wouldn't say exactly how he'd come by them.

"Rousted some dealers," was all he said, and Dennis knew he was lying. But his plan to study the drugs at work was the truth, and Dennis hoped Vincent would clue him in on the result.

Since it was a hot, sunny day, Dennis snatched up one of his poetry books and decided to run to a nearby park where he could sit and read for a while.

That decision would change his life forever.

Vincent spent much of the day analyzing the drugs he'd gotten from Franky. Every sample contained the same additive he'd found in the marijuana, so he focused his energies on that specific chemical compound. It was synthetic, as opposed to naturally occurring, so its inclusion in the drugs was intentional. The creator expected a specific outcome from users taking the drugs laced with this compound. But what outcome? Joe had said something about the drugs making people "dumber." Wasn't that what he'd said? Okay, but all recreational drugs destroyed brain cells, especially meth. So what was the bottom line here?

They were forbidden by UCLA ordinance from experimenting on animals, and he was uncomfortable with that idea, anyway. What he needed were some brain scans of users, people who'd been doing drugs laced with this compound. Then he could compare and contrast those scans with the ones from volunteer users who weren't taking the laced drugs. This project allowed for anonymous volunteers to come in for MRI's of the brain in exchange for one hundred dollars, and Chin had a large number of images already on file. But the only person he knew for sure that was taking these laced drugs was Franky.

Franky could certainly use the money, but minors weren't allowed to participate in the study without parental permission.

Knowing he might be crossing a line he could never take back, Vincent considered sneaking the boy into the lab and taking pictures of his brain. He knew how to circumvent security since he'd worked late many nights over the past few months. And Chin had entrusted him with other necessary codes, including the combination to the safe containing the drugs.

But should he do that?

Sitting back from his computer screen, his body slumped with fatigue. It had been a long week and he couldn't think clearly about such a crucial decision. He'd continue with computer models for now, projecting the likely effects of this compound on the brains of children and adults.

He'd only involve Franky as a last resort.

Wearing workout shorts and a tank top, Dennis ran to Ridge Park. He'd tied his hair into a small ponytail to keep it out of his eyes and clutched the book in his right hand. The air was hot and dry and he worked up a good sweat. Running and sparring with Vincent seemed to be the best medicine when he felt lonely or down, but lately Vincent had no time to spar, so running was his main source of exercise.

The park sloped upward and Dennis ran to the top where a lone bench overlooked the Valley below. Sweaty and panting because he'd pushed himself, he plopped onto the bench and surveyed the vista beneath him. Houses and trees and lots of greenery filled his vision.

He'd lived in Porter Ranch since fifth grade, but still missed his friends from the old school. He'd kept in contact with a few of them via social media for a while, but then lost touch. He'd made lots of new friends in the Valley, especially Jackson and Kenny. They'd included him in their circle and introduced him to everyone they knew.

Everything had been good. Until his parents were ripped from his life. Then came the PTSD. Then the moodiness. Then the obsession with creating Invictus. He'd sucked Vincent into the project and now he, the creator, was just an accessory, like a heated car seat that provided comfort, but wasn't necessary.

He glanced at his poetry book. Yes, today he would read "the poem" for the first time since his parents' headstone was put in place. He had to become stronger. He had to move beyond their deaths. It was the PTSD that made Vincent think he was weak and fragile.

That's not true. He always thought you were weak.

Dennis pushed that thought aside. He wasn't weak. He was strong and smart and capable. He just needed to prove it to his brother.

He opened the book to John Donne's *Death Be Not Proud*. He cleared his throat and glanced around to make sure no one was watching. The warm breeze dried the sweat on his arms and face. His hands shook slightly as they held out the paperback, and he fought to control them.

"Death be not proud," he read in a strong, clear voice. He would not stumble this time. He would get through the whole thing. "Though some have called thee mighty and dreadful, for thou art not so, for, those, whom thou think'st thou dost overthrow, die not, poore death, nor yet canst thou kill me."

"What'chu reading, kid?"

He whirled around in shock, startled more than afraid. Standing behind him were three Asian guys, Vincent's age or a little older. They all had shaved heads except for a thin rattail dangling down their backs. The one in front, who was Vincent's height, wore a tank top revealing thick, muscular arms folded across his chest. The smirk on his face annoyed Dennis big time!

"Poetry," he replied tightly, wary that there were three against one and no other people in sight.

The guy grinned. "Hey, I'm down with poetry. To be or not to be or somethin', right?"

He laughed and the two guys laughed with him.

"That's from a play," Dennis stated, but he remained seated and made no threatening moves. Could he take all three of them? Doubtful. Vincent could, but not him.

"Oh, we got us a schoolboy here, Demon," one of the other guys sneered.

Dennis flinched at the name. Could it be?

"S'okay, Ricer," Demon replied firmly. "We can always use some smart guys."

The one called Ricer backed down and fell silent and Dennis understood that Demon called the shots.

"What's your name, kid?"

"Dennis."

The three of them laughed and Demon took a step closer. Dennis jumped up from the bench and took two steps back.

"Don't worry, *Dennis*," Demon said in a mocking tone. "I won't hurt you. But that name sure as hell will. I don't tell nobody my real name. Not even these fools know it. Enemies get too much power over you when they know your real name."

Dennis considered what he heard. They sounded like a gang, but weren't banged out in their clothing style. All wore tanks and jeans and looked like any other young people out in the summer sun. Could this be the same Demon Vincent was looking for downtown? What would he be doing all the way out here?

"They call me Dreamer," he said, pulling up the nickname his mother gave him when he was five.

"Dreamer it is. We got us a good gig going. Could use some new blood. You want in?"

"What kind of gig?" Dennis's whole body was prepped for flight.

"Come on and find out."

Dennis thought of Invictus. "I have to be home when my brother gets back."

The three youths sniggered derisively and Dennis felt his ears burn red.

"Okay, be a weak-ass pussy," Demon grunted. "We're outta here."

He nodded his head at the other two and they followed him across the sloping grass.

Dennis froze. Those cutting words, "weak-ass pussy," struck him to the core. He considered the ramifications of this guy being *the* Demon his brother sought. This was his chance, likely his *only* chance. This was his moment to do something even Vincent couldn't do.

"Wait up," he called out before he could change his mind.

The three faced him.

"Well?" Demon called out. "Ain't got all day."

Dennis sprinted around the bench to join them.

When Vincent entered the house at five-thirty and called out, "Dennis, I'm home," he was met with a creepy silence. Entering the family room, he saw the television off and the game controllers tossed haphazardly on the couch where they'd been when he left for work.

Odd.

"Dennis?"

He stopped at the bottom of the stairs and tried again. "You up there?"

Silence.

A chill wrapped itself around his heart and soul. He dashed up the stairs two at a time and entered Dennis's room. Still messy. Computer off. Bed unmade. Then his eye caught sight of something and he froze.

Dennis's phone lay on the desk beside the keyboard.

Calm down, Vince, think this through. Dennis always has his phone unless….

Then he had it! Dennis had gone running. That was the only time he refused to take his phone because he wanted to forget everything and just enjoy the run and soak up the sounds of nature.

His pounding heart slowed a little, but not completely. Sure, it was light out till almost nine, but Dennis was usually back from a run by now.

Vincent retreated to his own room and dropped the backpack onto his neatly made bed. Then he headed downstairs to prepare something for dinner. Without Dennis's help, dinner would likely be leftovers. Just as he reached for the refrigerator handle, the backdoor into the yard burst open and Dennis bounded through, winded and flushed, clutching a small paperback book.

Upon seeing him, Dennis pulled up short, wide-eyed and looking like he'd been caught red-handed.

"Vince, you're home," he said lamely as he kicked the door shut and stood beside the counter as though unsure what to do.

Vincent felt tremendous relief, but also uncertainty. Dennis wore a tank top and running shorts, but his behavior was…weird. "Where did you go?"

Dennis made eye contact, but just barely. "Took a long run. Needed the exercise."

Vincent wasn't good at detecting lies in most people, but he knew Dennis better than anyone. And Dennis was lying.

"I'll run up and change and then help you with dinner." He hurried across the kitchen to the family room entry. "I want real food tonight."

He laughed, but it sounded hollow and forced. And then he passed into the family room.

Vincent watched him disappear, heard the tromping of his sneakers up the carpeted wooden stairs, and then the house lapsed into silence once again.

As he rooted through the pantry and fridge for potential dinner items, he couldn't help but worry about his brother's odd behavior. Could he have a girlfriend, maybe? The look on his face when he'd burst through the door almost looked as though he'd been caught making out on the couch or something.

Dennis had never shown much interest in girls, at least no particular girl, that Vincent knew of, and they'd talked about girls and relationships only a few times. Usually it was Dennis telling him he should get his nose out of his science books and find a girlfriend, or Dennis trying to play matchmaker.

He supposed it was *possible* Dennis had been out with a girl, but had a feeling his brother would tell him something like that. They had never kept secrets from each other.

Except you're keeping one now, he thought as he pulled out some eggs and milk to make omelets, one of the few items he could cook.

You're not telling him about Joe and Franky.

He set the items on the counter and reached into a cupboard beneath for a large bowl.

You're trying to protect him, he assured himself. *You don't want him hurt anymore.*

Still, a lie was a lie. And now Dennis had lied to him. What was happening to them?

He decided not to push the issue when Dennis returned wearing a tee shirt and a clean pair of shorts. They worked together on dinner and Vincent told him about the strange ingredient he'd found in the drugs and how they'd never seen anything like it in any of the samples they had been testing.

Dennis listened with keen interest and asked some questions about what Vincent thought the purpose of the additive was, and they conversed as they normally did. After dinner ended and the dishes were done, Vincent retreated to his room to get ready while Dennis fired up his computer. Since it was Friday with no work or school the next day, Invictus had a long night ahead of him.

CHAPTER FIFTEEN

AM I HERO OR VILLAIN?

Hoping to get a line on Demon, Invictus headed for downtown where most of the action seemed to happen.

Once again, he parked and camouflaged the bike so he could jump roof-to-roof and alley-to-alley looking for trouble. He'd barely spotted an older lady waiting at a Metro bus stop before a tall, lanky guy sprinted out of the shadows of a nearby building and snatched the purse right off her arm. She spun around and cried out, but had the good sense not to grab hold of the bag or she'd have been thrown hard to the sidewalk and seriously hurt.

Invictus hurled his shield at the retreating mugger. The shield struck the sprinting man behind the knees and he buckled, tossing the purse into the air as he dropped and tumbled onto the pavement, flinging out his hands to break his fall.

Invictus trotted over in time to snatch the purse out of the air and then grab his shield from where it landed on the sidewalk.

The mugger eyed him with fear. His knees were split open from the impact and gushed blood all over the cement.

Invictus jogged back to the lady just as her bus arrived, and handed over her purse. She snatched it from him and entered the bus. Once again, he felt a punch to the gut. On the top step, the lady glanced back and offered a crooked smile before the doors closed.

Stunned by that tiny gesture of gratitude, Invictus ran back to secure the mugger.

While searching for Franky, he spotted two pre-teen kids, probably no older than twelve, a boy and a girl, sitting in a doorway passing a joint back and forth.

He snuck up and loomed before them so fast the girl screamed and the boy let loose with some choice profanity.

Invictus snagged the joint and tamped it out on his shield before slipping it into a belt pouch. "Go home and use your brains for something useful."

The kids were up and running down the street before he even finished speaking.

While cruising past Olympic Boulevard, he heard shouting from a crowd up ahead. He slowed to assess his surroundings. The long line of people wrapped around the corner from what had to be the LA LIVE movie theaters, a towering fourteen-screen complex. He suspected the theater had tons of security and the shouting would soon be addressed. Easing the throttle forward, he spotted from the corner of his eye a big, broad-shouldered man shoving somebody out of the line. He couldn't make out if the person shoved was male or female, but the victim toppled hard to the asphalt and rolled around in obvious pain.

Invictus rode his bike to the sidewalk and killed the engine. Hopping off, he locked it and sprinted forward along the line of patrons.

People reacted with surprise upon seeing him. He heard exclamations like, "Look, it's the vigilante guy" and "Wow, look at his shield." He ignored them.

By the time he arrived to where the victim had fallen, he saw that it was a man, small, mid-twenties, and that the man's date was trying to help him up. He leaped forward to lend a hand.

"Are you all right?"

The woman gasped and the man stared at him with his mouth open.

"These guys pushed them out of line," Invictus heard a woman say from behind him, and he turned to look.

The broad-shouldered man, even larger than the biggest of the thugs who'd taken over Dennis's school, stood beside another tall guy, though the second one was not as broad shouldered.

"That wasn't nice," Invictus admonished, his anger controlled. Bullying infuriated him.

The bigger of the men laughed. It was a harsh, grating kind of laugh. "You hear that?" he said to his smirking friend. "It wasn't *nice*."

The tall guy jeered, "What're you gonna do about it, shorty?"

Invictus smiled. He'd long ago learned that his lack of height was not a problem. Noting that the crowd of people was backing away from the altercation, Invictus made his move. He swung the shield hard at the broad-shouldered man while kicking out at the tall one. Both men were caught by surprise. With loud grunts they went down. But just as quickly, like raging bulls they were up and coming at him.

Invictus didn't wait for them. He charged and leapt into a spinning kick, connecting with the tall guy's face and sending him spiraling backwards onto the pavement.

The broad-shouldered guy grabbed him by the arm and tried to lift him, but Invictus swung the shield up and around, clocking him on the side of the head. His grip faltered and he let go, stumbling back. Invictus punched him in the stomach, sending air whooshing from his lungs in a loud grunting exhale. Then he spun once more into a kick that connected with the guy's chest, sending him sprawling back to tumble over his partner. The two of them lay on the sidewalk, stunned and entangled.

Someone shouted, "Here comes security!"

Invictus looked toward the corner of Olympic. Several uniformed security guards and a cop sprinted toward them.

"Enjoy the movie." He took off at a run toward his motorcycle.

As he leapt onto it and gunned the engine, he heard something from the crowd that nearly stopped his heart – applause. He glanced up to see the people clapping and whistling, some pumping their fists into the air. As he sped away, Invictus did something he hadn't done before – he smiled.

Before the night ended, he'd foiled two attempted-car break-ins and busted up another drug deal. Unfortunately, the sellers got away and the buyer claimed not to know Demon, but said, "Probably looks like your fool ass seein' as how youse all look alike."

Invictus flinched, but didn't overreact. "I could send *your* fool-ass to jail," he threatened in a stern, solid voice, which he hoped sounded serious. He must have because the young man, who couldn't have been more than twenty-five, took a step back.

"Please, man, I'll go back to the pen for violating." The guy's tone had completely changed from the moment before. "I'm sorry for what I said, okay? It just slipped out."

"Racism never just slips out," Invictus replied evenly. "We let it out."

The guy was wide-eyed and fearful, but made no response.

"Get the hell out of here," Invictus admonished. "I find you buying again, you're going in."

The guy looked so relieved that Invictus wondered what had happened to him in prison. He watched as the man sprinted off down the street.

He made sure to swing behind the restaurants he'd made deals with to verify they were keeping up their end of the bargain. The ones he checked shortly after two a.m. had set out the leftover food as promised. Invictus observed scores of homeless scooping it up and heading back to their tents or wherever they'd sleep for the night. A few spotted him watching from the shadows and nodded in recognition. But no one spoke.

He didn't see Franky or Joe the entire night, which surprised him. As he headed home, he said a silent prayer for their well-being.

Dennis once more lay slumped over his desk when Vincent entered the room. He'd removed the hot, uncomfortable costume and hung it up in his bathroom to air out. It needed to be washed again – all his exertions and sweat were raising a ripe smell that would alert the bad guys to his presence a mile before he got there. He couldn't recall what setting to use on the washer, so he decided to wait for Dennis to wake up in the morning before attempting to clean it.

As he eased his brother into bed, Dennis groaned slightly, but did not wake up. Vincent covered him and then scanned the desk. Spotting the poetry book Dennis was clutching when he'd burst into the kitchen earlier, Vincent picked it up and opened to the marked page. He froze. The page was marked with one of the prayer cards given out at his parents' funeral mass. The poem on that page he knew all too well. In his dreams, he still heard Dennis's haunted voice, tremulous and soft, reciting these lines at the gravesite.

Death, be not proud…

Vincent's heart pounded and he snapped the book shut. Dennis was *officially* diagnosed with PTSD, but he wasn't the only one suffering from it.

He navigated his way back to the door and flicked off the light before heading down to his own room to crash.

When he awoke at noon and trudged downstairs, he found Dennis in front of the television switching from news channel to news channel. Almost every channel was talking about him. Well, about Invictus, anyway.

Dennis waved him over. "Check it out, bro. You're all over the place."

Clad only in his workout shorts, Vincent had planned to check on Dennis before jumping into the shower. But the news broadcasts intrigued him so he scooted around the couch and plopped down beside his brother.

"What's the consensus?" he asked. "Am I hero or villain?"

"Still up in the air," Dennis replied as he switched the station to Channel 4 News. An attractive African American lady with the words "Sharon Farmer Live" on the screen stood with a microphone in front of the LA LIVE movieplex interviewing people who'd witnessed Invictus's fight with the bullies.

"I thought it was awesome," a teenaged girl gushed.

An older lady leaned in to the microphone. "I think he should have let security handle it. That's what they're paid for."

The man beside her piped up. "I agree with my wife. It could have escalated into a brawl and gotten people hurt."

The reporter aimed the microphone at a young couple in their twenties. The lady said, "Those big guys were out of control and there was no security people anywhere. I think Incident did good."

"His name is Invictus," Sharon corrected, and the young woman giggled.

"It's a weird name."

People around her laughed.

Vincent exchanged a look with his brother.

Dennis shrugged. "Hey, we both agreed on the name."

Vincent nodded. It felt odd to hear people talk about him when they didn't even know they were talking about *him*. He felt split in two, and that feeling was disconcerting.

Sharon continued her report from the studio, detailing some of the known sightings of the "Asian vigilante known as Invictus." The news station ran a clip of Captain Torres from a press conference that morning.

"I have Detective Stevens and Sergeant Janson on the trail of this vigilante," he announced proudly, indicating James and Janson standing behind him. "He will be arrested on sight."

A reporter off-screen called out, "On what charge, Captain?"

Torres glowered into the camera. "We'll start with interfering in a police operation at the gun store. Other charges might be filed depending on what else we find this clown has done."

In the studio, Sharon gazed straight into the camera. "With all of the questions people seem to have about this Asian vigilante, Channel 4 is offering him complete anonymity to contact us for an exclusive interview. I can promise the location will be undisclosed and only my cameraman and myself will be present. So how about it, Invictus? Do you want to formally introduce yourself to the world? We'd love to meet you."

As a phone number flashed onscreen, Dennis killed the volume.

Vincent knew what he was thinking. "It could be a trap, set up by Torres."

Dennis paused. "I don't think so. You've been on every station, but this lady seems to be the one who loves you the most. I bet she knows you're hot and just wants to meet you."

Vincent chuckled. "Yeah, right." He considered the woman's offer. Doing the interview might be the best way to get his message across, especially if it was picked up and blasted all over the Internet.

"It's a golden idea, bro," Dennis affirmed as though reading his thoughts. "We can get our message out there faster."

Vincent eyed him. "You can contact her so she can't trace your number?"

"No sweat. You want?"

Vincent hesitated a moment. "Has to be at night and in an out-of-the way place. Let her know if it even smells like a trap, I'm gone."

"You got it." Dennis rose and started toward the stairs.

"Hey, Dennis," Vincent said, suddenly remembering what he'd come downstairs to ask.

Dennis turned, eyebrows raised.

"Heard any chatter on that Demon guy yet?"

Dennis flinched.

Vincent saw it.

"Uh, no, not a word." He tromped up the stairs out of sight.

Vincent sank back against the soft couch pillows. Another lie. But why lie about something like that?

Unsure how to handle this new development, he retreated upstairs to shower.

Dennis heard the shower turn on in the bathroom next door as he used his encryption and scrambling software to set up the call to Sharon Farmer. And he pondered his changing relationship with his brother. They had always been pretty close, despite the gap in age, and always straight up with each other.

At least until Invictus arrived on the scene.

But he was your idea, fool!

Even though he'd known his role in the venture would be limited, deep down Dennis had secretly hoped that at some point he could be part of the action. He'd even designed a costume to disguise his identity. Of course, he'd never told Vincent about the costume, especially since his brother was adamant about him staying home.

But you lied to me, Vince, he thought. *You do want kids helping you out there. Just not me.*

Okay, he had to admit that those kids were already out on the streets, so it wasn't like Vincent brought in some noob and threw Dennis under the bus.

Am I just jealous?

Yeah, he had to admit he was. Still, Vincent should have at least told him about Joe and Franky instead of lying about where he got the drugs. Was that enough reason to justify his own lie about Demon? Technically, it wasn't a lie since Dennis hadn't heard any chatter about the drug-dealer from the police or 911.

It's still a lie, Dennis, he heard in his father's quiet voice. He felt guilty, and yet he also felt empowered.

He sat back a moment to reflect on yesterday.

Demon and his posse drove around the Valley scouting the best locations to sell their drugs. They never came right out and told Dennis that's what they were doing, but all of their stops were middle and high schools and Demon queried Dennis about each of them – did he know if the kids had money, were there gang problems, drug problems – questions like that. Ricer, the stubby one with the goatee, took notes on everything Dennis told them.

As they sat across the street and watched Parker Middle disgorge its summer school students, Dennis scooted down in the back seat so he wouldn't be spotted. He noted several of Ms. Ellis's students sauntering off down the street, particularly DeAndre, the kid who'd insulted him.

Bet you'd never have the guts to infiltrate a drug ring, he thought as DeAndre moved on down the sidewalk with his friends.

Dennis thought it odd that Demon never invited him to officially join his group, but figured the drug lord was feeling him out, testing the waters, as it were, to determine if Dennis might be interested.

They'd dropped him back at the park because he didn't want them knowing where he lived, or neighbors like Linda seeing Demon's car. Demon drove a very expensive, jet-black Mercedes coupe that would attract attention, even in his neighborhood.

Before they drove off, Demon asked, "You wanna hang out with us again, Dreamer? You don't talk much and I like that."

Dennis hesitated only a second before nodding.

"I can't on weekends, though." He felt weak and childish, but knew he couldn't take the chance with Vincent around the house.

Ricer sniggered. To Dennis's surprise, Demon silenced him with a glare and gave Dennis the chin raise. "Next week then."

"Uh, how will I find you?"

"Kick it here, same time. We'll find *you*."

Dennis nodded as Demon gunned the engine and roared off down the street.

Now, sitting and staring at Sharon Farmer's cell number on his computer screen, Dennis considered his options. He could go back to the park, wait for Demon and get more heavily involved, or he could simply stay away and Demon would never find him again.

But then I can't learn more about him, he thought, *or where he gets the stuff he's selling.*

But what if Demon insisted he sell for them? Could he do that, sell drugs he knew were going to hurt kids?

No. He couldn't intentionally hurt anyone, which was why he wasn't as aggressive at martial arts as Vincent.

But I can gain some intel and pass it along to Vincent, he decided. *I can prove I'm not weak.*

Having made his determination, he called Sharon and set up the interview.

CHAPTER SIXTEEN

AN IDEALIST, OUR HERO

Vincent loved that Dennis set up the interview in Skid Row because viewers couldn't help but see how much assistance the residents required. His brother was a genius!

They chose a quiet corner so the police—who would study it closely—couldn't tell where the interview originated from and harass the homeless people for information. Sharon promised Dennis the station would blur out any visible street signs.

Dennis set it up for nine p.m. and explained that Invictus would find *her*. She assured him only her boss would know the location. The interview would be taped and go on the air at eleven o'clock Saturday night. On Sunday, the interview would be repeated throughout the day and then offered to national news outlets.

Invictus studied the Channel 4 News van from across the street, his motor-cycle idling beneath him. Homeless people, alone or in groups, hovered around the van, eying it with curiosity.

Sharon Farmer stood beside the van with a man resting a large video camera on one shoulder. They chatted, but kept glancing around nervously at the home-less. Invictus didn't blame them. A large number of these people, if not most, suffered from mental illness, and their behavior could be unpredictable, even dangerous at times.

Dennis had spent two hours prepping him for this interview and he was ready as he'd ever be. Gunning the throttle, he rode toward the van. Sharon glanced up at the sound.

Invictus rolled to a stop in front of them and shut off the engine. He glanced around at the people watching. He recognized some from the previous nights he'd spent in this area, but didn't see Jasper or the old lady.

Invictus saw the red camera light switch on.

"I'm Sharon." Her voice was perky and light. She extended a hand and they shook.

"I know. I've seen you on TV."

She looked to be about thirty with alert eyes, prominent cheekbones, and mounds of curly hair. She wore little makeup, which he suspected better suited the HD video cameras.

"Thank you so much for agreeing to this interview," she went on, her voice clear and professional, her diction perfect.

"Thank you for inviting me," he replied, always remembering his parents' lifelong lessons about courtesy.

"Let's begin, shall we?"

He nodded.

She faced the camera. "This is Sharon Farmer reporting from Los Angeles. I have with me the mysterious Asian Vigilante who arrived on the scene in spectacular fashion two weeks ago when he foiled the takeover of Samuel Parker Middle School."

She turned to Invictus and the cameraman followed her movement.

"Welcome," she began, her demeanor serious and business-like.

"Thank you for this opportunity to introduce myself." Normally camera-shy as Vincent, wearing the mask of Invictus erased those insecurities to the point that he actually felt comfortable. It was a liberating sensation.

"Why don't we begin with your name," Sharon went on. "Invictus is unusual. What does it mean?"

"It's the title of a poem," he answered. "Part of it goes like this – it matters not how strait the gate, how charged with punishments the scroll, I am the master of my fate, I am the captain of my soul."

"I like it," she said, but Invictus suspected she didn't understand the meaning. "So tell us why you're out here every night."

"I'm using the skills and abilities I have to make things a little better for people."

"By being a costumed superhero?"

He laughed. "I'm just a regular guy, not a superhero. But I know the law" – he used the air quotes for "law" – "doesn't like regular citizens getting too involved, so the costume keeps my identity a secret. I also figured it would catch people's attention and maybe motivate them, too."

"Motivate them how?"

"Everyone has skills and talents and abilities of their own," he replied, looking her right in the eye. "And everyone has time they can give to others. I happen to be good at martial arts, and a few other things that I won't say right now. Look around you, Sharon."

She paused and glanced around. Invictus pointed out the clusters of homeless standing in their threadbare clothes holding each other in solidarity.

"I helped these people out a week or so back," Invictus went on, "in a way that will hopefully continue. I can't say how because I was told there are city ordinances prohibiting what I did. That's part of our problem, Sharon. Too many laws hurt more people than they help. *I'm* against the law, but these people around you welcomed my help, and more importantly, they *needed* it."

"So what are you saying, exactly? That everyone should break the law?"

"Only if the law is immoral."

"But who makes that determination, Invictus?"

"If a law benefits the powers that be and hurts regular citizens, it's probably an immoral law and should be changed."

She studied him a moment. "Are you calling for a revolution?"

"If you want to call it that," he replied. "A revolution of volunteerism. Again, let's take this area right here. How many people in this city are carpenters, plumbers, clothes-makers, you name it. If they gave a little of their time to these people, made clothes, built tiny houses, offered mental health services part time for free, can you imagine how much better Skid Row would become. What could the city do then, arrest all of us for not getting permits or obeying every ordinance? Not likely. Not if there are enough of us."

She looked surprised, as though she'd never considered the idea before.

"And what about the children?" Invictus went on passionately. "I've found so many on the streets at night, buying drugs, hanging out with gangs. Artists, teachers, photographers, athletes, regular people like me, could be offering some of their time at Boys and Girls Clubs or YMCAs or after school programs teaching kids new skills and keeping them engaged so they won't drift into these negative behaviors. Every single person in this city has a talent he or she could share for free."

"To play the Devil's Advocate here, Invictus, why would they want to do that?"

"Because it's the right thing to do, Sharon. The one thing in life that's free is kindness. If more people gave of themselves to the community, whether what they're doing is technically *legal* or not, if it's *moral* then most of our problems could be solved."

"A lofty goal." She looked impressed.

"But an attainable one."

"To shift gears a bit, it's been noted that you're Asian. Do you see yourself as a special hero to the Asian community?"

He shook his head. "No. I'm doing this because it needs to be done. Why can't people just use their talents and be who they are? Why do they have to represent an entire cultural heritage, as well?"

"That's a good point, Invictus," she acknowledged. "Any other thoughts you'd like to share?"

"I'm tired of hearing people say we need to make things better in this city and in this world, but they never step up to do anything about it. Yes, it takes personal sacrifice. I'm not a bad guy like the police keep saying. I'm just doing what needs to be done. Now it's everyone else's turn. I don't want to be alone out here. Does that make sense?"

"It makes perfect sense to me," she replied. "Convincing the police might be another matter."

"I'm not out here to win *them* over, though certainly people in power can and should see the value of what I'm doing," he asserted with confidence. "For now, it's the average citizen I hope to inspire. After all, apathy is the evil that will destroy the world."

"Thank you so much for your time, Invictus. Keep in touch."

He smiled. "Thank *you*, Sharon."

The camera light went off and Sharon gushingly thanked him for this "scoop" and acted like a teenaged girl at her first rock concert. He laughed and bade her good night. Then he was onto his bike and roaring off down the street.

"How'd it go?" Dennis said into his ear when Invictus called him.

Steering the bike toward Franky's neighborhood, Invictus replied, "I think I did well. Practicing with you really helped. I didn't even feel nervous."

"Awesome."

"It's an odd sensation."

"What is?"

"I don't feel shy behind this mask," Invictus went on as he cruised the streets. "That's a feeling I'm not used to."

"Maybe it's because people can't see the real you," Dennis suggested.

Invictus considered a moment. "Maybe." He turned a corner. "Anything down here I should follow up on?"

There was a brief pause. "Not at the moment," Dennis replied. "Where you are seems pretty quiet."

"I'm going to ride around a bit and see what's going on, maybe bust up some drug deals, try to get a line on Demon."

There was a long pause. Dennis did not respond.

"Dennis? You still there?"

"Uh, yeah, bro," Dennis answered quickly. "Sounds like a plan. I'll call if I have something. Out."

Invictus heard a click in his ear and then there was only wind. *Odd*, he thought as he turned the corner toward Franky's Laundromat hangout. Something was definitely up with Dennis. But what?

Franky wasn't in his clothes "bed" and there was no sign of him anywhere in the surrounding area. Feeling a sense of loss at not finding him, Invictus rode off in search of crimes to foil.

He broke up several drug deals, confiscating the drugs and tying the dealers to lampposts for the police to collect. The buyers, who were all teens, he let go with the implied threat that next time he would turn them over to the cops if they didn't find something better to do with their time and money.

The sellers were clearly gang members of varying ages, and they threatened him with retaliation from their homies.

He questioned them about Demon. One guy with a heavily tatted face and thick forearms snorted with anger.

"That slant is gonna pay for cuttin' into our business!"

His homeboy scowled. "He be hiding. Too afraid to face us."

"Hiding where?" Invictus asked, hoping to finally get a lead. He chose to ignore the racial slur.

"In the Valley somewheres."

Invictus nodded. That information was valuable. Hearing the approaching sirens, he realized Dennis had already called the police.

He didn't even warn me!

"Your ride is coming," he told the two gangsters, who struggled in vain against their restraints. "Do yourselves a big favor – become part of the solution, not the problem."

He sprinted away down the street. He just managed to duck into a shadowy doorway before two police cruisers, lights flashing and sirens blazing, sped on past. Then he ran to his bike and roared away into the night.

On impulse, he decided one last time to search Franky's neighborhood. He wasn't sure why, but it frightened him when he'd go a whole night and not see the little boy. He also worried that Franky would become too gung ho in his "Robin" job and get himself hurt.

He was about to give up when he spotted two figures in the darkness of a quiet street walking side by side. One was tall and the other small. He slowed his bike so the engine wouldn't spook them and eased along the street toward the pair. The tall one spun around, gripping the hand of the smaller boy and preparing to bolt.

When he saw Invictus, Joe visibly uncoiled and released Franky's hand. Franky shivered and bounced on his heels.

"'Sup, Super Hero?" Joe asked, offering the chin raise.

Invictus rolled to a stop. The street was empty. He glanced at Franky. The little boy munched on a burger. But his eyes darted everywhere and his feet wouldn't stop moving.

"He's high again?"

"I found him this way. Guess he had a relapse."

Invictus climbed off his bike and approached. He crouched down so he could look into Franky's face. The eyes were large and dilated, but they widened further with recognition.

"Batman!"

Invictus felt that tightening of his chest. "Hey, Robin."

"Joe brought me food," the boy went on rapidly. "I was super hungry."

Invictus eyed Joe. The teen was wearing his white tank top and tight jeans again. "That was nice of you to feed him. Where'd you get the money?"

Joe glanced down. "A customer, a regular. He treats me okay and pays good."

Invictus realized he must look disgusted because Joe bristled.

"I gotta make sure Franky has food," he snapped. "If he doesn't, the meth'll eat him up!"

Invictus flinched at the sharp tone.

Joe's expression softened. "It's okay, Super Hero," he added quietly. "I close my eyes and pretend it's someone else's body."

Invictus felt his mouth go dry.

Joe stared at him silently, the unasked question right there on his dark features – when will you find me that home you promised so I don't have to do this anymore?

But Joe didn't ask, and Invictus had no answer anyway. He'd been so busy this past week he hadn't even begun trying to fulfill his promise.

He cleared his throat. "So, uh, Robin, have you seen Demon around?"

Franky swigged from his Coke while dancing and spinning in place. He shook his head and swallowed the soda. "Heard he's gone. Young Z runs the hood now."

"Where do you usually buy from Z?"

Franky spun around and around and wouldn't stop. Invictus got dizzy just watching him. He reached out and gripped the boy by both shoulders.

"Whoa, pal, slow down."

Franky stopped and stared at him with those wide, dilated pupils. He'd lost another tooth since Invictus last saw him, and that saddened him even more.

"So where can I find Young Z?" Invictus tried again as he let go of Franky and waited. The boy stared at his half-eaten hamburger as though it were an alien, and then shoved it all into his mouth.

"Not so fast, Little One," Joe exclaimed, his voice rising in alarm.

He squatted and helped Franky sip some of the Coke. His cheeks bulged like a chipmunk in winter and he chewed rapidly. Invictus heard his teeth clicking against each other and watched the two boys, anxiety tugging at his heart.

Joe kept a hand to Franky's throat and lightly massaged it as he swallowed the large amount of food.

"He could choke easy when he's this high," Joe explained as he gave Franky another sip of soda and kept one arm wrapped around his shoulders.

"He hangs at Mack Park a lot," Franky blurted, turning those huge eyes on Invictus, as though he'd just recalled he'd been asked a question.

"That's street for McArthur Park," Joe added when Invictus looked confused.

Invictus placed a hand on Franky's shoulder. "Thanks, Robin."

The little boy grinned, but his eyes were distant, his mind slipping off to someplace far, far away.

Invictus felt helpless. "What can I do for him?"

Joe shrugged. "Nuthin'. I'll stay with him till the worst passes and then take him home. I know his pad."

Invictus felt his quads cramping and stood to stretch them. Joe stood beside him, one arm still draping Franky's small shoulders.

"You might lose your bed at Runaway House if you stay out here," Invictus suggested, trying to make this irrational scene somehow rational.

"Franky's more important." He grinned. "Sides, I can always get back in. That old man likes you now. Said what you did for those homeless people was *stu*pendous." He used air quotes for "stupendous."

Invictus knew Joe was trying to lighten the mood, but his whole body felt like it was made of lead. The sadness filling his soul threatened to immobilize him on the spot because he understood Joe's implicit meaning – when will you keep your promises?

Joe slipped a hand into his pocket and pulled out a small plastic bag. Invictus took it and eyed the contents. White powder.

"He saved some for you," Joe explained. "Told me to give it over if I saw you."

Invictus shifted his gaze from the skinny African American boy with the baby face to the small Latino with the grownup one.

"Thanks, Robin," he murmured, knowing that Franky was lost inside himself and no longer even aware that anyone was with him.

"You better go," Joe said quietly. "I'm gonna take him back to his little bed and keep him safe." He paused. "Work fast, Super Hero. I don't wanna lose him."

Invictus understood Joe's meaning. Franky needed a real home, and he needed it soon. So did Joe. He felt an urge to grab both boys in an intense hug and just hold them close. But he couldn't allow emotions to control him, especially out here.

Mounting his bike, he glanced back to see the bigger boy leading the smaller one by the hand down the street and flashed back to himself walking Dennis home from his first day of school. And once again he wondered what his brother was hiding.

Dennis watched the interview on the eleven o'clock news with an upsurge of excitement. Finally, Invictus had been formally introduced to the world and the campaign could kick into high gear.

He'd coached Vincent well and was happy to see that his brother mostly followed through.

That Sharon is one Lois Lane, he thought, as she followed up the recorded interview with a live response from the mayor, Captain Torres, James and his new partner. Even in his thoughts, Dennis choked up on the word "partner," and chose to not look at that man at all.

"I applaud his desire to help the homeless," the mayor said into the camera in front of City Hall. "As you know, Sharon, that has been a huge focus of my administration. However, I agree with Captain Torres that we can't allow people to roam the streets and play Batman. Someone will get hurt."

"So far, Mr. Mayor, people have only been helped."

Captain Torres leaned forward and Sharon thrust the mic in his direction.

"Pure luck," he growled. He looked straight into the camera. "We know you ride around on a black motorcycle with no plates, and we know where you've been spotted. We will arrest you sooner rather than later. If you're a smart vigilante, you'll cease and desist before then. In the meantime, the city is offering a reward for any tips leading to the apprehension of the Asian vigilante. Call this tip line if you spot him."

A number flashed onscreen, and Dennis sucked in a breath. He muted the sound and sat back on the couch. He knew the cable channels would get the interview tomorrow and then the debate would kick in big time. But he pondered Torres's threat. It probably wouldn't be hard to get a line on Invictus, especially when the city was offering money. Anybody could call it in and he might not know until the police were on the move.

He turned off the TV and retreated to his room to monitor police activity and await his brother's return.

Cat and Demon stood in front of her wall of video screens. The largest of them was tuned to Channel 4 News and the Invictus interview. The sound was low, almost inaudible, but Demon knew she'd already watched it numerous times. He wished she'd allow him to take the guy out of the picture. Her obsession with this vigilante still angered him. He'd informed her that the Valley operation was shaping up, that he'd recruited some new blood who knew the terrain, but she only seemed interested in the Hero and his stupid ideas!

"An idealist, our Hero."

"He is breaking up our sales, Mistress." Demon tried to make the situation sound more serious than it was.

"Of course, he is, Demon," she replied. "He's trying to save the world." She looked him in the eye. "He doesn't realize that it's already too late. Our product will soon go national and we'll have set in motion the destruction of a generation. There's nothing the Hero, or anyone else, can do to stop it."

Her smile grew larger, but she said no more.

CHAPTER SEVENTEEN

VINCENT, ARE YOU ALL RIGHT?

Dennis complimented Vincent when he appeared in his room at two a.m., telling him the interview was great. "Except you messed up one thing I told you to say."

"How?" The voice sounded robotic.

"You were supposed to say, apathy is the evil that will destroy the world if we let it. You forgot 'if we let it'."

Vincent shrugged. He held the mask in one hand and looked tired. No, not tired, Dennis realized. He looked downcast, almost depressed.

Like I look like sometimes in the bathroom mirror.

"What happened, Vincent?"

Vincent shook his head and plopped down on the bed, throwing himself back onto the pillow.

Dennis put the computer to sleep, set aside the comic book panel he'd been drawing, and crawled onto the bed beside his brother. Silence weighed them down and Vincent's erratic breathing scared Dennis. He reached out and wrapped one arm under Vincent's head and cradled him the way Vincent had cradled him when he'd had nightmares as a child.

"Tell me."

"There are so many lost kids out there, Dennis," Vincent whispered, his voice raspy and tight. "So many who need so much and there's no one to help them."

Dennis listened and tried to make sense of what his brother was saying. "The people will step up, Vince," he said in as strong a voice as he could. "They *will* get our message. We can't give up."

There was silence for a moment. Then Dennis heard, "It's just so hard to see."

Dennis didn't respond. He didn't know what to say anyway. If the reality out there affected stoic Vincent in this way, it must be truly horrific.

He reached out with his free arm and switched off the lamp. Then he scooted closer as Vincent's even breathing told him his brother had fallen asleep.

Dennis lay there in the dark listening to Vincent breathe, and wondered if his brother was talking about Joe and Franky. Or about the other kids he'd referenced in his interview. In any case, it must be a lot worse than he ever imagined.

The following day, Vincent sat with Dennis for part of the day watching news coverage of Invictus's interview and highlights of his heroics. The cable news shows had pundits debating the pros and cons of vigilantism in general and Invictus in particular.

For his part, Vincent wouldn't talk about the kids he'd mentioned before falling asleep, but he did bring up Demon. Dennis flinched beside him and hoped his brother didn't notice.

"A…," Vincent began, hesitating a split second, "buyer told me Demon's not working that neighborhood anymore, that there's a new guy. Have you heard the name Young Z?"

Dennis squirmed under his brother's intense scrutiny. "No, not a peep."

He forced himself to maintain eye contact so Vincent wouldn't think he was lying, which he wasn't this time. He'd never heard of Young Z. Vincent nodded and retreated to his room to do homework.

Dennis continued watching various channels and noted how each one covered the Invictus story. He figured maybe he could help spin things in certain directions once he knew how the wind was blowing.

Vincent holed up in his room all day and didn't even come downstairs for lunch, which worried Dennis. When it became clear his brother wasn't coming down, Dennis made a tuna sandwich and brought it upstairs with a glass of water. He knocked, but there was no answer.

Cracking open the door, he saw Vincent drooped over his desk, books spread out around his head, computer screen-saver melding different views of the human brain one into the other.

Dennis tiptoed into the room, which was spotlessly clean, of course, and set the plate and glass onto a shelf above Vincent's computer. He didn't want his brother waking up and accidentally knocking the glass onto the floor.

"Hang in there, bro," he whispered.

Then he retreated back down to the family room to watch more news reports. He was surprised to see Ms. Ellis interviewed by Sharon Farmer. Even though it was Sunday, the interview took place in her classroom as she prepared her lessons for the week. The charcoal drawing of Invictus still sat on an easel up in front by her large wooden desk.

She was in the middle of saying, "and my students will all be creating their own interpretations of Invictus throughout summer school and writing about how they view his impact on the city."

"What do your students think of Invictus?"

Ms. Ellis looked serious. "I plan to show them your interview tomorrow. I hate to lump you into to this statement, Sharon, but you did it in your interview so I have to. Because you in the media so harp on race, many of my students have focused on the fact that Invictus is Asian, and because he's Asian, and not black or Latino or white, he doesn't represent them."

Dennis was surprised to see Sharon look abashed, as though no one had ever called her on anything she'd said before. "I hadn't intended to imply that with my question, Ms. Ellis."

"I'm afraid you were playing the race card, Sharon," Ms. Ellis answered, shifting slightly. "Like the media always does. As an African American, I see that condescension all too well, as you probably have, too. This man–" She pointed to the charcoal drawing. "–is clearly not about race or ethnicity. He's about helping people and inspiring them to help others. That kind of truth is universal."

"I understand you are putting together a coalition," Sharon went on, looking anxious to move away from the race issue. "Tell us about that."

"I've created a Facebook group for fans of Invictus," Ms. Ellis explained, sounding more excited with every word. "Anyone can join and learn from the example this man is setting. For any members here in the Los Angeles area, we are exchanging phone numbers and will keep in regular contact, sharing ideas and ways of paying it forward like Invictus is doing."

"Will you be organizing actions in support of Invictus?"

"That depends," Ms. Ellis went on, sounding hesitant, as though she was afraid Sharon might snitch on her. "We definitely don't support the official police position. But right now there aren't enough of us to make serious noise. If I have my way, there will be."

Sharon thanked her for the interview.

Dennis clicked off the TV and sat back to ponder what he'd seen and heard. Ms. Ellis starting a support group was awesome and definitely a step in the right direction. But ultimately, he knew, that group wouldn't become large enough just because she wanted it so. No. If the people were to come out in large numbers, it would be Invictus inspiring them to do so.

Dennis so wished Invictus could go out before dark, to drop by Boys and Girls Clubs and after-school programs to encourage the kids and the adults tending those kids. His "vigilante" status with the police was a serious roadblock to The Dream becoming a full-fledged reality.

Maybe if Invictus broke up Demon's drug ring, that would be huge news and the police would have to accept that he's helping, not hurting, the city.

But that means I need to get a lead he can use, Dennis thought as he switched the flat screen input to game mode and fired up his Xbox. As he engaged his on-screen enemies, Dennis wondered what to do about his real ones. Or *were* they his enemies? They'd befriended him when they didn't have to, after all. Sure, they're looking for sellers, not friends.

And they're getting kids hooked on drugs!

That thought ran through his mind as he killed one enemy after another.

Be a weak-ass pussy!

Demon's words burned through his heart and stabbed at his pride.

I'll show you who's weak when I take your ass down!

He focused on the game for now.

Invictus did not find Franky or Joe that night, despite riding around the area numerous times in between Dennis's 911 calls. He was tempted to go to Runaway House and ask for Joe, but he didn't want the police hassling the kid any more than they already had. So he headed for MacArthur Park in search of Young Z.

With only a name and the knowledge that he was Asian to go on, Invictus hid his bike and moved stealthily through the shadows of the enormous landmark between Sixth and Seventh Streets in the heart of Los Angeles. Even on a Sunday night, the site teemed with activity, mostly street people and local residents. He sought to avoid pools of light as much as possible, but even so a number of the homeless gazed wide-eyed at his costume. He'd left the shield with his hidden motorcycle because it called too much attention to itself and this was primarily a reconnaissance mission.

Across Wilshire Boulevard from the park, a fountain set within a large lake shot sprays of water into the air. The water landed with splashing sounds that intermixed with the omnipresent traffic noise. The area surrounding the lake was where most of the drug "deals" went down. He spotted several obvious sales in progress, but the sellers were all Latino or Caucasian. Before becoming Invictus, he'd not have known a drug deal in progress from a random gathering of people, but now he knew the signs: cautious movements of the hands, surreptitious glances side-to-side, obvious attempts at "accidentally" running into an acquaintance. To name a few. If one continued to observe, the exchange would happen. Always subtle. Always casual. Then the two parties would shake or high five and move off in opposite directions.

Police in patrol cars cruised past with regularity and Invictus made sure to hide any time one drifted by. After watching a number of transactions from behind several large palm trees, he was about to depart when he spotted three Asian guys strut into the park from the direction of Seventh Street. All three were bald except for thin, dangling rattails trailing down their backs, very similar to the guys he'd mixed it up with in that alley. Even their clothing style was the same – long sleeve shirts and jeans.

Invictus studied the trio intently. As they moved through the pools of park lighting, he saw their faces briefly: impassive and determined. This was no casual visit. They were there to do business.

Two African American kids, no older than Dennis, approached the group from the side and Invictus watched the "Fancy meeting you here" fake greeting. He couldn't hear what they were saying, but he knew the drill. Slinking from behind the tree, he crouched low and crept from tree to tree, closing the gap until he was about six feet behind the Asians. He stood and leaned around the tree, one hand in a belt pouch.

"Hey, Young Z," he said loud enough for the Asians to hear.

All three whirled around quickly.

Invictus stepped from behind the tree with care. One hand was buried within the pouch at his side. "You get off on selling to kids?"

Two of them reached beneath their shirts. Invictus didn't hesitate. He whipped up his hand and flung one shuriken star at the closer of the two, snatching another from the pouch almost simultaneously and flinging it through the air at the second.

The two young men cried out in agony as the shuriken ripped open their hands and forced them to drop the guns they'd pulled. The two buyers bolted down the pathway. So far, the altercation had only drawn the attention of a few homeless, but that would soon change.

Invictus charged. He jumped into a flying leap and his feet landed squarely in the chest of the closest Asian, sending him sprawling backwards to roll over several times before landing in a daze. Hand spewing a river of blood, the second Asian jumped up and connected with Invictus's stomach, knocking the air from him and forcing him to his knees. The guy rushed him, but Invictus head butted him in the midsection and then used the guy's momentum to toss him up and over. The guy landed with a loud grunt on the grass behind him.

The third guy dashed behind Invictus so fast he barely saw the movement. Strong arms wrapped around his throat and cut off his air supply. White dots danced before his eyes as his hands clawed at the forearms, futilely trying to dislodge them.

"You wanted Young Z, Hero," he heard whispered into his ear as the pressure grew stronger. "Well, here I am. And yes, I get off on selling to kids. What'chu gonna do about it, huh?"

Rage filled him and Invictus struggled all the harder, but Z was strong and the pressure on his windpipe increased.

"Let him go!" somebody yelled from off to one side. Sounded like a girl.

Invictus heard a loud *thud* behind him and a grunt of surprise from Z. Whatever struck him loosened his grip, and that was all Invictus needed. He reached back and grabbed Z by the rattail and yanked him up and forward, simultaneously rolling his shoulders and lurching upward. Like a wrestler on WWE, Z rolled over Invictus's head and slammed down hard onto his back.

Invictus instinctively held on to the hair and Z shrieked with agony as the rattail tore loose from his scalp with a horrifying *rip* and dangled loosely within one gloved hand. The ends were bloody, with bits of flesh attached.

Invictus gulped for air, his chest heaving as he watched the wounded drug dealer roll around on the grass clutching at the back of his head and mewling with pain.

Franky's sallow face and chapped lips flashed before his mind, and Invictus saw the wounded Z in a new light—as a monster sucking the life from a child.

"You lowlife," he hissed, swinging out with one booted foot and connecting hard with Z's side. "You sell to children!"

He stomped down again and heard the snap of bone as his foot connected with Z's right elbow. Another shriek of pain poured forth, but Invictus didn't care. All he could see was Franky and all the other Franky's this guy was killing.

From the corner of his eye he saw movement and spun as one of the other Asians lunged at him, He elbowed the guy in the ribs and then used a double fist to slam hard into his back, sending him crashing to the ground.

By now a crowd had formed, and Invictus knew that the cops were on their way. Someone would've called. But he couldn't get Franky out of his mind. He dropped down and punched Z in the face, breaking his nose and splattering blood all over the grass.

"Who do you work for?"

Z groaned, but didn't answer.

Invictus pummeled his face several more times. Somewhere in his rage, he knew if he didn't stop he'd pound Z into unconsciousness, but he didn't care. This was the first time he'd ever lost control and it felt liberating.

"Cat," Z mumbled though bloody lips. "I work for Cat." He chuckled, and blood gurgled forth. "And she'll kill you for this."

Invictus froze. Cat. A woman?

He heard sirens approaching.

"You better bail, Hero," a voice spoke from behind him. The same voice from before.

Invictus turned to find a young girl, obviously homeless, eyeing him with wide, frightened eyes. She held a large rock in one hand. He lurched to his feet. The three dealers groaned and rolled around on the grass surrounding him. The sirens grew louder.

"Thanks for the help."

The girl brushed dirty brown hair off her face.

He bolted.

Racing across the grass, he dodged between trees until he left the park and dashed across the street to his bike, parked in a dark alcove. Just as he jumped on, a black Mercedes careened around the corner. He heard someone on the sidewalk shout, "Scatter, it's Demon!"

Demon!

Invictus spun the choke and the throttle. The engine stalled.

No!

He tried again.

A *click click* sound was all he got.

He heard another voice from across the street, cold and commanding. "Throw them in the car. Cops are almost here!"

Invictus recalled Joe's instructions and executed them.

Vroom!

The bike sprang to life and he pulled away, bouncing off the sidewalk back toward the corner of the park. He spotted two men tossing a third into the back seat of the Mercedes and leaping in after. The Mercedes peeled out and raced away down Seventh Street. Invictus sped after it. Lights flashing, several police cars rounded the corner onto Seventh. The Mercedes, with Invictus in pursuit, sped right past them.

Glancing back, Invictus saw the first cruiser screech to a halt and spin around to follow.

Oh, no!

Keeping his head low, he cranked up the speed as the Mercedes raced down Seventh in the direction of Hoover Street. Even on Sunday night there were plenty of cars. The Mercedes weaved in and out of lanes to pass cars going either direction, forcing Invictus to do the same.

Horns honked, tires screeched, but he didn't hear any telltale "crash" sounds, for which he was grateful. He focused on the road and not hitting cars or pedestrians. A pickup truck slowed down and forced him to veer off onto the sidewalk.

He called out, "Look out!" as people scattered to avoid being run down.

This is a bad idea, he told himself as he swerved back into the street. *Somebody's going to get hurt.*

But if he lost Demon now, he might never get another chance.

He heard the bullet strike his shield almost before he heard the shot itself. He ducked down lower, barely spotting a head and arm leaning out the back window of the Mercedes and pointing a gun.

Ping, ping, ping!

Three more bullets ricocheted off his shield.

From the corner of his eye he saw pedestrians duck and dive for cover. He heard their cries of terror.

The shooting continued. The sirens behind him grew louder as more police vehicles joined the chase.

Invictus glanced around. Too many cars. Too many people. Someone would be killed or wounded if he let this go on.

You'll get Demon some other time, the voice of reason assured him. *It's not like you have to get him tonight.*

He wasn't sure if the cops would follow him or Demon—likely both—but he couldn't be the reason innocent people got hurt. That would negate the entire purpose of him being out there. And Dennis would never approve. Invictus felt a sharp stab of guilt for losing his temper with Z and beating him so severely, despite obtaining valuable information. That also went against their code.

Just then his earpiece vibrated and he tapped it.

"Vincent," Dennis's frantic voice called into his ear. "The cops saw you!"

Invictus could have invoked sarcasm, but that wasn't his style. "They're right behind me. Any suggestions?"

"Report is they're chasing you and a black Mercedes," Dennis said breathlessly. "If you veer off suddenly they might stay on the car."

Exactly what I was thinking, Invictus thought.

"Did they dispatch a chopper?"

"Yup."

"Okay. Hang on. About to make my move."

He glanced up ahead and saw Vermont Street looming large with a green light in his direction. The Mercedes barreled through the intersection. Invictus swung a hard right onto Vermont, tires slipping. The motorcycle skidded sideways and almost entered the oncoming traffic lane. Horns blared. Tires screeched. The bike wobbled and shook, but he maintained control and poured on the speed.

His move caught the police by surprise and all three cruisers sailed though the intersection after the Mercedes. He wasn't sure if any would turn around to pursue him, but thought it more likely they'd send backup. And the helicopter would be alerted.

Ordinarily, he avoided freeways, but this time he decided the best hiding place would be in plain sight, at least for a short while. He sped through Little Bangladesh and Koreatown until the 101 Freeway rose above him in the night like a concrete anaconda stretched out across the city.

Weaving in and around cars, he whipped in front of an SUV and entered the onramp. As always, the freeway was packed and Invictus was forced to slow down and match the speed of traffic.

People in their cars reacted with surprise. Windows went down and phones came up.

Crap! He hadn't thought about that!

"Why are you on the freeway?" he heard in his ear. "Everybody'll Snapchat you all over the net."

"I know, I know," Invictus called into the wind. "Hold on."

He considered his options. His best bet was to transition to the 170 Freeway and then exit quickly so he could take side streets from there to home. Knowing he could be drawing more attention than less, Invictus sped up and darted between cars. The traffic seemed to be moving at around fifty-five miles per hour. He zipped through and around the other vehicles at seventy. His lack of experience riding between cars unnerved him and he gripped the handles fiercely, keeping the motorcycle as steady as possible.

"I'm getting off the freeway ASAP, Dennis," he called out. "Alert me if they know my location."

There was a pause. "You lost the guys downtown, but they know you're on the freeway. Chopper's on its way and cops will converge as soon as they have your location."

That's when Invictus heard it.

Whup, whup, whup!

Glancing up he saw the helicopter behind him, about a half-mile back, soaring low over the freeway. He knew the cops would be using night vision scopes to spot him, which meant he had to get off this freeway!

The next exit was Lankershim, adjacent to Universal City, and he darted across three lanes of traffic to fly onto the off-ramp and circle around to surface streets. A yellow light flashed ahead. He gunned the engine, darted between cars and ran it just as the red took over. Passing underneath the freeway, a red light barred his way forward and he screeched to a stop.

"Vincent, you all right?"

"Hold on, Dennis."

Whup, whup, whup.

It was right above him! Looking up, all Invictus could see was the concrete underside of the 101. Which meant the cops in the chopper couldn't see him either!

For once he was thankful that a red light took forever to change, and listened with growing relief as the *whup, whup, whup* grew fainter. The chopper pilot still thought he was on the freeway!

Phew!

Drivers and passengers on either side of him stared in awe. They were so surprised to see him that no one even took his picture. The light turned green and he sped through the intersection.

"I lost 'em," he said to the wind, and the brother in his ear.

"How?"

"Red light."

"Huh?"

"I'll explain later. On my way home."

He ended the call.

This night had revealed several significant truths. He had a name to go with the shadow drug ring. Cat. And he'd seen the face of who he could become. And that face terrified him.

CHAPTER EIGHTEEN

HOW COULD YOU DO THAT TO HIM?

THEY STOOD IN THE SLEEPING quarters on the ground floor. Demon had brought Z and his team back to the warehouse after losing the cops in South Central, and now The Mistress stared at Z writhing in pain on his cot. Arms folded across her chest, she looked amused by his suffering, rather than angry, as Demon would've expected.

"The Hero did this, Mistress," Demon hissed, leaning in to her. "We have to take him out."

She eyed him with disdain. "When he's turning out better than even *I* expected?"

"Look what he did to Z!" Demon insisted, his head throbbing with imagined pain as he glanced again at the bloody patch of missing scalp.

"Exactly," she replied calmly. But there was an edge of excitement there, too, that Demon didn't understand.

"What do we do?" Demon asked, fighting to control his breathing. The sight of his best friend twisting in pain filled him with rage.

"Continue with my plans," she explained evenly, turning to face him. "You will kill Z and make sure the body isn't found."

Demon froze. "What?"

Her face remained impassive, like a porcelain doll. "Was your hearing damaged? I said kill him."

Demon couldn't believe his ears. Of course, he'd seen her dispose of failures in the past. But Z? Z was his friend!

Z watched the exchange with wide-eyed fear. His eyes pleaded: *Don't do this!*

"Mistress, Z has been one of your most loyal subjects." Demon fought to keep his voice steady. He knew how fast she was with those blades she carried. "And he's my...." He trailed off as her eyes narrowed.

"Friend?" She sneered with disdain. "There's no room in my organization for friends. Or failures."

She slipped a sharp throwing knife from its sheath along her upper thigh and held it out to him, handle first.

He didn't take it. He'd killed for her before. But those had been strangers, or snitches. He'd never killed anyone he considered a friend.

Her eyes became venomous slits. She flicked her wrist and the knife flew from her hand. Demon heard a grunt followed by a low gurgling sound. He spun around to see Z gagging and choking on his own blood. The hilt of her knife protruded from his jugular vein, the blade buried deep within the flesh of his throat. Blood gushed forth in torrents, staining the pillow and pooling on the floor beneath the cot.

It wasn't the gagging or splashing of blood that would forever haunt Demon. No, it was the stunned, disappointed look in his friend's eyes, the look that said, "Why didn't you save me?"

The hand vainly clutching at the knife handle stopped twitching and dropped loosely to his side. Z was gone.

"Make sure the body isn't found," she stated coldly as she stepped forward to remove the knife. It slid forth with a tiny sucking sound. She wiped the blade against Demon's hoodie, smearing it with blood. He fought not to shiver at a level of callousness he'd never seen from her before.

Her eyes held his. He couldn't look away even if he'd wanted to. She had a way of mesmerizing him.

"Disobey me again, Demon, and it will be the last thing you do on this earth."

He nodded numbly.

Slipping the knife back into its sheath, she left the sleeping quarters. The clicking of her heels against the warehouse floor faded, and silence reigned.

Demon stared at his dead friend. Images of his brother dying in his arms flooded in and threatened to send him to his knees. Something was happening he didn't understand, something with The Mistress. And it was the Hero's fault!

He stepped closer to the bloody, unmoving form on the cot, his heart pounding. "He will pay for this, Z. I swear on your blood."

He dipped his fingers into the blood covering Z's ravaged throat and smeared it on his own face. Then he set about the grisly task of body disposal.

Shoulders slumped, sweat-filled mask in hand, Vincent trudged into the family room to find Dennis perched on the couch, eyes riveted to the flat screen. Dennis glanced up and his eyes widened even further.

Vincent saw the pain, the uncertainty, the myriad questions in those brown eyes. Without even tuning his ears into the broadcast, he knew it was about him.

Dennis muted the sound and looked at him as though he were a stranger. "How could you do that to him?"

Vincent felt like a knife stuck him in the heart. If he lost Dennis's love, he'd lost everything. He faced the screen. Cell phone video of his fight with the drug dealers unspooled before his eyes. He watched as Z wrapped both arms around his neck in a vise. And he cringed when he threw the man over his head, causing the rattail to tear loose from his scalp. Watching himself rising to his feet, bloody strands of hair gripped in one gloved hand, he felt nauseous and dropped onto the couch.

"People are shocked, Vincent," Dennis went on. "They didn't expect you to do something so…" He trailed off.

Vincent met his brother's pained expression. "So vicious? Me, either. It just happened, Dennis, I swear. I thought I was going to die. When I flipped him I forgot to let go of his hair."

Dennis nodded, but still eyed him like he was the bad guy. "And you also forgot you weren't supposed to beat the crap out of people who couldn't fight back?" The tone of reproach and disappointment in Dennis's voice shook Vincent to his core.

"I lost control."

"That was obvious."

"Uh, what did the witnesses say?"

"They said those guys were regular drug dealers and that they pulled guns on you first," Dennis replied somberly. "But you still looked like The Punisher out there and that's not what we wanted."

Vincent sagged. "It's just so…." He paused, his thoughts and feelings jumbled up and confused. "It's not like comics or TV, Dennis. It's bigger and worse and… overwhelming. I thought I could stay detached, but… That guy, Z, he bragged about selling drugs to kids. I don't know, Dennis, if I can…."

"Yes, you can," Dennis insisted, his voice strong and filled with vigor.

"I keep seeing little kids strung out on drugs," Vincent went on. "Who's going to help them?" He shivered. "I keep hearing the sound of Z's hair ripping off his scalp. I'll never forget that sound."

The next thing Vincent knew Dennis was right beside him, arms wrapped around him. "They will come, Vincent, and those kids will get help. You're the key. You're the inspiration people need."

"After what I did tonight?"

Dennis pulled back and forced their eyes to meet. "Yes. You'll keep going and you'll save more people and you'll not lose your temper again and everyone will forget about tonight. You'll see."

Vincent wasn't sure Dennis was right. His body felt numb with fatigue and shame, but his brain spun like a whirlwind. He had a full day tomorrow, and sleep was unlikely.

"You still have those pills the doc gave you, the ones to help you sleep?"

Dennis pulled back, aghast. "No, Vincent. You're not weak, you're strong."

Vincent stared at him vacantly. "No. I'm just human."

Dennis looked at him with compassion. "Okay, but only one. Come on, I'll help you off with the suit."

He stood and used the remote to click off the TV. Feeling the weight of every human degradation on his shoulders, Vincent followed his brother upstairs.

The sleeping pill helped a little, but not much, and the following day Vincent slogged his way across campus from the parking structure to Professor Chin's class. He was surprised to find Lisa waiting for him in front of the building. He never had called her and only just remembered that fact. He figured she'd waited to yell at him, but she didn't seem angry at all. Instead, she made a strange request.

"Could you untie you ponytail, Vincent, so I could take some photos of your amazing hair?" she asked, holding up her phone.

Surprised and too tired to ask questions, he set down his pack and slid the band off his thick tail of black hair, allowing it to fall loose about his back and shoulders. "Like this?"

She smiled. "Perfect." She snapped off a number of shots from different angles and then slipped her phone into her backpack. Noting his confused look as he retied his hair, she laughed. "Sorry, but your hair is so gorgeous. Photography is kind of a hobby."

He retrieved his backpack from the walkway. "You spend your free time photographing guys with long hair?"

"Only the cute ones."

Still confused, he followed her into the building.

After the lecture and copious pages of notes, Vincent followed Lisa outside and they sat on a nearby bench to chat for a few minutes before they had to separate for their respective classes. His body felt like dead weight and he wasn't sure he'd even be able to get back up.

"Since you study the brain, I want to pick yours about something." She dropped her backpack onto the ground and plopped down beside him.

"Okay, but I study the brain, remember, not the mind. That's psychology."

She tilted her head in that way he liked. "Okay, be a purist. I wanted to know what you thought of Invictus's interview the other night. You must've watched it because they ran it, like, all weekend."

Immediately his guard went up and he leaned slightly back from her, studying her face carefully. But she just seemed curious.

"Yeah, I saw it," he replied, twirling his ponytail in his hands nervously. He had to be extremely careful here. "I love what he said, and what he's doing."

She looked surprised. "Really? I thought a super serious guy like you would say he was a foolish dreamer."

Now he tilted his head to regard her. "Why would you think that?"

"I don't know. You have a rep for being all about clinical science and not about emotion or, oh, I don't know, *human* stuff, I guess."

Vincent was taken aback. Was that how his fellow students saw him, as cold and clinical and not in touch with emotion? Was he that way by nature? He had to acknowledge that he was. Invictus was changing him, however.

"I guess I do focus a lot on science and what it teaches us, but I'm not a robot."

Her face fell. "Oh, I didn't mean that. I just meant, what Invictus is trying to do, inspire us to think of other people instead of being selfish all the time, well, it seems almost impossible to me. People today are all about themselves. Do you think one person like him can make a difference?"

"Sometimes it only takes a snowball to start an avalanche." That analogy had just come to him, but he thought it a reasonable one.

"I guess that's true," she replied, obviously mulling the idea over in her head.

"Would you give up some of your time and talents to help others?"

She paused. "I suppose."

"Even after you become a doctor? Would you give away medical treatment for free, say to the homeless or just poor people in general?"

"I hadn't really thought much about it before, even though I know lots of doctors do that," she responded. He heard the honesty, and a trace of shame in her voice. "But now that Invictus put it the way he did, yes, I think I would. What about you?"

He felt himself turn red around the ears and twiddled more with his hair to distract her. "Uh, well, right now there's not much I can offer except the research I'm working on."

"What if some day you discover an antidote to addiction or a cure for cancer?" she went on excitedly. "Would you patent it and make money or give it away so everyone could be helped?"

"I'd give it away," he answered without hesitation. And he was surprised that he hadn't hesitated.

"Really?"

He reflected a moment on all the addicts he'd seen on the streets, especially the children. "Really. Why should one person control something that can help millions who can't afford it and desperately need it? Doesn't seem right to me."

"That's awesome. I had a feeling you weren't as cold as everybody said you were."

"I'm shy and stick to myself, so that's why they don't know me well. I'm not too social."

"I think I figured that out." Then her face clouded over. "Invictus did scare me last night when he tore that guy's hair off and then beat him up."

Vincent fought to keep his face neutral. "It looked bad, I know, but he was fighting for his life. Everybody said so."

"That's true," she agreed.

"I'm giving Invictus the benefit of the doubt."

But am I giving Vincent that same benefit?

She gazed wide-eyed at him, as though seeing him in a new light. Then she grinned shyly. "You're not all clinical."

"Dennis keeps me human."

"How so?"

Vincent considered a moment. "He's like an old soul and a young soul mixed into the same person. Maybe it's all the poetry he reads and writes, but he understands people better than I do. And he helps me understand them, too. I don't know what I'd do without him."

She smiled. "That's sweet. He seemed like a nice boy when I talked with him."

Vincent froze. "When did you talk to him?"

She looked startled, as though caught red-handed, and then quickly relaxed and gave him a mock shove. "The night he called to cancel our date."

He let himself breathe again. He'd already forgotten. He glanced down, embarrassed. "Oh, yeah."

"You still haven't called me, Vincent."

He lifted his head, expecting to see her glowering or angry. Instead, she leaned in and kissed him on the lips, lingering barely a wisp of a moment before pulling back and leaping to her feet.

"Gotta get to class." She scooped up her backpack. "See ya, Vein Boy." Then she hurried away along the path.

Vincent soon lost sight of her among the milling, chattering students. Dumbfounded, he forced himself to his feet and schlepped his way to class.

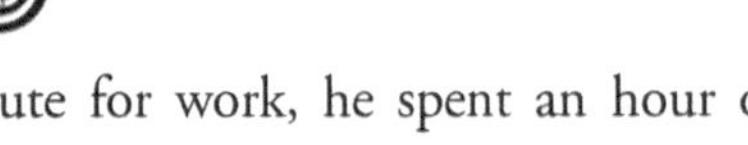

Before heading to the Neurology Institute for work, he spent an hour on the phone with Department of Children and Family Services and other foster care agencies. Unfortunately, everyone he talked to echoed what both Joe and Franky had told him. For every child, there was an attempt at reunification with the birth parents, which Joe adamantly did not want. All kids had to go through the courts for many months, especially if there were birth parents, before any adoption could take place. And that meant living in foster or group homes.

Because Joe and Franky were street kids, one of the social workers asked Vincent if he knew whether or not either was HIV positive. Startled by the question, he admitted that he didn't know, and then he panicked that it might be so. Either boy could've been infected given how they'd been living.

Also, he was told, the younger boy would have to go through an intensive detox program in a medically supervised setting before anyone could take him home. In addition, the older boy being gay and the younger being an addict made them less adoptable than other children and both would likely remain in foster care until they aged out of the system.

Every agency gave him the same spiel because they all went through DCFS. Some agencies only worked with infants or through a mother who'd decided to give up her baby for adoption.

The brief moment of joy he'd felt at Lisa's kiss, and the implicit message that she had not given up on him, faded quickly amidst this sober realization that he'd made a promise to two boys in desperate need that he couldn't keep. By the time he sat down at his computer station in Chin's lab, his heart felt heavy and his soul despondent.

He noted the professor eyeing him, clearly observing his lethargy. Chin frowned and returned to his own work.

Vincent spent most of the day on the official DEA drug samples and only a short amount of time on the street ones. He sought to compare analyses of the two, especially how the drugs glommed onto brain cells and the extent of the damage done to those cells. It looked more and more like the drugs Franky gave him—drugs the little boy ingested daily—destroyed brain cells at a vastly accelerated level.

He knew he needed to share his findings with Chin. He'd simply have to tell his boss that a kid on the street had given him the drugs and leave out the other details. He'd also have to alert the police. Somehow, he needed to bring James in on this, but he wasn't sure how without revealing the truth. And James would *definitely* not be on board with *that* truth.

Lisa sat in front of her computer struggling to focus on her fast approaching anatomy midterm. But the pictures she'd taken of Vincent filled her screen underneath the anatomy graphics she was supposed to be studying, and she kept switching back to them. She'd made a collage of the images so they covered her entire monitor.

He did have gorgeous hair, she thought for the umpteenth time. And he was cute, especially with the round, Harry Potter glasses. But that hair… She knew she'd seen it somewhere before. Somewhere recently. On someone else.

Lisa, all Asian guys have black hair, she kept telling herself. And she knew it to be true. There were tons of Asian guys at UCLA and many had long hair. She knew because she'd checked them out when they weren't looking. But a niggling feeling kept nudging her brain that UCLA was not where she'd seen this hair before.

She switched to her anatomy screen and studied the various muscles of the throat and esophagus, a key area for her midterm. The human body only had two hundred and six bones, she'd long ago learned, but the number of tiny muscles that all worked in concert with one another still amazed her. Her eyes held on the windpipe, and she gasped.

Switching the screen back to Vincent, she studied the hair for a long moment. And then she knew where she'd seen it before.

CHAPTER NINETEEN
HE'S BEEN ACTING WEIRD

DENNIS STAYED HOME ALL DAY. He scoured the news shows for reports on the guy Vincent had injured, but there was nothing. Demon had not taken them to a hospital. So where were they? It was mainly this uncertainty that prevented him from running to the park to find Demon and hang out with him.

The debate raged on TV and the Internet about Invictus and the incident regarding Young Z. The support seemed to be split. Those who liked the sentiments he'd expressed in his interview gave him the benefit of the doubt. Those who didn't felt he'd crossed a line and should be taken down by the police.

And everyone speculated on the whereabouts of "the victim," as the media had taken to calling Z. He was a drug dealer who preyed on children and he'd attacked first, but because Invictus ended up hurting *him*, suddenly the criminal became the victim. This, Dennis knew, was how the media spun every story—they drove the conversation and never allowed something as mundane as the truth to get in their way. In this regard, he knew Invictus had to win the media over to his side or their dream was dead before it even began.

The first thing Vincent asked upon returning home was, "Any word on Z?"

When Dennis told him no, Vincent looked somber. "That could mean he's okay and they didn't want him arrested or…."

"Or what?"

"Or they got rid of him," Vincent replied, his voice heavy with guilt.

That surprised Dennis, but later he realized it shouldn't have. "You think?"

"Word on the street is Demon killed his first man when he was twelve."

Dennis flinched, but kept his face neutral. "You were defending yourself, Vincent."

"I lost control," Vincent admitted. "That's something daddy taught us never to do."

The mention of his father sent Dennis's heart to pounding. "He also taught us to fix our mistakes. So just don't lose control again."

Vincent eyed him with gratitude. "You remind me so much of mom."

Dennis froze, images of Vincent running into the entry hall, calling their parents that he was late, the police at the door. His palpitating heart threatened to burst from his chest.

"I've gotta finish dinner."

He hurried to the kitchen before his brother could say anything else.

That night Dennis sent Invictus to a 911 call about a liquor store robbery in progress, and he arrived before the police. Parked across the street, he observed through a large plate glass window at least two men pointing guns at someone hidden from his view. Knowing he couldn't approach directly or the robbers would spot him—and likely shoot the storeowner—Invictus pulled his small grapple gun from the motorcycle storage compartment and climbed up a fire escape to the roof of the building across the street.

Hearing no sirens, he took careful aim and fired a grapple at the building that housed the liquor store. The four hooks snagged onto a brick ledge above the store awning and held. He couldn't see in the window, but since no one came out to check, he decided the robbers hadn't heard his grapple. He tied it off around an air vent pipe jutting up beside him and hurriedly wrapped his small zip line wheel around the steel cable stretching above the street to the other building. With his shield attached to his back, he gripped the handle and kicked off from the roof.

His stomach dropped. The street seemed to fly up at an alarming rate and the store window loomed larger by the second. Feet outstretched, he smashed through the glass, shattering it and sending shards in all directions. He let go of the zip handle and landed on his feet, did a quick roll over and leaped up to connect with a fist to the first gunman, knocking the weapon from his hand and sending him to the floor with a heavy groan.

Almost simultaneously, he whipped the shield off his back as the other two fired.

"Get down!" Invictus shouted at the storeowner, who ducked behind the counter.

The bullets shattered bottles. Glass sprayed everywhere. The smell of liquor permeated the air.

Invictus heard sirens in the distance.

He charged the two assailants, slamming the shield into both and knocking the guns from their hands. They stumbled. He lowered the shield and kicked out hard, connecting with the first guy's lower back. The robber crumpled with a strangled cry of pain.

Using a display table for leverage, Invictus placed one arm on the table and flew upward, snaking his legs around the neck of the third robber and flinging him hard down to the floor. The robber's head struck the linoleum with a loud *crack* and he lay in a daze.

Movement caught his eye and Invictus whirled to face another assailant blocking the front entrance, his gun poised to fire. He flung his shield and leapt to one side. Bullets struck the glass cooler behind him and he heard a loud *grunt* as the shield struck home.

He jumped up and charged the stunned gunman. As the man rose to his feet, Invictus knocked the weapon from his grasp with a sharp punch to the wrist, and then he pounded a fist into the man's abdomen that sent him to his knees.

Remembering his promise to Dennis—and to himself—he maintained control and did not beat the man. He spotted an extension cord and yanked it from the wall, binding the dazed robber's hands behind his back.

He stood and surveyed the store. Broken bottles and spilled liquor abounded. The cooler door had blown out and beer cans littered the floor around it. The other three gunmen moaned and rolled on the floor.

The sirens grew louder.

Invictus approached the owner. "I'm sorry about your store, sir."

The man, who looked Korean, stood to his full height behind the counter and grinned. "Insurance."

The sirens were almost there.

"I have to go."

The storeowner pointed at his own eyes. "You one of us. These people are bad." He pointed at the robbers.

Invictus took a moment to look them over. Despite wearing ski masks over their faces, their dark hands indicated they were all African American or maybe Latino. He turned back to the owner.

"Please don't condemn an entire race for the actions of a few," he asserted with sincerity. "*We* wouldn't want that, would we?"

The man was surprised and said nothing more.

Invictus scooped up his shield and bolted from the store. Using the metal awning, he clambered up above the shattered window to wiggle his grapple free from the bricks. Then he was onto the sidewalk and across the street. From the opposite roof, as he hauled his grapple back to him, he watched cops converge on the liquor store. He spotted James and Janson exit their unmarked car. Janson entered the store, but James paused and glanced around. Invictus barely managed to duck down out of sight as James scanned the rooftops. Then he was across the roof and down the fire scape to the street where he retrieved his bike and sped off into the night.

A short time later, he spotted Joe on his way to Franky's Laundromat lair and pulled up alongside. Joe gave him a chin raise and gratefully accepted a ride. When they arrived at the dumpster behind the Laundromat, Franky's pile of blankets and clothes was there, but not him.

"He'll be along soon," Joe announced as he dismounted.

"How do you know that?" Invictus climbed off and kicked out the stand.

"He made another score last night so his mom'll be crazy high," Joe explained as he plopped himself down onto the dirty blankets.

Invictus envisioned the pile crawling with bugs, but shoved that thought aside.

"He'll jet outta there fast so he won't get beat up."

Invictus reluctantly sat beside Joe and decided not to think about the lice that might end up in his costume.

"He's been acting weird, lately," Joe commented, his voice tinged with worry.

"How so?"

"His memory's gone to crap, for one thing."

"That's pretty standard with constant drug use," Invictus answered cautiously, recalling Chin's research data on the long-term effects of addiction.

"Yeah, but this is worse," Joe insisted. "Member how I told you about the super drug?"

Invictus nodded. Two people shouting angry epithets at one another from one of the tenement buildings distracted his attention and he forced himself to focus on Joe.

"Franky couldn't remember his name the other night."

"What?" Invictus tuned out everything else.

"He didn't even know me at first. Kept saying he was Robin, like you call him, and that he was waiting for Batman. When I told him I was Nightwing, that's when he looked at me funny and said, 'No, you're Joe'. It was weird."

Invictus felt his whole body tense, and his heart pounded. "No, it's the drugs. I've been analyzing them. There's something in there that destroys brain cells at an accelerated rate."

"You got your own Bat Cave for doing stuff like that?"

Invictus nodded absently, his mind on Franky. "Something like that. We need to get him clean, Joe."

"I know, dude, but how?"

"Is he still trying to wean himself off?"

"He goes back and forth. I think mom forces him to take more than he wants."

Invictus felt a chill envelop him. How could a mother do that to her child? He pictured his own mom - strong and loving and protective.

"She's probably afraid to be an addict by herself," he suggested, surprising himself for having said it. It was something Dennis would say.

"Maybe," Joe replied, running a trembling hand through his 'fro. "But it freaks me out how he's acting."

They sat in silence a few moments. The screaming couple kept up with their tirade, but Invictus focused on Franky. He had to move fast or he'd lose that boy. Then he had an idea.

"Say, Joe, you know any Asians?"

Joe grinned in the shadowy darkness. "Yeah, you."

Invictus smiled. Joe's grin was infectious. "I mean besides me."

Joe considered a moment. "Yeah, there's a coupla dudes I know out here. Why?"

"I have a plan. It's not a great one, but it'll at least keep Franky away from the super drug for a few days. If it works."

"I'm all ears."

Invictus explained his idea and Joe listened intently, nodding his head every so often.

"So, what do you think?"

"I think it's dangerous," Joe answered soberly. "Lots could go wrong. Demon could find out. Franky's mother could find out and beat him even more. My Asian friend could end up dead."

Invictus deflated. Everything Joe said was true.

"But out here, man, it's all life and death anyway," Joe added. "I say we go for it. For Franky." He raised a fist.

Invictus eyed the fist a moment, his heart filled with dread. He'd known the plan was dangerous the moment he uttered it. But what choices did they have? He paused, once again torn with how the concepts of right and wrong seemed to be so blurred out here, how the only colors of morality were shades of gray. He bumped Joe's fist.

"You better hurry up and find him that home, Super Hero," Joe added as he pulled back his fist. "That's the best cure."

"I know. It's just… not as easy as I thought."

Joe nodded. He clearly knew this already.

Invictus studied his young, drawn features. "I haven't forgotten my promise to you, either."

"Nobody'll adopt a queer kid, 'specially a black queer kid."

He sounded so resigned to his fate that Invictus felt an urge to hug him. But his natural reticence kicked in and he held back. "I will find someone. I promise.

Joe nodded again, but said nothing more.

They waited in silence until Franky showed up. And then Invictus put his plan into motion.

At first, Franky wanted to do more "Robin stuff" and follow the dealers back to where the drugs were made.

Joe and Invictus both blurted, "No!" at the same time.

Franky looked confused, but Invictus explained that Robin could only do that if Batman was with him. He briefly considered abandoning his original plan in favor of this new one, but somehow felt that Cat would be too savvy to allow him to tail her puppets.

Cat. Was that short for something or a nickname?

When Invictus told Franky they would take a ride to the Bat Cave, the little boy's eyes became huge and his chapped lips formed an "O" of surprise.

"For real?"

Invictus nodded.

"Did you hear that, Joe?"

Joe mock punched the boy. "Lucky you."

It took Franky a bit longer to accept being blindfolded for the journey, but Invictus explained that Robin had to learn his way around the Bat Cave before he could go there on his own.

Franky scrunched up his dirty face and considered that. "Don't worry, Batman. I'll make you proud."

A lump formed in Invictus's throat. The little boy's eager, sallow face gazing up at him with such need ripped into him worse than any bullet ever could.

"You already have," he whispered, placing one gloved hand on the scrawny shoulder.

And then they were onto his motorcycle and speeding toward UCLA.

CHAPTER TWENTY

GET OUT, NOW!

INVICTUS KNEW THE ALARM CODE to the building and the one for the lab. The real trick would be staying under the radar of roaming campus security and late night students out for a stroll.

He kept the bike in quiet mode as he navigated his way past the darkened parking structure toward the Neurology Institute. It was already past midnight and night classes had ceased over two hours ago. He knew there were only sixty or so campus security officers patrolling four hundred-sixteen acres of campus, so unless he attracted undue attention, he should not be noticed.

Dark shadows leapt at him from backlit trees and the breeze shifted those shadows from side to side. He'd often thought there wasn't any place more perfect for a horror film than a school campus at night.

Franky sat in front of him, clutching the handlebars and enjoying the ride. Being blindfolded seemed to relax him.

Invictus slid the bike into a dark alcove where the poor lighting should obscure it if a security vehicle cruised past. He slid the blindfold off Franky's head. A gust of wind kicked up. The boy shivered in his threadbare tee shirt as he took in the back entrance to the building. Invictus detached his cape and wrapped it around Franky's trembling shoulders. Franky's eyes almost popped out as he clutched the cape around him like he would never let it go.

"C'mon, Robin."

He led Franky to double glass doors and punched a code into the keypad. With a low click, the doors swung outward. Invictus entered, Franky trailing behind, and strode to a wall to the right of the entrance. Another keypad, punctuated by a large red light, was affixed to the wall at chest height from the floor.

Invictus typed in a series of numbers and the red light turned green. There were security cameras within the building, but these only activated if someone entered without disarming the alarm.

Franky watched the double doors close behind him and then followed Invictus along a series of corridors to the lab. Another keypad, another code. They were in. Chin had his own security cameras installed because the lab housed so many drugs, but the professor trusted Vincent and a few others with that code, as well. Making certain to stay out of range of the camera, Invictus punched in another series of numbers. Now they could move about freely.

The lab seemed haunted in the pale moonlight streaming through its only window. Every computer monitor looked like a monster rising up from the floor. Franky pressed against Invictus, his eyes darting everywhere at once.

Part of the nervousness came from the drugs in his system. Paranoia was a standard symptom. It was the actual destruction of brain cells that Invictus sought to map, and hopefully arrest.

"Over here," he whispered, navigating his way between tables. He didn't dare turn on the overhead lights because of the window. They moved slowly toward the Connectome scanner in the far corner. This was a super MRI machine modeled after one in Boston. It featured a gradient field eight times more powerful than a standard MRI and produced images four to eight times more detailed. It would give a very accurate picture of Franky's brain and what the drugs were doing to it.

It would also leave an energy footprint behind, as it did each time it was used. Vincent was ninety percent sure he could erase this one use of the machine from the computer records, but it would certainly be reflected on the monthly power bill.

I could lose my job, he thought as he turned the machine to "ready" mode. *Chin is almost sure to find out eventually.*

He observed Franky glancing furtively about in the dark.

Courage can be costly.

Is helping this little boy worth the risk?

Yes.

He powered up his computer, making sure to dial the screen brightness down to almost nothing. He pulled up his private file in which he'd compiled all of the data on Franky's drugs and linked it to the MRI machine. Fortunately, this super MRI was both faster and quieter, so Franky would only have to be inside for about fifteen minutes.

Franky eyed the MRI machine with unease. "What's that?"

"That's called a superhero MRI machine," Invictus replied, throwing in the extra word in the hopes it might make Franky less anxious. "It will take pictures of your brain."

Franky stared at him with wide eyes. "I have to go inside that?"

"It's kind of fun. You feel like you're inside a big cannon or something."

Franky walked slowly forward. He stared at the shadowy table and into the long dark tube. Invictus moved to his side and squatted down. Franky faced him.

"You need me to do this?"

"Yeah, I really do."

"Then I will." Franky sounded brave and terrified at the same time.

Invictus offered his best smile as he lifted the boy and set him on the sliding table.

"I have to strap your head and arms down so you don't move," he explained, indicating the straps. "And your feet."

"Go ahead," Franky whispered as he lay on his back.

Once strapped securely onto the table, Invictus instructed him to not move his head or even sneeze. Franky giggled and Invictus pressed a button on the machine. The table slid inward and Franky's head vanished from sight.

"You okay in there?"

"Great," echoed the small voice. "This is fun."

"Okay. You'll hear noises, but that's the machine working."

"'Kay."

Invictus switched on the machine and returned to his monitor as the images started to appear.

You'll get fired for this kept running through his mind as the machine clanged and rattled and took pictures of a young boy's very damaged brain.

And possibly arrested as Vincent, not Invictus.

Not only was this illegal, it would likely be considered unethical. But was it? Was helping this boy the wrong thing to do, or just illegal? A few years ago he'd have said "wrong." Now he sided with "illegal." As he'd said in his interview, everything legal wasn't good for people, especially children.

While the machine mapped Franky's brain, Invictus moved to the safe where Chin kept all of the drugs. The drugs were catalogued and weighed upon arrival, and apportioned to each grad student as needed during work hours. If he took too much, the loss would be noticed.

He input the combination and the safe door popped open with a slight hissing noise. Reaching into his pocket, he pulled out some of the meth he'd confiscated from dealers, not knowing if it contained the "super drug" or not. Squinting in the dark, he found a small baggie that contained a similar amount and slipped it out of the safe. He replaced it with the one he brought and dropped the DEA meth into his pouch. Locking the safe, he scurried back to the MRI.

As soon as the machine ceased its rattling noises, Invictus slid Franky from the tube. The boy had such a big grin on his face that Invictus laughed.

"That was fun, Batman. Can I do it again?"

Invictus glanced at the wall clock. Almost one in the morning. And he had early class.

"Uh, not tonight, Robin," he answered as Franky sat up. "Maybe some other time."

"Cool." Franky slid himself off the table. He stumbled when his feet hit the floor and Invictus had to whip out both arms to secure him around the torso.

"You okay?"

"Just coming down now."

Invictus felt his chest tighten as he released the boy. He saved all the brain images in his private folder. He'd examine them the following afternoon.

He logged into the MRI database and deleted this one session from its record before returning the machine to "idle" mode. As he powered down his computer, his earpiece vibrated. He tapped it.

"Vincent!" Dennis was so loud Invictus flinched. "What are you doing at the lab?"

"Don't yell," he whispered, and Franky eyed him peculiarly. "I had to check on something."

"Security spotted your bike. James is on his way."

"Oh, crap. How close is he?"

There was a pause. "He's coming up Veteran now, moving fast."

"Got it. Thanks."

"But Vince—"

Invictus ended the call with a slap to the side of his head. "We're outta here, Robin."

He scooted the boy forward around the tables and made for the door. Keeping them both out of sight of the security camera, he reset the code and practically dragged Franky into the hall. He closed the door and tapped in the code to lock it.

"Where now, Batman?" Franky whispered.

Good question, Invictus thought, considering his options. The guy who spotted his bike was probably right outside watching it. He had to distract him somehow. Then he had it!

"C'mon," he hissed and started along the corridor. Franky trailed behind him like a puppy.

Skittering along the darkened corridor, Invictus and Franky stopped in front of another door. This lab studied spinal cord injuries. Reaching into his pouch, Invictus fumbled a moment until he came up with a small jimmy-tool. While Franky watched, he stuck the metal edge between the door and the jamb and wiggled it around. The door didn't even need to snap open before a loud claxon filled the building like a cry of pain.

Franky jumped at the alarm sound and Invictus placed one hand on his shoulder to calm him. Slipping the tool into his pouch, he led Franky back the way they'd come while his earpiece vibrated again beneath his mask. As he led Franky down another dark corridor, he answered the call.

"Yeah?"

"James is inside the campus, coming fast," Dennis reported with urgency. "Get out now!"

"Working on it. Hold on."

He hoped the guard who'd been watching his bike had entered the building to check out the alarm. And he hoped there was only one of them. He spotted the door he sought just ahead in a dark corner. It was an emergency exit that would sound another alarm if the person using it didn't have the access code. He did. Franky clung to him as he punched in the numbers with one gloved finger. The door popped open and he pushed Franky through. Darting after, he closed the door and re-armed it with the code.

They were out on the side of the building now. "Any other UCLA security on their way?" he asked Dennis as he led Franky along a concrete path.

"Like, all of them," Dennis replied soberly. "And more cops are coming."

"Got it."

Scooting to the edge of the building, Invictus craned his neck to see around the corner. The back entrance he'd used was unguarded, which meant his bike was, too.

"Go, go, go," he hissed at Franky and then bolted around the corner at a run, the small boy on his heels. He stopped at the alcove where his bike was parked.

Unguarded.

Phew!

He swung around, snatched Franky off the ground, and lunged for the bike. He practically leaped onto the seat and swung the boy up and in front of him. Just then the security guard appeared in the rear lobby, which meant the diversion had worked.

The guard saw Invictus at the same moment Invictus spotted him. Invictus gunned the throttle. The guard made a mad dash for the doors and they swung open just as Invictus got the bike in gear and roared away from the building.

He heard, "He's getting away!" before leaving the Neurology Institute behind and roaring off across campus.

"Where's James now?" he called into the wind.

"You talking to someone?" Franky asked, twisting his head back and up.

"Phone," Invictus replied.

"Who's that?" he heard in his ear and then cursed his stupidity.

Damn!

"I'll explain later," he quickly replied.

But how?

"Where's James?"

There was a long pause. "Heading up Westwood Plaza now."

Right where I'm headed!

He decided the direct approach was best. Catch them off guard. As he approached Westwood Plaza Road, five UCLA security carts veered at him from multiple directions.

You fool, you put Franky in danger!

He had no time for recrimination as he swung the bike a sharp left onto Westwood Plaza. Oncoming headlights blinded him and Franky covered his eyes.

"Hold on tight, Robin," he cautioned, and then increased his speed.

The headlights filled his vision and Invictus heard the roaring of the car engine approaching. But he saw nothing but bright light. Hoping his memory of the entrance was accurate, he swung right onto Medical Plaza Driveway. James's sedan roared past. Invictus sped around the circular driveway where patients and visitors were dropped off for the medical facility.

He heard a screeching of tires somewhere in the distance. James was turning around. He cranked up the speed. His cape around Franky's shoulders kept flapping upward and distracting him. He made a complete circle and burst back onto

Westwood Plaza as James's car bore down on him. He turned right and the bike flew forward, sedan and security vehicles in pursuit.

He gunned the engine, hoping his pursuers would think he planned to shoot straight through the light onto Westwood Boulevard. He plowed into the intersection and swung the bike a hard right. With a screech of rubber against asphalt, it tilted precariously close to the pavement. Franky cried out in terror and clutched even harder to the handlebars. Invictus fought the controls. His right foot left the pedal and struck the pavement. Pain shot up his leg. The tilting continued. Invictus kicked against the pavement with his throbbing foot. Frankie pressed back against him, mewling with fear. More pain drove up his leg, but he righted the bike and swung back into the westbound lane of Le Conte Avenue.

He glanced back in time to see James rip through the intersection onto Westwood Boulevard. He'd bought himself a few seconds. Invictus soared up and over a small hill and down to Levering Avenue, a lightly trafficked street that led into residential areas of Westwood. Glancing back, he saw no signs of pursuit and sped along Levering until he reached the more heavily traveled Montana Avenue. Confident he'd lost James, he slowed and backtracked toward Los Angeles.

"Thanks, Dennis, for the heads up," he said into the earpiece, his thumping heart beginning to slow down.

There was no answer.

Thinking the wind had cut off his voice, he tried again. "Dennis? You there?"

He listened, but there was nothing. Dennis had hung up.

Oh, no…

James swung his sedan into a screeching U-Turn on Westwood Boulevard, thankful for the light traffic at this hour. By the time he got back to Le Conte there was no sign of Invictus. UCLA security vehicles pooled near the entrance to the school and he pulled over.

"Aren't we pursuing, Stevens?" Janson barked. He already had his gun out.

James eyed him with anger. "Pursue where, Sergeant? He got away."

"We need to try."

"And engage in a high speed pursuit through residential neighborhoods? No. We're not endangering anyone for a non-violent offender."

"But–"

"That's an order, Sergeant," James snapped as he turned off the ignition and popped open his door. "Now let's do our job and find out why he was here."

Janson mumbled something James didn't catch and exited the car.

As he approached the uniformed campus security, James felt a sense of disappointment. Despite leaving his idealism about the goodness of human nature in the dust decades ago, he still believed some people were genuine. Too many fellow cops thought everyone was up to no good. James knew better. He'd encountered enough decent people along the way.

He'd had hope this Invictus was the real deal. A guy out to make the world better. But breaking and entering on a college campus? That made him just another perp, and perps had to be taken down.

CHAPTER TWENTY-ONE

YOU DOWN TO CHILL, DREAMER?

DENNIS SAT STARING AT THE map of UCLA and the flashing light that indicated James's car. Vincent had long since vanished. With the kid he had with him.

A kid who isn't me.

Was it Franky or Joe? It didn't matter. All that mattered was that it wasn't him.

Dennis snatched up his poetry book and flipped to his favorite Shakespeare sonnet, the one he always read when he felt worthless.

"When, in disgrace, with fortune and men's eyes, I all alone beweep my outcast state...."

He mumbled his way though the poem, his heart pounding, his sense of unworthiness mounting. By the time he reached the end, his resolve had hardened. He would seek out Demon tomorrow, and every day thereafter until he learned something important, something Vincent didn't know. He'd prove to his brother that he could do more than sit at this desk. He'd prove himself strong, one way or the other.

Invictus almost gasped when Franky confirmed that the abandoned tenement building was his home. He'd followed the boy's directions and felt sure the drugs had muddled Franky's mind. Seven stories high, it sported broken windows, tattered remnants of draperies billowing from the openings, a dirty brick facade, and a pungent odor of decay. It looked like a haunted house!

"You live here?" His voice came out quiet and uncertain.

"Lots of people do."

"But there's no lights or heat," Invictus objected, knowing the moment he said it how dumb he sounded.

But Franky didn't laugh. "We got blankets and it's better than the streets. At least till mama gets crazy with me."

Feeling guilty at the thought of sleeping in a real bed when he got home, Invictus climbed off the bike and set Franky on the cracked pavement.

He'd gone through a fast food drive-thru and picked up food. The girl at the window giggled nervously and asked if she could take a selfie with him. Knowing his reputation needed shoring up after the Z incident, Invictus leaned in to the window while she stuck her head out and snapped a couple of photos. He knew those pictures were all over social media by now.

They'd parked in a quiet alley while Franky hungrily consumed the food. Invictus watched with heaviness clutching at his heart.

I have to keep my promise!

Now, standing before this tenement that had a "Condemned by Order of the City" sign affixed to its front, that promise loomed ever larger in his consciousness.

Only a wrecking ball could fix this place, he thought as he stared at the remains of what looked to have been an old apartment building.

How can people live like this? And why do we force them to?

With reverence, Franky removed the cape and held it out like it was the Holy Grail. "Thanks for letting me wear it."

Invictus choked up again. He reached out and took his cape from the dirty fingers clutching it. So rattled by the building and Franky's casual acceptance of his lot in life, he nearly forgot about the money. As Franky started around back, Invictus called to him. The boy turned, his wide eyes lit with expectation.

"Uh, I gave Joe some money for you." Invictus forced his voice to sound steady and strong, even though he felt anything but. "He'll give it to you tomorrow night."

Franky broke into another of those angelic smiles. "Thank you, Batman."

"Use some of it for food," Invictus felt compelled to say. "Please."

Franky considered a moment. "Depends on mama." He started back toward the building, and then spun around quickly. "I'll try."

He hurried around back and Invictus lost him in the gloom. Weighed down by a deep sense of failure, he clambered onto his motorcycle and started for home.

It was later than usual when he entered the house. He knew, once again, he'd be living off caffeine to get through the next day. The house was quiet. He'd seen Dennis's lamplight spilling through the upper window as he pulled into the garage, and suddenly he remembered. He'd been so preoccupied that he'd forgotten about Dennis hearing Franky's voice on the phone!

What am I going to say to him?

He didn't have an answer as he trudged up the stairs, mask in hand. Dennis's door stood open. Light spilled onto the hall carpet, but there was no sound from within. Not even the squawking of the police scanner.

Vincent pushed open the door and saw his brother sprawled out on his bed, face buried within the voluminous pillow, fast asleep. He'd not even removed his clothes.

Vincent stepped around the piles of clothes and video game cases to stand beside his brother's bed. He didn't know how long Dennis had been sleeping, but the pillow beside his face glistened with dampness. He'd cried himself to sleep.

Vincent stood paralyzed with indecision. He glanced down at the wastebasket and spotted some artwork. Stooping, he quietly lifted out the crumpled sheets and spread them open. Invictus, in full costume with shield in one hand, stood beside a taller figure, also in costume, wearing a mask over the top half of his face. The figure had no cape, but on the left breast was an attenuated "S" in black. The costume was shaded a dark red, almost maroon. The figure had a name beneath it – Solitude. And then at the bottom of the page, Dennis had scribbled: 'Big Brother and Me. Someday'.

Vincent trembled as he set the paper down beside the computer. He spotted the open poetry book and picked it up. Silently, he read the marked Shakespeare sonnet:

'When, in disgrace with fortune and men's eyes,

I all alone beweep my outcast state,

And trouble deaf heaven with my bootless cries,

And look upon myself and curse my fate,

Wishing me like to one more rich in hope,

Featured like him, like him with friends possessed,

Desiring this man's art and that man's scope,

With what I most enjoy contented least.'

His gloved hands trembled as he set the book down and faced his brother. He knew that sonnet well. It was always Dennis's go-to poem when he felt alone or worthless or a failure.

And I made him feel that way. But I didn't intend to!

Memories flooded in to rebuke him.

You used to joke about his weak martial arts skills.

I was a kid then!

Did that matter? He'd never forgotten unkind words thrown his way in school, so why should Dennis forget jibes from his only brother?

Vincent fought back tears. He hadn't cried since the funeral. Even then he'd only cried in private, and felt weak for doing so. He'd had to stay strong for Dennis. But now he felt an intense need to reach out and touch his sleeping brother. He wanted to wake Dennis and tell him how important and amazing and special he was. But the words weren't there. He could explain the functions of the human brain quadrant by quadrant, but the emotions of the human heart continued to elude him.

"Dennis," he whispered. "You have no reason to curse your fate. I know you're mad at me, but you didn't do anything wrong. I just can't lose you. I can't. If protecting you by keeping you home means you hate me, then I accept that. But I can't lose you. I'm sorry."

Dennis lay still. There was more wetness on the pillow near his eyes. Was he crying in his sleep?

Feeling as though he'd failed at everything his parents ever taught him, Vincent switched off the light and plodded from the room. Too disheartened to even remove the suit, he crashed onto his own bed and lay in the dark, sad, lonely, and lost.

When his alarm woke him the following morning, he found his pillow stained with tears.

By the time Dennis left his room, Vincent had departed for school, which was why Dennis had lingered. He didn't want to talk to his brother. What would be the point? More lies and deceptions? There'd already been too many of those.

He'd play video games till after lunch and then run to the park. Hopefully, Demon would come looking for him.

When Vincent arrived at school, students throughout the campus were on their phones or reading the L.A. Times. He suspected it was because of "Invictus" being on campus the night before. But when he asked a random young man reading the paper what was going on, the guy showed him the headline: "Dramatic Intervention by Asian Vigilante Foils Armed Robbers."

And there, right below the headline, was an incredible photo of Invictus on his zip line smashing through the liquor store window. The photographer caught the image just as his feet pushed the glass inward and glittering shards floated in the air like snowflakes.

"Pretty cool pic, huh?"

Vincent forced himself to breathe. "Uh, yeah, it's amazing. Do they, uh, know who took it?"

"Somebody sent it into the paper anonymously. Didn't even ask for money. Sent video into the news stations, too."

Vincent gasped. He hadn't seen anyone lurking by the liquor store. Who had captured these images?

"The Asian vigilante also broke into a building here last night," the young man went on, but Vincent had already started toward class at a brisk pace.

"You're welcome," he heard from behind him. But he was too shaken to respond. Was someone following him? Or did somebody just happen to be there to catch him on camera?

Students glued to their phones – more than usual – unnerved him as he passed. He had a feeling he knew what he'd see, but stopped a girl anyway and asked what she was watching. She pulled out her ear bud and aimed the phone at him. Video footage of him zip-lining into the store unfolded. The camera moved in toward the shattered window and captured Invictus defeating the robbers. It even lingered long enough to capture his muffled conversation with the storeowner. As Invictus turned toward camera, the image jerked to the left and went black.

"Pretty amazing, isn't he?"

Vincent glanced at the girl and mumbled, "Thanks for showing me," before stumbling away.

It could have just been someone in the right place at the right time. But if so, why not cash in? Those photos and that video could have fetched thousands of dollars from the media. What was going on?

He found Lisa huddled with some of his classmates watching the same video, and greeted them disinterestedly. Lisa broke away and linked her arm in his to enter the building.

"Did you see Invictus in that video?" she asked, breathless with excitement. "Incredible."

He nodded, still shocked and afraid. If someone was following him, did they know about Franky? Did they follow him here last night?

"Heard there was a break-in last night," he offered, fishing for information.

They passed through the double doors into the coolness of the building and dodged milling students as they made for the stairs.

"It was your building, Vincent," she explained as they ascended. "Looks like he got caught before he could steal anything." She paused a moment, which was good because he was formulating his jumbled thoughts. "Why would Invictus want to break into a science building?"

He shrugged and tried to sound nonchalant. "No idea. But seeing as he wants to help people, he must've had a good reason."

She stopped and gave him a long look. "That's what I told my roommates, but they weren't so sure."

"Uh, we better get inside."

He ushered her toward the open door into the lecture hall. Taking a long, slow breath to calm himself, he followed.

When he arrived to work that afternoon, Vincent found police still on the scene. Head down and deep in thought as he entered the building, he nearly collided with two men.

Janson snapped, "Watch where you're going, kid!"

Startled, Vincent glanced up and froze at the sight. "James!"

"You know him?"

James glared at Janson. "Yes. He's the closet thing I have to a son. Now wait in the car, Sergeant."

Janson was clearly annoyed by the chastisement, but didn't argue. Vincent watched him strut down the path.

"I was hoping I'd run into you, Vince."

Vincent swung his head around sharply. "Why?"

James looked taken aback. "Because I haven't seen you for weeks, that's why."

"Oh." Vincent adjusted his glasses and slipped his falling backpack up onto his right shoulder. "So, how's it going?"

"Not great. Captain wants this vigilante apprehended so I've been on night patrol. I'm sure Linda told you."

"Yeah, she did. So what brings you here?"

James reacted with surprise. "You didn't see the news? The Asian vigilante broke in here last night, tried to get into one of the labs. But security spotted his bike and called us."

Vincent squinted against the morning sun. "Any idea what he was after?"

James shook his head. "But now the captain has a genuine crime to hang on his head, breaking and entering. It just got real, Vince."

A horn honked. Janson sat in the passenger seat, staring at them through the open window.

"I hate that guy," James announced with disgust. "Anyway, captain gave me Thursday night and Friday off. He's got a big meeting scheduled for Friday night, but until then I'm free. So we can spar Friday when you get home. Been too long."

He grinned, and Vincent forced himself to look excited. "Yeah. That'd be great."

James sprinted down the walkway to his car.

Vincent watched the vehicle pull away and then entered the building.

Professor Chin was examining equipment along with the other grad students when Vincent clocked in at two. Knowing this could be the moment of truth, he approached Chin. Had he left any traces of his presence the night before? He'd had to depart so quickly he worried that he might have.

"Hey, Professor, everything okay in here?"

Chin studied him a moment.

Was it a long moment or am I being paranoid?

"You heard, obviously."

"Yes," Vincent admitted, pulling his slipping backpack up again. "Did he get in here?"

Again, Chin studied him. No, something *behind* him. Vincent turned, but there was nothing but a lab table.

"Something wrong, Professor?" he asked, returning his gaze to the older man and forcing himself to hold it steady.

"Your hair, Vincent, it's not tied back today," Chin replied, his voice slow and methodical, his eyes riveted to Vincent's trailing hair that draped over his shoulders and down his back like an oil spill.

Oh, crap! Chin had a rule about hair!

Vincent dropped his pack to the floor.

"I'm sorry, Professor." He fumbled in the front pocket of his pack for a hair tie. "I was in a hurry and rushed out today. Forgot to tie it." He found a rubber tie and yanked it out, holding it up before his boss. "I'm sorry, sir, it won't happen again."

He grabbed his damp hair and flung it behind him, securing the mass into his standard ponytail. He gazed sheepishly at Chin, hoping his faux pas would be forgiven.

But Chin had an odd look on his face, as though he was struggling to recall an elusive memory. Then he seemed to come back to himself and nodded stiffly.

"Make certain it doesn't."

"Yes, sir."

Vincent grabbed his pack and headed into the small room where the lockers were situated. He slipped on his lab coat and tossed his bag into the locker, spinning the dial to secure it. Then he hurried to his station to fire up the computer.

Dennis wore long sweats this time and a regular tee shirt and jogged lightly to the park so he wouldn't be sweaty. And he left his book at home. Today wasn't about reading or exercise. Today was about measuring up, about becoming a hero in his own right. Upon arriving at the park, he stopped jogging and strode casually up the hill toward the bench. The air was warm, with no breeze, the sun shining brightly. The warmth on his skin improved his mood and helped him feel human again.

He felt like a baby, what with crying himself to sleep like he had, and vowed not to let that happen again. Vincent hadn't even cried during the funeral, while *he* had bawled his eyes out. That was embarrassing. And all the PTSD reactions? He had to control those, too.

I need to toughen up, he told himself, *especially if I'm going to get the goods on Demon.*

As though his thoughts had gone live, he heard, "Well, look who's back."

He turned to find Demon sauntering across the grass with his two lackeys in tow. Dennis jumped up from the bench and strode to meet them.

"'Sup, Demon?"

Keep your voice steady, Dennis!

"You down to chill, Dreamer?"

"Sure."

Demon jerked his head sideways and led his posse back toward the parking lot. Dennis sprinted forward to flank them.

Demon put him in the shotgun seat and indicated the others climb in back. And then they just cruised. Summer school had already let out for the day, so Dennis wasn't sure where they were going or if any deals would go down in his presence. But he decided to fish for information.

"You run this business, Demon?"

Demon cast a hard look his way. "Why you wanna know?"

Dennis shrugged. *Look casual!* "Just wondered."

"You don't need to wonder, Dreamer. You're with us, you follow orders. Got it?"

Dennis decided to back off. "Yes, sir."

"Better.

They drove in silence for a few moments, with only hip-hop music drifting out of the speakers. The music wasn't cranked, which Dennis figured was to avoid confrontations with police over noise pollution regulations. You never knew where those might be enforced.

"You got family, Dreamer?"

"Just a brother."

"Older or younger?"

"Older."

Demon glanced over. "He treat you good?"

Dennis was unsure how to answer that given everything that had changed. He shrugged and remained silent.

Demon returned his eyes to the road. "I had a big brother once. The best."

Detecting a wisp of sadness in Demon's voice, Dennis asked, "What happened to him?"

He heard one of the guys in back gasp, but Demon held up a hand to prevent whichever guy it was from speaking.

"He got smoked, Dreamer, by some strung out junkie."

Demon glanced over and Dennis felt a lump in his throat. Most people probably couldn't detect the pain in those few words, but he wasn't most people.

"I'm sorry, man." Then he recalled what Vincent had heard about Demon, and asked, "What did you do?"

"I cut the bastard's throat," Demon answered dispassionately. "Ear to ear."

Dennis felt his insides clench with fear. "Uh, like, how old were you?"

"Twelve."

Dennis swallowed hard, his whole body tensing up. Demon didn't notice.

"If you become one of us, we got your back, Dreamer," Demon went on casually as he turned a corner to avoid a police cruiser in the oncoming lane. "If anybody messes with you, including your brother, we'll take 'em out."

Dennis shivered. "Uh, thanks."

They stopped at a public park. Dennis was ordered to stay in the car.

"Watch and learn," Demon told him.

So he did.

Demon was good. Dennis had to hand it to him. If he didn't know a drug deal was going down, he'd never have suspected. It just looked like friends meeting each other at random and kicking it for a while in the park. He couldn't even see the exact moment of exchange. Even if he wanted to actually sell drugs, he was way too clumsy. He'd be spotted by somebody and that would be that.

But he had to make himself useful. As long as they found him useful he might be able to meet the boss, or at least get a name or location. He could be the lookout! That might work.

And what will you do with the information once you have it? Give it to Vincent so he can take his street kid friends into battle and leave you home?

Just the thought made him angry. He'd cross that bridge when he came to it. Maybe he'd figure out how to get James the info anonymously.

Demon led the others back to the car. Pulling out his phone, Dennis glanced at the time. Five-thirty. Vincent would be home soon. As Demon neared the car, Dennis slid the phone back into his pocket. The driver's door popped open and Demon dropped in behind the wheel.

"Whadda ya think, Dreamer? Could you do that?"

Dennis looked sheepish and shook his head. "I couldn't even tell when the handoff happened. I'm too clumsy, Demon. I'd blow it."

Demon glanced over the back seat at the other two. "Then why are you here if you can't be useful?"

"But I can," Dennis pleaded, hoping he sounded desperate and anxious to join. "I have good eyes, the best. You'll never need another lookout besides me."

Demon seemed to mull that over in his mind as he started the car engine. "Maybe so, Dreamer. Maybe so."

Dennis relaxed slightly as Demon pulled out of the parking lot.

He knew he should get home soon so Vincent wouldn't be suspicious, but he didn't want to look weak in front of Demon, so he said nothing.

They cruised along in silence, with Demon bumping some tunes through the car speakers.

Dennis sat and wondered how many other people Demon had killed.

CHAPTER TWENTY-TWO

THE HELL HAPPENED TO YOU?

Vincent trudged in through the back door at close to six. Work had run longer because of Chin's decision to check every nook and cranny of the lab for anything amiss. Fortunately, he seemed satisfied that "the vigilante" hadn't gotten in. Chin apparently didn't like to call a criminal "Asian" and so left that part off. Vincent phoned Dennis to let him know he'd be late, but the call had gone to voicemail and his brother never called back.

The kitchen was empty. No smells. No cooking utensils or apparatus in sight. He dropped his backpack onto the counter beside the sink and entered the family room.

"Dennis?"

No answer.

It was possible Dennis had gone running again. Maybe he'd left a note upstairs.

Exhausted, and knowing that more caffeine was imperative, Vincent plodded up the stairs to Dennis's room. Pushing in the door, he frowned. It looked exactly as it had the night before. Dennis's computer was off, all the piles of stuff untouched.

Vincent navigated his way to the desk. The crumpled drawing of Invictus and Solitude was back in the wastebasket. Poetry book was closed. No cell phone.

So, he's not running.

Then where was he?

A door slamming caused him to turn. Footsteps pelted up the stairs at a run and a breathless Dennis burst into the room.

Vincent studied him. "You okay?"

Dennis didn't meet his eyes. "Yeah. Sorry for being late. Just out with some friends."

His breath hitching, he moved past Vincent to turn on the computer.

"Jack and Kenny?"

Dennis shook his head. "No. You don't know these guys."

Vincent felt his chest tighten. More secrets? Dennis had never hidden his friends when their parents were alive.

What should I say? He tried to think how his father would respond, but not wanting to trigger the PTSD, he decided not to mention either parent.

"Call me, please, next time you're going to be late. I get worried."

Dennis swiped damp hair off his forehead, and gave him a peculiar look. "You do?"

Was that sarcasm in his voice?

"Yes, I do."

Dennis continued his hard stare a moment longer, and then his face resumed its usual softness. "Okay."

He turned away to type in his password.

Vincent knew Dennis's attitude had to do with last night, but didn't know how to broach the subject. "Uh, I'm gonna start on dinner."

"Sounds good."

Dennis pretended to check his Instagram messages. Vincent backed away and silently left the room.

Dennis didn't come downstairs for dinner. Vincent made some hotdogs that he thought tasted decent, ate three of them and some salad, because he'd missed lunch, and then took a plate up to Dennis's room.

The door was closed.

He knocked. After a bit of shuffling within, the door opened and Dennis stood wearing a Batman shirt and running shorts. When he didn't say anything, Vincent offered an awkward smile.

"You didn't come down for dinner so I, um, made you this." He pulled the plate from behind his back. Dennis stared at it without saying anything. "I know it's not that good, not like you can do, but I, well, you need to eat."

He held out the plate and Dennis took it in one hand. He looked uncertain how to respond—unusual for him.

"Thanks." He displayed no emotion. "You gonna go out soon?"

"Yeah. Gotta suit up."

Dennis waited, but Vincent didn't know what for. Scratch that. He *did* know what for. Dennis wanted to know about last night. But Vincent didn't know how to explain it without going into everything. And that would make matters even worse.

"Let me know when you're leaving and I'll log into the police mainframe." He stepped back into his room and closed the door.

Vincent felt like he'd lost his parents all over again. Only this time, he was losing the one person he needed more than anyone else. And that hurt beyond measure.

Invictus left the house feeling empty and drained. He downed an energy drink, but didn't want to consume too much because the outfit didn't have a zipper, and that meant urinating was a major ordeal.

Mostly, it was Dennis's detached attitude as he'd said, "Good luck" that cut into his heart like a knife.

With the money—and the drugs he'd taken from the lab—in his belt pouch, he headed east. He needed to get to Joe before Franky did.

As he cruised down Saticoy approaching Lankershim Boulevard in North Hollywood, he noticed a bright orange glow lighting up the night sky, and heard the sound of approaching sirens.

Must be a fire.

Since the burning building looked to be in the next block over, he decided to zip past in case anyone needed help. The sirens sounded like they hadn't arrived yet.

He slowed as he came upon groups of people huddled together in the street. A rectangular-shaped, two-story apartment complex was engulfed in flames. His adrenalin kicked in and he stopped the bike. He paused a moment to recall whether his outfit had been fireproofed or not, and then he remembered that it had. Dennis had thought of everything.

He locked the bike and grabbed his shield before trotting over to the crowd of residents. Some were clad in bathrobes, others in underwear and tee shirts. They'd obviously had to evacuate quickly. The crackling of the flames assailed his ears and the heat from the inferno nearly forced him back. About three fourths of the structure was burning, with the last section going up fast.

"Everybody okay here?" he asked in his deepest, most hero-like voice.

People stared at him silently. He heard a woman gasp. He saw kids pointing at him. But no one spoke. They just stared at him as though trying to decide if he was real.

Then a woman shrieked.

Invictus saw a lady being held back by two men as she fought and kicked and struggled against them.

"My baby!" she screamed. "My baby's still in there!"

"You can't go in there!" one of the men shouted, but she fought all the harder to escape their grip.

Invictus ran over. "Which apartment?"

The men stared at him like he was crazy, but the woman pulled one arm free and gripped his hand.

"There!"

She pulled his arm up and pointed at a first-floor apartment. Flames licked at the door. The number had partially melted off. Invictus saw what was left of a seven, but couldn't make out the rest.

Then he heard it.

A baby squalling.

The woman keened liked a wounded animal. Makeup streaked her face from her tears. Invictus squeezed her hand and let go. Then he raised his shield and sprinted toward the apartment door.

"No!" a male voice shouted, but he ignored it.

Shield up against his shoulder, he raced forward and slammed as hard as he could into the burning door. The wood splintered and the door caved inward. Heat assaulted him and flames licked at his arms and legs.

The baby squalled again—this time in pain.

Invictus sprinted down the burning hall, stooping low, keeping one arm in front of his nose and mouth. Smoke billowed around him. His eyes watered and his lungs burned. But the crying baby was like a beacon. He followed the sound as creaking, groaning, and popping sounds increased around him. The building was in its death throes and about to collapse. He didn't have much time.

The crying grew louder. He stopped before a closed door. Flames had begun eating it away. He raised one foot and kicked it in. The flaming wood shattered. Smoke filled the room, but he spotted the crib in the corner. He leaped forward. Fumbling in the murky smoke, his hands found the screaming infant and he scooped it into his arms, covering it with his shield.

Glancing around the room, he momentarily lost his bearings. There was a window. He'd seen it when the door caved in.

But which direction?

His lungs felt scorched, and his skin enflamed. He smelled singed hair and realized it must be his.

There!

The window lay just ahead. A low chest of drawers sat beneath it. The drawers were aflame. Taking a moment to focus and tune out the screaming child, he prepared himself and then sprinted forward. He leaped up as high as he could into a somersault right over the chest of drawers. Snapping his eyes shut, he rolled head first through the window. Glass shattered. He fought to keep his balance as fresh air filled his lungs. His eyes popped open as the somersault carried him outside the building. Rotating a full three-sixty degrees, he landed on his feet in a low crouch and then burst forward like a track star as the building collapsed in on itself with a rending of wood and shattering of glass.

Invictus kept his footing and jogged to the waiting crowd. He was dimly aware of flashing red lights and fire department vehicles, but his vision was still obscured by smoke, his breathing raspy. He stopped before the gesticulating woman. He took a moment to catch his breath. Pulling aside his shield, he saw the dirty, blackened face of the squalling infant and grinned.

The lady snatched the baby from his arms and cradled it. Then she shocked Invictus by leaning in and kissing him on the cheek.

Fire fighters suddenly surrounded them. Some led the woman and her baby away while others attacked the inferno. Invictus felt a hand slapping his lower back and spun to find a young, female firefighter in full gear.

"The ends of your hair were on fire," she explained, matter-of-factly.

He recalled the smell. "Uh, thanks."

She stared at him in amazement. Everyone stared at him in amazement.

"You want us to check you for burns?" she asked.

His lungs felt like he'd inhaled a coal mine, and the skin beneath his outfit screamed as though sunburned. But then he recalled Franky. And he heard more sirens approaching.

"Thanks, but I have somewhere to be. And I don't think the police want to shake my hand."

"I do." She stuck out her hand.

Momentarily stunned, he stared at her outstretched hand. Then, with a shy grin, he reached out to shake it. Letting go, he sprinted back to his bike. As he did, he heard the crowd clapping. He stopped and stared. Even the fire fighters were clapping. He had to admit, the appreciation felt good.

Franky had been gone forty-five minutes and Invictus was worried. When he'd first met up with Joe, the teen looked aghast at his appearance.

"The hell happened to you?"

Invictus explained about the fire.

Joe sniffed the air. "Costume smells nasty, and you burned your hair." He stepped behind Invictus and pulled up his dangling hair. "That's one way to get rid of split ends." He chuckled. "I don't get 'em." He pulled on his curly 'fro. "Your hair kicks butt, but mine is easier."

Invictus had grinned, despite his anxiety over what they were about to do. Joe seemed to have that effect on him. He'd handed off the drugs and Joe went in search of his "other Asian friend," as he called Samuel. That had taken thirty minutes because, as Joe intoned when he got back, "the fool wasn't where I told him to be." But he assured Invictus that Samuel knew where to be at what time to intercept Franky before the real dealers arrived.

Invictus was surprised to find that Joe had a cell phone.

"Just got it." He'd laughed and shook his head in disgust. "Crazy ass government. Gives homeless people phones, but not a place to live."

Invictus wasn't surprised. The government often got things wrong, which was in large part why he was out here. He'd given Joe his "Invictus" cell number and said to call when he gave Franky the hundred dollars.

"Remind him to save at least fifty for food."

"I got it."

And off he'd gone.

Now the two of them sat behind the dumpster atop Franky's makeshift bed awaiting the little boy's return. Invictus found he no longer minded the smell of rotten food emanating from that dumpster. When he'd first started coming here, he had to stay back from it because the smell made his stomach lurch. Now, that smell was ordinary. He supposed this was how people like Joe and Franky so casually accepted their fate. Given enough time, even the most dysfunctional lifestyle could seem "normal."

Joe sat fiddling with his new phone while Invictus twirled his shield out of nervous boredom.

"That big-ass shield hits me in the head, Super Hero, and we gonna get down," Joe said, mimicking the tone of so many street kids out there.

Invictus stopped twirling. "Sorry." Joe studied him so intently that he squirmed and had to force himself to maintain eye contact. "What?"

"Nuthin'. It's just cool how you care about him like I do."

Invictus nodded and sat beside Joe, his mind twisting with fear. What if the real dealers caught Samuel, or if Franky met the real ones first, or if Franky met up with Samuel and *then* the real guys found them? The number of ways this plan could go wrong were endless.

And Franky wasn't back yet.

"He'll be okay." Joe placed one hand on Invictus's forearm in a comforting gesture. Invictus noticed for the first time how long and slender Joe's fingers were, like those of a pianist. That's what a kid his age should be doing, playing music or sports or going to the movies with friends. Not selling himself to evil men and protecting ten-year-old addicts.

Invictus smiled as best he could.

Joe pulled his hand back and stretched out his long legs. His sneakers were starting to get holes in them.

And then Franky rounded the dumpster, high as a kite and grinning from ear to ear. "Hi, guys!"

His voice sounded higher than usual and reedy. By now Invictus understood this to mean that the boy had snorted meth, as opposed to ingesting it some other way. The reediness came from restricted airflow through his damaged nostrils.

Joe sat up and Invictus rose to his feet. He studied the boy for any signs of injury, but found only the usual layers of dirt and grime beneath tattered clothes. Franky's Adidas looked even worse than Joe's shoes.

"You okay?"

Franky nodded dreamily. His eyes were wide and dilated, like those of a cat.

"Did you save some for food like I told you?" Joe asked, his tone firm and commanding.

"Yeah, 'cept I'm not hungry now."

Joe glanced at Invictus. They both understood why Franky wasn't hungry.

Franky eyed Invictus peculiarly. "You smell funny tonight, Batman, and your costume is dirty. Better have Alfred wash it." He burst into gales of laughter, as though that was the funniest thing he'd ever heard.

Invictus felt sick to his stomach. It was the drugs *he'd* supplied that were making Franky act this way. Yes, his supply was "cleaner" than the super drug, but it was still killing the boy one brain cell at a time. Not to mention the damage the drugs were doing to his heart.

He watched Franky twirl around and try to break dance.

Joe dropped to the ground.

"Watch me, Franky."

Invictus watched with his mouth hanging open while Joe executed some drops and spins and twirls and other break dance moves that were astonishingly smooth and athletic. Even Franky ceased his twitching movements to focus on Joe spinning on the dirty ground, hoisting himself up with one skinny arm, and then whirling on his head.

In moments, the performance ended and Joe rose to his feet, panting, brushing dirt from his 'fro. "I'm outta shape, Franky, but that's how it's done, little bro."

Franky's grin was even bigger than his eyes and he clapped wildly. So did Invictus.

"You got moves like that, Super Hero?" Joe grinned.

"Hell, no!" He held up one gloved hand and Joe high-fived him.

Then Joe held his hand out to Franky and the boy's small hand slapped it.

"You guys going to be okay tonight?" Invictus asked.

"Yeah, we're good," Joe answered. "I'll stay with him till he's not flying so high." He put one hand over Franky's heart. "Heartbeat's racing. Don't want anything to happen."

Invictus felt his chest constrict with fear. How easy it would be for a child as small and lightweight as Franky to overdose. The boy seemed to know his limits, but the super drug was more potent.

"Okay." He was reluctant to leave them, but understood there was nothing he could do. Just like every other night.

As he rode out of the alley, he observed Franky on his back on the dirty pavement and Joe spinning him around like an upended turtle. Franky laughed with delight. Kids were kids, he realized, no matter how they were forced to live.

Demon found Cat in her room lounging on a king-sized bed and reading a book.

Clad in a long, kimono-like robe, her slender legs peeked out from between the folds and tempted him. He forced his eyes up to her face before she noticed them drifting.

"Reporting in, Mistress."

She set her book down onto the lush bedcovering and focused her attention on him. "And?"

Demon recounted the sales and listed the numerous Valley gangs whose turf he'd encroached on with their "less expensive product." She looked pleased. That was all he wanted, to please her.

"How's the new boy, Dreamer?"

"He's weak, Mistress," Demon replied, fighting to mask the tone of disgust in his voice. "He refuses to sell and asks too many questions. I think we should get rid of him."

She wrapped delicate fingers around a television remote and clicked on a flat screen mounted to her bedroom wall. Images from the afternoon unspooled on screen, images from his body cam, and the one mounted to the dash in his car. She had the sound off, but Dreamer sat in the shotgun seat looking like the little pansy he was. Demon hated weakness in anyone, especially males, and this kid reeked of it. He never would've considered approaching him if—

"I think he's cute," she commented, interrupting his thoughts.

He stared at her aghast.

"Does he offer any services of value?"

"Says he could be lookout."

She regarded him a moment. "Lookout it is."

"But, Mistress–"

She raised her well-trimmed eyebrows.

"Yes, Mistress."

He was about to bow and leave when there came a knock at her door.

"Come."

The door opened and Rocket entered. Short, muscular, and Japanese, he'd taken over Z's turf. Just the sight of him clinched Demon's stomach and made him angry about Z all over again.

"Yes, Rocket?"

"Mistress, please forgive the intrusion, but something happened tonight I thought you'd want to know."

"I'm listening."

So was Demon.

Rocket explained how some Asian guy who didn't work for her had pretended he did and sold some stuff to one of their regulars, a kid named Franky.

"Little Franky?" Demon asked in surprise. "With the tweaker mom?"

"Yeah. Bamboo saw the drop and called me. By the time I got there, the Asian dude was gone. Franky, too."

Cat appeared thoughtful, but not concerned. Demon had never seen her lose that cool facade. "Would Bamboo recognize the interloper if he saw him again?"

"Yes, Mistress."

"Assemble a team, Demon. Take Bamboo. Scour the city until you find this renegade. Then kill him. Make it bloody and make sure the body will be found. We want our enemies to know we mean business."

"Yes, Mistress."

When he arrived home, Vincent found Dennis downstairs watching CNN. He was shocked to see footage of himself running into the burning building, but then realized he shouldn't be surprised with so many people out there wielding phones. He had to admit that his flip through the window to the sidewalk looked pretty dramatic.

Dennis leaped up the moment he entered the family room. "You okay, bro? I mean, your hair was on fire and all!"

He pointed to the screen. The female fire fighter slapped Invictus's back to put out the fire.

Vincent shrugged. "Guess we need to figure out how to fireproof the hair, huh?"

Dennis grinned.

That grin from his brother lifted Vincent's spirits like nothing else could.

"You were amazing, Vince," Dennis gushed, sounding like a little boy again. Almost like the boy he'd been before all of this started. "Even the firefighters clapped."

"I know. Felt kind of good."

"Let me see your hair."

Dennis reached around to lift his hair. "Not too bad. I'll trim off the burnt part."

"Thanks, Squirt."

"The people will come now, Vincent," Dennis insisted. "You'll see. How can they not when they saw you holding that baby out to the mom? It was freakin' awesome!"

Vincent laughed and they high-fived. All the misunderstandings that had passed between them seemed to fade away in that one high-five.

"You hungry?" Dennis asked with a raise of his eyebrows. "I made some real food."

Vincent chuckled. "Rub it in."

"Okay. Your cooking sucks."

Vincent's mouth dropped open and Dennis laughed. They went into the kitchen together and sat down at the small table. Vincent was exhausted, and he had a full day of work tomorrow. But he ate Dennis's delicious broiled chicken with potatoes and they talked about the fire and how the pundits on talk radio and TV were leaning more in the "Invictus as hero" direction and dropping the "Asian vigilante" moniker.

They talked about the weekend and how they should go see a movie or do something fun. But they didn't talk about the subjects Vincent knew they should, the ones that had driven a wedge between them. He wanted to, but Dennis obviously didn't. It was on his face and in his voice that he just wanted to pretend everything was the same between them as it had been before. And he was so excited about the response to the baby rescue that Vincent chose not to spoil the mood by bringing up Joe and Franky or asking more questions about Dennis's new friends.

He hoped he wouldn't live to regret that choice.

CHAPTER TWENTY-THREE
IT'S YOU, VINCENT!

THE FOLLOWING MORNING, DENNIS ROSE to make breakfast for both of them before Vincent headed off to work. Dennis seemed quiet again and thoughtful. The excitement of the previous night had worn off. Still, Vincent didn't bring up the elephant in the room that both of them were conspicuously avoiding. It was his job, he knew. He was the adult and he was the one who'd let Dennis down, even though he hadn't done so deliberately. But he simply didn't know how to broach the subject.

He chugged his last gulp of orange juice, told Dennis to have a good day, and then hopped into his car for the drive to UCLA. Only when he was underway did he realize he'd forgotten to tell Dennis to pick out a movie for the weekend.

Do it when I get home, he thought, and focused on his driving.

It was mid-morning when he felt a phone vibrating in his pocket. His regular phone was in his locker. This was his Invictus phone and he only kept it on him for emergencies. Dennis knew to call that number if there was a major problem he couldn't handle.

Chin had strict rules about phone use in the lab, even during off-duty times. Vincent slipped it out and saw a text fill the screen: 'CALL ME.' The text was from Joe.

Glancing around the lab, he noted Chin with his back turned. Standing, he nodded at Byers seated at the next table over.

"Bathroom break."

Byers, a short, stocky guy from the Midwest, returned the nod and Vincent scooted his way around tables to the door. He glanced back, but Chin was still engaged with another student. Vincent pushed open the door and stepped into the coolness of the hallway. No one was around so he walked a short distance from the lab and pressed Joe's number on his phone.

The ring in his ear unnerved him. Why would Joe be calling him? As he had with Dennis, he'd told Joe never to call unless it was an emergency.

"Super Hero?"

"Yeah, it's me," Vincent replied, keeping one hand over the phone to mask his voice if people happened to pass. "What's wrong?"

"Samuel's dead!" the boy hissed into his ear. He sounded terrified.

Samuel? Who was…? *Oh, no!* The Asian guy who sold the drugs to Franky!

"Tell me."

"His throat was sliced open, man, and he was cut up like crazy," Joe went on, his breathing raspy. "Demon did it. That's the word out here. I'm scared, Super Hero. What if Samuel told him about me?"

Vincent's heart raced with fear. What had he done? "Does Demon know who you are?"

"No, but it's not hard to find the skinny-ass black kid who puts out for money," Joe replied, his voice trembling. "And what if Demon goes after Franky?"

No!

"Listen, Joe, you need to stay calm," he said, trying to assure himself to do the same. If anything happened to either of those boys… "Can you get to Franky today and hide him somewhere? I don't think Demon'll look for him until tonight, if he plans to at all."

There was a pause on the other end. "I think I know a place we can chill," Joe said. "How we gonna find out if Demon's looking for me?"

That was a good question. "I'll have to find Demon first."

"How?"

Vincent considered a moment. "They say he's working the Valley, so I'll patrol out there. If you hear anything, let me know right away. Okay?"

"'Kay." Pause. "You're not gonna let him kill me, are you?"

Vincent's breath hitched. "No."

The line went dead.

Heart pounding, Vincent slid the phone back into his pocket and returned to the lab. Chin eyed him sidling back to his desk, but said nothing. It took every ounce of concentration for Vincent to focus on his work.

He'd never even met Samuel. And yet he'd killed him all the same. Would Samuel be missed? Did he have people somewhere who would mourn? Or was he just another young cast-off who became a nobody on the streets, but was now a somebody because he'd been murdered? He was a homicide, a homicide the cops would chalk up to drug wars and file in the "we're too busy to solve this one" drawer. His dad had told him about such cases his whole life, and now he was the cause of one.

He'd need *two* of Dennis's sleeping pills tonight.

At least.

Dennis followed the news reports all morning and felt elation that the baby rescue seemed to have shifted the public sentiment away from the Young Z incident and the alleged UCLA break-in. Of course, Vincent had not volunteered to explain the break-in, as he'd promised he would, and Dennis wasn't surprised. Vincent was all about secrets these days.

His plan had been to meet Demon at four-thirty, but Linda called and invited them over at five for a sparring session.

"Didn't Vincent tell you?" she asked when Dennis expressed no knowledge of the plan. "James ran into him at school the day of the break-in."

Something else he didn't tell me about!

Dennis tried to beg off the sparring, claiming his martial arts weren't near as good as hers and the men, but she wouldn't take no for an answer and he didn't want to make her suspicious.

He could still hang out with Demon for a few hours and be back by nine or ten. Vincent didn't need him anyway.

He told Linda he'd see her at five and hung up.

Vincent got home at four forty-five. He looked exhausted, stressed, and worried.

"You okay, Vince?" Dennis asked uncertainly as he muted the sound of the video game he was playing.

Vincent did a double take. "Oh, hi, Dennis. Didn't see you."

"Huh? The game was blasting when you came in."

Vincent stared at the muted images on screen. "Didn't notice. Tired, I guess."

Dennis saw his brother looking seriously despondent, and all his anger at the secrecy fled. He leapt up from the couch. "Something happened. What?"

Vincent gazed long and hard at him. He looked guilty and sad at the same time. "I don't know where to begin."

Maybe this was the moment of truth. "How about you start with—"

A knock distracted him, and Dennis turned to find James opening the front door. He was dressed in his workout clothes and grinning. "Well, boys, time to get your asses whupped."

Vincent groaned. "Oh, man, James, I'm wiped."

"Nothing a good workout won't fix. C'mon, get changed and let's go."

Dennis exchanged a look with Vincent, who nodded weakly. "Okay. We'll be right down."

He hefted his backpack off the floor where he'd dropped it and led the way to the stairs. Dennis halfheartedly followed.

Vincent was slow, his reflexes cumbersome, and James pressed the advantage every chance he got. James's three-car garage had been re-imagined as a training center with mats, kicking bags, punch mitts and other accouterments for martial arts training. Linda sometimes gave free classes for neighborhood kids during the summer months, depending on her schedule at the studio.

She and Dennis sparred because he wasn't good enough to take on Vincent or James. Vincent didn't mind sparring with him, but Dennis always knew Vincent pulled his punches and kicks so as not to hurt him, and that made Dennis feel worse about his abilities, not better.

On this occasion, James had insisted he spar with Vincent, and Vincent was too tired to argue. Tired and anxious. He'd not heard back from Joe all day, despite texting him after work.

Please, God, let them be safe!

James kicked and connected with his chest. Vincent tumbled to the mat, panting and sweaty.

Barely winded, James shook his head in surprise. "You really *are* tired, Vince. I've never seen you this slow."

His pride kicking in, Vincent leaped up and swung into his signature roundhouse kick – up and around. As he spun, his bare foot poised to connect with James's chest, he expected a counter attack. But James's mouth opened in stunned shock. The kick connected and James flew backward to land hard on his butt.

"Whoa, nice move, Vince," Linda offered as she deflected Dennis's punch and slipped into a wrist hold that held him in check.

When James sat on the mat staring at him with open-mouthed shock, Vincent relaxed his fighting stance.

"What? I kick you too hard, old man?" He tried for a jesting tone, but deep down he knew what James's expression meant.

Linda released Dennis, who rubbed his shoulder, and gazed at James. "What's wrong?"

James ignored her. "It's you, Vincent!"

Swallowing hard, Vincent feigned ignorance. "It's me, what?"

"You're the Asian vigilante!"

Linda gasped. "What?"

"Dammit, Vincent, it *is* you!" James spat as he jumped to his feet.

Linda threw one hand to her hip and swiped a wisp of errant hair off her forehead with the other. She regarded her husband uncertainly. "What are you talking about, James? Vincent couldn't be–"

"That's his move, Linda," James insisted, his voice rising in pitch. "His trademark kick. You saw him use it against those scumbags at the school. Damn it all to hell, Vincent!"

Linda regarded Vincent with wide-eyed realization. "He's right, isn't he, Vincent?"

"Yes."

She put one hand to her mouth. "Oh, my God…." She sat on the mat in shock and studied him. "Why didn't you tell us?"

Vincent pushed back his shoulders and stood straight, despite the fatigue dragging him down. He could not appear weak in front of James. Not now.

"Because I knew James would be mad."

James took a step forward, his face livid. "Damn right I'm mad!"

He flew into a kick. Vincent jumped to one side and parried with a kick of his own.

"James, listen to me–"

"What the hell's wrong with you?" James threw a punch. Vincent pushed it aside.

"If you just let me explain," Vincent tried again, but James spun into a kick. Vincent ducked underneath it and swung out with one leg. It hooked around James's ankle and nearly toppled him. They squared off again.

"You knew about this, Dennis?" James barked, casting a sideways glance over at Dennis.

"Of course. It was my idea."

James glowered. "I thought you had more sense!"

"I do," Dennis retorted angrily.

James executed another kick at Vincent. Vincent parried with one of his own. "What the hell's gotten into you, boy?"

Vincent's anger rose. "I'm not a boy anymore, James!"

He connected with a solid kick to James's thigh, but the bigger man only stumbled. He did not go down.

"Then stop acting like one!" James retorted, practically shouting. "What is this, some damned Filipino thing?"

Vincent took a step back, fists raised, legs spread apart. "James, will you stop swearing at me? Or is that some damned African American thing?"

"I oughtta kick your butt right through that wall!"

"Yeah? Try it!"

Vincent readied another flying kick and James prepared to deflect it.

"My name is Ozymandius, king of kings," Dennis intoned. "Look on my works, ye mighty, and despair."

Both men froze.

James glowered. "What the hell are you saying, Dennis?"

Vincent understood, and those words had the desired effect. He inhaled and forced calm into his lungs.

"It's from a poem. He's telling us we're both acting like arrogant jerks, and he's right."

Linda rose to her feet. "He *is* right, James."

James inhaled and exhaled, forcing oxygen into his body. "Okay, I'm calm. Now tell me why."

"Because you and daddy said it couldn't be done," Dennis offered from the sidelines.

James looked at him, and then back at Vincent, mouth agape. "Huh?"

"You both said no one would sacrifice any part of their lives for the betterment of the community," Vincent explained, keeping his voice steady. "You said no one would ever come forth to set the example that others might follow. You both said that. And we're proving you wrong."

James exchanged an astonished look with Linda. It was obvious they recalled the conversation.

"You're risking your life to prove your dad and me wrong?"

"No," Vincent replied with conviction. "We're doing it because it needs to be done. Like I explained in my interview."

"And people will follow, James," Dennis added, his voice filled with the sincere, child-like conviction Vincent hadn't heard from him lately. "They will come. You'll see."

"Linda, is it just me or is all this crazy?"

Without even awaiting her response, he turned back to Vincent, his temper rising again.

"You're gonna get yourself killed, Vincent! Hell, I'm supposed to arrest your dumb ass. Do you know the position you're putting me in?"

"Yes. I'm forcing you and everyone else to choose between the letter of the law and the spirit of the law."

"We're not crazy, James," Dennis added quietly.

"You stay out of this, Dennis!" James snapped. "Sounds like you've done enough damage, filling his head with comic book nonsense!"

"James!" Linda exclaimed.

Dennis looked furious. He snatched up his Nikes and strode across the garage to the door leading into the house. He pushed it open and slammed it hard, vanishing from sight.

"Thanks, James," Vincent said, the weariness flooding in on him again. "I'm already having enough drama with him."

He started across the mat to follow, but Linda stopped him. "What drama? How can we help?"

James stepped forward aggressively. "I should arrest you right now."

Linda looked stunned. "You wouldn't!"

Vincent stared aghast at James's surly features. "Is Invictus really that big of a criminal? Is what he's doing so egregious that you'd arrest someone you helped raise?"

James's anger seemed to falter on his face, almost flicker in and out like a bulb struggling to stay lit. "You broke into your own building."

"I didn't break in, James. I have a code." Vincent wanted to go after Dennis and fidgeted with apprehension.

"What about that lab door you jimmied?" James studied him, as though trying to decide whether or not to stay angry.

"I only did that to distract the security guard watching my bike." Vincent paused. He could see James considering his words with care. "I didn't steal anything, James."

"Then why were you there?"

Vincent hesitated. He knew he had to tell them everything. They were his family, after all, and now that the truth was out they needed to hear it all. But he had to deal with Dennis first.

"I watched how you and dad could turn it on and off all of my life."

"Turn what on and off?"

"The job." Vincent felt his insides tighten up. "You'd go out there and deal with all the stuff going on and then come home and just turn it off."

James nodded. "We have to. If we get too involved, we lose our perspective."

"Or maybe by not getting involved, people lose their humanity," Vincent replied, his heart heavy. "I can't do what you do, James. I thought I could. Mr. Robot here, right? The kid who never showed emotion except the desire to win every martial arts match he ever entered."

Linda stepped closer, her eyes filled with love. "What are you trying to say, Vince?"

"That I'm part of those people out there, and they're part of me. I care about them. I can't just turn it off."

"What's this have to do with the break in?" James asked, mystified.

"I was there to help someone," Vincent admitted. "I did my best to cover my tracks, but I'm sure Chin will figure it out one of these days and then he'll fire me."

Linda gasped.

James looked stunned. "You risked your career, Vincent?"

He nodded.

"Who could be that important?" Linda asked.

Vincent choked up as he saw in his mind's eye Frankie's dirty face and angelic smile. "A little boy."

"Oh, honey." She stepped forward and wrapped her arms around him, which was good because he felt like crying at that moment and tears would not go over well with James.

When she stepped back, Vincent noted James eyeing him more with awe than anger.

"James, I know I owe you both the whole story, and I promise to tell you everything. But right now, I need to find Dennis. He and I... have been miscommunicating a lot these days and he's mad at me and I need to fix it before something terrible happens."

She pulled him into a hug. "We'll fix it together, as a family. Won't we, James?"

Vincent pulled away and faced his surrogate father.

The man was clearly conflicted, his emotions at war with one another. "Vincent, please, I beg you to stop what you're doing."

"We have to finish what we started, James." Vincent replied. "You and dad taught us that." He paused. "You still plan to arrest me?"

James almost deflated. "I could never do that. But we do need to figure this out."

"I'll tell you guys everything, I promise," Vincent asserted, his mind tingling with worry over Dennis. "Soon as I can."

James nodded. "I'll keep Janson off your tail for now until we decide what to do."

"Thanks."

He hurried from the garage without looking back.

Dennis burned with fury as he stalked out of James's front door and started down the street toward his house. He paused to slip on his Nikes before stepping onto the hot asphalt. How dare James belittle him that way and make him feel stupid? He already felt useless enough with Vincent. He didn't need more garbage from James!

A car cruised up the street and stopped him in his tracks, distracting him from his anger.

Demon?

How the hell does he know where I live?

"Yo, Dreamer," Demon called out the rolled down front window of the shiny Mercedes. "You live around here?"

Dennis stopped in front of the car. He was tempted to look back over his shoulder, but didn't. "Just visiting friends."

Demon squinted in the late afternoon sun. "Been cruising this hood hoping to find you. Got lookout duties. You in?"

Dennis's mind raced a moment. He was supposed to be home when Vincent hit the streets…

But he doesn't need me, his anger told him. "Yeah, I'm in."

Before he could change his mind, he popped open the back door and slid in beside Runner, the Japanese kid with the badass manga tattoos. Dennis gave him the chin raise and then Demon gunned the engine and sped off down the street.

Determined to come clean about Franky and Joe and everything he'd experienced, Vincent sprinted across the street and entered the house. The family room was empty.

"Dennis?"

No answer.

Vincent took the stairs two at a time. Dennis's room was empty. A cursory inspection revealed his phone resting on the table beside the computer.

Oh, no!

He picked up the phone and tried to unlock it, but Dennis had changed his password. Vincent's heart sank even lower. They had always allowed each other access to their phones because they had no secrets between them. Now Dennis had locked him out. Why?

Vincent considered his options, suddenly realizing that he didn't know any of Dennis's friends' numbers, not even Jackson or Kenny. His parents had always known his friends' numbers. Dennis's friends, too. While he'd resented it growing up, he now understood the reason why. And he'd never had any real friends anyway, just acquaintances or study buddies. Dennis had been the social one and his parents kept close tabs on all those he interacted with.

Now I'm the parent, Vincent suddenly understood, *and I'm not doing my job.*

"I'm sorry, Mom and Dad," he whispered.

He replaced Dennis's phone next to the computer and left the room.

"Okay, lookout, don't screw up!" Demon snapped when they arrived at their first meeting site at Lake Balboa Park. Demon handed him a phone to text a heads up if trouble showed up. Then he and the others left Dennis in the parked Mercedes and sauntered into the park.

The first deal went smoothly. But as the second buyer approached Demon and his crew, Dennis spotted a police cruiser sliding into a parking space not far from his and he rapidly typed the alert code into the phone. Demon veered away from the buyer. Runner whipped up a Frisbee and they tossed it around like regular park-goers.

Not surprisingly, the cops exited their cruiser and headed his way. A kid in a hot, expensive car like this, even riding shotgun, was always suspicious to police. As the officers approached his window, he eyed them casually. His heart pounded like crazy and he felt sweat break out on his forehead.

Chill, Dennis.

"Nice ride, kid," the taller cop observed as he stopped by the rolled down window. He looked maybe forty.

His partner wandered around toward the back of the car.

"Yours?"

"I wish." Dennis laughed. "My big brother's. He went off with his girl. Told me to wait. They're probably making out somewhere in the park."

The cop chuckled. "I remember those days."

Dennis smiled. "So, you like being a cop?"

The man studied him a moment, sizing him up. "Most of the time."

The other officer circled completely around the car and stood beside his partner.

"You got a name, kid?"

"Well, my mom calls me Dreamer."

"Why?"

"Because I dream big things." He offered his best smile.

The two cops exchanged a look and the tall one chuckled. "You're okay, Dreamer."

"I think so," Dennis replied with a big grin and the cop laughed.

"Don't let your brother damage this ride. It's a beaut." Slapping the side of the car, the cop started back toward his cruiser, the other one following.

Dennis watched them enter their vehicle and take a slow turn around the parking lot, clearly studying the people wandering around. He held his breath as they paused to observe Demon and the others chasing the errant Frisbee. Then the cruiser passed out of the parking lot and vanished down the street.

The phone in Dennis's hand vibrated. He opened the text from Demon: 'Good job, kid.'

He observed Demon and his posse stroll casually toward some picnic tables where the buyer sat staring at his phone. The exchange went off without a hitch.

Flustered and angry over finding out that Vincent was the vigilante, James entered the station at seven-thirty for his assigned briefing with Torres.

Janson had already arrived and the briefing room was jammed with officers of all ranks, mostly patrol officers.

What the…?

"Come in, Detective, and take a seat," Torres barked from a podium situated in front of a large virtual map of Griffith Observatory and the surrounding grounds.

Griffith Observatory?

"We're about to begin."

James took a seat as far from Janson as he could find. He adjusted his tie and focused on that Griffith Observatory map. Numerous lights flashed at roads and exits along the perimeter. He had a bad feeling about this.

"Let's begin, shall we?" Torres announced. His voice sounded like it was coming through a bullhorn. "In conjunction with the Chief and Sergeant Janson—" He pointed to Janson, who smirked at the officers behind him. —"We have devised a plan to lure the Asian vigilante to Griffith Observatory and capture him."

James jumped slightly in his chair, making a scuffing sound as the leg scraped against the floor.

Torres glanced at him irritably. "Was that a comment, Detective?"

"Uh, no, Captain." James knew he had to tread very carefully from this point forward. "Just shifted position." How dare Janson go behind his back?

Torres eyed him a moment longer and then went on to explain his plan. "Since the vigilante seems to favor busting drug dealers, we think this will lure him in. We figure he's listening to our police calls, so we'll trap him at his own game."

As Torres laid out the plan, James grew anxious and fearful.

"The area around the observatory is remote enough should there be any gunfire."

James couldn't let that pass. "Excuse me, Captain, but Invictus doesn't use a gun."

"Maybe not, Detective, but he's pretty damned accurate with that shield of his. If he throws it at one of my men, it's open season on him."

James felt his heart thundering in his chest. There was a real possibility if Vincent was cornered, he'd use the shield. And it was standard protocol to shoot if an officer was physically assaulted in any way. He had to warn Vincent!

As Torres assigned each unit to their roadblock or perimeter location, James found his mind wandering.

I'm forcing you and everyone else to choose between the letter of the law and the spirit of the law.

Vincent's words replayed themselves over and over in his mind. Sure, he'd interfered with police operations on several occasions, but he insisted he'd only been helping a little boy at UCLA and hadn't stolen anything, and he had definitely helped people on the streets. Then James recalled the video of Vincent ripping the hair out of that drug dealer's head, the sheer brutality of it.

Is that the boy I know and love, the one I helped raise? Are his offenses so egregious that he deserves jail time? If you warn him about tonight, aren't you an accessory?

James had never wavered from his duty and believed in law and order above all else.

He's Loy's son, his desperate mind reiterated. *You swore to protect him! Yes, I did, Loy. And I will.*

Once the briefing disbanded, Janson sidled up to James. "Ready to roll, partner?"

James glowered, but not as fiercely as he wanted to. He had to be careful. "Yeah. Gonna hit the john and I'll meet you at the car."

"Right-O, Detective." His whole tone rubbed in the fact that he had Torres's ear on this case.

James didn't give a rat's. He'd never played the kiss-up game before and didn't plan to start now. He exited the briefing room.

In the hall, he bypassed the bathroom as too public and ducked into a janitor's closet. Then he whipped out his phone and speed-dialed Vincent. He heard ringing as he placed the handset to his ear.

"C'mon, Vince, pick up!"

The ringing became Vincent's voicemail: "Hi, this is Vince. Leave a message and I'll return your call. Thanks."

"Vincent," James hissed, keeping his voice low. "Don't go near Griffith Observatory tonight, whatever you hear. It's a trap. We'll talk tomorrow."

He ended the call, breathing heavily. He hoped Vincent would get the message in time.

Pressing his ear against the door, he listened for footsteps outside. Hearing none, he cracked the door open. The corridor was empty. He darted out of the closet and set out to meet Janson.

CHAPTER TWENTY-FOUR

DENNIS, I NEED YOU!

Vincent finally got in touch with Joe as he prepared his meager dinner.

"One of my old customers is letting Franky and me stay for tonight."

That set off alarm bells in Vincent's mind. "He won't expect you or Franky to…." He couldn't even complete the thought in his head, let alone with his mouth.

"No," Joe assured him. "He's doing it to help out. Says he got the idea from 'that Asian guy, the one in the costume.' Guess he got your message."

Vincent shivered. Maybe he *had* gotten the message. But this was still a man who picked up boys on the street for sex. Just the idea made his skin crawl.

"Okay. But if he tries anything, you call me," he ordered. "I will beyond kick his ass if he touches either of you!"

Joe made a sound on the other end. Vincent thought it might be what a grin would sound like if a grin was audible.

"Thanks, Super Hero."

The call ended and Vincent set down his Invictus phone to finish making dinner. His regular phone lay charging upstairs. No one but James and Linda ever called that number anyway, and after what happened this afternoon, he doubted they'd call any time soon.

He attempted to study after dinner, but the longer Dennis was gone, the less he could concentrate. At eight o'clock, he decided to suit up and search for Demon. He considered searching for Dennis, but honestly had no idea where to even begin. But he couldn't just wait around the house. He could cruise around the Valley looking for drug deals and might get lucky enough to find Demon. Or even Dennis out wandering the streets in anger.

Once he slipped on the boots and gloves and picked up the mask, he ducked into Dennis's room. He knew it was irrational because he would've heard something, but in his mind he hoped and prayed he'd find his brother seated before the computer ready to begin their nightly adventures.

But the room was empty and sad-looking, the computer off and Dennis's phone silent. Vincent clicked on the police band scanner in case there was something interesting he could check out.

The scanner squawked with static. Then he heard, "All units in the vicinity of Griffith Observatory. Apparent gang activity. Likely drug sales in progress. Approach with sirens off."

Vincent reached over to turn off the scanner.

Griffith Observatory?

He mulled over the police call. It was an odd place for gang activity, but if drugs were involved, maybe Demon would be, too.

He left the room and grabbed his shield.

As he rode off into the night, his thoughts were on Dennis.

Please be all right…

Griffith Observatory sat on the south-facing slope of Mount Hollywood in Griffith Park. In addition to being a spot to star gaze, the site also afforded a wonderful view of Los Angeles.

Invictus rode up the hill toward the observatory entrance and reflected on all the activities he used to do with Dennis when they were growing up. Sometimes, after he'd gotten his license, he drove them to the observatory and they'd gaze up at the stars, each of them lost within his own thoughts.

As the three huge domes of the observatory came into view, brightly lit and eerily beautiful beneath the summer moonlight, Invictus realized a startling truth – Dennis was his best friend. His only friend.

Dennis, where are you?

He eased to a stop in front of the astronomer's monument - a towering white obelisk with what looked like a metallic rendition of Saturn topping it. He scanned the area around him. The place was deserted. It was Friday night.

Shouldn't the observatory be open? What were the hours?

He glanced at the small digital clock on his motorcycle dash. Nine-fifteen. Something was wrong.

He felt an intense desire to get out of there. His internal alarm shrieked.

That's when bright lights snapped on all around him, big searchlights, like at movie premieres. He froze. Cars roared up from all directions, headlights blinding him along with the searchlights, surrounding him with brightness that would give the sun a run for its money.

A voice bellowed out of the darkness, "You are surrounded, vigilante! Do not move and you won't be hurt!"

Torres!

Did it mean James was there, too?

Why didn't you warn me, James?

With such an instant infusion of brightness, he felt like a mole sticking its head out in broad daylight. Careful to move slowly, he slipped two shuriken from one of his pouches. He squinted against the lights. Without even seeing, he knew that cops crouched behind those lights, likely pointing guns at him. His shield was still attached to the front of the bike. His only hope was to distract them and escape.

He switched the shuriken to his other hand and reached back into another belt pouch for one of his smoke bombs.

"This is your last warning, vigilante!" Torres sounded mad. "Hands in the air now!"

Invictus raised his arms slowly above his head. His vision was still useless and he blinked against the harshness of the lights. But he hoped his sense memory of where the searchlights snapped on was intact.

"Now off the bike! Slow and easy-like!"

Invictus had no intention of getting off the bike. They'd have him for sure. Thinking of Dennis, he offered a silent prayer and flicked his wrist. The first shuriken flew from his hand. Glass shattered, breaking the silence. A searchlight went out. He flicked his wrist again. More glass shattered. A second light died. A hole of darkness filled the circle of light and he crushed the tiny smoke bomb between thumb and forefinger.

Billowing white smoke engulfed him and he made his move. He switched off his headlamp, gunned the engine, and shot toward the black hole.

"Hold your fire!" Torres's voice thundered through the night. "Too much smoke!"

Invictus raced toward that opening of black, the smoke in his eyes adding to the punishing irritation of the lights. He hoped he would not run somebody over!

He barely caught sight of a cop crouched low as he blasted his way between two police cruisers. Then he was past the perimeter of vehicles and shooting down Observatory Road toward Griffith Park.

Since this was obviously a well-planned trap, Torres would have blocked all means of escape, even within the park.

He needed Dennis!

Screeching tires and wobbling headlights from behind told him the chase was on. He tapped his earpiece. "Call Dennis Villanueva!"

He heard the phone ring. And ring. And ring. "This is Dennis. Go for it." Then a beep.

"Dennis, I need you! I'm in Griffith Park, cops everywhere. Call me back!"

He tapped his ear to end the call and scanned the darkened road ahead. On either side of him were steep declines down the mountainside, but no roads. Just hiking trails. He squinted into the darkness ahead. Something glinted in the moonlight – a windshield.

Crap!

He slowed down to scan the slope on his right side. Steep. But then, he was at a high elevation. In a moment of blind panic, he pictured himself pitching forward, losing control, and toppling down the mountain.

But he had no choice. He gunned the engine and rode through an opening in the barrier. A sudden drop—like a steep waterslide he'd done once at Raging Waters—almost sent his stomach into his throat as the bike tilted at a forty-five degree angle and barreled down the mountain.

His teeth rattled as he fought to keep the bike steady.

Bump! *Thump*!

His tires spun in loose dirt, causing the bike to skid.

The muscles in his arms burned.

His hands gripped the controls with desperate intensity as he fought to keep the bike upright.

Only the moon lit his way, and it provided meager light at best. He switched his headlight back on. Screw it if the light gave him away! He'd die without it. The light revealed a steep decline made up of rocky, brushy terrain interspersed with trees. Hopefully, at the bottom, he'd find the park and a way out. But there was no way he could use his GPS under these conditions.

He needed Dennis!

Torres had ordered all units in pursuit. Relieved that Vincent hadn't been shot, James leaped behind the wheel and Janson clambered into the passenger seat.

James finally understood what it meant to be trapped between a rock and a hard place. He had to follow orders. But what if something happened to Vincent in the process? He'd never forgive himself. And Linda wouldn't forgive him either.

As James slammed the sedan into gear and took off, Janson unholstered his gun and lowered the window.

"The hell, Janson?"

He kept his eyes on the road. They were still watering from Vincent's damned smoke bomb!

"You heard the captain," Janson said in his usual know-it-all tone. "Under no circumstances let the vigilante escape."

James glanced over a second. "We will not shoot an unarmed suspect, Sergeant."

"Just prepared, Stevens," Janson shot back as James focused on the dark road ahead. "In case he throws that shield."

James fought to control his pounding heart.

Please don't do anything stupid, Vincent!

The radio crackled. Torres voice slammed into the car like a grenade: "All units. Suspect has left the road and heading down the mountainside. Regroup in the park below. All park units look alive. Do not let him slip past you!"

Even as he floored the accelerator, James silently hoped Vincent knew a way out.

Dorothy Ellis sat at her computer inviting people to join her Invictus Facebook group. She'd named the group "Holding Out for A Hero" after an old song she'd always loved. The title fit the theme – this city needed Invictus and she determined to generate as much support for him as possible.

Her police scanner sat beside her computer in the living room of her apartment. She had the volume down low, but the word "vigilante" caught her ear and she cranked up the sound.

"Try to keep him contained within the park. If he escapes, Operation Overpass will go into effect."

Oh, no…

She sent out a group message that Invictus was in trouble.

Invictus thought he understood what being inside of a cement mixer must feel like. He bumped and skidded and slid from side to side as he made his precarious way down the mountainside. He wanted to try Dennis again, but didn't dare remove one hand from his handlebars to tap the Bluetooth. And he'd sound like he was stuttering if he did make contact.

His forearms throbbed from the strength needed to keep the bike steady. Ahead in the moonlit darkness, he discerned a flat expanse of grass and knew the park was finally within reach. But even there, which direction should he go? He'd totally lost his bearings and had no idea where the road was, or even the bike paths. He couldn't hear any pursuit so the road must be far behind him. But what lay ahead?

Dennis, where are you?

Dennis served as lookout on eight deals before Demon drove him home. While Dennis felt guilty participating in these crimes, he had learned some important information about how the group operated. Each deal went down smoothly. He noted that, other than Demon and his boys sporting the shaved heads and rat-tails, they all dressed preppy style, which Dennis surmised they'd adopted for the Valley because they were dealing with more rich kids than might have been the case downtown.

After the final deal, which took place way out in West Hills, Demon complimented Dennis. There had been two other instances of police cruising past their locations and both times Dennis had alerted Demon ahead of time so the deal could be delayed until the cops moved on.

"You did good, Dreamer," Demon told him as he and the others gathered around the car. "Especially the way you handled those cops in Balboa. You might fit in, after all." He snapped his fingers.

Runner peeled off around back and popped the trunk. He returned a moment later with a pair of battery-powered hair trimmers.

"You're not all in till we see you fight," Demon explained. "But you earned the hair cut."

He nodded at Runner, who stepped forward and pulled open the door.

Dennis froze. He didn't want his hair to match theirs. He'd been growing it out since the funeral. It was already brushing past his shirt collar and he'd come to love how he looked.

But if he refused, he might lose all chance to find out where the drugs were made and who called the shots. So he forced a smile to his face.

"Go for it."

When it was done, he felt naked and exposed, as though everyone would know he'd joined a group of drug dealers. So lost was he in thought that he didn't realize Demon had stopped in front of James's house.

"Figured I'd drop you close to home."

Dennis shuddered. "Thanks, man." He stepped from the car and closed the back door.

"Later," Demon said through the open window, and then with squealing tires tore off down the street.

With no idea of the time, Dennis crossed the street and entered his house.

He heard his ringtone as he started up the stairs. A sudden premonition washed over him, almost like that night his parents were killed. He took the stairs two at a time and burst into his room. Leaping over his piles of clothes, he grabbed for the phone and saw the number.

"Oh, hell…."

Invictus had survived the mountain, but now he shot across a large expanse of dirt in near-total darkness with no idea where he was going except that he was heading east. He tapped his earpiece again, hoping and praying Dennis would finally pick up. The phone rang. And rang. And rang. And then… someone answered!

"Dennis, are you there?"

"Yeah, Vince," came Dennis's out-of-breath response. "What's wrong?"

"Hurry, get into the police mainframe. Griffith Park. They have me trapped. Roadblocks and cops everywhere. I need to get out!"

"Okay. Computer's starting. Turn on your GPS."

"It's on. Hurry!"

Up ahead in the dark he saw the Greek Theatre looming large. There should be a show going on in there, his brain told him. There should be people. But it was dark and quiet and empty. The cops planned all this, he realized. They made sure no one would be around to help him escape, or get hurt if they should take shots at him.

Which meant they planned on shooting, he understood with a sick feeling in the pit of his stomach. How could they want him that badly? Was what he was doing such an egregious violation of law that he should be shot for it? He supposed it must be. Shaking up the status quo always angered those in power.

His mind randomly replayed police shootings he'd seen on the news in which the suspect hadn't been armed or done anything violent. His dad and James had shared plenty of horror stories about police training tactics and the "shoot first" mentality of officers today. Yes, he understood. They would likely shoot him if they had the chance.

Dennis practically jumped up and down in his chair as the computer took its sweet time booting up. He glanced at the time on his phone. Almost nine-forty.

Vincent's in trouble and I should've been here!

His desktop finally active, Dennis clicked on the link to the police mainframe. Once open, he typed in Griffith Park and a file popped up called "Target: Vigilante." A map of the park sat in one corner of his screen. He clicked it to enlarge.

"Holy crap!"

The park was littered with red dots, each indicating a police vehicle. It looked like a freakin' Christmas tree! Some dots were moving along Vermont Canyon Road, heading for the Greek Theatre. His GPS tracking of Vincent superimposed him as a green dot about to intersect the oncoming red ones.

He snatched up his phone. "Vince!"

"Yeah?"

Invictus passed the sad and silent Greek Theatre. A large paved road was about to cross his path. He spotted wavering lights some distance to his right.

"Cross over that road, go through the trees and cross another road. Then jet across the golf course!" Dennis shouted into his ear. "Cops are almost on you!"

Invictus didn't need Dennis to tell him that. He twisted the throttle and revved the engine. To his right bright headlights bore down on him like laser beams. With a squeal of tires he turned slightly left and bolted across the road into another copse of trees. He heard brakes screeching, but didn't dare turn back to see if they were pursuing. Would they destroy a perfectly good golf course just to get him?

A gunned engine not far behind gave him his answer. He poured on the speed, keeping low in his seat in case of random gunfire. He zigzagged between the trees until he saw the second road Dennis mentioned. To his left, he spotted a massive roadblock. Headlights flicked on, nearly blinding him. He sailed past the waiting cops onto the well-trimmed grass of the golf course, and heard cars in hot pursuit. Lights flitted in and out of his peripheral vision and confirmed their presence.

He'd never been on a golf course in his life and had no idea what to expect except grass and putting greens.

And sand traps.

Crap!

He swung the bike a hard left to avoid pitching headlong into the first sand trap.

Damn, that came out of nowhere!

The light from his headlamp made the course look dark and deadly.

"Any suggestions, Dennis?" He had to shout against the wind and his roaring engine.

"I'm working on it," Dennis answered in his ear. He sounded harried. "Keep heading east. Stay on the course. Some cops are trailing you, but most of them are on the roads all around it."

Invictus felt a brief moment of resignation.

Just give it up and turn yourself in.

Then Franky's face intruded.

And Joe's.

And the woman with the baby.

No!

Giving up would be selfish.

He focused on avoiding traps and other obstacles, and hoped he wasn't doing too much damage to the golf course.

CHAPTER TWENTY-FIVE

HE CAN'T POSSIBLY GET AWAY

James had to take the long way around the golf course because of the steep mountainside Invictus had used. He was sweating beneath his jacket and tie. Never before had he been this panicked during a pursuit. His heart pounded with dread that one of Torres' men would get trigger-happy and shoot Vincent.

Disgusted with Janson, he snorted. "Great plan you cooked up, *partner*!" He practically sneered on that last word. "Without telling me, I might add."

Janson had his gun ready and leaned forward in his seat to squint into the darkness ahead. "I had the idea and happened to share it with the captain. He loved it."

James fought his temper. "And both of you forgot this big-ass golf course?"

Janson chuckled. "Oh, no. We have men stationed everywhere, with nets, I might add."

James's blood ran cold. "Nets?"

"Yep. *Big* nets. Black, hard to see. But big enough to capture a guy on a motorcycle."

James glanced over to see his partner grinning like he'd just won the lottery.

"We'll get the SOB, Stevens."

James focused on his driving.

Invictus plowed through the darkness, rising and falling as he traversed the fairways and dodged the sand traps.

"What's up ahead?"

"Not good, Vince," Dennis responded. "Cop cars are all over the course. They probably have their lights off so you can't see them. You're coming up on one pair in about a hundred yards."

Invictus squinted ahead in the black. His headlight wasn't strong enough to project more than three hundred feet. Why two cars with their lights off?

"How much space is between the two cars?" he called into the driving wind.

There was a pause. "Twenty-five. Why?"

"Why that distance?" Invictus called out, not expecting an answer.

"I don't know," Dennis called back. "But you can get between them and continue toward North Commonwealth Avenue. Once you're there, I think I can get you out of danger."

"Okay."

His eyes having adjusted to the darkness, Invictus stiffened as he made out what was dead ahead. A net. His lamplight glinted momentarily over a huge, black net directly in his path.

That's why the cars are spread apart!

"Oh, crap...."

"What?"

"Hold on."

Knowing he had seconds to formulate a plan, Invictus scanned the area in front of the net. He spotted a bench that golfers must use to sit on while awaiting their next turn. It sat at ninety-degrees to the rapidly approaching net. And it was his only hope.

Fumbling in one pouch, he whipped out the small airsoft pistol. Unlike at the school takeover, this one was loaded with corrosive, thermite-based pellets. He took quick aim and fired at the closest legs of the bench.

Bam! Bam!

With a slight sizzle sound, that side of the bench dropped to the grass, creating a narrow, but acceptable launching ramp. Slipping the pistol back into his pouch, he revved the engine and aimed right for it.

"I'm dead," he mumbled.

"What was that?" he heard in his ear.

"I said, hold on."

He gripped the handles with knuckle-whitening intensity and leaned down even more to lessen wind resistance. The bench loomed before him, closer and closer and then... with a stomach-dropping rush he was up the ramp and airborne.

The net flashed beneath his headlamp as he rose higher into the air. He barely cleared it by an inch or two. His stomach remained in his throat as the bike wobbled against the wind and plummeted downward. He so wanted to close his eyes!

The front wheel hit the ground hard, seconds before the back, and nearly pitched him forward over the windscreen. He grunted with pain, expelling the air from his lungs.

"Vincent?"

Invictus's butt had risen into the air and he felt a panicked sensation that he was about to fly off the bike. His breathing stopped in that split second until he felt the seat once more planted firmly against his buttocks. But the bike wobbled furiously and he fought with all his strength to keep it upright.

"Vince, are you all right?"

He heard from behind, "He got over the net," as he regained control of the bike and raced across another fairway.

"Vince, what's going on out there?"

Dennis sounded panicked.

Not as panicked as me, he thought. His heart still raced. "Just a minor heart attack."

"Huh?"

"Never mind. Where to now?"

"Stay on the golf course," Dennis called into his ear. "Keep going east until–"

The call went dead.

"Crap!" Invictus narrowly avoided pitching into yet another sand trap as he reached up to redial. The trap had risen out of the darkness like a sea monster. He slapped his upraised hand back to the handlebar and gripped both securely. His front wheel slid down into the sand, but a quick lurch to his right snapped it up and back onto the fairway. He allowed himself to breathe again. Then he tapped the earpiece.

The phone rang. And rang. And rang.

"C'mon, Dennis!" Then Dennis's voicemail came on. When he heard the beep, Invictus hissed, "Call me back! Hurry!"

He ended the call and pressed forward into the darkness. He had no idea if he was headed toward freedom or incarceration.

Dennis stared at the dark screen on his phone and cursed. Dead battery! He shoved papers and comics off his desk in desperation.

"Come on, I know it's here somewhere!"

But his charge cord was nowhere to be found.

And Vincent needed him.

James raced down Commonwealth Canyon Drive, circumventing the golf course, and heard through the radio, "Suspect just jumped the net, headed toward Commonwealth."

"Roger that," came Torres's booming voice. "All units, Phase Two is in effect. Repeat, we are at Phase Two."

Janson picked up the mic. "Got it, Cap."

James glanced over. "Phase Two?"

"I told you we had everything covered," Janson replied, that smugness back in his voice. He clicked a switch on the mic. "All units, this is Sergeant Janson. Allow suspect access to Commonwealth Avenue. Make sure he turns onto Los Feliz. Janson out."

Now James felt genuine panic. What was going on here?

"Los Feliz?"

"Drive, Detective," Janson ordered, that haughty air infuriating James. "We need to catch up to the vigilante on Commonwealth."

"Now just—"

"Like I told the captain, he can't possibly get away. I want to be there for the capture. Don't you?"

James grunted and floored the accelerator.

Invictus spotted another net and numerous police cruisers as he roared across the golf course, but no one made an effort to engage or pursue him. That lack of action raised alarm bells in his mind. He had called Dennis back three more times and got the voicemail every time.

What could he be doing?

A large road loomed dead ahead. Glancing at the small GPS screen mounted to bike dash, he saw it was Commonwealth and ran north-south. There would be roadblocks in both directions. He had in his mind to race across it into the residential district beyond, but as he neared the road, the darkness lit up with flashing red lights to his north and more straight ahead. Cops! He glanced to his left and spotted a full roadblock barring all vehicle passage in a northbound direction. Straight ahead, his path was blocked by more police cars with their lights flashing. He made out shapes of men crouched around their vehicles pointing weapons at him.

With only one option, he veered sharply to the right the second he hit the pavement, and roared down the empty street. They obviously wanted him headed in this direction so there had to be a trap someplace up ahead. He decided he would veer left or right and get off the road the first chance he got.

But that chance never materialized. Police cars lined both sides of Commonwealth wherever there was a road or path he could take. They wanted him to stay on Commonwealth.

That couldn't be good!

Dennis tore his room apart. It had previously looked like a junkyard. Now it resembled a war zone.

Nothing!

Where the hell is my cable?

Downstairs! He'd had it downstairs charging in the kitchen, hadn't he?

He burst from his room and flew down the stairs to the kitchen. Flipping on the lights, he scanned all the outlets along the countertop. Nothing!

Damn Vincent! He must've found it and put it away somewhere!

He leapt for the first drawer and yanked it open.

Gotta be here somewhere!

Invictus felt his stomach twisted into knots, and his heart hammered with dread.

They're gonna get you, his frantic brain kept shouting. *You're finished!*

But still he sped forward, determined to escape at all costs.

If I get arrested, what will happen to Dennis?

With that thought uppermost in his mind, he scanned the GPS. Los Feliz

Blvd lay dead ahead. It was a major thoroughfare. While he didn't want to endanger any drivers, he hoped he could get lost amidst the traffic there.

Wait a minute! Where were the cars along Commonwealth?

Oh, no…

Too late he realized the situation. Los Feliz was right in front of him, but there were no cars moving in either direction—just an empty intersection with flashing police lights on the opposite side and to his right.

They want me to go left, he thought as he swung into a left turn onto the eerily empty Los Feliz. He spotted people along the sidewalks watching the chase. Lots of people. And then he heard the cars behind and realized he was under pursuit.

Why now?

He glanced back to see a black sedan turn the corner off Commonwealth and several black and whites joining it. They bore down on him with calm deliberation.

He revved the throttle, squeezing hard, hoping to coax just a bit more speed out of the bike. As though knowing his life depended on it, the motorcycle responded. He shot forward, eyes scanning the GPS screen as best he could. A Golden State Freeway overpass lay dead ahead.

And then he got it!

They're gonna trap me on the overpass!

The six-lane Los Feliz Boulevard looked like something out of an apocalyptic movie with its absence of cars, but every side street flashed red as waiting police cruisers blocked his escape. They wanted him on this street. And they wanted him on that overpass!

Traffic noise rose into the night as he rapidly approached the overpass and the heavily trafficked freeway below. He glanced back. The pursuing cars were in no hurry, since he had nowhere to go. They hung back and cruised slowly in pursuit. He was sure the sedan belonged to James.

James desperately wanted to swing the car sideways and block the others from access to Vincent, but he couldn't do that. It would be dangerous and put him on the wrong side of the law. Vincent had broken the law. And this was the consequence.

But I can't let anything happen to him!

His heart thumped with dread. Even when facing down an armed suspect, he'd never been so afraid.

Vincent was going to be caught. James knew that. He'd figured out the plan and there was no way Vincent could get off that overpass. He had to hand it to Janson, the plan was well thought out and executed. He had no idea how Torres had cleared Los Feliz of traffic, but the plan was working perfectly.

He glanced over and saw Janson with his head and arm out the window, gun poised and ready.

Please, Vincent, don't throw that shield!

Invictus spotted the roadblock at the opposite side of the overpass long before he even arrived at the freeway. Several cars, lights flashing, blockaded the road. Cops with guns drawn crouched beside their vehicles. They made no movements. The only sounds were made by heavy traffic below.

Invictus slowed his bike and rolled out onto the overpass. Over the low retaining wall, he saw the cars and trucks rushing past beneath him. The eerie silence of Los Feliz had given way to a cacophony of noise.

He noted a large number of open-bed trucks passing beneath him in the southbound lanes. He glanced to his right and observed the flashing lights of the sedan and police cruisers bearing down on him. Again, they moved methodically. Why not? There was nowhere he could go.

Or was there?

Another of those open bed trucks caught his eye as it passed beneath him.

Squinting in the darkness, he was sure he saw the truck bed filled with fruit of some kind; something round, anyway, just piled in there with no cover, no boxes, no anything.

Fruit was soft.

And soft might just work.

He whipped his head around and spotted another of those fruit transport trucks approaching in a southbound direction. It was crazy, but it was all he had.

Fumbling in his pouch, he yanked out the air gun again and popped in four pellets. He glanced back. The truck was getting close. He glanced side to side. The cops on the opposite side remained in place. The ones on his side of the pass kept coming.

It was now or never.

He raised the pistol and took aim at the base of the concrete retaining wall. He fired twice.

Bam! Bam!

The pellets struck with a flash and a sizzle as the corrosive chemical ate away at the concrete.

He fired two more times half way up.

Bam! Bam!

More sizzling, more weakening concrete.

He replaced the gun and pulled out his small grapple. He'd lose this for sure and it might get traced back to him, but he had no choice. He threw the grapple at the wall. It snagged itself over the top and caught. Releasing the handlebars of the idling bike and planting one foot firmly against the asphalt, he gripped the rope with both hands and tugged it toward him.

"What the hell's he doing?" Janson muttered, head still out the window.

James leaned forward in his seat, straining to make out what Vincent was doing. There were four flashes, and then Vincent threw something at the top of the barrier. He pulled and a section of the barrier crumpled inward, scattering chunks of concrete all over the overpass.

A section large enough for a small motorcycle to pass through.

Oh, hell, no!

He pressed on the horn in panic.

As the section of wall tumbled inward and concrete chunks spread out on the ground before him, a honking horn drew his eye to the oncoming police. Was that James driving? Why was he honking?

No time to wonder. He glanced over his shoulder. The fruit truck was almost beneath the overpass.

Never one for impulsivity, he knew if he hesitated he'd be dead or captured. This way, he might only be dead.

Go for it!

He gunned his engine and shot toward the opening. All he could think of was

Dennis alone without him as his wheels left the asphalt of the overpass and the bike sailed out over empty space.

His stomach flew into his throat. He felt the air whoosh up around him. He dropped toward the speeding cars at an alarming rate. He snapped off the engine.

The fruit truck emerged from beneath the overpass as he fought to keep the bike from twisting in midair. He held his breath. The world around him seemed to vanish. The fruit-filled truck loomed closer. His terrified mind swirled with images from those crazy-ass James Bond movies he used to watch with his dad. He tried to breathe, but his free-fall sucked the air from his lungs. The truck bed grew larger and larger beneath him. He snapped his eyes shut.

Splat!

He sank beneath a sea of red.

James gagged and slammed on the brakes. The black and whites behind him screeched to a halt. Janson leaped from the car and sprinted toward the shattered retaining wall. James whipped off his seatbelt, jumped out and followed.

Certain he would see his best friend's son splattered all over the pavement, he gripped the retaining wall and looked down. The traffic moved along with ease. There was no one on the pavement. No motorcycle. No… nothing.

The hell?

Janson pulled his head back and eyed James with suspicion, as though Invictus escaping was his fault.

"How the hell did he get away?"

James shrugged, his heart still pounding.

"Janson, do you have him?" Torres's voice called out over the car radio.

With a disgusted sigh, Janson holstered his weapon and strode back to the car. He snatched up the microphone and put it to his pursed lips. "I don't know how, sir, but… he escaped."

Torres cursed. "He can't possibly get away, huh?" His words were laced with derision.

Janson returned the mic to its cradle.

James stared at the busy freeway below and finally allowed himself to breathe.

CHAPTER TWENTY-SIX

CAT WON'T LET YOU, WILL SHE?

INVICTUS EXPERIENCED A PANICKED SENSATION of drowning. He'd had the foresight to shut off the engine while the bike was in midair so it wouldn't plow forward and slam him into the back of the cab, but the sudden sensation of claustrophobia overwhelmed him. His heart palpitated with wild abandon. Tomatoes crushed and squirted all around him. Juice poured into his eyes and up his nose. His breathing hitched and sputtered.

The bike wheels slammed down onto the bottom of the truck bed and he fought to keep it upright. His momentum pressed him forward and the wheel banged hard into the front wall, but the thousands of tomatoes kept the bike from tipping. He planted one foot on the bed floor, his heart hammering and his breathing erratic.

In those first few seconds of blind terror, he thought his head would remain below the tomatoes and he'd suffocate. But then he realized he'd crouched low in the seat for safety purposes. He sat up straight and his head broke the surface.

Blessed warm air filled his lungs. His heart rate slowed as he realized he wasn't going to die. He glanced back over his shoulder, but the overpass had receded into darkness. Had the cops gotten the plate number of this truck? Would they be waiting at the drop-off point? The driver must've heard him slam into the bed.

I have to get out of here!

He could barely move with so many pounds of tomatoes crushing in on him from all sides. Even if he could turn the bike around, he'd have to get the back of the truck bed open so he could escape, and he couldn't make any such attempt until the truck exited the freeway.

Damn!

His frustration mounted as the truck continued at a high speed with no signs of slowing. Where was it going?

He thought about Dennis. What had happened? Had Dennis hung up on him in his time of need?

Is he that mad at me?

That scenario didn't seem likely. Dennis was too good to want anyone hurt if he could prevent it. So what happened?

He froze with dread. The irrational thought that someone had broken in and hurt Dennis filled his heart and soul like lead. Forcing his arm back up to his head, he pushed tomatoes out of the way and tapped the earpiece once again. The redial option kicked in and Dennis's phone rang. And rang. And rang. Then the voicemail came on again. Disgusted, he ended the call.

He scanned the passing cars and surrounding area as the truck transitioned from the Golden State Freeway onto the 110 toward Los Angeles. He observed the bright lights of downtown L.A. before his driver exited onto the 101 Freeway heading southbound.

Where is he going?

Glancing back, he saw no sign of police pursuit, so hopefully they'd failed to get the truck's plates. That might be his only break of the night.

The truck finally exited the 101 onto surface streets and headed into the downtown warehouse district. Traffic diminished and he observed other trucks headed in the same direction. They peeled off onto different streets, apparently making deliveries. The open-bed trucks he'd seen on the freeway were lined up to enter the receiving dock of a huge processing plant just ahead. His truck fell into line behind them. Lighting was meager, but as he neared the entrance, he spotted someone with a clipboard at the front of the line checking off each truck as it entered the lot.

Oh, hell…

The driver had to know something fell into his truck and would be sure to alert the man with the clipboard.

He was trapped.

After several anxious minutes, his truck finally reached the checkpoint. He heard laughter from the man with the clipboard and figured his driver must've said something funny.

Then, to his shock, the clipboard holder waved him through.

Invictus glanced around as the truck entered the largest parking lot he'd ever seen. The driver pulled to the most secluded corner of the lot, well away from the loading bays where the others were backing in to deposit their cargo.

The truck screeched slowly to a stop. Then the cab door popped open and the driver dropped to the asphalt. Invictus pulled his head down so he wouldn't be seen. Tomatoes surrounded his face. He kept his nose tilted above the fruit to get air, but kept the rest of his head hidden.

Muffled clanging sounds came to his ears. Hearing beneath a load of tomatoes was almost like being underwater, but he could tell the driver was unlatching the back of the truck. He heard locks released and then creaking as the rear door was lowered to the ground.

Almost like one of those comedy movies where someone opens a closet and tons of stuff tumbles out, the tomatoes *whooshed* past him in waves, rolling out the back of the truck like draining water. Once his head and shoulders were free, he turned to watch the river of fruit pour into an open vat set below ground level. The tomato tsunami continued, accompanied by clanging and rolling sounds and hollow thudding as they poured down into the underground vat. Within seconds, only smashed and broken tomatoes lay piled around the wheels of his motorcycle. The driver stood just outside the truck watching his load slide into the hole, and then grinned at Invictus as though he'd just hit the jackpot.

Not sure what to expect, Invictus used the space once filled by tomatoes to ease his bike around. After several three point turns, he was able to face toward the rear of the truck and the silent driver.

With the last of the tomatoes rolling their way into the open pit, the driver reached out and pressed a button attached to a panel. The pit sealed itself up with metal plates.

It was now or never.

"Uh, hi," Invictus offered lamely.

"Well, how do, young hero?" The driver wore a dark flannel shirt and jeans and looked middle-aged, from what was visible in the shadowy darkness.

"You're probably wondering why I'm in your truck, huh?"

The man laughed. It was a hearty, happy laugh, which confused Invictus. "Got me a CB radio. Heard about the whole police chase. 'Sides, I saw you fly off that overpass and land in my truck like you was Evel Knievel!"

Invictus sat unmoving on his bike, overwhelmed with confusion. He had no idea who Evel Knievel was and he didn't understand why the man helped him escape.

"Why didn't you radio the cops that you had me?"

"Hero, you are the most kickass thing to happen to this state in forever. My kids'd kill me if I turned you in."

Flabbergasted, Invictus felt his breathing stop for a split second. Then the man's words sunk in and he grinned.

"I don't know what to say except thanks."

"Thanks'll do it."

Invictus observed the destroyed tomatoes around his wheels. "But I ruined your cargo."

"Don't sweat it, kid." He offered a casual wave of his hand. "Happens sometimes. That's why we have this vat. Turns the ruined fruit into juice."

Invictus wanted to laugh, but held himself in check. "May I know your name, sir?"

"Conner Martin."

"Thank you again, Conner Martin. If there's anything I can ever do for you, let me know."

"Just keep doing what you're doing. My kids and their friends, they need good role models."

Invictus felt a rush of emotion fill him. "They certainly have a good one in you, sir. And I'll keep doing what I can."

"That'll do. Now you best clear on out before anyone sees you." Mr. Martin chuckled. "You kinda need to clean up, too."

Invictus laughed. "I sure do. Thanks again."

He turned the key, twisted the choke and then the throttle. The motorcycle spluttered to life, expelling chunks of tomato from itself like the belching of smoke. He eased it down the ramp into the parking lot, and circled around to eye Mr. Martin. The man had one hand raised and pointed at an open back gate. Invictus raised a hand in farewell and then roared off in the indicated direction.

Demon cruised through the downtown streets bumping some tunes and relishing a good day's work. His foot soldiers sat in back rapping to the beat and chattering on about how chill "that Dreamer kid is. Best lookout we had in a long minute."

Demon had to admit the kid had eyes like an eagle. Easily got them out of several dangerous situations today. The Mistress had been right about him, like always.

He spotted something through the windshield that set his heart to pounding. He pressed the "Off" button to the sound system and eased up on the accelerator. From the back seat he heard, "Hey, Demon, what's–"

"Silence!"

He stared through the windshield at a motorcycle parked off the street, at the corner of an alley. And bent over the engine was the one person he hated more than anyone – the Hero!

He rolled forward a few more yards and stopped the car. His breathing sped up and his blood pounded with rage. Z's battered face and ravaged hair played out in his infuriated mind.

"Uh, Demon?"

That was Panda. Big. Looked fat, but faster than lightning when aroused. Demon understood his unspoken message. The Mistress could see and hear everything. She forbad him engaging the Hero. But there was Z. Didn't matter who threw the knife. The Hero was responsible.

Dare I disobey The Mistress? She would kill anyone else who did, but would she kill me?

He recalled her eyes, the purse of her lips as she watched video images of the Hero in action. Doubts filled him.

He forced himself to calm down. She promised him he'd have his turn at the Hero and she had never lied to him. Better to play it her way. He'd just started the engine when the Hero glanced up from his bike and stared straight at him.

Demon knew he wasn't visible through the windshield tint, especially beneath the streetlights, but the Hero must've recognized the car because he leapt up and snatched the shield off the front of his motorcycle.

With no other choice, Demon floored the accelerator and zoomed straight at his enemy. Tires squealed and the twin exhaust roared as the Mercedes shot forward like a rocket.

The Hero flung the shield. Demon tried to swerve, but the shield struck his windshield with a loud crack, imploding it and showering the entire interior with pebbled shards of glass. Demon closed his eyes to protect them and the car veered onto the sidewalk, sideswiped a mailbox, and then struck a light post a glancing blow before he was able to brake to a stop.

He slammed the gearshift into park and leaped from the car, his soldiers right behind him. They had their weapons raised, but the Hero stood before them with his damnable shield back in hand!

Demon stared long and hard at his enemy. Then he noticed the Hero covered in red juice of some kind, and the sight amused him.

"Have some trouble with ketchup, Hero?" He sniggered, and the other two chuckled behind him.

The Hero stood his ground. "Why'd you kill that Asian guy, Demon? Wasn't he one of yours?"

"He was an interloper," Demon answered. "Trying to cut in on my turf. Had to send a warning to the other wannabes." Then a thought occurred to him. "Was he a friend of yours? I hope so."

The Hero noticeably flinched, and Demon knew he was right. There was a connection.

"He was just a guy who needed some money. He didn't deserve to die."

Demon knew he was lying. "Anyone who messes with me dies, Hero."

"Including me?"

"Especially you."

The Hero shifted the shield slightly, but kept it in front. "Then let's do it. I've had a bad night and I need some ass to kick!"

Demon froze, fighting another upsurge of anger. His fists clenched and unclenched. He wanted this. He wanted it bad!

Panda slithered up beside him and pointed at his chest. Demon understood. The camera. He had no choice but to back down. Jaw clenched, he mumbled, "Not tonight, Hero."

"Why not?" The Hero sounded confused. He paused a moment. "Cat won't let you, will she?"

Demon flinched. He knew about The Mistress! For the first time since he was a child, Demon was unsure what to do. He snapped his fingers. Panda and Runner eased behind him. He heard the car doors open and close.

He mad-dogged the Hero. "We *will* get down, Hero. That's a promise."

He backed toward the open driver's door.

"But only one of us will get back up."

He jumped behind the wheel and pressed the start button. The Hero started forward. Demon snatched his gun off the passenger seat and fired out the shattered windshield.

Pop! Pop! Pop! Pop!

The Hero did a tuck and roll behind his shield and crouched low as bullets struck the shield, the pavement, the building behind him.

Demon floored the accelerator and stopped shooting. Tossing the gun aside, he gripped the wheel as the car ripped out into the street. Regaining control, he roared past the crouching Hero and sped off down the street.

Invictus watched the black Mercedes careen around the corner and vanish from sight.

Damn!

He rose awkwardly to his feet. The sudden tuck and roll had been slightly off. His right ankle and shoulder throbbed with pain. He lifted the shield and limped back to his motorcycle.

So it had been Demon directing the alley fight he'd busted up a few weeks back. He recognized him, and the rattail he sported. Picturing Z's torn and bloody hair in his hand sent shivers up his spine. Obviously, the hairstyle was a symbol of Cat's organization.

I almost had him!

But at least it sounded like Demon wasn't after Joe or Franky. That part relieved his mind.

Frustrated, he bent to tinker with the throttle. The bike had stalled several times since leaving the food processing plant and he'd finally had to pull over.

He turned the key and twisted the throttle forward. The engine sputtered to life and them hummed normally, as though nothing untoward had occurred. Shaking his head in amazement, he refitted his shield to the front before mounting the bike and resuming his journey home.

With the wind in his face, he calmed down and considered his encounter with Demon. His comment about Cat had been a wild guess, but Demon's reaction proved it was the right one. This Cat, whoever she was, wanted him alive. Why?

Then another image pounded through his fired up brain – Demon's partner pointing discreetly at Demon's chest. Had there been a glint of metal beneath the streetlight?

There had been!

He's wearing a camera!

Another flurry of questions assailed him. Was Cat that paranoid about betrayal or disobedience? Was she a control freak who had to be in on the action no matter what? Or maybe she just got off on watching her foot soldiers deal drugs and kill people who got in their way.

That thought sent a painful stab into his heart. Even though he'd never met Samuel, the young man's death was his responsibility and he'd have to live with it for the rest of his life.

He felt overwhelmed. The only person he had to confide in was Dennis, except a wall had arisen between them, a wall he'd partially built. But Dennis wasn't communicating either. Unless they could get back to how they were before, when they talked freely about everything, he feared something tragic would happen. That premonition of doom impelled him to increase his speed.

He needed to get home.

CHAPTER TWENTY-SEVEN
WITHOUT ME, YOU'RE NOTHING

By the time he entered the kitchen from the garage, Vincent's shoulder throbbed and he sagged with exhaustion. Then he froze. A fully clothed Dennis sat at the table, his head down, fast asleep. The silent police scanner rested beside him. Every drawer hung open. Items were tossed haphazardly around the floor and all over the countertops. The kitchen looked like a tornado had blown through it.

Vincent stepped forward and placed a hand on his brother's shoulder. He noted the beanie covering Dennis's head and thought it odd. Dennis sat up in startled fright and raised his fists defensively.

Vincent jumped back. "Whoa, bro, it's me."

Dennis blinked uncertainly and then seemed to jolt himself into awareness. "Thank God you're okay!"

He leaped up and threw his arms around Vincent, startling him. But Vincent didn't return the hug. He wanted an explanation.

Dennis must've sensed his diffidence because he pulled away. He eyed the sticky juice coating his arms, and then looked at the floor in embarrassment. "My battery died. I couldn't find the charge cord."

Vincent eyed him a moment before glancing around the kitchen. The cupboards were closed. He strode to the one nearest the fridge and pulled it open. Within were spices and condiments and other additives for cooking. A coiled white phone cord lay just inside, easily visible to anyone who opened the door. He snatched it up in one gloved hand and faced Dennis.

"It was hanging out of the couch cushion when I got home," he explained. "I put it there because I knew you'd find it when you made dinner."

Dennis's mouth hung open. Then he lowered his eyes again. "I got home late. Didn't make dinner."

Vincent stared at him. His anger simmered. He struggled to control it.

Dennis raised his head slightly. "Uh, what happened? You're, like, covered in… something."

"I had to jump off a freeway overpass into a moving tomato truck," Vincent replied tightly. "And I had to damage the overpass to do it. They'll charge me with destruction of public property on top of everything else."

Dennis's eyes widened, but he said nothing.

"Where were you?"

Dennis stiffened. "Out."

Vincent squeezed the mask between the fingers of his right hand. "Out? I almost died tonight, Dennis!"

He knew his voice had risen, and fought to control it.

Breathe, Vince!

Dennis bristled. "I helped you get away, didn't I?"

Vincent took a step forward.

Dennis retreated.

Vincent stopped.

He's afraid of me?

He took a deep breath and exhaled. "Dennis, I'm putting my butt on the line every night. You need to be on top of things here. That's your job. You being late almost got me killed!"

His voice had risen, despite his best efforts at control.

Dennis's soft brown eyes squinted with anger and he took an impulsive step forward.

"Don't yell at me, Vincent! We wouldn't even be doing this if it weren't for me. It's all my plan, my ideas. I came up with your hero name, I designed and made the costume. Hell, I even fire retarded it and treated it with your freakin' color changing chemical. So don't get all high and mighty with me, Vincent. I created you!"

Vincent stiffened. He'd never heard Dennis so angry, never seen such callousness in his eyes. And those words pierced to the heart of his insecurity.

"You created Invictus, Dennis, not me."

Dennis sneered. "Same difference. Without me, you're nothing."

Vincent's anger vanished. Pain and self-doubt replaced it. "That's not true."

Instead of backing down, Dennis dug in his attack. "Who's the one who always found friends for you, huh? You lost 'em, yeah, but I was the one who started talking with 'em because you wouldn't do it otherwise. Older kids that *you* needed, not me. I had plenty of friends. So, tell me, Vincent, who *are* you without me?"

Vincent lowered his head and stared at the floor. He struggled to control his breathing.

"I'm Vincent Villanueva, a super shy kid who hid his insecurities behind books and martial arts. Then overnight I had to become a parent to take care of my brother because my mom and dad died, except I don't know how to do that. And now I'm supposed to be a superhero who's going to save the world, but I don't know how to do that, either. I don't even know how to be a grownup yet. I just know I envy my little brother for his big heart and ability to understand people, and I always wanted to be like him." He paused a moment, his body tight with coiled emotions he didn't understand and couldn't control. "That's who I am, Dennis. I thought you understood me."

When Dennis didn't respond, Vincent raised his head.

Dennis no longer looked angry. He looked stunned. "I never heard you open up like that before."

"That's because I was too busy hiding. Invictus forced me to see myself, weaknesses and all."

Dennis stared at him, on the verge of tears.

"Dennis, what's happened to us?"

Dennis's eyes filled with water. "I gave us a life, Vincent, a life we could share together," he whispered as the first tear spilled from one eye and dribbled down his cheek. "Then you cut me out of it!"

He bolted through the double doors into the family room, leaving Vincent silent and paralyzed with sudden comprehension.

He stood a few moments in shock, digesting all that had occurred. Then he tossed the mask onto the table and hurried after his brother.

He heard Dennis's door slam and the lock cinch into place as he arrived at the foot of the stairs. Limping up to the second floor, he stopped outside the closed door and stood a moment to regain control. His hands shook – not with anger, but with fear. He raised one hand and knocked.

"Go away," came the muffled response.

"Dennis, please let me in. There's so much we have to talk about, so much I need to tell you."

Silence filled the hall, the same silence he'd felt at the funeral home with his parents laying side by side in their open caskets.

"Dennis, please, I know I've let you down, I know that. There's a lot I kept from you, about what it's like out there. I wanted to protect you, not cut you out."

Silence remained his only answer.

"Please, Dennis, don't cut *me* out. I need you. *Now* more than ever."

He listened, but nothing moved within. And the door remained locked. He stared at the closed door with an empty heart and a guilty soul. Feeling like he'd lost the most important thing in his life, Vincent shuffled down the hall to his room. He loved Dennis so much and wanted to rush back to his door and shout out the words.

But he didn't.

"You made a wise decision, Demon," Cat purred.

Demon still trembled with rage at what the Hero had done to his car, and because he'd looked weak for not fighting him. But the look on Cat's face told him he'd made the right choice. She wore an expression of cool amusement, but her eyes told the real story—had you disobeyed me, I'd have cut your heart out.

"Thank you, Mistress." He bowed with deference.

Once again, he'd found her lounging atop her bed watching the video screen present a slideshow of activity from her servants' cameras.

While he stood at attention, she raised the remote and pressed a few buttons. The images on screen skipped around until the Hero appeared leaning over his motorcycle, his back to the camera.

Demon stiffened.

She allowed the scene to play out, turning the audio up extra loud as though to accentuate his inability to take action. Demon stared dispassionately at the screen. His body temperature rose along with his anger, but he knew she was studying him, not the screen, and he determined to prove himself up to whatever task she had planned for him.

Once the camera sped off down the street, Cat froze the image.

He made eye contact with her, but said nothing.

"It's time to see if Dreamer can fight."

Demon raised his eyebrows in surprise.

"Tomorrow night."

"Yes, Mistress."

"There's more. Listen carefully." She smiled and explained her plan. It didn't make sense to him, but he would follow orders. As long as she left the Hero to him, he didn't care what she did.

Despite his exhaustion, Vincent barely slept all night. He tossed and turned and drifted into fitful moments of dreamless bliss. But then he'd wake up. Thoughts of his parents, Dennis, Franky, Joe, even Lisa kept intruding. All the people he'd failed in one way or another. But mostly, thoughts of Dennis kept sleep at bay.

He finally arose at eleven, but Dennis's door was still closed and locked, so Vincent slogged his way downstairs wearing just the workout shorts he'd slept in. He dragged the costume with him. He'd rinsed it off in the shower, but traces of tomato lay stuck within the course material and he needed to get it out. Squirting dish soap into the kitchen sink, he absently scrubbed the suit section by section with a small brush.

A key rattling in the door to the backyard caught his ear and he looked up to see James step silently into the kitchen. Dressed in sweats and a tee shirt, James closed the door and stared at him. Vincent offered a chin raise and returned to cleaning his costume.

"You almost got your dumb ass killed last night."

Despite his lethargy, Vincent's temper flared. He did not need a lecture right now.

"But I *didn't*."

James said nothing more until Vincent finally met his gaze.

His father's oldest friend didn't look angry or even chastising. He looked scared. "You okay?"

"I'll probably never eat another tomato, but yeah, I'm fine."

"Vincent, I'm asking you, as your friend, as your father's friend, please stop this."

"I can't, James," he replied solemnly. *Even though I want to!* "I have to finish what I started."

James sagged slightly, almost caved in on himself as though he were a balloon losing air. Vincent had never seen the big man look so desperate. "I was never so afraid as I was last night."

Vincent saw the truth in his eyes, and heard it in the anxious tone of voice. This man wasn't his enemy. This man was the closest thing he had left to a father.

"I'm sorry, James. I was scared, too. And I still owe you and Linda the whole story." He paused, and then on impulse added, "If you're so worried, why not become my partner out there?"

The wrinkles around James's eyes creased inward as he squinted. "This isn't a game, Vincent. Dammit, I wish I could make you understand that. Something's going to happen, something bad. Linda and I are coming over later and have that sit-down. Make sure Dennis is here."

He yanked open the door and stomped out of the kitchen. Vincent eyed the open door a moment before feeling the sensation of being watched. He whipped around to find Dennis standing in the doorway to the family room, staring at him with an expression of disbelief.

Oh, no! Did he hear what I said to James about being my partner?

Wordlessly, Dennis strode forward and roughly pushed him aside. Vincent was shocked by the gesture. "You don't use dish washing soap on Kevlar, fool!"

"How do you know?" That was all he could muster.

Dennis glared a moment before dropping down to the cupboard beneath the sink and extracting a box of baking soda.

Vincent stood helplessly to the side as Dennis drained the sink and refilled it with warm water. Then he sprinkled in the baking soda and scrubbed the sticky patches.

Vincent watched a moment. Dennis was fully clothed, but not in his usual shorts and tee shirt or tank top. No, he wore jeans and a button down shirt and that beanie again. It was supposed to be in the nineties today!

But he had more important concerns. Dennis deserved the truth.

"Uh, Dennis, there's a lot I need to tell you before we talk with James and Linda."

Dennis pretended to scrub, but Vincent knew he was listening.

"It's a lot different out there than we–"

A loud car horn sounded from outside the house. Dennis stopped scrubbing and dried his hands. "Gotta go. Those're my friends."

Caught off-guard, Vincent stood paralyzed as Dennis headed toward the family room. "Uh, hold up."

Dennis stopped.

"Why don't you invite them in so I can meet them?" He had a bad feeling about these 'friends'. "Dad always wanted to meet our friends."

Dennis soft features turned feral. "You're not daddy!"

He entered the family room. Vincent chased after him. His ankle still ached, but he ignored it. Running around the couch, he blocked the front door so Dennis had no choice but to stop.

"What's with you? Don't you think I miss them too? But whenever I say anything about them you go off on me. Why?"

"Because you were late, Vincent, like always!" Dennis hissed, his voice keening with pent up anguish. "It's your fault they died! Why'd you have to be late?"

Vincent stood frozen as Dennis brushed past him out the front door. He vaguely heard a car door slam and then a high-powered engine roar off down the street.

CHAPTER TWENTY-EIGHT

YOU CAN'T STOP ME

The truth of Dennis's words hit Vincent like a truck.

In his mind's eye, he saw himself leaving late from work, speeding home to pick up Dennis to meet their parents for dinner. He'd rushed through the front door, lab coat still on, to find Dennis at the foot of the stairs reading a comic book.

"Vincent, we're gonna be late."

"I'll call." Vincent vividly recalled the cell phone in hand, speed-dialing his father as he raced up the stairs to his room. Dennis's words drifted after him, "Mom always says you'll be late for your own funeral."

Now Vincent stood in the entry hall, shirtless, wearing workout shorts and no shoes, front door hanging open, and finally understood so much of Dennis's attitude since the crash.

And the truth of his brother's words.

The crash *was* his fault. He'd called and delayed their parents' departure for the restaurant. If not for that call, they'd still be alive.

His stomach clenched with anguish. "Oh, God, what did I do?"

Linda stepped through the open door. "Vincent, who were those guys with–" She stopped in surprise. "Oh, honey, what's wrong?"

"Dennis is right. It was my fault!"

He grabbed her in a tight hug and she wrapped her long arms around him with the kind of gentleness only a mother can display.

"What was your fault, honey?"

"The crash!" Vincent blurted, spluttering between breaths. "I was late, like always. I tried to pretend it wasn't my fault, but it was. Dennis is right. I killed them, Linda!"

He heaved with sorrow and allowed tears to erupt from his eyes. He wept more than he had during those difficult days and weeks following the crash. Linda led him to the sofa and eased him down, all the while keeping her arms wrapped securely around him. After they sat, she pulled back to make eye contact.

"Sweetheart, Dennis is a brilliant boy, but he's still a boy. All he can see is that you were late and your parents died. He needs to blame someone."

"But he's right, Linda. If I'd been on time they'd still be alive."

She offered a gentle look. "Vincent, you have to face it. Your parents died because they were in the wrong place at the wrong moment."

"But I put them in that moment, Linda. If I hadn't called they'd have left earlier and never gotten hit in that intersection."

She drove her gaze right into him. "You stop that talk right now, Vincent Villanueva. It happened. Period. It was horrible. I lost my best friends. You lost your parents. But it was no one's fault except the drunk driver who hit them."

Vincent sniffled. The tears felt so cathartic he didn't feel weak shedding them. He studied her gentle face. Even the crow's feet beneath her eyes seemed to radiate love and security. "You really believe that?"

"Yes, because it's true."

He sagged back against the couch and she released him. "I've felt guilty for so long." He leaned in and wrapped his arms around her. "I love you, Linda."

"I couldn't love you more if you were my own."

They held each other close for a few moments until Vincent felt he'd gotten his emotions under control. Then he pulled back and searched her face with anxiety. "Please don't tell James I was crying. He already thinks I'm acting like a little kid."

"Men cry, Vincent. And James is very proud of the way you stepped up to take care of Dennis. He just doesn't wear his emotions on his sleeve."

"Thanks."

"James wants us all to talk today. When will Dennis be back?"

Vincent froze. "I don't know. I don't even know who he's with."

She frowned. "I didn't like how fast that car took off down the street, but Dennis has always been good at choosing friends. I'm sure they're all right."

Vincent bit his lower lip with worry. "I'm not so sure."

She offered him an encouraging look. "If it helps, I understand why you guys are doing what you're doing."

"Glad someone does."

She shivered. "But seeing you fly off that overpass into the tomato truck scared the hell outta me."

Vincent stiffened. "You saw that?"

She nodded. "Someone filmed it and sent the video in to the news."

"Who?" There was no one around. How could someone on the freeway below have filmed something that happened so fast?

"No idea. Video was sent anonymously."

He saw fear in her wide brown eyes.

"Am I interrupting something?"

Vincent turned in shock toward the open front door. Lisa stood just inside looking as beautiful as ever in shorts and a tee shirt, gazing at them with uncertainty. Vincent jumped to his feet, wiping tears off his face in embarrassment.

"Lisa. What are you doing here?"

Linda stood and smiled at the newcomer. "Hello, Lisa, I'm Linda, Vincent's other mom. Nice to meet a friend of his. Please excuse his abruptness. He's had a rough morning."

She kicked him in the ankle. He winced, but got her point.

"Yeah, sorry, Lisa," he stammered. "Nice of you to drop by." Strapped for what else to say, he added, "I didn't know you knew my address."

Another kick to the ankle. He winced again.

"Would you like to stay for lunch, Lisa?" Linda offered. "I was just about to make something. My son hasn't been eating well lately."

Lisa brushed strands of blonde hair off her face and eyed Vincent. "You sure I'm not intruding?"

"Not at all," Linda assured her. "You're just the breath of fresh air Vincent needs. Come on in. I'll be in the kitchen."

She tossed Vincent a knowing smile and vanished into the kitchen.

Lisa closed the door and approached, studying him with amusement. "Nice outfit."

Vincent froze and glanced down at his bare feet and naked torso. He muttered, "Excuse me," and dashed around her and up the stairs. He heard her light laugher wafting up after him.

Within moments he was back wearing a clean tank top he'd yanked from his drawer. He found her gazing at the family portrait atop the curio table.

"This is a beautiful photo."

"Yeah, it's my favorite." He paused, fumbling for something to say. "So, what brings you to my neighborhood?" He tried for a light tone, but it came out stiff and unnatural.

"I wanted to make sure you were all right," she replied. "After yesterday and all."

Vincent frowned. His heart beat wildly, as it always did in her presence, but the comment confused him. "Yesterday? I was at work."

Her face shifted ever so slightly, as though correcting itself, and then she said, "I meant the whole week, really. You seemed so down. Hardly talked to me at all."

She smiled again and that relaxed him a bit. He wasn't used to people worrying about him. It felt nice.

"Vincent," Linda called from the kitchen. "Could you come in here for a minute?"

Oh, crap! The costume!

"Uh, feel free to, well, have a seat and relax. I'll be right back." He fled into the kitchen.

Under Linda's watchful eye, in case Lisa became curious enough to peek in, Vincent finished cleaning his costume and took it out to the garage to hang dry. He realized he'd never asked Dennis if it could go in the dryer because his brother had been the one cleaning it all along.

He returned and hung out with Lisa until Linda announced that lunch was ready. Vincent found himself more comfortable around Lisa at home than he had been at school. At school he felt open and exposed, whereas at home he felt secure and safe. He shared with her some of his drama regarding Dennis and she assured him her own brother went through similar behaviors at that age.

She made it sound like everything would be fine, and Vincent wanted to believe that. But he knew this was different. It was his decisions that had led to Dennis's behaviors and only he could make it right between them.

Linda had made hamburgers and the ladies did most of the talking. They seemed like they'd known each other forever, and Vincent felt good about their easy closeness. He also felt good about not having to hold up his end of the conversation. His mind was too troubled, dominated by Dennis's words and the look on his face when he'd run from the house.

By the time lunch ended, Lisa had agreed to take some martial arts classes with Linda in exchange for teaching Linda photography.

"I take shots of more than just cute Asian guys with long hair." She winked at Linda, who laughed.

Vincent looked down at his food.

Once they were gone, he stood in the family room staring at Dennis's Xbox and worrying about his brother.

Who were these new friends that he kept hidden? The fact that he was rebelling indicated they probably weren't "safe" kids like his old ones had been. For the first time in his life, the thought of Dennis getting into partying or drugs shot through his head and scared the hell out of him! Especially with those new, more destructive drugs on the street.

He took the stairs two at a time, ignoring the dull throb in his ankle. Dennis's door was closed, but thankfully could only be locked from the inside. He threw open the door and fixed his eyes on the computer desk.

Damn!

Dennis's phone sat charging beside the computer.

Now there was no way to contact him, even to ask his forgiveness.

He spotted a photo of himself and Dennis dressed in martial arts garb and sparring. He navigated his way through the mess and picked it up. Dennis had drawn a line from himself with an arrow pointing at Vincent. Beneath it he'd scrawled a line from that Shakespeare sonnet: "Desiring this man's art."

Fatigue descended on him once more.

Not fatigue. Dejection.

"I'm sorry, Dennis," he mumbled.

He sank onto the bed and shoved all the comics onto the floor. Then he laid his head down on the pillow and stretched out. Glancing over at the chest of drawers, he spotted a framed picture of him, Dennis, and their dad grinning broadly with the ocean churning behind them.

"Oh, Dad," he murmured. "You always knew what to do when one of us was in trouble. But I don't. I'm really messing things up. I lost you and mom and now I'm losing Dennis. I don't know what to do, Daddy. I need you."

His eyes welled with tears for the second time that day and he shut them to cut off the sight of that photo.

I'll just lay here for a bit in case Dennis comes home.

He was asleep within minutes.

Linda kept her word and told James nothing about Vincent becoming emotional, but she did let him know how Vincent blamed himself for his parents' death.

"That's crazy, Linda." James laid out his clothes for his nightly patrol. His badge and gun lay on the bed beside them. "Vincent's smarter than that."

He'd already been downtown that morning for a debriefing on last's night's failed operation. Torres had been beyond livid, especially with all the time and planning and expense that had gone into it.

James had remained silent since the operation had been Janson's plan and he'd had to take most of the heat for it failing.

After that, he'd had a few hours to sleep before resuming normal patrols tonight.

"Smarts has nothing to do with it," Linda went on, interrupting his thoughts. "He feels responsible and that's all that matters. I tried to explain that it wasn't his fault, but I'm not sure I got through."

James grunted as he slipped on a dress shirt and buttoned it. "We need to have that sit-down. He still thinks this hero thing is a game."

"He knows it's not a game. They both do. But they learned from you and Loy to always finish what they start."

"Linda, something is going to happen. I feel it in my gut. That's why I'm going out alone tonight. Then tomorrow, we corner them and have that family talk."

"What'll I tell Janson when he calls?"

James's face became stormy. 'Tell him to go f—"

She placed a warning hand over his mouth. "You know how I feel about cussing."

She removed her hand.

"Tell him I got called out on an emergency and to patrol without me. He loves running his own anyway."

Vincent awoke to a car door slamming just below the window. Lethargy overwhelmed him and he couldn't quite get his bearings. Only when he heard, "What are you doing in my room?" did he sit abruptly up on the bed and take in his surroundings. The room was darker – it was dusk already.

"Who said you could touch my stuff?"

Dennis swooped in and snatched a photo from Vincent's grasp. Only when his brother stood back holding the photo did Vincent remember it—the one of them sparring. He'd been holding it when he fell asleep.

Dennis glowered as he clutched the photo to him.

"I'm sorry," Vincent offered in a soft voice. "I guess I fell asleep."

"Do that in your own room."

Vincent stood warily, fixing his gaze on the surly face before him. A car horn sounded. He stepped around Dennis and peeked out the window. A brand new black Mercedes, an exact twin of the one that had attacked him the previous night, sat idling in the driveway. And, despite the windshield tint, Vincent clearly made out Demon, impatient fingers drumming against the dash.

He turned to Dennis, aghast. "That's Demon!"

Dennis rolled his eyes. "Duh. I've been hanging with them for weeks."

Vincent's stomach clenched like a fist. "What?"

"They found me by accident one day. Soon as I heard the name I knew he was the one you wanted. Since you refused to let me help you on the streets, I joined them. Figured I could find out where the drugs came from."

"Dennis, that's crazy! Demon just sliced up an Asian guy the other night. He'd kill you in a second."

"Doubtful. He likes me."

"You didn't tell him about me, did you?"

Dennis looked like he'd been punched, and Vincent wished he could take the words back.

"*I* don't betray people."

"I didn't betray you, Dennis." Vincent finally took note of the beanie on his brother's head. A beanie in midsummer? Dennis rarely wore them even in winter. "Why are you wearing that beanie?"

Dennis hesitated, as though he wasn't going to respond. Then he reached up and yanked off the beanie.

"Your hair!"

It matched that of Demon and his cohorts, even to the rattail brushing past his shirt collar.

"They treat me like a friend." Dennis paused and gazed a long moment at him. "I don't have anybody."

"You have me."

Dennis scoffed. "Yeah, right. You're never here, and out there you have Franky and Joe. And you asked James to join you, too. I heard it this morning. You want everyone out there but me."

Vincent's entire body froze with guilt. "Dennis, I was going to tell you about Joe and Franky this morning, and I only said that to James to get him off my back."

Dennis shoved the photo into his pocket and reached out to snatch his cell phone off the desk. "I don't believe you. You think I'm weak and can't handle myself. I'm gonna prove you wrong."

Another stab of fear shot through Vincent. "What are you going to do?"

"They're gonna jump me in tonight and then I'll be official. I'll find the drug house and bring down this Mistress they keep talking about."

"No!"

Dennis stared at him with disdain. "You don't own me, Vincent. And I can fight good enough to get in."

"I won't let you." Vincent's entire body trembled. This was the tipping point. He'd either bring Dennis back from the brink now or lose him forever.

"You can't stop me."

Dennis headed around scattered debris for the door.

Vincent panicked. Short of tying his brother to the bed, how could he stop him?

"I can tell you the truth," he blurted, hoping the desperation in his voice wasn't too evident. "The whole truth about what it's like out there, about Joe and Franky. I've been meaning to for the longest, but I just didn't know how."

Dennis stopped and hesitated. He turned slowly around. He looked tempted.

Vincent studied his brother's face and saw indecision behind the anger. Dennis was still in there, the gentle soul who hated hurting anyone or anything.

"Hey, Dreamer, hurry up, man!"

Vincent flinched. "That's what mom called you."

"I gotta go."

"Dennis, please don't." Vincent didn't care if he sounded like he was pleading. "You have it wrong on that photo. *I* need to be like you. *Please.*"

Dennis hesitated and Vincent thought for a hopeful moment he would relent. Then he bolted from the room.

"Damn!"

Vincent strode to the window and watched as the back door to the Mercedes popped open and the person he loved more than anything in the world disappeared within. The car backed out onto the street. Vincent got one last glimpse of Dennis's gentle features as he gazed out the open window at him. Then the car peeled off down the road with a screech of tires. He leaned out to catch the plate number, but there was no plate. The car rounded the corner and vanished from sight.

Vincent felt tears burn his eyes as he ran from the room to suit up.

CHAPTER TWENTY-NINE

HE'S NOT BREATHING!

HE CALLED JAMES FROM HIS regular cell as he pulled on the costume.

"Is that other guy with you?"

"No," he heard from the speaker. The phone lay on his bed. "I'm patrolling alone. Where are you?"

Vincent pulled the suit up over his waist and slipped his arms through. "Home. Dennis is in trouble."

He gave James the short version and a description of Demon's car.

"Dennis thinks he's helping, but he could get hurt or…." He couldn't say the rest.

James's voice sounded calm, but tense. "Where should I look?"

Vincent considered a moment as he pulled on his shoes. Demon had obviously been dealing in the Valley. That was how he found Dennis, or vice versa. But a gut instinct told him Demon would likely jump in Dennis somewhere more familiar, like maybe that alley where they were jumping in that Chinese guy.

"I think they're downtown." He rattled off a few neighborhoods Demon had been known to frequent, including that particular alley cross street. "I'm heading out now."

"I'm on it," James said. This time Vincent heard fear. James stopped talking. All Vincent could hear from the phone was the car engine and street noise. Then, with a quiet urgency, James added, "Thanks for trusting me."

Vincent felt his chest tighten. "I should have from the beginning. We have to save him, James."

"We will. Call if you find him and I'll do the same."

Vincent hesitated only a moment before giving James his Invictus number and then hung up. Nothing mattered now except Dennis.

Invictus headed for downtown to roust any of Demon's followers he could find. If they didn't tell him the location for Dennis's induction, he'd beat the truth out of them.

On route, he received a call from Joe. Panic swept over him. "You guys okay?"

"Yeah, we're good, Super Hero," he heard in Joe's typically deep voice. "My guy kicked us out, but it's cool. I guess his being nice only went so far. Word on the street says Demon's not looking for me."

"I heard that too, but you still need to lay low."

"Plan to," Joe agreed. "Franky needs to see you."

"What about?" Invictus turned a corner in North Hollywood and headed south.

"Didn't say." Invictus could almost hear Joe shrug. "But he was writing something while we was at Lloyd's place that he said only Batman can read. And he says you need to read it now."

A wave of indecision swept over him. He had to find Dennis. "Does it have to be now?"

"He says so."

Invictus considered. "Has he stayed clean?"

"Pretty much. Barely touched anything since I been with him. He's kinda shaky right now, you know, coming down."

Invictus glanced at the time on his phone. Eight p.m. Demon's cohorts didn't usually hit the streets till after nine. He'd swing by that alley first, but suspected the "jumping in" wouldn't happen until later at night, like that other one he'd stumbled upon. "Okay. Be right there."

He ended the call and roared through the night, his heart and soul heavy with the feeling that Fate was about to play another cruel trick on him, one even more costly than his parents' death. He cranked the throttle and sped up.

He found Franky and Joe playing handball against the back of the Laundromat with an old, semi-flat tennis ball. The ball bounced everywhere except the spots they aimed at and the two boys laughed themselves silly each time.

"Yo, Batman," Franky crowed. "Robin is ready."

"You're in a good mood, Robin," he observed, squatting down to face the boy. "What's going on?"

Trembling from withdrawal, Franky fished around in the pocket of his tattered shorts and pulled out a piece of rumpled paper that had sweat stains all over it. He held out the paper. Invictus took it and Joe leaned over his shoulder to see.

Opening the folded paper, Invictus squinted in the poor light at the ungainly, childish scrawl.

'Mama. I love you, but I cant do no more drugs with you.

And I cant live with you no more or buy you no drugs. A friend

said he wud find me a real home, but I know he cant. Nobody

wants a tweaker like me.'

Invictus stiffened because he knew which "friend" Franky was talking about.

'But see, Mama, I dont wanna be a tweaker no more. I wanna

be Robin and that means I gotta be clean. I know you dont

know what I'm talkin about and thats okay. But I gotta leave.

Im sorry, mama, sorry if you be mad, but I gotta take care a me.

Joe says that and so does Batman. Please get clean, mama.

Your son Franky.'

Invictus felt his mouth go dry. "Robin, I…." He stopped, glancing at Joe, who looked stunned by what Franky had written.

Franky reached up to take back the letter. He twitched and squirmed.

"It's okay. I'll go with Joe to Runaway House. I'm not mad or nothing cause you didn't find me a home. But I really wanna be clean so I can still be Robin with you." He paused a moment and looked down at his dirty shoes. Then he raised his wide eyes. "You still want me to be Robin, right?"

Invictus felt his breath freeze. All he could do was nod. Between Dennis and this, he was at the breaking point. He made a fist and held it out. "I wouldn't have anyone else."

Franky bumped. "I'm gonna take this note to my mama and say goodbye. I got her this, too." He held up a bag of white powder. "Last bag. Will you wait for me?"

Invictus hesitated. He slipped out his phone and checked the time. Eight-thirty. The alley had been empty when he'd cruised by, as he suspected. It wasn't even fully dark yet. "Sure."

Franky sauntered out of the alley and vanished from view.

Invictus found Joe gazing long and hard at him.

"Was that note your idea?"

Joe shook his head. "You got to him, gave him a reason to come clean. You're all he talks about." He paused. "But I'm pissed you didn't find him a home like you promised, even if he isn't."

Invictus flinched. He opened his mouth to tell Joe what he'd done, but hesitated. What if it didn't work? Giving Joe and Franky more false hope than he already had would be worse than their anger.

"It's complicated."

"I heard that one before."

Joe strode to the pile of blankets and old clothes and plopped down onto them. He refused to look at Invictus. Instead, he pulled out his phone and focused on the brightly lit screen.

Invictus sat down and leaned against the dumpster. Tonight it smelled like rotting bananas. The minutes ticked away and he became increasingly alarmed. Franky shouldn't have been gone so long. And Dennis could be fighting at this very moment. James hadn't called, so obviously he hadn't found him. Invictus rose stiffly and walked over to Joe.

"He should be back by now."

Joe eyed the time on his phone and leaped to his feet. "Yeah. He should. Let's check on him."

Relieved to be doing something tangible, Invictus climbed onto his cycle and Joe slid easily into the seat behind him. Invictus cranked the throttle and engaged the engine. They roared off down the street.

Franky only lived three blocks from the Laundromat so they arrived at his abandoned tenement within minutes. The windows were mostly dark, but some flickered with candlelight and others glowed faintly with what must have been lantern light or flashlight beams.

Invictus parked his bike behind the building and locked it. "Do you know which place is his?"

Joe nodded and set off for a back door that had a wooden sign affixed to it: 'Condemned. Do Not Enter.'

Joe pushed one side of the double doors inward. The sign remained affixed to the other door.

"Better turn on your phone light. It's dark in here." He pressed a button on his phone and the flashlight sprang to life.

Invictus did the same. He didn't know why, but a sense of dread had enveloped him on the ride over. Something was wrong.

"Let's go."

Joe entered the tenement. Invictus followed.

Even with the flashlight engaged, it still took a few moments for his eyes to adjust. The mask didn't help. In thick darkness, it limited his peripheral vision. He followed Joe through a dirty, crumbling rear lobby, skirting broken pieces of furniture on his way to the back stairs. Joe didn't hesitate. He started up them at a rapid pace and Invictus sprinted after. He sensed Joe knew something was wrong, too, and that speed was necessary.

They exited the dark stairwell on the fifth floor. Joe waved his flashlight in both directions.

"What?"

Joe eyed him. "Never know when some crazy junkie might jump you in this place."

Invictus nodded and followed Joe down the musty corridor with peeling wallpaper and a dirt-stained carpet. The moldy light fixtures looked as though they hadn't been lit for years.

The wavering beams from their phones provided the only illumination, and the whole scene put Invictus on edge. Something *was* wrong. Something had happened. He felt it. He knew it.

The absence of people further twisted his nerves into knots.

Joe must've read his thoughts. "At night people lay low in here. Safer that way."

Invictus followed the boy around a corner past more closed, decrepit doors and crumbling wallpaper. Finally, Joe stopped before a scratched and pitted door and gripped the knob. He glanced back as though for permission. Invictus nodded and Joe turned the knob. Pushing open the door, he shined his light into the dark apartment. Invictus stepped past him and entered the void.

His flashlight moving in all directions, he scoured the empty living room. The smell of decay and human waste assailed his nostrils. There were some blankets and food wrappers and scattered old clothes lying around, but no sign of Franky or his mother. Invictus exchanged an anxious look with Joe before heading down a short hall past a tiny kitchen to the first door. Glancing in, he saw a dirty, crud-encrusted bathroom. The sink was blackened and the toilet filled with feces. His stomach heaved and he pulled back into the hall. Joe seemed nonplussed.

The only other door at the end of the hall was closed. Heart pounding, Invictus held out his shield in a defensive position and approached. The eerie silence further jangled his nerves. Joe was right. In a dark contained place like this, anyone could leap out of the blackness and attack. What would he find behind this door? He hesitated only a moment as images of Dennis fighting against a group of grown men kept intruding. He grabbed the knob and swung the door inward.

Raising his light, he gasped in horror. Sprawled on the dirty carpet was a woman in tattered pants and a threadbare shirt. Scattered on the floor around her unmoving form were assorted pen bodies, razor blades, straws... and Franky's note. In her hand she clutched an empty plastic bag.

But Invictus only scanned her body for a moment. His gaze riveted to the child wrapped in her arms. He lay beside her, dirty features sprinkled with white powder, as though it had been shoved into his face and mouth. Her eyes were open. His were closed.

"Oh, my God!"

He bolted forward and bent to examine Franky's unmoving form. Joe squatted anxiously beside him. Ripping off one glove, Invictus felt Franky's neck for a pulse. He panicked when he couldn't find it. He shifted the position of his fingers. There it was! Faint. Dangerously weak. But still there.

"He's alive. Just barely." He fought for control.

Please don't die!

Joe was leaning over to examine the woman. "Mom's not."

"Call 911. Tell 'em to meet us out front."

Invictus told Joe the address and handed him the glove and shield. He leaned in and gently extricated Franky from his mother's arms. Her hands were still warm so she hadn't been dead long.

"Hello? Hey, I got a kid here OD'd on meth," Joe hissed into his phone. "Please hurry!"

Invictus scooped up Franky's frail, limp body. His tiny legs dangled as Invictus rose to his feet and headed back down the hall.

Joe gave the address in a trembling voice as he trailed behind, and then silence returned.

Invictus trotted through the empty living room and into the hallway, Joe at his heels.

"Will he be all right?" Joe whispered as they rounded the dark corner back toward the stairs. His voice sounded terrified. Joe's light illuminating the dirty carpet in front of them was all they had to see by.

"He has to be." Invictus felt his whole body numb with fear. First Dennis and now Franky. Was everything about to crumble around him? How could he have messed things up so badly?

Joe's light wavered unsteadily on the stairs as they descended. Stains and the reek of urine were all Invictus noticed as he focused on not losing his footing. Franky didn't move and it wasn't obvious if he was even still breathing.

Please don't die!

Finally they set foot on the ground floor and Joe darted ahead to push open the rear door. He ducked beneath the 'Condemned' sign and held open the door. Invictus bent and eased Franky through, and they were outside at last. As they sprinted around the corner to the front of the tenement, people spilled out of the building and others approached from dark alcoves and shadowy doorways.

Invictus became aware of them, but his focus was on Franky. He laid the boy down onto the sidewalk in front of the building and squatted beside him. Joe joined them, his youthful face etched with fear.

"He's not moving."

Invictus leaned down and felt for a pulse. He froze. Nothing. Pressing his ear to Franky's face, he listened and felt no breath coming out of the boy's nostrils.

"He's not breathing!"

"No!" Joe hissed.

Remembering his high school training, Invictus launched into CPR. It was all he could think to do. He placed a hand behind Franky's neck to tilt it up. Then he used thumb and forefinger to pinch closed the nose. He wiped powder from the boy's mouth and bent to place his lips over Franky's. He blew in air and saw the chest rise. He repeated this. Then he released the head and began chest compressions. With one hand over the other, he pressed as hard as he dared. Franky was so skinny and frail he could do serious damage if he pressed too hard. Thirty rapid compressions. He repeated the breathing, and then the compressions.

He heard a siren in the distance.

"Super Hero." Joe's voice sounded panicked. "There's people all around us."

Invictus noted shadowy, shifting forms in his peripheral vision, but Franky was his focus.

Two breaths. Thirty compressions. Two breaths. Thirty compressions.

"C'mon, Robin!" he hissed in desperation as sweat filled the inside of his mask. "Batman needs you!"

The siren blared in his ears and flashing red lights rimmed his field of vision.

Two breaths. Thirty compressions.

The siren stopped. The lights continued flashing.

Two breaths. Thirty compressions.

"Paramedics, let us through!"

Invictus bent to listen again at Franky's chest. His heart nearly stopped because Franky's was beating! Faint, but beating! The small chest rose and fell almost imperceptibly.

Then the paramedics were there. Two of them. They swept in, eyed Invictus a split second with surprise, and squatted down beside Franky. Sweaty and panting from his exertions, Invictus stood to give them room.

"What kind of drugs?"

"Meth," he wheezed.

Joe stepped to his side and pressed up against him. Invictus lifted one arm and wrapped it around Joe's shoulders, pulling him in, relishing that human contact he so needed at this moment.

While the two paramedics worked, Invictus fought for breath. He eyed the sea of spectators surrounding them. All were clearly street people, likely the 'residents' of this abandoned building. They stared at him without visible emotion. Living like animals seemed to deprive them of the ability to feel much of anything.

"Pulse fifty," one paramedic intoned, while the other ran a blood pressure test.

"Blood pressure eighty-two over fifty-four."

A third paramedic rolled a gurney through the crowd.

"Is he gonna make it?" Joe whispered.

The paramedic who'd taken the blood pressure looked grave. "I don't know."

Joe's eyes welled with tears and he pressed his head against Invictus's shoulder.

They watched as Franky was lifted gently onto the gurney and wheeled through the onlookers to the boxy red vehicle with the flashing lights. More sirens could be heard bearing down on them.

Invictus broke away from Joe and dragged the boy forward. As Franky was slid into the back of the vehicle and one of the paramedics leaped up with him, Invictus approached the other two.

"I know it's not the letter of the law, but in the spirit of the law, please let Joe ride with Franky."

The first paramedic opened his mouth to speak.

"That little boy has no one except us," Invictus continued, before the paramedic could object. "If he wakes up, he needs to see the face of someone who loves him. Please."

The paramedics exchanged a look of uncertainty.

"It's against the law, like he said," one of them reiterated.

"Yeah, but so's he," the other one replied, pointing to Invictus.

The men were young, probably new to the job.

"C'mon, guys, we gotta go!" barked the one in the back of the vehicle. "We're gonna lose 'im!"

The first paramedic studied Invictus a long moment. "Oh, screw it." He looked at Joe. "Get in, kid."

Joe didn't hesitate. He thrust the glove and shield at Invictus and clambered up into the back, crouching beside Franky.

The second paramedic grunted and hurried around to the driver's side.

Joe locked eyes with Invictus. The desperate need in those eyes was gut wrenching. "You coming?"

"I have to save my—"

Joe's eyebrows rose, and his wide eyes grew even wider, as though with sudden understanding.

"—someone who's in trouble. Call me."

Joe looked even more afraid and nodded.

The first paramedic slammed the rear doors shut. Within seconds he was in the passenger seat, the siren had been engaged, and the vehicle thundered off down the street, lights flashing.

The other sirens drew ever closer. He turned to the crowd. "His mom's upstairs. She didn't make it. Please tell them."

He threw a thumb back toward the approaching sirens. Not awaiting a response, he sprinted through the silent crowd back to his motorcycle.

CHAPTER THIRTY

WHAT'CHU LOOKIN' AT, DREAMER?

INVICTUS CRUISED THE STREETS. IT was close to ten p.m. and so far he'd come up empty. His frustration mounting, he finally spotted three Asian men with baldheads and rattails.

They hadn't seen him yet so he swerved into an alley and killed the engine. Then he jogged down the street and ducked into a shadowy alcove as he heard their voices approaching. They would strut past any minute and he would be ready. He pressed up against the building and his costume shifted color to match. He fought to control his breathing so they wouldn't hear him.

Their voices wafted over the warm breezy air like ghosts, gradually growing louder as they neared his location. First an arm appeared, and then all three passed his hiding place. Invictus leapt out of the shadows and side kicked the first in the right kidney. He grunted and dropped. The other two spun around, but Invictus was too hyped up to hold back. He spun into a kick and his foot impacted with the second guy's face. The guy twisted in a grotesque imitation of a pirouette and toppled. The third guy rushed in, but Invictus raised the shield and slammed it into his face. He heard the crack of shattering bone and the guy crumpled to the pavement, clutching his destroyed nose as it gushed blood everywhere.

Invictus spun and grabbed the first guy by his shirtfront. Still clutching his side, the man barely had time to raise his arms before the enraged Invictus slammed him up against the wall. He cried out in pain. Invictus threw one gloved hand around his throat.

"Where's Demon?" His voice sounded like a growl, even to him.

The guy glared in fury. "Fu–"

Invictus kneed him in the groin. The man cried out in agony and would have collapsed but for Invictus propping him up. "I'll only ask one more time before I kill you. Where's Demon?"

He heard a groan and glanced back to see the second guy starting to rise. He kicked backward and felt his foot strike flesh. There came a loud "Oof!" and then the sound of a body dropping to the ground.

He squeezed his captive's neck. The guy's face turned red.

"Seventh street overpass," he spluttered, gasping for air. "Near the river."

"They gonna jump in the new kid down there?"

The guy gave a tiny nod, fighting for breath.

"What time?"

"Ten… thirty," the guy croaked, and Invictus loosened his grip a bit. "After… the… sale." He gulped for air.

Invictus ran that information through his frantic brain. Demon must be waiting for a buyer to show. After that would be Dennis's turn to prove he had what it took to be one of them. Invictus released his hold and the Asian slid down the wall to crumple near his feet. He pulled out his phone to check the time. Ten after ten. That overpass was close. Less than five minutes.

He ran, leaving the three Asians beaten and groaning. He got back to the alley within seconds and jumped onto his bike. He turned the key, cranked the choke and threw the throttle forward.

The bike stalled.

No!

He tried again.

Another stall.

Again.

Stall.

No!

He pounded the handlebars so hard his hands hurt.

You can't do this to me!

He whipped out the phone and checked the time.

Ten fifteen.

No time left.

He leaped off the bike, locked it, snatched up his shield, and set off running.

Dennis stood behind Demon gazing up into the dark at the graffiti-covered concrete overpass extending out over the L.A. River. The ground beneath his sneakered feet was all dirt and gravel, and the cars belonging to Demon and his men were parked nearby for easy access. There'd been no traffic across the overpass, which seemed odd to Dennis, but he did hear the sound of cars in the distance.

Several of Demon's cohorts had climbed up onto a short stone tower and disabled the two large lights that illuminated the overpass entrance. The area had plunged into near darkness and, though he attempted to study their movements, Dennis was unable to discern just what the three were doing atop the light tower.

"Nervous, Dreamer?"

He spun around and raised his fists.

Demon chuckled. "Chill, homie. You'll get your chance."

Heart racing, Dennis lowered his fists slowly. "What are they doing up there?"

Demon smiled. Even in the dark that smile sent a chill up Dennis's spine. "Preparing."

"Preparing what?"

Demon's phone vibrated. He pressed the green button and held it to his ear. "Yeah?"

Dennis heard a muffled, "He's coming."

"Good," Demon replied. "We're ready."

He hung up and eyed Dennis in the dark.

"Who's coming?" Dennis asked. Suddenly, all of this didn't seem like the great idea he'd presented to Vincent.

"The buyer, of course," Demon answered with a smoothness that screamed "lying" to Dennis. "You'll make the sale, and then it's time for you to prove yourself."

Dennis nodded. His mouth had gone dry. Now that he was actually about to sell drugs that could hurt people and then fight against three men bigger and stronger than himself, all of a sudden he wished he was home alone playing *Call of Duty*.

"So, who taught you how to fight?" Demon asked casually.

Dennis sensed movement around him as the other cohorts placed themselves at strategic points at the foot of the overpass. Did they expect trouble? Shooting?

"Uh," he fumbled, pushing those thoughts aside to focus on Demon. "My father and brother."

"I hope they taught you well. I like you, Dreamer. Would hate to lose you."

That tone again. Truth masked by lies.

"You still think about your brother?" Dennis asked, not sure where the thought had come from.

Demon squinted in the dark and Dennis feared he'd go off. But then his face softened. "Every day."

Going on intuition, Dennis asked, "Do you think he'd be proud of you?"

Demon stared at him, and then shook his head quizzically. "You ask weird questions, kid. Maybe that's why they call you Dreamer."

"Maybe." But Dennis had seen something in Demon's eyes, in the slight shift of facial expression. His question had hit a nerve.

"Your brother proud of *you?*"

That question caught Dennis by surprise. But his answer didn't. "I want him to be."

Demon grunted and looked away.

Clutching his shield to him, Invictus sprinted along a darkened street. Hair flying, cape fluttering, his breathing became more ragged as he increased his pace. He'd never been a long-distance runner and his lung strength was built for martial arts and hand-to-hand competitions. A stitch formed in his side and his heart raced wildly. How much time had passed? Was he too late? Up ahead, in the distance several blocks away, he spotted the Seventh Street overpass jutting out across the L.A. river. The lights on his side of the span seemed odd, as though some had gone out. He summoned reserves of strength he didn't know he had and plowed onward with a vengeance.

I'm coming, Dennis!

Dennis felt his hands going clammy, and sweat broke out on his forehead. He could see the three guys up on the tower, moving around, but they were just silhouettes against the moonlight and he couldn't make out what they were doing. It looked like they unfurled something and then stood beside the blacked out light fixtures, silent and unmoving.

He scanned the area around him. Demon's men stood beside their cars, guns drawn. Dennis wiped his sweaty hands on his jeans. The area was deserted. Remnants of tents and a few battered shopping carts attested to the homeless frequenting this desolate area, but Demon must've scared them all away. Just for a deal? Dennis had already witnessed over a dozen deals. None had been so clandestine as this one.

Something was wrong. He sensed it. Demon had only told him part of the truth. They were waiting for someone. But who?

The vibrating of Demon's phone nearly made Dennis jump. Fortunately, Demon was too occupied answering the call to notice.

"Yeah, Creeper. He pass your checkpoint yet?"

"Yeah," cracked over the phone. The cell connection wasn't so great down here. Dennis leaned closer to hear. "'Cept he's running. No bike."

Dennis gasped. Demon turned to eye him and Dennis forced himself to cough. "Sorry. Summer cold."

Demon focused on his call. "Why the hell's he running? Is he still headed for the overpass?"

"Looks like," crackled the voice over the phone.

Demon ended the call and pressed another number while Dennis stood by with a sick feeling in the pit of his stomach. No bike? Could that mean—

"Chanster," Demon said into the phone.

Dennis spotted movement up on the bridge tower.

"Yeah, Demon," he heard over the phone.

"He's headed your way." Demon's tone reeked of expectation. "Everything ready?"

"Yes, sir," came the muffled response.

Demon ended the call.

Despite his best efforts not to, Dennis found himself staring at the drug dealer with growing alarm.

"What'chu lookin' at, Dreamer?"

"Nothing."

Dennis lifted his gaze toward the road above, the one leading onto the overpass, the one leading someone into a trap. Was it Vincent? Why else would they be surprised about "no bike?" He'd turned off his cell earlier in the evening, per Demon's orders, but even if it was on there was no way he could text Vincent without Demon seeing him.

Please, Vincent, don't be headed this way!

The overpass loomed large in the semi-darkness. Traffic sounds could be heard in the distance, but this area was desolate and Invictus decided that was why Demon chose it. He stopped running and doubled over to catch his breath. The stitch in his side stabbed at his innards, and his heart pounded with frantic unease. He sucked in air, smelling rotten water and diesel fumes. Train tracks were nearby.

Raising his head, he felt sweat dribble down the inside of his mask and sting his eyes. Blinking furiously, he scanned the road leading onto the overpass. It was empty. He recalled a detour sign a while back, directing drivers to take an alternate route. Had the city put it there, or Demon? From what he'd seen of this organization, the mysterious Cat seemed to wield a lot of power.

Holding the shield in front of his body, Invictus started toward the overpass. The absence of homeless people spooked him, and further suggested that Demon had control of the area. Why? Who was this buyer that so much set-up was required?

He saw no one. Nothing moved. As he'd noted from the distance, the lights on the right side of the overpass entrance were out. Only the two on the left side burned, but those only offered a feeble illumination of the roadway. Invictus decided to stick to the darkened side. His costume would blend in with the blackness and hide him from view.

Maybe the meeting was taking place down by the riverbed? He considered this possibility as he inched closer to the darkened tower. He knew something was wrong. Had Demon been alerted that he was coming? He should've tied up the others so they couldn't raise the alarm.

His heart pounded anew with the dreadful possibility that the meeting had been moved and Dennis might be in for the fight of his life somewhere else. He sprinted the last few feet onto the overpass roadway and pressed up against the tower. Darkness surrounded him. He leaned over the concrete railing and peered into the blackness below. Moonlight illuminated several cars parked down by the riverbank, but nothing moved. Invictus couldn't see well enough to know if the cars were old or new or abandoned or just parked. It seemed odd they would be there at all. He glanced into the river, but the absence of rain had left it dry and forlorn.

Pulling back from the railing, he scanned the roadway. He stepped away from the tower and gazed off into the distance across the span of the bridge. He heard nothing and saw nothing.

Something was *very* wrong here.

Crouched behind the Mercedes, Dennis could see nothing going on atop the overpass. Demon hunkered beside him texting away, but Dennis couldn't see well enough over his shoulder. What was happening? The quiet freaked him out. He couldn't take it anymore. He raised his head ever so slightly and peered through the car windows, but the roof of the Mercedes blocked his view of the upper roadway. He caught stealthy movement of someone in black, but could only see the feet and dark pants. Was it Vincent?

"Get your head down!" Demon hissed and Dennis twisted his neck to find the drug lord glaring at him. He lowered his head as Demon returned to his phone. Because Demon turned his way, Dennis saw the phone.

Demon typed one word: 'now.'

Invictus scoured the darkness surrounding him. Every one of his senses tingled with dread. There came a faint rustling from above, like the fluttering wings of a dove. He jerked his head up, but it was too late. An enormous net, easily large enough to hold a boatload of fish, swooped down on him. He tried to leap aside, but the net engulfed him and his roll became a frantic struggle to free himself. The shield slipped from his grasp and struck him on the side of the face when his arms and legs became entangled.

Two shadowy figures shimmied down ropes from the light tower and a third strode out from behind it. The three young Asians held guns aimed straight at him.

"I told you I'd get your ass, Hero," he heard from below.

He stopped struggling and rolled over so he could see between the slats making up the concrete barrier. Two stories down, Demon rose up from behind a dark car like a vampire from its coffin.

"And now I have it."

Invictus froze, his breathing on hold. A figure rose from behind the same car into a shaft of moonlight and gazed up at him with horror. It was Dennis.

No!

Invictus thrashed against the net, not even caring that the three Asians could shoot him dead on the spot. His only thought was to get to Dennis.

Dennis stared up at him, frozen with indecision.

Demon raised his handgun and pointed it at the back of Dennis's head, but Dennis was staring up at the overpass and didn't notice.

Invictus felt his heart race. "No!"

His voice echoed through the night.

Dennis looked confused.

Demon pushed the gun closer.

A searing *screech* of tires cut through the silence like a bomb blast. Two black sedans roared to a stop at the overpass entrance and four large, dark figures leaped out to fire at the three Asians.

Pop! Pop! Pop! Pop!

Invictus heard the first Asian drop dead behind him as bullets flew back and forth over his prone form. He wrestled against the net and looked at Dennis down below.

Demon pulled the gun back from Dennis's head and pointed it up at the bridge.

Dennis blurted, "What's happening?" He dropped back behind the car.

"Thug Boyz trying to horn in."

Demon fired up at the new arrivals. One of them clutched at his chest and toppled. An Asian behind Invictus shot a second newcomer in a splatter of blood, causing the man's head to explode.

Invictus activated the blade on his shield and sliced through the net.

James cruised the downtown streets immersed in thoughts of Vincent and Dennis and the very real possibility that he could lose both of them.

"All units in the vicinity of the Seventh Street overpass," crackled over his radio. "Multiple gunshots reported. Possible gang fight. Approach with caution."

Dread engulfed him. James flipped on his siren and spun the wheel to head in that direction.

The shooting continued. The newcomers crouched beside their cars and exchanged gunshots with the Asians behind Invictus. More shots flew up from below and Invictus could make out two of the newcomers firing downward. He fought and sliced and tore at the net.

A huge figure emerged from one of the cars, much bigger than the others. He looked like an NFL linebacker wearing a hoodie and carrying a large handgun that gleamed in the moonlight. He approached the concrete barrier.

"This is for you, Demon!"

He raised his weapon.

Invictus twisted his neck around to look through the barrier.

Demon yanked Dennis to his feet and used him as a shield.

The huge man fired.

Pop! Pop! Pop! Pop!

"Noooo!" Invictus screamed.

The bullets ripped into Dennis's stomach and blood blew out of him like an erupting volcano. He looked up and Invictus felt those wide, startled eyes fix on him a split second before Demon shoved him to the ground and opened fire on the big man. His bullets struck the guy in the face, dropping him in a shower of blood and brain matter.

Invictus went wild. He slashed and tore and yanked the net apart, heedless of bullets flying, not caring about his own safety. His only thought was to get to Dennis.

Both Asians behind him stopped firing and Invictus figured they'd been hit. But he didn't care. He heard sirens approaching as his peripheral vision revealed the gangsters jumping back into their cars.

Finally free, he leaped to his feet with the shield in hand and leaned over the rail. His heart lurched.

Dennis lay unmoving in a vast pool of rapidly expanding blood that reflected the moon like a ghastly mirror.

"Demon!"

Demon spun and raised his gun. Invictus held up the shield. Bullets bounced off and whizzed away into the dark. When the shooting ceased, he lowered the shield and saw Demon sprinting for his black Mercedes.

Invictus looked down. Too far to jump. Catching sight of a broken section of concrete along the rail, he snatched up the net and hooked it over the jagged piece. Then he jumped up and over the railing, clutching the net and dropping toward the ground at an alarming rate of speed.

Demon reached the car and jumped behind the wheel.

Invictus flung the shield as hard as he could. As he continued to drop, the shield slammed into the windshield, cracking it and ricocheting back up toward him. The net pulled taut and nearly tore his arm from its socket. He heard the net rip as concrete above broke loose. He went into free fall. The shield arced toward him and he flung out a hand to snatch it from the air. His feet plowed into the dirt alongside the riverbed and he tried for a tuck and roll. The impact was too great and he flew sideways, slamming into the hard earth and gasping for breath.

He heard a car engine roar to life.

Staggering to his feet, he saw Demon glaring furiously at him through the cracked windshield. Invictus stumbled forward. Agony ripped up his leg from his ankle. He ignored it.

The Mercedes plowed toward him. Without even time to raise the shield, Invictus snatched a handful of powder from a belt pouch and tossed it at the on-coming car. He leapt to one side.

The Mercedes roared past him. The sirens grew so loud as to be almost deaf-ening.

The other cars raced after Demon's and vanished up the road.

Invictus rolled over and rose to one knee. One of Demon's men lay in a large pool of blood, his face unrecognizable.

A few feet away Dennis lay on his back, unmoving.

"Dennis!"

Invictus grunted as he struggled to his feet and staggered past the dead Asian to drop down beside his brother. He yanked off his mask and stared in horror at the jagged bullet wounds peppering Dennis's abdomen. Blood rolled out like small rivers and even in the dimly lit darkness, Dennis looked deathly pale.

"Dennis," he panted, barely able to breathe. "Oh, God, Dennis, be all right! Please, you have to be all right!"

Footsteps pounded on the gravel toward him, but he didn't look up.

"I called the paramedics," James exclaimed breathlessly.

Invictus felt James squat beside him, but couldn't pull his eyes from his brother's face. He looked so peaceful.

The eyelids fluttered open. "Vincent?"

"I'm here."

"Hang on, Dennis," James begged, his voice cracking. "Help's coming."

Dennis kept his eyes fixed on Invictus. "It…hurts."

Invictus took his hand and squeezed gently. "You'll be okay." His voice cracked.

"You were right… not friends… sorry… for what I… said. Not… your… fault…. You're… a good… brother."

Tears obscured Invictus's vision.

"It's okay, Dennis. You're gonna be fine. You and me, we're a team, remember? Together forever."

Dennis's eyes seemed to glaze over a moment, as though he couldn't see either of them.

"You hear that?" His voice had dropped to a whisper.

"What?"

"Mommy," Dennis replied, a tiny smile crossing his lips. "She's… calling me."

"Oh, God…," James muttered.

Terror engulfed Invictus and tears rolled down his cheeks.

"No, Dennis! You can't go to her! You can't leave me. You're all I've got. Please. I need you!"

Dennis's eyes seemed to clear and he focused on Invictus's anguished face. "They… will… come," he whispered. Blood gurgled up from his mouth and dribbled down his chin. "The dream… is… everything…"

His eyes closed and his head lolled to one side.

"No! Dennis!" Invictus gripped his brother's hand while James leaned in and placed two fingers against his throat.

"He's alive, but just barely."

Invictus glanced at James.

More sirens approached.

James glared with disgust. "Get out of here, Vincent."

Invictus released Dennis's hand, ignoring the blood on his glove. "I'm not leaving my brother."

"Go!" James snapped. "Before they arrest your ass. I'll take care of Dennis."

Invictus looked at him, but James kept his eyes locked on Dennis.

The sirens became thunderous.

Invictus felt more lost and afraid than ever. His whole body was cold and numb.

"James, I–"

"Go!" James snarled, looking up and casting him such an angry glower that he recoiled.

Rising to his feet, Invictus eyed the flashing lights of the second paramedic vehicle he'd seen that night. Three men leaped from the truck and sprinted down the slope toward them. He cast one more look at his unmoving brother, snatched up his shield, and staggered away.

CHAPTER THIRTY-ONE
PAYBACK IS JUSTICE

Vincent slouched in a chair by Dennis's bed in the Intensive Care Unit at County USC Medical Center. Clad in latex gloves and a sterile mask, his head was bent in desperate prayer. He'd made it back to the alley where he'd left his motorcycle, but there was no sign of the three Asians he'd beaten up.

Not even caring if anyone saw, he'd stripped off the costume and stood in his boxers as he fumbled though the bike's storage compartment for spare clothes. Yanking out short pants and tank top, he'd practically leapt into them and slipped on the black running shoes that he wore as Invictus. Shoving the sweaty costume into the compartment, he'd jumped onto the bike and prayed it would start. One twist of the choke and turn of the throttle was all it took. Why it had stalled out before didn't even matter. What mattered now was getting to the hospital. Shield firmly in place, he'd roared out of the alley and down the darkened street.

He'd hidden the bike and concealed it beneath the camouflage cover before sprinting down the block to the Emergency Room entrance. He found James pacing the waiting room. Dennis had been rushed into surgery. James refused to look at him, and Vincent understood why.

He paced alongside James, the two of them silent and pensive. Linda arrived a short while after and engulfed Vincent in a tight, motherly hug. He stiffly accepted it, but honestly felt she should slap him or yell at him or otherwise reject him outright for what he'd done. Or just give him the silent treatment like James. But she didn't.

"This isn't your fault, Vincent," she assured him.

James cast her a defiant look and Vincent said nothing. She said those words because she loved him, not because they were true.

Hours passed until the doctor finally entered the waiting room. Exhausted and spent, he wore his facemask around his neck and still sported his surgical scrubs. Vincent stared at the bloodstains adorning them.

He couldn't even speak. James did the talking.

"How is he, doctor?"

"Alive, but extremely critical. He'd lost an enormous amount of blood."

Linda reached for Vincent's hand. He reluctantly allowed her to take it.

"The bullets did extensive damage to his abdominal cavity and upper GI," the doctor intoned, as though giving a lecture. Then he seemed to notice how afraid they were and his features softened. "The spinal cord was also traumatized."

"Oh, God," James muttered. "Is he paralyzed?"

"I'm afraid so, from the waist down." He must've seen their horrified faces and heard Vincent's groan of anguish because he quickly added, "Of course, spinal cord trauma differs from person to person. Dennis's wasn't severed, so I can't say for certain he won't regain some use of his legs. Some day."

Vincent forced himself to speak. "Can we see him?"

"He's in recovery now. Once he's moved to ICU, you can visit. But only one at a time and only for brief periods. The next twenty-four hours are critical." He paused and looked grave. "We almost lost him twice."

Linda squeezed Vincent's hand.

James stood so stiffly he resembled a statue. "Thank you, doctor."

The doctor left the waiting room. James gazed a moment at Vincent, his eyes narrowed with accusation. Then he strode from the room without looking back.

Linda's eyes glowed with love and compassion. "He gets like that when he's afraid."

Vincent shook his head. "No. He hates me. I hate me, too."

She let go of his hand and gripped his shoulders hard. "He loves you, and so do I. We'll get through this, as a family. But right now, Dennis needs you more than anyone. As soon as they let you, Vincent, you sit with him. Read him that story he loves. Talk to him. Tell him how much you love him. That's what he needs right now."

Vincent shivered and his throat went dry. "I never have before."

"Never have what?"

He swallowed. "Told him I loved him."

And now I may never have the chance.

She met his gaze straight on. "Then it's time you did."

So here he was, sitting beside the brother he cherished, hoping and praying that Dennis would live, and hating himself for destroying such a gentle soul.

He'd already read through *The Velveteen Rabbit* twice after downloading it to his phone. He had never understood why Dennis felt less than real, why this story of the toy that longed to become a real rabbit so appealed to him. True, their dad had never been very affectionate, but mom had always hugged them and said she loved them.

Then he saw the photo of himself and Dennis in his mind's eye.

Desiring this man's art…

And he thought of all those times he felt someone staring and he'd look up to find Dennis watching him. His mind raced with images of Dennis excitedly showing him some school project he was proud of, or demonstrating a new martial arts move he'd learned or sharing a poem he'd written. The memories tumbled over themselves in his head, each new one fighting the others for supremacy. In every single recollection, he was immersed in a book or practicing his martial arts. Had he even acknowledged Dennis all those times? Had he ever said, "Good job, Squirt" or "I'm proud of you?"

Vincent raised his tear-streaked face and stared in horror at his brother's slowly rising and falling chest.

"Oh, God, Dennis, it's me!" The realization washed over him, and he felt like he was drowning. "You needed *me* to make you real all this time and I ignored you!"

He reached out and took Dennis's limp hand in his. The gloves prevented him feeling any warmth, and that scared him even more.

"Dennis, I hope you can hear me. I'm sorry, I'm so sorry! You think I don't love you, but you are so wrong! I know you always wanted to be like me, but I always needed to be like you. I was just too proud to admit it." His breathing hitched as the tears resumed. "Dennis… I need you. Don't die on me!"

There was no response. Dennis's eyes remained closed, his soft features impassive.

Vincent bowed his head and sobbed.

He cried until he had no more tears left in him. So much pain. So much anguish. So much guilt. Maybe this was why he'd always tried to avoid people and their drama. Life was too painful. Emotions made him feel weak and helpless.

A knocking against glass caused him raise his head and turn.

Linda stood at the window with someone. A boy. A tall African American boy.

Vincent blinked.

It was Joe!

He stiffened, panic assailing him. How? How could Joe be here?

He couldn't know about me!

Linda waved for him to come out into the hall and he stood. With trembling fingers, he grasped the knob and stepped from the room, leaving the symphony of machine noises behind him. Buzzing activity surrounded him as nurses and orderlies hurried past. He removed the facemask and forced himself to look at Joe without emotion. What the hell was going on?

"Vincent," Linda offered causally, "This is Joe, a friend of Dennis."

Vincent's heart thundered so loudly he was sure everyone would hear it.

Dennis's friend?

He stared at Joe without comprehension. The boy gazed back, those wide brown eyes giving away nothing, just as they gave away nothing on the streets. He was dressed in the same jeans and baggy t-shirt he'd been wearing when the paramedic vehicle took him away.

"I was in Dennis's class at Wilton Park," Joe said. "Back in the day, before you all moved to the Valley."

The hell? Could that be true? Vincent's mind chased illusive memories. Could he even remember Dennis's friends back then?

"Joe's friend is in here," Linda went on somberly. "Just down the hall."

Vincent fought for composure. Franky! He'd been so worried about Dennis he'd forgotten!

"Uh, what happened to your friend?" His voice came out hoarse and raspy. The crying had tightened his throat.

Joe studied him. "OD'd on meth."

Vincent felt his lower lip tremble. Struggling for control, he asked, "Will he be all right?"

"Don't know. Docs won't talk to me. Said I'm not family and just a kid anyway."

Vincent nodded, afraid to speak.

"I told Joe I'd go with him to Franky's room and try to convince the nurse I'm family," Linda explained, giving Joe a look of deep compassion. "Joe said the boy's mother is dead and he has no one."

He has me, Vincent thought. But he just nodded again.

Linda eyed him as though she wanted to hug him again. He hoped she wouldn't. He didn't deserve it.

"Can I spend a few minutes with Dennis?" she asked. "Before I go with Joe?"

Vincent suddenly realized he'd been monopolizing Dennis. He'd been in the room ever since the doctor allowed it and Linda hadn't been inside once. Or James. He didn't even know where James had gone.

"Course. Sorry, Linda."

"Don't be sorry for loving your brother." She reached for the mask dispenser.

But I didn't love him, he thought as she slipped the sterile mask over her head and around her mouth. *Not the way he needed.*

He and Joe stood silently as she pulled on a clean pair of latex gloves and entered the room.

"Maybe you oughtta sit a minute," Joe said after an awkward silence. "You look beat, man."

Vincent stripped off the gloves. Tossing them into a trash receptacle, he followed Joe to the waiting room down the hall and they sat on old plastic chairs. The room was empty and Vincent wondered where everyone had gone. The place had been packed earlier. He felt Joe's eyes on him and reluctantly met them.

"You don't remember me, do you?"

Vincent flinched. "What do you mean?"

Joe studied him a moment. His time on the street made his face unreadable.

He'd probably clean up in a poker game, Vincent thought as he waited for the other shoe to drop.

"Dennis always said you never noticed people much," Joe went on, his voice sounding far away as he reminisced. "I guess I saw that back at Wilton Park."

"I'm sorry." Vincent was unable to think of anything else. He was too afraid of giving something away.

"I think you were my first crush, Vincent," Joe went on, his voice soft and serious.

That caught Vincent off guard. "Huh?"

"I used to love watching you pick Dennis up from school," Joe went on. "Especially when you wore tank tops like that one." He pointed toward Vincent's shirt. "I didn't understand it then, not till I got older."

Vincent just stared, wide-eyed, and Joe offered a shy smile.

"I never talked to you, though. I was too scared." He paused, his young face thoughtful as he remembered. "Dennis and me were best buds back then."

Stunned, Vincent digested this new information. Joe had crushed on him? He and Dennis were friends? Had Dennis tried to tell him about Joe and he'd ignored it like everything else?

"I used to get messed with," Joe went on soberly. "By a kid named Tommy. Dennis always took my side, used that martial arts you all taught him to keep Tommy away."

When Vincent gaped in amazement, Joe said, "He never told you?"

Vincent shook his head again. Dennis stood up against Tommy. And he still felt bad when Tommy was sentenced to prison.

"He was pretty badass," Joe went on sadly, as though Dennis was already gone. "After you moved we pm'd a lot, but then I guess he got new friends. Last year, my parents decided to move to Mississippi and I didn't wanna go. After my dad found out I was gay, all hell broke loose. I ran and they moved."

Vincent swallowed with difficulty. His throat was parched. He needed water. "I'm sorry."

"Not important now." Joe paused, his brown eyes wide with fear. "You think Dennis is gonna make it?"

Vincent froze with sudden fear. "He has to."

Joe nodded and a heavy silence fell between them.

"What about Franky?" Vincent finally asked. "How bad was he when they brought him in?"

Joe's face clouded over with even deeper anguish. "Real bad. The superhero kept him alive till the paramedics got there. He'd be dead otherwise."

Vincent flinched again, despite his best efforts at composure. "The super-hero?"

Joe stared at him as though he could see his every secret.

Or is that my imagination?

"The vigilante," Joe explained. "That's what I call him, even though he says he's not."

Vincent chose his words carefully. "How do you, uh, know him?"

"Everybody on the streets knows him," Joe replied. "'Specially me and Franky. It's like, finally somebody cares about us out there, you know? He's real important to a lot of people, man." He paused and screwed up his face in thought. "Don't think he knows it, though. Sure, he kicks ass on drug dealers and muggers and stuff, but that's not what makes him a superhero. It's the way he makes people like me feel real, like we're important."

Vincent realized his mouth hung open and he quickly closed it. He felt confused and guilty in equal measure. He'd made promises to this boy. And to Franky down the hall. Promises he hadn't been able to keep. But had he truly inspired that many people out there? Even if he had, it wasn't worth Dennis's life. Dennis would say it was – that was what made Dennis so special. That's why he'd come up with the Invictus plan in the first place.

And to get closer to me, Vincent finally realized. *So I would be proud of him.*

Linda stepped into the room, stripping off her latex gloves, the mask dangling from her neck.

"Any change?" Vincent blurted, leaping to his feet.

She shook her head.

Joe stood and placed a hand on Vincent's shoulder as though they'd known each other forever.

"He's tough, Vincent. He'll make it." The look in his eyes reeked of sincerity and youthful hope. He stepped away and approached Linda. "Can we see Franky now?"

She looked across the room at Vincent. "You going back in with Dennis?"

"Yes."

She left the room. Joe paused in the doorway. With a knowing look in his eyes, he said quietly, "Invictus was wrong."

Vincent's eyes went wide with uncertainty. "How so?"

"If he ain't a superhero, no one is."

He vanished down the hall, leaving a shocked Vincent behind.

It took a bit of persuasion, but Linda managed to convince the nurse that she and Joe were the only family Franky had, that his real mother was dead and there was no one else.

The head nurse finally broke and told them, "That boy is lucky to be alive. They pumped his stomach, but his heart almost stopped twice since they brought him in. He's on a breathing machine and very fragile."

"Can we go in?" Linda asked, her voice filled with urgency. She didn't even know this boy, but just the thought of a ten-year-old alone and unloved and drug addicted tore her heart to pieces.

The nurse studied them both a moment. "One at a time. No more than ten minutes each. Mask and gloves at all times."

She pointed to the mask and glove dispensers affixed to a nearby wall. Joe was so excited that Linda's heart lurched. He ran to the dispensers and pulled on the sticky latex gloves with difficulty. Then he popped out a mask and slipped it on.

"Can I go first?" His voice sounded muffled beneath the mask.

Linda nodded and he practically ran for the door.

The nurse looked almost frightened. "I have a son who's ten," she muttered. "What's happened to our world?" Obviously not expecting an answer, she headed back to her station.

Linda drifted over to the window. Joe looked so small and helpless as he sat beside the bed. The boy beneath the tubing and oxygen mask appeared younger than ten, more like six or seven, tiny and frail. She couldn't hear Joe's words, but saw him bend his head and weep.

"Linda!"

She turned to find James striding down the corridor toward her.

"What are you doing here? The nurse by Dennis's room told me where you went."

"Sorry, honey. I forgot to tell you." She explained about Joe and Franky.

"Jeez!" he muttered, staring into the room. "Ten?"

She nodded gravely.

"Any change with Dennis?"

She shook her head. She knew he knew what she was going to say. "He needs you."

James stood tautly. "What could I possibly say to him?"

"James," she whispered. "You act like Vincent wanted this to happen."

"I warned him, Linda," James hissed. "I told him something would happen."

She held his gaze with her own. "So now you feel vindicated?" She reached out and took one of his hands in hers, startled to feel it trembling.

"James, that young man is like our son, same as Dennis. And he's hurting a helluva lot more than either of us. He needs you. Talk to him. Don't judge him."

James stared at her for a long moment. He squeezed her hand and nodded.

James flashed his badge to the head ICU nurse and asked for a private room. She showed him a small, empty office and told him he could use that. He thanked her and went to Dennis's room. Donning a mask and gloves, he opened the door and stuck his head inside.

Vincent sat in the chair, head bowed.

"Vincent."

Vincent turned his head. His eyes went wide with surprise, and then lowered with guilt.

James cleared his throat. "We need to talk."

At first he thought Vincent wouldn't come. The elder son of his best friend sat and stared at the tile floor beneath his shoes. After a long moment, he rose and stepped forward, but refused to look James in the eye.

James backed out of the room and Vincent followed. They discarded their gloves and masks and James led the way to the empty office. There was a desk inside with two wooden chairs and framed certificates adorned the walls. He sat while Vincent stood in silence at the door.

"Close the door, Vincent."

Still keeping his gaze averted, Vincent slowly closed the door. It clicked shut and cut off the hallway sounds. Head bowed, hair dangling around his face, Vincent whispered, "Go ahead. Say it."

"Say what?"

"I told you so."

James flinched because those very words were on the tip of his tongue. "I wouldn't say that to you."

But you almost did!

The full weight of what had happened slammed down on his head and pounded into his soul. As a cop he'd seen plenty of dead kids. But as a parent… Nothing could compare.

"This is my fault, too," he finally admitted. "Once I knew what you were doing, I should have stopped you. Somehow." He choked then, unchecked emotion bubbling up from deep inside to pull at his heart. "Oh, God, Vincent, how did we let this happen to him?"

Vincent raised his head. "James, please believe me, this was never… he was never… I was the only one who was *ever* supposed to be in any danger. Dennis was never, ever supposed to be out there!"

"I know."

"But I drove him to the streets," Vincent went on, pacing the room, his voice pungent with remorse. "I ignored him, just like I always ignored him. He needed me to love him, to be proud of him. And I neglected him. That's why he hung around with—"

James stood. "Vincent, don't do this to yourself."

"James, he's all I have left!"

Vincent engulfed him in a desperate hug.

James felt awkward, especially since he knew Vincent was right. This happened because of choices he'd made, and ones he hadn't made. James lifted his arms and awkwardly enveloped him.

"You always have me and Linda."

"Oh, James, if he dies…."

"He won't!"

James couldn't imagine life without Dennis and refused to even go there. He gently eased Vincent down into a chair and stood before him, searching for the right words. And then suddenly he had them.

"You did what you thought was right at the time. We all make choices. Some don't work out the way we hope. It's done, Vincent. And it can't be undone."

Vincent visibly stiffened. He sat for a long moment, his head bowed and body motionless, as though weighing a momentous decision. He slowly lifted his head and James almost recoiled. Vincent wore an expression of raw rage.

"It's not done yet." Even his voice sounded cold. All trace of sadness and remorse had vanished.

"What do you mean?"

"That kid at Dennis's school had it right. Payback *is* justice."

Vincent stood and started for the door.

Fear engulfed James. "Vincent, where are you going?"

Vincent faced him, his expression steely. "Dennis and I were wrong. You and daddy were wrong. Even Batman is wrong. The law, that kind of justice doesn't work anymore, if it ever did."

James felt his heart pounding with dread. "What are you saying?"

Vincent locked eyes with his. "I'm going to find Demon. And I'm going to kill him."

He opened the door. James lunged forward and tried to slam it shut, but Vincent's foot blocked it.

James said, "You can't do that."

Vincent's face darkened and James thought he might throw a punch.

"Listen to me, Vince. You'll be going against everything your father ever taught you, everything you and Dennis believe in, the whole reason you started this thing in the first place."

"Step aside, James."

James removed his hand from the door and stepped back. Vincent flung it open and stepped into the corridor.

"If you do this, Vincent, you'll lose yourself forever."

Vincent stopped and twisted his head around. The movement was so deliberate and his expression so savage that James couldn't help but think of that head-turning scene in *The Exorcist* movie. Vincent looked like a man possessed.

"I'm already lost without him."

"He's still here," James pleaded. "And he needs you to be here when he wakes up."

Vincent hesitated a brief moment, and James hoped he'd gotten through. Then Vincent started down the corridor toward the exit.

"I could arrest you," James said as loudly as he dared.

Two nurses glanced over from their station.

Vincent stopped, but didn't turn around. "You do what you have to."

He strode forward and vanished around the corner.

Cursing under his breath, James ran to get Linda.

CHAPTER THIRTY-TWO

WELCOME, HERO

JAMES BARELY GAVE LINDA A second to give Joe her number before dragging her from the ICU.

"Call if anything changes with Dennis or Franky."

Clearly confused, Joe nodded and slipped his phone back into his pocket.

Nurses eyed James with alarm as he pulled her by the arm to the bank of elevators.

"What's wrong?"

He let her go and punched the down button. "Vincent's going after Demon. We have to stop him."

She gasped.

The elevator door popped open and they darted inside.

As James pulled out of the hospital parking lot onto Zonal Avenue, he suddenly realized something. "Damn. I don't know where he's going."

He stopped as the traffic light turned red and glanced over at Linda, sitting pensively in the semi-darkness.

"How does *he*?" she asked thoughtfully.

"Huh?"

"If he knew where Demon was before, why didn't he tell us or break up the operation himself?"

James considered her words. The light turned green and he sped off down Zonal. He replayed in his mind everything he'd seen as he'd approached the

Seventh Street overpass. Vincent had cracked the car windshield. The car had tried to run him down. And–

"I know where he went!"

He swung a hard left onto State Street and switched on his siren.

Traffic at five a.m. was light and James arrived at the overpass in less than ten minutes. By then, he'd killed the siren because he didn't want to spook Vincent.

"Look, there he is!" Linda called out as she pointed through her window at the area alongside the riverbank.

James stopped the car and leaped out, sprinting for the concrete barrier. Vincent stood in front of his motorcycle, in full Invictus attire, attaching some kind of red gel to the headlamp. The red light cast him in a grim silhouette.

"Vincent!" James called out as Linda joined him.

Vincent looked up, but the mask covered most of his face and the red light made his eyes unreadable.

"Don't do this, Vincent!" Linda called down, her voice rife with fear.

Vincent paused for a moment. Then he tilted the headlamp down so the red light splashed along the ground.

James noted an odd glow coming from the pavement. Vincent remounted his motorcycle and sped away from the scene.

"Damn!"

"James, did you see the ground glowing?"

"Yeah. Any ideas?"

"Knowing Vincent, it's probably some phosphorescent chemical that's only visible under red light."

"Grab the emergency flasher from the trunk."

She ran to the car.

Invictus followed the glowing traces of red along the darkened streets, his wrath building with each speck of crimson. Images of Demon with that gun to Dennis's head filled his mind and heart. The gangsters showing up hadn't been part of the plan. Killing Dennis had. It was premeditated! Why? To get to him? He knew Dennis would never have given away his identity. Maybe Demon just suspected Dennis was a plant? It didn't matter now.

Visions of Dennis's stomach erupting with blood like a volcano from hell kept intruding and Invictus had to force them into retreat. He needed to focus on the roadway. The powder he'd thrown was beginning to diminish. It would only have stuck to Demon's tires for a limited distance. He hoped it would be far enough to find Cat's lair and finish this once and for all.

James drove slowly while Linda leaned out the passenger window with the flashing beacon. In strobe-like fashion, the light illuminated speckles of glowing powder leading away from the river toward the warehouse district. His detachable police flasher would provide more light, but would also attract more attention and he didn't want to endanger Vincent or themselves.

He should call for backup. That was protocol. That was the law. The letter of the law. But he couldn't risk Vincent getting hurt in a firefight. The spirit of the law reminded him that Vincent was his son and not a criminal. At least, not yet.

Invictus saw the massive warehouse looming before him. The chemical tracks were faint, but led straight to that building. It was three stories high, with only a few windows near the top, large bay doors and loading docks, and silence all around. It was already after five in the morning and he'd seen big rigs loading up at some other warehouses in the area. Nothing moved at this facility because there was nothing to be picked up. This was the place, all right.

Anger surging, he rode around behind the building and found some dumpsters. He stopped the bike and climbed off, easing it behind the dumpsters as best he could. The rear tire stuck out, but he didn't care. After tonight it wouldn't matter. Without Dennis, Invictus was dead anyway. Without Dennis, life in prison would be exactly what he deserved. But Demon would pay for what he'd done. And so would this woman, Cat, who pulled the strings.

He strode along the sidewalk until he came to a regular sized door. He tried the knob. Locked. Furious, he spun into a kick and slammed his foot into the wood. The door rattled, but held. Cursing, he reached into a pouch for several of his thermite pellets and stuck them around the knob. Using a small rock he picked up off the ground, he smashed each pellet. Sizzling sounds broke the early morning quiet as the chemical burned its way into the metal. The knob slipped out with ease and so did the locking mechanism.

Invictus tossed them aside and shoved open the door with his shield. It slammed into the wall with a loud *thud.* He didn't care if they heard him. He'd kill everyone in this place to get to Demon. His loss of control barely registered in his mind. Fury filled him. His entire body shook with it, like he would explode if he didn't expel it. And the only way to expel it was to beat Demon to death.

He stormed into the dark unknown.

James approached the warehouse and told Linda to kill the flasher. She did. Being the end of July, sunrise would not be for another hour or more, so darkness, broken up by sporadic streetlights, filled the area.

"This is the place," James murmured.

"I'm going in with you," Linda insisted.

James wanted to protest, but one look at her determined face told him it wasn't worth it.

"Let's go."

They exited the car and hurried toward the building. James led the way, gun out and ready.

Janson had gotten the message from Stevens' wife and welcomed the opportunity to patrol alone. He didn't understand why, but Stevens had gone soft on the vigilante case and would be more of a hindrance than a help. Janson had swung by the scene of that gang firefight by the river, but there was no indication the vigilante was involved, so he'd left.

It was practically morning and he was almost ready to call it quits. Then his headlight beams caught a glimpse of something behind a row of dumpsters. This warehouse district was known for clandestine drug deals and the vigilante seemed drawn to those, but so far all had been quiet.

He stopped and backed up the car. His lights illuminated the rusty blue dumpsters. A wheel jutted out from behind them.

A motorcycle wheel.

Could it be?

Gun drawn, he stepped from the car and surveyed the dark street. Nothing moved. He approached the dumpsters with caution, giving them a wide berth in case someone lurked behind them. As he moved around toward the rear, the beam of his flashlight revealed the whole of the motorcycle. Black. No plates. He grinned.

"Bingo."

He sprinted back to his car to call for backup.

Dorothy Ellis lay in bed unable to sleep. Her second floor apartment sweltered during the summer and made sleeping a chore unto itself. All was quiet. She checked the time on the clock beside her bed: five-fifteen. The only sounds were the low chatter from her police scanner sitting beside the clock. She reached out to raise the volume. Might as well find out what was going on.

Her Facebook group had grown into the thousands since she'd created it and had spawned numerous similar groups. Invictus had become wildly popular on social media, and the world was starting to take notice, too.

"Attention all units," crackled over the scanner. "Asian vigilante spotted at a downtown warehouse."

She sat straight up in bed and jotted down the address.

"Per Captain Torres – surround the building, but do not attempt to enter. Sergeant Janson is on scene. He is in command until the captain arrives."

Dorothy leaped from the bed and sprinted for her computer, cell phone in hand. Her army was ready.

The Mistress stood before her monitors when Demon burst into the chamber. She wore her fighting attire, like she was expecting to go into battle.

"He's here, Mistress."

She raised one slender arm and pointed at the screens. "I think I know that, Demon."

He strode to her side and scanned the monitors. Each screen displayed different areas within the vast complex. The Hero stood on the ground floor, looking at the catwalks above him.

"Demon!" shouted The Hero, his voice potent with rage. "I know you're here!"

Demon had never seen him like this before. "Why's he so pissed?"

"Dreamer was his brother."

Demon froze. "You never told me that."

Her gaze remained pinned to the screen as the Hero stalked back and forth.

"It was best this way."

Demon didn't respond. He watched the screen. The Hero kicked down an office door and charged inside, but there was no one there. Then he stormed back out and raised his eyes.

"Demon!"

Demon flinched. That anger. The visceral fury and animalistic body movements. Just like his twelve-year-old self when his brother had been murdered right in front of him. He understood The Hero's pain. Finally, something they shared in common. Was the Mistress right? If he'd known Dreamer was the brother, would he have agreed to execute him? No way to know for sure. And it no longer mattered.

"I will finish him now."

He started to leave.

"Wait."

He paused.

"I want to see how close to the edge he really is."

Not understanding, Demon stood and observed.

One of her men appeared on a separate screen, creeping along a catwalk. The Hero could be seen through the perforated metal walkway on the floor below, looking side to side. The man climbed over the railing and jumped.

Invictus looked up as the man plummeted toward him. He jumped aside. The man landed and tried for a kick to the head. Invictus bent and powered forward with a vicious punch to the groin. The man cried out in agony and stumbled. Invictus slammed his shield into the man's face, who toppled as two more jumped at him from the shadows.

He spun and kicked the nearest one in the face. The second tried for a punch, but Invictus slammed down on his forearm with one elbow. The man dropped in pain to the floor of the warehouse and Invictus stomped on his arm. The snapping of bone fed his bloodlust. He viciously kicked the man in the kidneys, sending him rolling over and whimpering in agony. Stepping over the fallen fighters, Invictus spotted stairs ascending to the next level and strode toward them like an out-of-control robot.

Demon flinched at the brutality. He pictured The Hero saving those guys at the school when he could have let them die. Then he thought of Z with his hair ripped out and his shattered arm.

It's his fault Z is dead!

Or was it? Had The Mistress planned that, too, just like she'd planned out the brother?

"He's nearly mine," Cat whispered, more to herself than to him. She was so engrossed in watching those screens that Demon decided she'd forgotten about him. Had everything been a carefully orchestrated game since the school incident? Or even before?

He observed The Hero sprint up metal steps to the second floor. Two more fighters leapt out at him, only to be pummeled and pounded and slammed with the shield. Even though the monitor, Demon heard grunts and groans of pain. Such sounds used to excite him. But not now.

For some reason—maybe it was Z, maybe it was Dreamer—what The Mistress was doing bothered him in ways he didn't think was possible anymore. He'd never even considered how she'd corrupted him. After he'd slashed the throat of his brother's killer, there'd been no going back. He had nobody. She took him in, educated and groomed him. Right and wrong became mere words that had no place in his world. But he had thought she honestly cared about him, maybe even loved him as the little brother she never had. Now he wasn't so sure.

His thoughts were interrupted as The Hero spotted a camera and strode toward it. His face grew large on one of the screens and Demon could easily see flecks of blood on his mask.

"Demon! Get your cowardly ass out here and face me!"

Demon flinched, but his pride asserted itself. "Let me break him now, Mistress."

"A few more moments," she purred.

Demon returned his gaze to the screen as more of her foot soldiers ran along the catwalk to challenge The Hero.

James heard the sounds of fighting from the parking lot. So much for the element of surprise. He aimed and fired at the door lock, shattering it with two consecutive bullets. Yanking open the door, he glanced back at Linda.

"Stay behind me in case they're armed."

She eyed him in the darkness. "And if they aren't?"

"They're all yours, baby."

She followed him inside.

James spotted the mewling, bleeding, badly wounded men rolling around on the floor. Fighting sounds came from above. He glanced up and froze. Vincent was on the second-floor catwalk fighting against three more. He watched Vincent grab one of his attacker's arms and slam it against the railing. The shattering of bone was louder than the attacker's scream.

"Oh, my God," Linda whispered from behind him.

"We've gotta get up there," James hissed and started for the steps.

A voice echoed all around them. "Intruders in the building. Take them down!"

"Behind me," James barked.

He felt Linda slide in behind him as five Asian men appeared from the dark reaches of the warehouse and formed a semi-circle around them. None brandished a weapon and James didn't give them time to arm themselves. He slid his gun into its holster.

"Let's get 'em."

They leaped forward as the Asians rushed in as a group. Linda ducked, then kicked the nearest one in the side. He grunted and staggered. James spun into a kick against one attacker while simultaneously punching out at a second, connecting with the young man's face. Another Asian grabbed Linda from behind. She dropped and pulled him up and over her head. He slammed into one of his fellow attackers and they both went sprawling.

Two of the fighters double-teamed James, but his size and weight overcame them both. One went down with a solid kick to the midsection, while the other took multiple punches to the face before crumpling to the floor.

James and Linda pressed up against each other, back to back, as the Asians regrouped for another attack.

Invictus stepped over the attacker whose arm he'd broken and slammed his shield into the next one, following it up with a brutal punch to the face and a knee to the midsection. Shoving that attacker aside, he faced off against the third. This one was taller and built like a football player, but he barely noticed. He marched forward and ducked as the guy took a swing. He spun into a kick, connecting with the man's knee. The guy shrieked in agony and dropped. Invictus threw up his own knee and connected with the man's chin. The attacker's head snapped up and he flew backward, where he lay rolling and pitching on the metal catwalk.

Invictus scanned the area for more threats, and then glanced down through the catwalk to see James and Linda engaging a group of fighters. More appeared from the shadows to join them, but he couldn't stop now. He wanted Demon and no one would prevent that.

A female voice echoed all around him: "Welcome, Hero. I've been expecting you."

Invictus peered at the nearest camera, and looked at the next floor up. Seeing nothing, he called out, "Cat? Where's Demon?"

"My name is Catherine," the voice purred, sounding seductive and admiring all at once.

"I know about the chemicals you're putting in the drugs," Invictus called out. "And I'm gonna stop you!"

She laughed. It was a mocking laugh, but enticing, too.

"Come to me, Hero. Up to the next catwalk and straight ahead. I'm waiting."

He surveyed the area and spotted steps leading to the next level. Sprinting over, he took those steps two at a time. Arriving at the top floor, he looked around. The catwalk led to a closed door straight ahead. Just like she'd said. He strode forward with reckless abandon.

CHAPTER THIRTY-THREE

SO, HERO, WE MEET AT LAST

CAT TURNED TO HIM, AND Demon saw such fire in her eyes that he stepped back. "Wait outside."

"But, Mistress–"

"Now!"

Her coldness felt like a knife to the gut. Had she finally decided he was expendable? He bowed and marched stiffly to a rear door that led to another catwalk. He pushed open the door and glanced back. Her gaze remained riveted to a screen on which The Hero could be seen approaching the opposite door. Demon ducked out onto the catwalk and closed the door. But not all the way. He wanted to hear her what she said. He *needed* to hear.

Invictus stopped in front of the door. He tried the knob. Locked. Cursing, he started to spin into a kick when the lock *clicked* and the door drifted inward. Lowering his leg, he raised the shield and shoved through the door into the room.

The vastness of this chamber caught him by surprise, as did the massive wall of video monitors. On one he caught a glimpse of chemical containers and conveyer belts – obviously where the drugs were made. Several displayed different views of James and Linda fighting on the first floor. There had to be ten men against them now, but he couldn't worry about that. They could take care of themselves. He focused on the woman standing before him.

Her stunning beauty nearly took his breath away. Soft features, long silky hair, light makeup that highlighted her brown eyes and sensuous lips. The skintight fighting suit revealed a taut figure, more panther than human. She smiled.

"So, Hero, we meet at last."

His rage momentarily displaced by shock, he stammered, "You're the one behind this operation?"

"In the flesh." The smile grew wider. She obviously enjoyed flummoxing him.

He fought to control his breathing. "Your chemical additives will lower the I.Q.'s of the users ten times faster than the drugs themselves. What can you hope to gain?"

She circled around, as though preparing to attack. He moved with her, keeping the same distance between them. "Revenge, Vincent. And power."

He froze. His ragged breathing paused and his heart pounded even harder. "How'd you… the name's 'Invictus.'"

She laughed and continued circling. "I am the master of my fate and the captain of my soul. I read poetry, too, Vincent Villanueva, son of Loy."

"Who are you? How'd you know…?"

She lunged and he parried her punch with one arm.

"I've been watching you for months, Vincent, contemplating your fate."

She threw out a kick. He raised the shield and her foot slammed into it. Hard. He staggered back slightly, suddenly realizing how exhausted he was. He hadn't slept for almost twenty-four hours.

"I knew who you were before you 'became' Invictus."

She lunged out and spun into a kick.

He jumped up and did a back flip, landing just out of range of her foot. She grinned and circled, the panther teasing the prey.

"Your father investigated the murder of my older brother."

Those words slammed into his brain, but only confused him further. "Huh?"

Her face became feral as she circled. "My brother was beaten to death by black men who didn't like his slanty eyes. Your father and his partner never bothered to get enough evidence to convict, so the killers went free. Is that justice, Vincent?"

Suddenly that case rose up in his memory and he recalled the conversation they'd had about the killing over Thanksgiving dinner.

"No," he blurted, "But–"

"I took my own revenge," she spat, cutting him off and spinning into another kick.

This time he wasn't fast enough and the kick connected with the edge of his shield. He stumbled back and dropped to one knee. He heard her approach and leapt up and around, shoving the shield out to block her next deadly kick. Her foot bounced off and she staggered slightly.

He backed away.

"That's why you're destroying the minds of kids, because my dad couldn't nail those guys?"

His mind replayed Joe's words: *"They never sell to Asians."*

Oh, my God…

She stopped circling and stared at him with fiery eyes.

"I'm not destroying anything. They are. No one's forcing them to use drugs. And no one forces them to hurl racial slurs at Asians. Tell me you haven't seen the rise in crime against Asians, not to mention efforts by universities to keep us out because, more than any other racial group, we *earn* the right to be there. I know you've lived your life in a book, Vincent, but don't tell me you've never been called a slant, or told to go back to your own country, even though this *is* your country, or had them pinch up their eyes to mock you."

Invictus fought to catch his breath. Was all she'd said true? He honestly didn't keep up with the news, so she might be right. But he *had* experienced prejudice, especially before moving to the Valley.

"Yeah, I've heard junk like that from stupid, ignorant people. All your drugs will do is make them more stupid and more ignorant."

She smiled again. "And more controllable. People hate us because we work hard and use our brains. Well, I'm using mine. Soon Asians will be the dominant race in this country and all those who mock us will take orders from us."

Invictus couldn't believe what he was hearing. Her plan was crazy and evil and… might work.

"You don't fight bigotry with bigotry. My father taught me that."

She lost the smile. "I'm sorry your father died in that crash. My original plan was to take you all out at the graduation."

"What?" The big picture was beginning to dawn on him.

She chuckled. "I still hoped to kill you and your brother so the *partner* would know the pain of losing someone he loved. Invictus foiled that plan. So I had to settle for *you* losing someone."

He felt the blood drain from his face and his knees grew weak. "Oh, God, no! Dennis?"

She grinned. "Those lowlife gangsters almost ruined that plan, but only just. From what I've heard, your brother will be dead soon enough."

Invictus felt like a marble statue, as still as the air around him. He could scarcely breathe as the enormity of her evil washed over him and almost sent him into a swoon.

She lunged again, spinning into a kick that connected squarely with his shield and pushed him back.

He stumbled, but managed to keep his feet under him.

"I want you on my team, Vincent. Demon has served his purpose. He's been loyal, yes, but weak when it comes to certain things. Had he known Dennis was your brother, he'd never have followed my orders. Too much childhood trauma. But you? You've never let emotions like love or pity rule you. You're what I need."

Anger surged through him once more. "I'm not like you."

He circled, looking for an opening to take her down.

"No? All my shattered minions below might say different." She chuckled. "It's fitting, don't you think, that there's no evidence against Demon? He'll walk away scot free, just like the animals who murdered my brother."

Invictus felt his blood boiling as he pictured Dennis in that hospital bed, tubes running in and out of him, machines keeping him alive.

"Where is he?"

"You want the same kind of justice I exacted. That's why you came here, isn't it?"

"Where *is* he?"

She grinned and raised one hand to point at a door behind her.

"He says he's going to kill you."

"Like hell!"

Invictus broke into a run and leapt into the air feet first. His feet connected with the door and sent it flying outward where it slammed into the catwalk railing and split down the middle. He landed on the metal catwalk with a *clang* that echoed all around him. Demon stood not ten feet away, fists raised, poised to strike.

Invictus lunged forward.

James and Linda had incapacitated five of the attackers, but the other five were fresher and not so easily defeated. James punched and kicked and leapt, but the smaller, lighter assailants managed to evade many of his moves. Linda fared better because she was small like them and could more easily duck under and attack from below. Kicks to the groin sent two of the men sprawling to the floor, clutching their privates and howling in pain.

Swiping sweaty hair from her eyes, she faced the next attacker.

Demon jumped aside to avoid the first kick, then spun and planted one foot into The Hero's back, shoving him forward into the railing. He'd heard everything The Mistress said. He was to be sacrificed. She *had* lost faith in him. But if he killed The Hero first, she'd have to keep him. She'd have no one else.

They exchanged vicious blows, with Demon barely managing to avoid the deadly shield. He ducked beneath it and slid on the catwalk, knocking The Hero's legs out from under him. The Hero stumbled and went down. Demon kicked him in the side and relished the grunt of pain that erupted from his mouth.

The Hero rolled along the catwalk and clambered to his feet, swinging up with the shield as Demon launched into a flying kick. His feet struck the shield and shoved the Hero backwards into the rail yet again, momentarily stunning him. He raised one fist and plowed forward.

But The Hero managed to lift the shield at the last moment and Demon felt his fist slam into the metal. His knuckles shattered and his arm went numb with pain.

James and Linda faced off against the remaining three attackers. There seemed to be a pause in the fighting, as though someone had hit the "freeze" button. James glanced up and spotted Demon and Invictus viciously exchanging blows and kicks.

"We've gotta get up there!" he hissed.

She glanced over. "Airplane spin?"

His eyes went wide with understanding. The three men rushed them. Linda turned her back on James and threw her hands back over her head. He grabbed them and she pressed her shoulders against his chest. He executed a spin while she raised both legs. The men were caught off guard by the move. Her feet slammed into each of their faces as James spun her full circle, and the three staggered back. He released her and moved in to finish off two of the men with a hard punch to the face. They crumpled to the floor and didn't get up. She struck out with one foot and kicked the third in the chest, sending him slamming into a wall.

James didn't hesitate. He ran for the stairway. Linda followed.

Seeing the blood spurt from Demon's fist enraged Invictus even more. He plowed into the man like a predator attacking a wounded animal. He punched Demon hard to the face and slammed the shield into his head. Demon staggered, but didn't go down. He tried to throw a punch, but Invictus snatched the wounded arm around the wrist and slammed it down across the railing. It snapped like a twig and Demon grunted with barely contained agony.

Invictus let go and watched the wounded Demon stagger backward, his face a mask of controlled pain. He saw Dennis in Demon's face, Dennis with his eyes closed, Dennis who might never open them again, Dennis who would never walk again even if he lived. He drove forward and leaped into a flying kick. His feet smashed into Demon's chest and sent him staggering back into the metal rail at the end of the catwalk. The railing snapped and dislodged itself. It sailed downward to strike the floor three stories below with a hollow *thud*.

Invictus watched Demon teeter on the edge of the precipice. Demon's eyes met his for one brief second before he toppled off the catwalk. Invictus rushed forward, expecting to see Demon's crumpled body on the warehouse floor below. To his shock, he found his enemy dangling from the catwalk, barely holding on with his one good hand.

Their eyes locked.

Cat's voice sailed out of nowhere and echoed in his ears. "Kill him, Vincent!"

Demon's eyes widened slightly, and Invictus saw pain in those eyes, pain and betrayal. Demon had trusted Cat, he suddenly understood. She had made him believe he was important. She'd said she was proud of him, but it was a lie, a way to control him.

Not sure why, he impulsively squatted down and reached out, wrapping his free hand around Demon's wrist and squeezing hard. Demon winced and his fingers slipped off the rail. Now only Invictus kept him from death.

"He killed your brother, Vincent," Cat's voice echoed all around him. "It is your right. It's justice!"

Invictus trembled at her words. He saw Dennis lying in that hospital bed.

Not dead, but crippled for life at the very least. He saw the angry teen at the graduation yelling, "Payback is justice" and spitting in his face.

"Vincent, no!"

He swiveled his head to see James and Linda on the catwalk, frozen in horror.

He faced Demon once again, and suddenly felt as though he were seeing through Dennis's eyes. He saw Dennis drawing an X across a Punisher comic, Dennis clutching *The Velveteen Rabbit*, Dennis feeding those stray cats, Dennis reciting poetry to diffuse anger and calm difficult situations, Dennis expressing sorrow about Tommy, Dennis saying all life was precious.

Dennis was everything to him and Dennis would never forgive him if he did this.

"I hate you," he hissed. "But he's more important."

He yanked hard and dragged his enemy up onto the catwalk, rising to his feet and letting Demon sag into a barely conscious heap.

"Your brother," Demon croaked, and blood spilt from his mouth onto the metal catwalk. "I didn't... know." He struggled for breath. "No... honor. Kill... me."

Invictus felt tears behind his eyes and fought them back.

"If I kill you, I lose everything."

And then Linda was there, her arms wrapped around him. He dropped his shield and returned the hug, giving into the tears.

She pulled him tightly to her. "That was the hardest choice you'll ever have to make, sweetheart. And you made the right one."

James rushed over to cuff Demon to the railing. Invictus released Linda and faced this man he respected above all others.

James placed one hand on his shoulder. "I'm proud of you, Vincent."

Invictus felt a surge of happiness rush through him at those few simple words. Now he understood what Dennis had always needed from *him*.

"What about the woman?" Linda asked.

"Probably gone, but I'll check it out." He drew his gun. "Vincent, you better go. We'll take care of everything. Dennis needs you."

Invictus nodded, suddenly anxious to be back beside his brother. If Dennis awoke...

NO! Not if. He will awake, and when he does I need to be there!

Reaching down, he snatched up the shield. He caught Demon's eyes one last time, but saw no enmity. More like admiration. He rose and sprinted for the stairs.

James burst into the video chamber, gun drawn. He wasn't surprised to find it empty. His gaze was immediately drawn to the bank of monitors. The exterior cameras revealed the entire warehouse surrounded by police cars, with officers pointing their weapons at the building. Torres held up his bullhorn.

Invictus stepped out the door James and Linda had used, and was blinded by a harsh light slamming into his eyes.

"Freeze, vigilante!" Torres's voice boomed out from the bullhorn. "You're completely surrounded. Lower that shield to the ground, slowly, and put your hands on your head. Your ass is under arrest!"

Invictus squinted against the light. He could only make out shadows of cars and people. But even in the harshness of his vision, he easily recognized guns pointed his way.

He was trapped.

James sprinted down the stairs to where Linda stood guarding Demon.

"Torres has Vincent!"

She gagged. "Oh, no…"

They ran for the stairs.

CHAPTER THIRTY-FOUR
DEATH BE NOT PROUD

THIS WAS IT. THE END. As best he could beneath the bright lights, Invictus surveyed his surroundings. Cops ringed him with their cars. He might be able to dive back through the door before they shot him, but what for? This had all been a waste. His life, his career in science, all gone. And Dennis… his life had been shattered, assuming he didn't die. Franky might be brain dead and Joe had no home.

Invictus was spent. He'd failed and he was tired. It was time to give up. For a kid who'd grown up hiding from emotions, he felt overwhelmed by them. He had nothing left to fight for. He was done.

He squatted very slowly and laid his shield onto the cracked pavement of the parking lot, then rose to his feet.

"I give up."

He started to raise his hands.

A voice cut through the darkness. "No!"

Startled, Invictus glanced to his right and stiffened with shock.

Hundreds of tattered, limping, wheezing people approached the phalanx of police, with Jasper leading the way.

The homeless stopped just outside the police perimeter. Wearing the same dirty blue beanie and fingerless gloves, Jasper limped toward Torres.

"Get outta here!" Torres shouted, clearly furious. "All of you. You're impeding a police action."

Jasper continued his approach and several officers aimed their guns at him.

Invictus stood paralyzed, terrified the old man would be shot.

Jasper stopped four feet from Torres and locked eyes with him. Without turning his head, he raised one arm and pointed at Invictus. "He's our friend."

Torres snorted. "He's a wanted criminal."

Standing beside him, gun pointed at Jasper, was Janson.

Jasper stood his ground and continued pointing. "He's our friend and you need to leave him alone."

"You're nobody to tell me what to do. Any of you."

Invictus scanned the mass of impassive humanity filling the street. If they felt insulted by Torres's words, they didn't show it.

"Cause we's homeless?" Jasper shot back, his voice cracking. "Cause we can't vote? Don't matter that you got yourself a nice house and a job, you still gotta bully people like me and him." He again pointed at Invictus. "He's our friend and we ain't gonna let you take him away from us."

Invictus felt his heart swell.

Torres sneered and raised his bullhorn. "You will all be arrested if you do not disperse immediately!" His voice echoed all around them.

"Does that go for me, too?"

Invictus turned to see Ms. Ellis, Dennis's art teacher, striding across the parking lot.

Huh?

She pushed boldly through the police line. She didn't even seem to care that guns were trained on her back. Her eyes blazed with fire.

Behind her, several news vehicles roared to a stop outside the police line. Sharon and her cameraman leapt out of the Channel 4 van.

Invictus stared in confusion as Ms. Ellis stopped right in front of him.

"You can't give up," she insisted with passion, almost like she was reprimanding a student. "You have to finish what you started."

Invictus was stunned.

"Get the hell outta here, lady!" Torres bellowed through the bullhorn. "Who are you?"

She turned. The bright lights gave her an ethereal glow, like an angel come down from heaven.

"I live in this city," she replied, scanning the faces of the cops around her. "There's a lot of us citizens who appreciate what this man has been doing."

"You're obstructing justice," Torres shouted. "Arrest this woman, and take that vigilante into custody!"

Invictus heard running footsteps. James and Linda sprinted around the building toward him. The cops allowed them through the perimeter.

Ms. Ellis gave them no notice. She fixed her gaze on Torres.

"This city's riddled with drugs. Even my middle school kids are getting hooked. You and your kind didn't do anything till he came along. Now he's the closest thing we got like a hero in this city and we're not gonna let you touch him."

Torres was flabbergasted. "You and these homeless people?"

Dorothy looked defiant. "No, me and them and a whole lot more."

From the darkness behind the police, shadows moved into the light.

People.

A lot of people.

They pressed their way between police cars and around the cops, stopping directly in front of them.

Open-mouthed, Invictus stared at a row of civilians between him and the police.

Sharon and the news crews pushed their way past the police line to mingle with the new arrivals.

Invictus recognized familiar faces. There was the woman he'd saved from being carjacked, and the one from the alley; the McDonald's worker who'd served him and Joe; the Korean man whose store was robbed; people from the movie theater where he fought the bullies. There were even kids whose drug deals he'd busted up, kids he'd told to never be out on the streets again. He spotted the woman and her baby from the fire. Even two of those firefighters were present, and the paramedics who'd picked up Franky. And many more faces he'd never seen before.

At least a hundred people crowded in amongst the cops. The homeless also forced their way in, as though daring the police to shoot.

Invictus couldn't believe it.

Dennis was right.

They *had* come.

The police officers glanced at the flustered Torres, awaiting their orders.

Torres gaped at the scene surrounding him, clearly disbelieving what he was seeing. He raised the bullhorn. "Detective Stevens, handcuff this woman and that vigilante."

Invictus faced his father's partner.

James met his gaze a long moment, eyes wide with amazement, as though he couldn't believe this was happening.

Then he turned to Torres. "No, sir, I can't."

"I'll have your badge!"

James reached into a pocket and pulled out his badge. It glinted in the bright lights as he tossed it into the dirt at his feet. "Take it. If you and everyone else can't see that Invictus and us and these people are all on the same side, then that badge isn't worth the dirt it's lying in."

Linda slipped one arm through his and pulled him close.

Exasperated, Torres nodded at Janson beside him.

The sergeant raised his gun and started to turn. But an elderly lady stood in his path offering him a smile and a Tic Tac. He paused, and then lowered his weapon.

The cops glanced around at Torres, at James, at the people, and at the news cameras whirring away. Some of them gave Invictus a long look, as though "seeing" him for the first time. The officer nearest Ms. Ellis holstered his gun. Another followed. Then another, and another. Within moments, every gun was back in its holster.

Invictus stood like a stone statue, unable to move or even accept what was happening. His eyes teared up and drops slipped down the outside of his mask.

Ms. Ellis picked up the shield, stepping forward and holding it out to him.

"You see, we got your message."

She handed him the shield and then leaned in to kiss him on one cheek.

He gazed at her with wide-eyed wonder.

"Go now. Just don't go far."

The crowd burst into applause. James and Linda joined in. The cops followed suit, to the amazement of Torres and Janson.

Invictus knew he'd break any moment. He took one last look at the clapping citizens, gave Jasper a chin raise, and ran off into the darkness.

Vincent sat in a hard plastic chair slumped over the railing of Dennis's hospital bed. He'd once again ducked into an alley and stripped off the costume, replacing it with his shorts and tank top. He needed a shower, food, and sleep, but what he needed more than anything was his brother. So he'd sped to County USC and practically ran through the halls to ICU. Security guards eyed him suspiciously, but they obviously recognized him because they didn't challenge him.

He'd been both happy and sad to hear there was no change. Joe had been standing outside the room looking in when he arrived, and then headed down the hall to check on Franky.

So Vincent sat and prayed and shed more tears. After several hours, exhaustion overcame him and he'd swooned forward, resting his arms on the railing and falling into a deep slumber.

He heard a voice calling out to him from far away.

"Vincent."

It was almost a whisper, faint and parched.

He struggled to pinpoint it. Was he asleep or awake? He heard it again.

"Vincent."

His eyes felt glued shut. He forced them open. Everything was a blur.

"Vincent."

He knew that voice…

He sat up abruptly and shook his head to clear it. He looked down at his brother and saw those soft gentle eyes gazing up at him with uncertainty.

"Dennis!" He leaped to his feet and leaned over the rail. "Thank God!"

Dennis offered a strained smile. "Death be not proud," he croaked. "And not getting my ass any time soon."

Vincent wanted to shout for joy and scream "Thank you" to the rafters. But he just grinned and soaked in the sight of this boy he loved more than anyone in the world.

"They came, didn't they, Vince?"

Vincent's eyebrows shot up in surprise. "How'd you know?"

Dennis looked confused. "Dreamed it, I think."

Vincent choked up with emotion. There was so much he wanted to say. "Yeah, they came. Just like you said they would."

"Course they did. You rock, bro."

Vincent's heart pounded and he reached out to gently grasp one of Dennis's hands. "No, you do."

Dennis smiled again, this time with gratitude.

"Dennis, I'm so sorry." He struggled to keep the tears at bay. But they still trickled out and Dennis went wide-eyed with shock. "See? I do cry. And I *am* proud of you. I always have been and…" He trailed off and took a deep breath.

"I love you, Dennis, more than anyone on this planet. I was just too stupid to tell you."

Dennis squeezed his hand gently. "You're not stupid. You're my badass big brother and I love you."

Vincent could only nod and wipe away tears with his other hand.

Dennis realized right away that he couldn't feel anything from the waist down. Somehow he'd known he was paralyzed. He'd heard people talking while he slept, so the realization didn't shock him like it would have otherwise. Like his other injuries, he thought it was temporary. When told he'd likely never walk again, he'd fallen into despair. Once everyone left him alone, he struggled in vain to move his legs, and even just his toes. Sweat broke out on his forehead from his exertions. But nothing moved. He lowered his head and sobbed.

Courage can be costly, his father had said that one night, and Dennis now understood what he'd meant. It had cost him beyond measure. He put on a brave face for everyone who visited, especially Vincent, but continued to cry whenever he was alone. The frustration of not being able to do even simple things, like wiggle his toes or urinate by himself, sent him to dark places within his mind and heart. A few times, while pretending to sleep so he wouldn't have to talk to people, he heard Vincent crying by his bedside.

Was it worth it? The question kept flitting about in his head during the days and nights that followed. Watching news broadcasts proved what Vincent had told him, that the people *had* gotten his message and were stepping up to help those in need.

The Dream was becoming a reality.

He studied his unmoving legs beneath the blanket. Was this a fair trade-off? Not fair, no, but not the worst that could have happened. He could've died, or Vincent could've been killed. He cursed himself for his poor choices and wished more than anything for a time machine so he could go back and not make them. But he *had* made them, and now he had to live with the consequences.

Vincent told him what went down with Cat and Demon, and why he hadn't let rage push him over the edge.

"Because of you, Dennis. I thought about you."

"Yeah?"

Vincent nodded. "All life is precious."

Dennis's eyebrows shot up in surprise.

"I learned that from a very wise kid."

Dennis smiled at the compliment. Then his face clouded over. "You think Cat will be back?"

Vincent considered for a moment. "I don't know."

A few days later, Dennis was shocked to see his old friend Joseph enter the room. Had he dreamed Joseph was there before, right after he got shot? It seemed like he had.

Joseph was so happy to see him that his immediate problems vanished beneath the joy he felt at his friend's presence. Tall and lean with his trademark 'fro, just like he'd had in fourth grade, Joseph was what Dennis needed at that moment. He expressed sorrow when Joseph told him about the little boy who overdosed.

"How is he now?"

Joseph looked sad. "He's awake, but he doesn't know me any more."

Dennis scrunched up his face in confusion. "Why not?"

"They said the drugs trashed his brain."

He described the super drugs Demon had been selling, which made Dennis even sicker than he already felt.

I helped them sell that stuff, he thought.

"What's your friend's name?"

"Franky."

Dennis gasped and Joseph jumped up from his chair.

"You okay, Dennis? Need the nurse?"

Dennis shook his head slowly, but his voice had momentarily fled.

Franky.

And Joe.

Short for Joseph.

The pieces fell into place. Did that mean Joseph knew Vincent was Invictus? He didn't dare ask. Not here. Not now. But he recalled Vincent trying to explain, in his usual clumsy way, what it was like on the streets. Which meant he met Joseph on the streets, too, along with Franky.

"So where have you been these last few years?" he finally asked.

"You really wanna know?"

"Yeah, I do."

Joseph told him, and Dennis listened with compassion and friendship and disbelief. Despite his present predicament, Joseph's story reminded him how blessed his life had been.

"I'm sorry, man. I wish I knew. You could've lived with us."

Joseph offered a tight smile. "Never thought to check in with you."

"Will Franky be okay?"

"Dunno. Vincent called in the guy he works for."

"Professor Chin?" That news surprised him. Chin was about as cold a man as he'd ever met and he'd always feared Vincent would end up like him.

"Guess the guy's a brain specialist and studies drugs and stuff."

"That where Vincent is now?"

Joseph nodded. "James and Linda, too." He paused and looked down at the floor. "Some social worker lady's been checking on him. I think she's gonna take me away, too."

Dennis frowned, but didn't know what to say.

Vincent stood beside James and Linda listening to Professor Chin and Doctor Wang, Franky's neurologist, explain the harsh realities of the boy's condition.

"So he can't remember anything of his old life?" James asked.

Vincent almost said something snarky, but bit his tongue. He knew James didn't know Franky like he did and had been hoping the boy could testify against Demon. Doing his job, like always.

Wang, of average height, but built like a weight lifter with broad shoulders pressing against his white coat, shook his head. "As of now, no."

Franky had only just come out of his coma two days earlier and Vincent hadn't mustered the courage to visit yet.

"But," Chin chimed in, adjusting his glasses, "our studies are providing clues that might help him regain some of it. The potent chemicals in those drugs destroyed hundreds of thousands of brain cells. While those cells cannot regenerate themselves, we've often seen the brain switch gears, as it were, and other parts take over the job of the damaged ones. Pre-frontal cortex cellular loss is, however, the most pernicious."

Vincent barely listened. He already knew. He knew because of the work he'd done on those drugs all summer.

"What exactly does he remember?" Linda asked. "His name, at least?"

Wang shook his head. "Not even. He says his name is Robin and that he works with Batman."

Vincent jerked his head up and found Chin staring at him.

"He also thinks Batman will take him home to the Bat Cave," Wang went on, his clinical tone laced with sadness. "Our goal now is to stabilize him, to make sure his heart doesn't give out under the strain of not having a regular supply of meth."

Linda grasped James's hand. "Can we see him?"

"For a few minutes. He's still weak and I don't want him getting overly excited."

Wang led them down the hall to another ICU room. Vincent felt Chin's piercing gaze on his back the entire time, but his thoughts were on Franky. What would become of him now? Would they even let someone adopt him? He'd talked with the social worker who'd been assigned to Franky's case, but despite what he'd already set in motion, Franky's current medical condition allowed for little planning of his future.

Wang opened the door and ushered them inside. "Try to keep it under ten."

Chin led the way, followed by Linda and James. Vincent nodded his thanks to Wang and followed. Wang closed the door and vanished down the corridor.

Franky sat propped up in bed staring at the blank wall as though he were watching the most compelling action movie ever. His face was clean and his hair washed. He looked like a different kid.

Linda offered her characteristic smile. "Hello, Franky. I'm Linda."

He eyed her warily. "My name is Robin."

"I'm sorry, Robin. How are you feeling today?"

"I hurt all over," he mumbled. "Dunno why."

Chin stepped forward. "It's the drugs leaving your body, Fr– Robin. Eventually, you'll feel better."

Franky studied the professor intently. "Do I know you?"

"Yes, I've been in to see you these past two days. I'm Dr. Chin. I'm trying to help you. Vincent told me about you."

Vincent had been hanging back, out of Franky's line of sight. On hearing his name, he stepped forward and faced this wreck of a child he'd come to love.

Franky looked so thin and frail, but broke into that angelic smile. "Batman!"

Vincent stiffened. Chin frowned and Linda gasped.

Vincent forced himself to step over to the bed. "I'm Vincent."

Franky laughed, like Vincent was making a joke. "No, you're not. You're Batman. I know you." His face scrunched up in fear. "Where's your mask? Everybody's gonna see your face!"

Vincent was speechless. Was Franky delusional or did he really recognize him? He felt Chin's eyes boring into the back of his head.

"Uh, I think you have me mixed up with somebody else."

Franky frowned. "No, I don't. I know your hair and how you talk. Why are you pretending, Batman?" Then he seemed to realize a great epiphany. "Oh, cause *they're* here!" He pointed to the others conspiratorially. "Sorry."

"Not a problem."

Vincent raised a fist and Franky bumped it.

"When you gonna take me to live with you in the Bat Cave like you promised?"

Vincent felt everyone staring at him. He squirmed with discomfort.

"Soon, Robin. When you're better."

Franky tossed off that smile again. Somehow, without the dirt and grime on his face, it looked even more haunting.

"I think it's time we leave," Chin offered, extending a hand toward the door. "I'll be in to see you later, Fr– Robin." He strode to the door and pulled it open, ushering them all into the corridor.

Vincent felt Linda and James eyeing him curiously. They obviously had many questions. He had yet to tell either of them that Franky was the little boy he'd previously mentioned.

James cleared his throat. "We're going down to see Dennis. Coming, Vincent?"

The invitation was obvious. Not just the visit, but the need to talk.

"If I may have a few minutes with Vincent first?" Chin said to James.

James nodded and led Linda away down the hall.

"Follow me, Vincent."

Dread filled his stomach like a lead balloon as Vincent followed his boss down the hall and around a corner. Chin stopped at an office door and pulled it open, ushering him inside. It was sparsely furnished, as though no one used it full time. No family photos – just generic art on the walls. Chin strode to the desk on which rested a computer monitor and keyboard, but little else. He sat and pointed to the other chair.

Vincent shuffled forward and grabbed the wooden arms of the chair, lowering himself with deliberation.

Chin tapped on the keyboard while Vincent fidgeted. After a moment, Chin swung the monitor around and Vincent saw several MRI images of a human brain.

"These are images of Franky's brain, taken here at this hospital," Chin intoned as though giving a lecture. He tapped more keys and the screen split. Another set of MRI scans appeared of the same brain. "These images of Franky's brain were taken at UCLA. In my lab."

Vincent's heart pounded.

"Did you honestly think you could hide this from me, Vincent?" Chin went on, sitting back in his chair. "Or your clandestine research on those street drugs? As much as I trust you, I have security within security. Too much is at stake not to."

Vincent felt like he'd betrayed this man. He lowered his gaze and stared at his Nikes. "I'm sorry, sir. I'll write a letter explaining everything so they won't pull your grant. And you'll have my resignation in the morning."

Chin leaned forward. "I'll have no such thing."

Vincent looked up. "You won't?"

"It's because you think outside the box, Vincent, because you take risks. That's why I wanted you on my team. Not for your sunny personality."

Vincent's mouth dropped open. "But you could get in big trouble for what I did."

Chin removed his glasses and rubbed around the bridge of his nose.

"I could, but I didn't. Your research into those chemicals was brilliant, especially how you correlated the effect each compound had on different quadrants of the brain. I informed the DEA that it was my idea to expand our research and you were acting under my orders."

"You did?"

"Your work is going to help Franky and all the others these 'super' drugs have afflicted. I've arranged to have him transferred to UCLA as soon as he's strong enough so you and I can work more closely with him."

Vincent couldn't believe what he was hearing. "But, well, that's not what you always said in class. You said good researchers couldn't afford to get too involved with people or it clouds their judgment."

"That vigilante, Invictus, he got me thinking."

Vincent's eyebrows shot up. "He did?"

Chin nodded. "Why do we do research in the first place? To help people. And people have to come first if we're to be good researchers."

Vincent gaped.

"We have a lot of work to do, Vincent." Chin stood and moved to the door. "I need my best researcher back as soon as Dennis is ready to go home."

Stunned, Vincent stood and stepped over to the door. "Uh, thank you, professor."

"No, thank *you*," Chin replied. He offered his best version of a smile. "You have inspired me, Invictus, as you have so many others."

Vincent felt his stomach clench. "How did you find out?"

Chin reached around to lift his flowing hair. He'd forgotten to tie it into a ponytail again. "Your hair gave you away. Perhaps a man bun when you're Vincent?"

Vincent almost choked. "That's what Dennis keeps saying."

"Smart boy. Like his brother."

He pulled open the door. Vincent gazed at the older man for a long moment, feeling overwhelmed with gratitude. Then he brushed past Chin and hurried down the corridor.

CHAPTER THIRTY-FIVE
THE GREATEST SUPERHERO TEAM EVER

WHEN VINCENT RETURNED TO DENNIS's room, he found his brother propped up in bed surfing television stations with the remote.

"Where is everyone?"

"James and Linda took Joseph down to the cafeteria to make sure he eats something."

Vincent pulled up a chair. He sat and gazed at Dennis, wondering where to begin. As always, Dennis led the way.

"Joseph told me how you helped him on the streets."

Vincent flinched. "He did? I mean, he knows?"

Dennis considered a moment. "I don't know. He just talked about what Invictus did for him and Franky out there." He paused. "Why didn't you just tell me?"

"Because I didn't know how." It was a lame response, but it was the truth. "I'm not a poet like you. I say things and they come out wrong. Plus, I didn't want you to think I was choosing them over you." He met Dennis's soft eyes with his own. "I didn't want to hurt you, and ended up hurting you more than ever."

"Maybe it's time you told me everything."

Vincent did just that.

Fortunately, the others were gone a long time, as though they knew the brothers needed this time together. When Vincent finished, Dennis stared at him with deep compassion.

"You should've told me before, Vince. No one should carry that kind of burden alone."

"I didn't want you to think we'd made a mistake," Vincent confessed. "The dream meant so much to you. Invictus meant so much. I didn't have the heart to tell you I was a failure out there."

"But now you know you weren't a failure, don't you?"

Vincent nodded. Then his face clouded over. "Did Joe tell you about my promises?"

"What promises?"

Vincent explained, and Dennis listened.

"I know I should've asked you first," he concluded, "but when I found out that no one would adopt Franky, I offered myself."

Dennis leaned forward. "You did?"

"Yeah. I started the process weeks ago. Background check has been done. Home inspection was last week." He offered a wry smile. "Your room took forever to clean up, by the way."

"So, we're gonna have Franky living with us?"

Vincent nodded.

Dennis's smile became so large it lit up his face. "When?"

"Soon as he's released from the hospital."

Dennis raised a hand to high five. Surprised, Vincent slapped it.

"So, it's okay?"

"It's golden."

Vincent grinned, relieved that Dennis was so accepting. Then he frowned. "Um, there's more."

Dennis raised his eyebrows and Vincent plunged into the rest of his confession. By the time James, Linda, and Joe returned from the cafeteria, Dennis was happier than Vincent had ever seen him, despite the magnitude of his injuries.

"You two look happy," Linda said as she entered. "That's nice to see after so much drama."

She held out a wrapped turkey sandwich and bottle of water to Vincent. "You need to eat something."

As though on cue, Vincent's stomach growled and he sheepishly took the food from her. "Thanks." He set both on the table beside Dennis's bed.

"How you feeling, Dennis?" James asked, shuffling awkwardly. He was clearly uncomfortable accepting Dennis's condition.

Dennis lost his smile and glanced down at his legs beneath the covers. His unmoving legs.

Vincent felt that stab of guilt to the heart.

But then Dennis's optimism bubbled back to the surface. "Well, for a kid who got shot four times and almost died, I'm okay, James."

James nodded solemnly.

Dennis eyed his brother. "Does Joseph know yet, Vincent?"

Joe tilted his head and regarded Vincent. "Know what?"

A knock on the door distracted everyone and Ms. Valencia, the social worker, entered the room. Joe glowered when he saw her, but Vincent stood and introduced her to everyone.

"I brought the paperwork you need to sign, Vincent." An effusive, upbeat lady, she'd been instrumental in expediting the process.

As she reached into her shoulder bag to pull out a manila folder, James turned to Vincent. "What's going on?"

"Vincent's adopting Franky," Dennis blurted.

Linda threw her hands to her mouth in surprise and James went slack-jawed.

Joe gasped and stared at Vincent.

"For real, Vincent?" Linda looked excited. He nodded and she pulled him into a loving hug. "Oh, sweetie, your parents would be so proud of you."

She released him and he faced James. The taller man looked at him as though he were a stranger.

"It's hard for me to see a man in the boy you used to be, Vincent," James admitted with a shake of his head. "But a finer man I've never known except your dad. I'm proud of you."

Vincent felt like a real adult for the first time, and it was liberating.

"We'll help with him, of course," Linda chimed in. "We're family, after all."

"Thanks," he replied. "I'll need all the help I can get."

"Don't forget, you have me," Dennis said reproachfully.

"And *you* have me," Vincent assured him. "We're a team."

Dennis grinned. "Oh, yeah."

Ms. Valencia laughed and held out the paperwork to Vincent, indicating where he needed to sign.

Joe had stood silently to one side during the conversation, head bent, looking like he'd lost his best friend. So, when Ms. Valencia offered the same papers to him, he eyed them with confusion.

"What's that for?"

She glanced at Vincent. "You didn't tell him?"

Vincent felt embarrassment wash over him. "I wanted to talk with Dennis first."

Joe fixed his uncertain eyes on Vincent. "Tell me what?"

Before Vincent could respond, Dennis practically shouted, "You're gonna be part of our family, too, Joseph. We'll be brothers. Isn't that golden?" He paused as Joe's face collapsed in shock. "If you want to, I mean."

Joe stared at Vincent in disbelief. Tears glistened in his eyes and he fought to maintain his stoic demeanor.

"You kept your promise," he whispered, so low that only Vincent could hear.

Vincent was stunned, but before he could say anything, Dennis pleaded, "Please, Joseph, say yes."

Tears dribbled down Joe's cheeks like raindrops. He nodded, and Dennis grinned. After signing his name just below Vincent's, he handed the paperwork back to Ms. Valencia. "Uh, how long do I hafta wait to move in with them?"

"I pulled some strings to get Vincent temporary clearance until we finish his home study. You move in right away." She paused a moment. "There will be court hearings at some point to terminate parental rights. Your parents will be invited."

Joe looked worried and looked at Vincent with wide, anxious eyes. "You'll go with me to court?"

"Course, I will."

Joe looked like he'd collapse with relief.

Linda threw her arms around him and gave him an intense hug. "Welcome to the family, honey."

She released him and James shook his hand, looking even more astonished than before. "This family's getting bigger by the second. Any others you planning to take in, Vince?"

Vincent shook his head. "Not at the moment."

Ms. Valencia laughed. "We have a lot more children waiting, I can tell you. I'll be in touch, Vincent." She bade them goodbye and left.

Vincent found Joe staring at him in wonder and heard those whispered words loud and clear in his mind: *You kept your promise.*

Joe knew.

After two more weeks, Dennis was moved to a regular room and occupational therapy commenced. Vincent felt overcome with shame each time he saw his brother lifted out of bed and placed into a wheelchair like a helpless baby. He knew he was weak for doing so, but he tried never to be present when the OT therapist arrived. The attached catheter and colostomy bag freaked him out and he had to look away every time they became visible.

He and Joe arrived at Dennis's room one afternoon to find it filled with flowers. Joe asked Dennis who sent them and he said there was no card. There were sunflowers, carnations, and daisies, giving room a bright and cheerful atmosphere.

When Joe leaned in to hug Dennis, Vincent recalled what he'd forgotten. He'd been so busy these past weeks buying Joe clothes and other necessities, setting up his old bedroom (he had moved into his parents room) to accommodate the newcomer, not to mention preparing for the upcoming hearing in Children's Court, that he'd forgotten to ask Joe the most important question of all.

He cleared his throat. "Um, Joe, I've been meaning to ask you."

Joe sat on Dennis's bed and regarded him with raised eyebrows.

"How did you figure it out?"

Joe scrunched up his face in confusion.

"About me being, you know?" Vincent glanced at the open door nervously.

"The superhero?" Joe asked, and Vincent shushed him. "Sorry."

"I didn't tell him," Dennis insisted.

Joe considered a moment. "I remembered the name, Invictus, cause Dennis liked that poem even back in the day."

"That's true," Dennis put in. "You have a great memory."

Joe got off the bed. He approached Vincent and reached around for his hair. Once again, it hung loose down his back.

"Mostly, it was the hair." He stroked the sleek black hair. "I think hair is what makes dudes look hot, so I always notice. Yours is so kickass it's easy to figure out you're the same guy."

Exactly what Professor Chin told him.

Joe screwed up his face in thought. Then he released the hair and snapped his fingers. "A man bun! That's what you need."

Vincent scowled and cast a hard look at Dennis.

Dennis threw up his hands. "I never said a thing."

"What?" Joe asked, obviously confused.

A clearing throat drew everyone's attention to the door. Lisa stood just inside looking gorgeous in her shorts and tee shirt. She held a manila envelope in her hands. Vincent fumbled to smooth out his hair.

"Lisa, hi."

She tossed off a casual smile and stepped into the room. "I see my flowers arrived. I hope you like them, Dennis."

"They're beautiful. Thanks so much, Lisa."

"Nice to finally meet you in person, though I'm so sorry about what happened."

They shook hands.

"I'm dealing." Dennis eyed the silent Vincent and cleared his throat.

Vincent stared at her, unable to think of a single thing to say.

"Since my big brother is being all shy again," Dennis went on, "I'll introduce you to my *new* brother, Joseph."

Joe extended a hand and she shook it, wide-eyed and clearly confused.

Dennis went on to explain about Joe and Franky.

She listened, her face taking on a look of awe. "Always full of surprises, aren't you, Vein Boy?"

Vincent wore another tank top and Joe's gaze dropped to the prominent veins in his arms. "Hey, that's a great nickname for you. My pops—Vein Boy."

Dennis laughed and so did Lisa. Vincent squirmed with discomfort. Wearing the Invictus mask and being the center of attention didn't bother him. That was the whole point, after all, to be seen and to inspire. But as Vincent, he still preferred the shadows of obscurity because too much attention made him feel… vulnerable.

"Uh, thanks for the flowers, Lisa," he finally managed to get out. "They're really nice."

She looked amused by his tongue-tied demeanor. "You're welcome. I also brought you these."

She handed him the envelope. He undid the clasp and opened it. Reaching in, he gripped a number of photographs and slid them out. The first batch depicted adults working with kids at Boys and Girls Clubs or after school programs or YMCA's or public parks. The next few displayed groups of people handing out food and clothes to the homeless. There was one shot of a medical van parked at a corner. Homeless people were lined up while a woman dressed in a white smock held a clipboard.

Mystified, he glanced up at Lisa.

"Keep going, Vein Boy."

He uncovered the next photo and stiffened.

It was an image of Invictus with Joe and Franky. He continued rifling through the stack. These were the photos he'd seen on the news of Invictus during his various rescues, including when he rode his motorcycle off the freeway overpass.

Joe leaned in and took the stack, sitting back on the bed so Dennis could see them, too.

"You're the one who's been taking all these photos?" Dennis asked, clearly surprised.

Vincent stared at her, unable to speak.

"How'd you know where he'd be?" Dennis added, gazing at her in wonder.

She shrugged. "A girl has to keep some secrets, right?"

Dennis looked mystified.

"Invictus inspired me, Dennis, to do more than I was doing," she went on. "Yeah, I want to be a doctor and help people, but that's down the line. I'm also a good photographer and figured I could use that gift to help people right now."

"What are all these other pix of people helping kids and stuff?" Dennis asked.

"Since Invictus appeared on the scene, more people have been volunteering to work with kids, teaching them stuff like knitting, golf, art, music, photography, sports, just like he asked them to. Skid Row has also gotten a lot of attention. It's amazing. I shot all these for an online website I'm putting together to encourage more people to jump in and help."

Vincent finally found his voice. "You started all of this because of Invictus?"

"Yep."

He cleared his throat. "Um, so why bring them to me?"

She threw both hands to her hips. "Dennis, is he always this obtuse?"

"Yep."

Joe laughed.

"Vincent, I know you better than most," she said softly. "And I have a thing for cute Asian guys with long hair, remember? The hair's a dead giveaway."

Dennis stifled a laugh and Joe clapped a hand over his own mouth to keep from busting up.

Vincent scowled with disgust. Did everyone and his uncle know who Invictus was?

Lisa pointed to the pictures. "I wanted you to see those because, well, Invictus has been absent on the streets these past few weeks. He's been missed."

"He has?"

She shook her head in amazement. "Check the news once in a while, Vein Boy." She leaned in and kissed him on the cheek. "I gotta run."

She started for the door.

"Uh," Vincent stammered. "Am I gonna, like, see you again? I mean, I'll see you at school in the fall, that's not what I meant, I meant will I–"

She rushed back and pressed her lips to his, cutting off his words. Startled, he fought for breath. He'd barely begun kissing back when she pulled away and strutted to the door.

He must've had a comical look on his face because both boys laughed.

Lisa stopped and offered a mischievous smile. "You have way too much on your plate right now to be dating material. But… I'll see ya on the streets." Then she was gone.

"Smooth, pops, real smooth." Joe grinned and Dennis high-fived him.

Suddenly Lisa was back, sticking her head in the door. "I just had the most perfect idea. When you're Vincent, wear your hair in a man bun. I like taking photos of those, too."

Then she was gone again.

Joe stifled his laughter while Dennis purposely looked out the window to hide the smirk on his face.

Vincent burned with embarrassment. "Um, either of you know how to tie a man bun?"

The boys busted up. Joe raised his hand and Vincent reluctantly turned his back. He felt Joe's hands twisting and tying his lengthy hair until he could no longer feel it against his neck or shoulders. He felt naked. When Joe's hands retreated, Vincent turned around.

Dennis stifled a giggle and gave him the thumbs up.

Joe studied him. "I think it makes you look hot. Well, you always look hot, but you know, just as hot."

Vincent scowled. "Feels like a dead animal nesting on my head."

The boys cracked up and that's when James and Linda entered the room.

"Care to let us in on the joke?" She set her purse down on a chair and stepped forward.

Dennis giggled again and pointed to Vincent's hair.

James recoiled. "Oh, God!"

Linda elbowed him and stood with an appraising look on her face. "I like it, Vincent. Your long hair was a dead giveaway anyway."

The boys laughed and high-fived again.

"What?" she asked.

They didn't get a chance to answer because Rogelio, the OT guy, entered the room pushing a wheelchair.

"Whoa, party time in here," he said good-naturedly, pushing the chair past James and Linda to the side of the bed. Joe scooted out of the way. "Ready for OT, my man?"

Dennis caught Vincent's eye. "Look what I can do already."

Rogelio locked the brakes and pulled off one armrest from the chair. Lowering Dennis's bed with a foot pedal, he dropped the bed rail. Vincent watched with ever tightening guts as the brother he adored pushed and pulled and shoved himself out of the bed into the chair. Beads of sweat broke out on Dennis's forehead.

Clearly fatigued from the exertion, Dennis looked up as Rogelio adjusted his feet and the colostomy bag before returning the armrest to its proper place.

"Whadda ya think, bro?"

Vincent nodded tightly, his throat constricted. "Awesome." Feeling faint, he fled the room.

"Vincent, wait!" he heard Linda call out.

But he kept running. He hit the stairwell and took the stairs two at a time. Eight floors later, huffing and puffing, he arrived at the roof door. He wasn't supposed to be up there, but he'd previously used a bit of thermite to melt the lock. Sitting on the roof and looking out over the city was the only time he felt real anymore. He shoved the door open and stepped into twilight.

"What's wrong with Vincent?" James asked the room at large.

"I know," Dennis answered. "Rogelio, can you take me up to the roof?"

"Huh?"

James flashed his police badge. The chief had refused to accept his resignation after the warehouse incident, so James was back in business.

"You won't get in trouble. I promise," he assured the confused therapist. "Just show us how to get up there and no one will ever know."

Rogelio studied the badge a moment, then nodded.

Vincent sat on the parapet staring out at the sunset splashing his city with dappled shades of red and gold. The muted traffic sounds soothed him, while the twinkling lights coming to life warmed his heart and made him feel needed. Night was for Invictus. And Invictus is who Vincent was always meant to be.

He heard wheels crunching along the gravel of the roof and turned to find Joe pushing Dennis in the chair, with James and Linda flanking them. Joe stopped the chair right in front of him and Vincent faced his family.

"I knew we'd find you here," Dennis announced. "You just can't resist doing the Batman thing, can you?"

"No, I can't." He paused and met his brother's gaze. "I'm sorry for running. It's just… when I see you in this chair, struggling to do the simplest things, I… I'm *so* sorry, Dennis."

Dennis reached out and took his hand. Warmth shot straight into his heart.

"I'm still here, Vince, and we're still together. That's what matters."

"But you'll never walk again." He almost choked on those words. It was the first time he'd spoken them aloud, the first time he'd admitted the truth. "I ruined your life."

Dennis squeezed his hand. "We've been through this too many times already. We both made really bad choices. I never should've hung out with those guys."

"And I never should've neglected you."

"It wasn't your fault," Dennis asserted firmly. "Just like mom and dad wasn't your fault. I understand that now. We can't go back, so let's move on, okay?"

Vincent stared at him in amazement. "You're always so full of hope."

"Life *is* hope," Dennis replied, the old soul shining through the young one. He glanced down at his unmoving legs. "Without hope, I'd be crying twenty-four seven."

Vincent squeezed his hand. "There's nothing wrong with crying. Learned that from my badass brother."

"I know, right?" Dennis agreed with conviction. "And I'm not weak, Vincent. I don't care what those doctors say. I *will* walk again."

Vincent offered his brother a smile filled with love. "You're the strongest guy I know. And the most human."

Dennis beamed.

Linda leaned down and planted a kiss on Dennis's cheek. "That's the boy I know and love. Never a quitter."

Dennis released Vincent's hand. That twinkle of prescience he sometimes displayed flashed in his eyes, the same twinkle that begat Invictus.

"You know we can't stop now, right, Vince?"

"Uh, Dennis," James began, his voice cautionary.

Dennis held up a hand. "Here me out, James. I have a plan."

"What plan?" Vincent asked.

Dennis looked more excited than he had in months. "Well, Franky is your Robin, at least when he comes home with us. And we have Joe. He could be like Nightwing, but with a way cooler name and a kickass costume that I'll design. And Linda, well, Linda would be an amazing Catwoman type, but, you know, a good one, not a bad one."

Linda's eyes flew open and Joe stared at Dennis in amazement.

"And Lisa, well, if she wants to join the team she'd make a super-hot Bat Girl type, right? Bat Girl with a camera? That'd be golden."

Vincent exchanged uncertain looks with the others before focusing on his brother. "Uh, Dennis, what are you saying here?"

"A team," Dennis proclaimed. "The greatest superhero team ever. Us."

"Who would you be?" Joe asked.

"Remember how Barbara Gordon got shot and paralyzed by the Joker?"

Joe shook his head. "Never read much comics."

Dennis looked at Vincent. "You remember, right, Vince?"

Vincent nodded.

"Well," Dennis went on, his voice rising in pitch, "she became Oracle and used her computer skills to keep watch over the whole city. That's what I'm gonna do, except I'll have a different name, of course, a really powerful name like 'Visionary' or something."

"Sounds cool to me." Joe raised a fist and Dennis bumped it.

Vincent sat in silence, considering the proposal. He shrugged. "Dennis calls the shots on this team, so I'm in. Linda?"

She eyed James. He gave her a *you're not seriously considering this* kind of look. "Why not? I always wanted to be a superhero. James?"

"Yeah, James," Dennis challenged. "Vincent asked you before if you wanted to be his partner. You up for being part of our team?"

"I'm still a cop," James offered by way of skirting the issue.

"The cop can be your disguise," Dennis assured him. "Cop by day, superhero by night."

James studied him a moment. "After everything that's happened, you still wanna do this?"

"Yes."

"We have to, James," Vincent chimed in. "We have to finish what we started."

James glanced at Linda, but she just shrugged.

"I guess it's the only way to make sure you all don't get killed out there," he muttered. "Okay, I'm in."

Dennis threw both arms into the air and whooped. His voice echoed off the surrounding buildings.

James gave him another serious look. "Under one condition."

Dennis raised his eyebrows.

"I ain't wearing no tights."

Vincent chuckled. Joe and Dennis laughed. Linda threw one arm around James and pulled him close, resting her head on his shoulder as they looked out over the city.

Vincent gazed at his brother in wonder. "You're amazing."

Dennis smiled. "No. We are."

He extended his arms and wrapped one around Joe's waist. Vincent stood and allowed his brother to encircle his waist with the other.

They remained like that for a long time; six people who sought to make a difference in their city because one remarkable boy, for whom hope ran eternal, had showed them the way.

Vincent threw an arm around Dennis and pulled him in closer. He thought of their parents. Would they be proud?

Oh, hell, yeah…

ABOUT THE AUTHOR

Michael J. Bowler is the award-winning author of *A Boy and His Dragon*, *A Matter of Time*, THE LANCE CHRONICLES (*Children of the Knight, Running Through A Dark Place, There Is No Fear, And The Children Shall Lead, Once Upon A Time In America*), *Spinner*, The Film Milieu Thriller Series (*I Know When You're Going To Die, The Horror Film Killer*), *Warrior Kids*, and *Like A Hero*.

His screenplay, "THE GOD MACHINE," won First Place in the 2017 Scriptapalooza competition.

He grew up in San Rafael, California, and majored in English and Theatre at Santa Clara University. He went on to earn a master's in film production from Loyola Marymount University, a teaching credential in English from LMU, and another master's in Special Education from Cal State University Dominguez Hills.

He worked producer, writer, and/or director on several ultra-low-budget horror films, including "Hell Spa," "Fatal Images," "Club Dead," and "Things II."

He taught high school in Hawthorne, California—both in general education and to students with learning disabilities—in subjects ranging from English and Strength Training to Algebra, Biology, and Yearbook.

He has been a volunteer Big Brother to eight different boys with the Catholic Big Brothers Big Sisters program, a decades-long volunteer within the juvenile justice system in Los Angeles, and is a single father to an adopted child.

He has been honored as Probation Volunteer of the Year, YMCA Volunteer of the Year, California Big Brother of the Year, and 2000 National Big Brother of the Year. The "National" honor allowed him and three of his Little Brothers to visit the White House and meet the president in the Oval Office.

His goal as an author is for teens and middle schoolers to experience empowerment and hope; to see themselves in his diverse characters; to read about kids who face real-life challenges; and to see how kids like them can remain decent people in an indecent world. As society, and as individuals, we're better off when we do what's right, not what's easy.

***

Website: michaeljbowler.com
FB: michaeljbowlerauthor
Twitter: @MichaelJBowler
Tumblr: http://michaeljbowler.tumblr.com/
Pinterest: http://www.pinterest.com/michaelbowler/pins/
YouTube: https://www.youtube.com/chan-nel/ UC2NXCPry4DDgJZOVDUxVtMw
Instagram: @michaeljbowler

If You Enjoyed This Novel,
You Might Like My Urban Adventure/Fantasy Series,
THE LANCE CHRONICLES.

Here is a sample from Book 1:

CHILDREN OF THE KNIGHT

(Free at Amazon and other online sites)

A SMALL, LEAN BOY APPEARED AT the mouth of an alley and darted quickly into the protective shadows behind a large dumpster. A sheriff's car cruised slowly past the mouth of the alley and then continued on out of sight. The boy stepped from his hiding place and dusted himself off. Lance Sepulveda, a fourteen-year-old orphan, warily glanced around. Between avoiding gang members and cops, he lived a very cautious life.

The gang members liked to beat him up and the cops put him in juvy as a runaway. There was no place in Los Angeles for kids like him who didn't commit crimes, so they had to bide their time in juvy to wait for yet another group home to take them.

A smart, clever boy with unusually green eyes—which drew derisive comments from other Latinos—Lance preferred the freedom of the streets, living for a time with this friend or that friend, having no ties to anyone. He wore a pair of baggy overalls with the straps hanging down and a gray hoodie flipped up to obscure his face, clothes given to him by one of his friends. He lugged a bulging, ratty-looking backpack in one hand and an old skateboard in the other.

Lance continued warily down the alley. Tonight there were no unusual sounds save the occasional plane practically landing atop Lennox on its approach into LAX.

From the shadows around him loomed two large black youths. Lance was grabbed and spun around. The skateboard flew from his grasp and clattered to the concrete.

Broad-shouldered, muscular Justin sneered at the fear flitting over Lance's startled face. "What's the hurry, Pretty Boy? We got business wit' you."

Reaching out one arm, he slapped the hood off Lance's head, allowing the boy's long hair to tumble about his shoulders, and then snatched the old backpack away so hard it tore open with a loud ripping sound, scattering clothes, candy, and junk food onto the ground.

Taller and built more for basketball than boxing, Dwayne sneered at the junk. "Man, what a loser!"

Lance fought down his fear and glared at both boys, ignoring his hated nickname, "Pretty Boy." Justin grabbed him by the front of his shirt and practically lifted him off the ground. Lance fought and struggled, but he was no match for the muscular boy. "Mr. R. says he had a talk with you about workin' these streets for him."

"Yeah, he did, and I told him no. I don't want no part a that! I run myself."

"No problemo, Mexicano," Justin sneered, tossing Lance to the ground like a ragdoll. "'Cept Mr. R., he don't like guys who know too much 'bout his business. Especially guys who won't work for him."

Lance landed and rolled, leaping to his feet almost at once. His heart thumped wildly, his green eyes blazing with equal parts fury and fear. "I don't know nuthin'!" he spat angrily, visibly shaking with panic. "'Cept you jerks slang that crap for 'im! Who would I tell? What could I say anyway?"

Dwayne flipped open an evil-looking switchblade and pressed the razor-sharp point to Lance's throat before he could even flinch.

"You could just say no—to life, ya little runt!" He began slowly pressing the knife into Lance's throat, a wicked smile creasing his dark, tatted face.

A deep, harsh voice echoed from behind the three boys. "Unhand that lad, or forfeit your lives!"

Dwayne whirled to look over his shoulder.

From the shadows, confidently approaching, rode a man on horseback! The three youths merely gaped in astonishment. None of them had ever even seen a real horse before, much less one in this neighborhood. When the rider emerged from the darkness into a patch of streetlight, they gasped anew. He wore a full suit of knightly armor and carried a massive, gleaming sword that looked capable of slicing all three of them in half at the same time! The boys could not make out any facial features, as they were covered by a helm and mouthpiece.

The three stood frozen to the spot, Dwayne's blade pressed against Lance's throat as the knight halted his horse a few feet away.

Dwayne found his voice first. "Say what?" He couldn't believe what he was seeing! He needed to stop sampling R's stuff, that was a for sure.

"I do believe my intent was clear," calmly stated the knight in a strong voice tinged with something like a Southern accent. "Unhand the boy or forfeit your lives."

With speed seemingly impossible underneath all that armor, the knight flicked his sword downward and across, and Dwayne's pants dropped to his feet.

Startled, the boy reached down to retrieve them, and the knight swung the sword again, this time slicing open the hand holding the knife, causing Dwayne to curse and fling the blade to the ground.

Without pause, the knight just as swiftly swung the sword deftly back up, letting the point rest against Justin's throat. The muscular boy whimpered in terror.

"Okay, you win," he muttered fearfully, the tip of the sword already drawing blood. He stepped away from Lance.

The mysterious knight looked down at Lance. "Shall I kill these two for you, lad?"

Lance sucked in a sharp breath. He didn't know what to say.

Justin keened with fear. "Hey, man, ya'll can't kill us cuz my dad's a cop!"

Dwayne trembled, but he was too hard-ass to show it. "Shut up, fool!"

The knight ignored them, focusing his attention on Lance, who gawked like a fish out of water. "Well, lad?"

Coming back to his senses, Lance realized that the man wanted an answer. Would he really kill these guys if I asked him to? He didn't think he wanted to find out. "Let 'em go."

Without pause, the knight pulled his gleaming sword back from Justin's throat, but still gripped it firmly, ready to strike. He gazed down at the two older youths. "Methinks we shall meet again."

Always the bolder of the two, Dwayne spat viciously on the ground in front of the horse, causing it to neigh in annoyance. "Like hell!"

Then he and Justin turned and bolted, Dwayne struggling to keep his pants from tripping him up. They quickly vanished from the mouth of the alley.

Lance gazed upward at the knight, still speechless, staring at the horse, the sword, and the armor. His breath caught in his throat. He didn't do drugs, so it couldn't be that. So what the hell was going on?

The knight sheathed his sword as he stared down at the boy, his eyes shimmering slightly within the helm. "Have thou no manners, to not thank me for thy life?"

That helm and those hidden eyes creeped Lance out something fierce. "Oh yeah, sorry," he stammered. "Yeah, uh, thanks." He paused a moment. "Would you, would you really have killed them guys for me?"

"No. Not unless my life or yours be at stake. I wished merely to discern something of your character."

"Huh? You talk weird, mister."

The knight ignored Lance's comment. "What be thy name, lad?"

Lance's hackles instantly rose. "Uh, they call me, well, 'Pretty Boy'. I don't think I am, neither, but I guess it's the hair."

"Thou art a handsome youth, so the name appears to fit thee. Why doth you dislike it?"

"Cause they don't mean it like a compliment," Lance replied sourly. "They just do it to mock me."

"If it displeases you, I shall not use it. Hast thou no Christian name?"

Lance never shared his true name with anyone. On these streets, knowing one's true name could be dangerous. Yet somehow, this man's commanding tone and presence forced his guard down. "Huh? Oh, uh, Lance. Lance Sepulveda." It was practically a whisper. Then he felt his old boldness return. "What's it to you, anyways?"

The knight reacted with surprise. "Thy name be Lance?"

"Yeah, so?"

The knight squinted through the helm, studying Lance's shadowed face.

"Of course that be thy name, lad," he murmured, almost to himself, almost as if Lance wasn't even there. "All is as it should be."

Lance stood warily gazing up at him, a shiver flitting up and down his spine at those mysterious words, as though everything really was as it should be. But that didn't make sense. None of this made sense.

The man noted Lance's scattered clothes on the ground. "Tell me, young Lance, are these all your worldly belongings?" There was deep sadness in that voice.

Lance bristled. "What about it? I move around a lot." He set about picking up his stuff and shoving everything into the torn backpack.

"I see," the knight observed, his tone unreadable.

Lance retrieved his skateboard and stared at the knight, uncertain what to do next. His breathing had calmed, and he found himself deeply curious about this guy, even though curiosity on these streets could get you killed.

"Have you a place to lay thy head this night?" the knight inquired in a conversational tone.

Lance went rigid, his breath hitching in his throat, his heart pounding anew. "I always got places," he announced, prepared to leap onto his board and jet out of there.

The knight made no threatening gestures, nor did the magnificent white horse even shuffle its feet with impatience.

His body tight with tension, Lance still eyed the animal admiringly. It was the most beautiful thing he'd ever seen.

"Come with me," the knight offered. "I have a bed for thee."

Lance leapt back and whipped a knife out of his pocket. It was small and wouldn't do much damage, but even that short blade gave him a tiny sense of security. Sweat broke out on his face as he gazed upward and gulped. "You queer or somethin'?"

"How odd that after so many centuries, some words still retain their most common meanings."

Lance knew he was a smart kid—teachers had told him that since the first grade. But he didn't have a clue what this guy was talking about. What kind of English was he speaking, anyways?

"Huh?" was all he could muster, his heart still thrumming with fear.

"Be at peace, young one," the knight assured him. "The answer to thy question be nay."

Lance continued to eye him with great uncertainty. "Nay" sounded like "no," and that made him feel more at ease, slowing his heart a bit. "You got food at your place?"

"Yes, lad, all you could possibly eat. Now, if you get up on mine horse, we shalt be away."

Lance's extreme hunger did the deciding for him. Sure, he had the junk food in his pack, but real food was always better. "Okay. But if you try anything, I'll cut your throat."

"Agreed. Up with you now. We have a long journey ahead."

The knight reached down with a gauntleted hand. Lance eyed it for a long moment, then put away his pocketknife and reached up to do something he hadn't done since he was six years old—he grasped the hand of a stranger.

With strength and ease, the knight hefted the boy up and onto the saddle behind him as though Lance weighed no more than a stuffed animal. He was caught off guard by the man's physical power, and shook his head in admiration.

"Man, you're strong!"

The knight glanced back over his shoulder at the wide-eyed boy behind him. "As will you be, Lance Sepulveda."

The knight spurred his horse, and the large animal cantered softly down the alley, rounding the corner and disappearing into the dark streets of Lennox.

* * *

The knight, with Lance clinging tightly to his back, stopped at the edge of the Los Angeles River, and Lance gazed down into the dry, concrete riverbed. More of an aqueduct, the river seldom had much water coursing through it. The horse neighed approvingly.

"You weren't messin' with me about a long journey!" Lance exclaimed, sitting up to get a better view.

"Hold on," the knight intoned as he flicked the reins, and the muscular white mare began her descent to the riverbed below. Lance felt tight with fear atop such a large animal, but somehow the presence of this strong, confident man eased his fear.

"Does, uh, does your horse have a name?" he asked, trying to quell the nervousness in his voice. This descent was steep, and he wanted nothing more than to plant his feet firmly on cement.

"She hath been given the name Llamrei, after my first mount of long ago," the knight replied, his tone wistful.

Something about his melancholy tone silenced Lance. The mare reached bottom without even the slightest misstep and trotted along the riverbed, halting at an enormous entrance to the storm drain system, which wound underground throughout the Los Angeles basin. This cavernous maw looked large enough to drive a van through.

A metal grill guarded the entrance to the drain, but Lance noted that the aged lock had recently been broken. The knight reached out and grabbed one side of the grill, backing up his horse to ease it open. The metal screamed with disuse, and the sound sent chills down Lance's back. The dark, gaping orifice threatened to envelope him, and his stomach pulled up into his throat.

"We, uh, we're goin' in there?" He fought to keep his quavering voice steady.

"Have no fear, young Lance."

Lance bristled, his pride winning out. "I ain't afraid! It just don' look like no home to me."

"It doth be mine at present." The knight spurred Llamrei forward into the dark, forbidding tunnel, pulling shut the grill and sealing them within.

Lance squinted in the dark as the knight extended a gloved hand to grasp an old, weathered torch from a small alcove. With his other gloved hand, he dug into a leather pouch hanging from the saddle and extracted a pinch of some kind of powder, sprinkling it atop the torch. Flames sprang to flickering life, causing Lance to gasp with surprise as its warm glow cast weird reflections off the man's armor. He gazed in wonder.

That looked like something out of a movie! Who is this guy anyway?

"A mere trick, my boy, taught to me long ago by M—by an old friend."

The knight spurred his horse into the darkness of the tunnel. The man's quick change of subject was not lost on Lance. What had he been planning to say? All his street instincts told him to leap down from the horse and hightail it out of there. None of this made any sense, not here, not in his city, not in his sorry life. And yet he didn't jump. He didn't run. There was something about the guy…. Growing up as he had, Lance had a good gut when it came to people. No, this guy wasn't out to hurt him or kill him or….

Don't even go there!

No, he decided as they trotted along the dank underbelly of the city, this guy would not hurt him. But if he didn't want to hurt him, then what the hell did he want?

The two remained silent as Llamrei trotted along the damp and drafty storm drain. There were no sounds save the clop, clop, clopping of her hooves against the lichen-covered concrete. It surprised Lance that the horse seemed so comfortable underground. He always thought most animals, himself included, preferred above ground to below. She must be used to it, he surmised, which meant the guy was telling the truth. He really did live here.

Suddenly, Llamrei stopped. Lance had been so lost in his musings that he hadn't realized they'd left the tunnel to enter an enormous chamber.

"We are here," the knight announced, drawing Lance back into reality. As the man deftly dismounted, Lance's eyes bulged wide with wonder at his surroundings.

The immensity of the underground chamber awed him. It appeared to be some sort of central hub from which a multitude of tunnels branched off, each swallowed up by darkness. Lit solely by the light of numerous torches imbedded within the concrete walls, Lance gazed in amazement at what appeared to be the central hall of an old castle, the kind he'd only ever seen in books. What the hell? There wasn't such things in LA!

He observed bedrolls lining the walls and disappearing down each branching tunnel, old tables and chairs, wooden and rough-

hewn and not like any he'd ever seen. There was even a big-ass throne of some kind with huge arms and a really high back set against one wall, like right out of a frickin' old movie! What the…? And then his eyes fell upon the weapons, and his face lit up with wonder. Spread out before him were racks upon wooden racks of weapons—swords of all shapes and sizes, shields, short-handled dirks, knives, longbows and short bows, and arrows and quivers.

Carefully, eyes pinned to the armory before him, he dropped slowly off the horse, allowing his skateboard and backpack to fall to the ground unnoticed. Heart beating with excitement, he stepped forward into this wonderland, gaping in astonishment at the sight before him. He slipped the hood down, allowing his long brown hair its freedom. He shook his head in awe.

"Wow!" was all he could think to say, hurrying to the nearest of the weapons racks and gingerly touching some of the swords. He gripped the leather- bound hilt of a large broadsword and struggled vainly to heft it over his head. The blade alone was almost five feet in length.

The knight turned to observe Lance grappling with the weight of the sword.

"Each be forged of solid iron, lad, and honed to a fine edge. One day soon, thou shalt be hefting the largest of them with ease."

Lance fought the broadsword back into its place on the rack, watching curiously as the knight removed his gauntlets and laid them on an ancient-looking table. He then slipped the helm and face guard up over his head, revealing his face for the first time. His appearance surprised Lance, for he was a young man, probably not even thirty, with long brown hair cascading past his shoulders and a small, well-trimmed beard and moustache. Lance gazed at him open-mouthed, his hand still on the hilt of the sword.

"You're younger than I thought. How old are you, anyways?"

The knight smiled, a pleasant, reassuring sort of smile. "Much older than I look, I'm afraid."

Lance spread his arms wide at the myriad weapons with an enormous grin breaching his normally stoic young face. "This place is bitchin', man! What's all this stuff for?"

"A crusade, young Lance. Wouldst thou learn the use of these weapons?"

Lance's face lit up as he grabbed for a smaller sword and cut the air with it. "Hell yeah, but—" His smile dropped, his face clouding with suspicion.

"Why me?"

"Methinks, young Lance, that you require nourishment. There be much we must speak of this night if you are to understand."

Lance grabbed one of the knives and held it in front of him, sword in one hand, knife in the other. "Why me?" he repeated, hoping the hardness of his tone effectively masked the relentless pounding of his heart.

The young man studied him, but made not threatening moves. "T'were not by chance you and I met this night, but by design."

"Huh? You gotta start speakin' English or Spanish or something cause I don't know what you're saying!"

"It was decreed that you and I should meet, for I didst see thee in a vision, young Lance, a vision for the future."

Lance lowered the weapons, but kept them at the ready. "Who the hell are you anyways?"

The young man unsheathed his own large, gleaming sword, gazed regally down at the boy, gripped the ornately jeweled hilt, and raised the sword aloft.

"I am Arthur, once and future King of Great Britain, and this be Excalibur. Yours is a time and place of immense need, and thus, as 'twas foretold centuries past, have I returned to right the wrongs that plague thy homeland. Amidst the squalor and barbarism of this city, I shall rebuild my Round Table and change the course of history. And thee, young Lance, shall be my First Knight. Are you game?"

Lance's lower jaw dropped open and his wide green eyes bulged with amazement. For the first time in his life he understood the meaning of the word "dumbstruck."

"Huh?" was all he could muster.

Arthur grinned.